Origins

Origins

Varangian Book 3

Stuart G. Yates

This one for Sue, my good friend whose research and insight led me into a whole new world of adventure

Special thanks go to Miika and the team at Creativia who have laboured hard to save this volume from disappearing into the void.

The Northernmost Tip of the Byzantine Empire, 1042

In a small glade by the side of the River Dneiper, the Varangians rested; many huddled around camp fires, warming their damp clothes, sending up great trails of steam. Watching the river flow past, Hardrada stood, lost in thoughts of home, of what he had left behind, of what might face him. Sarah, the playing piece in a game of twisted desires and forgotten hopes, had returned to Constantinople without a word. Not a hint of regret for the moment of passion they had shared. Eyes like bottomless pools, bereft of life. How could she have changed so completely? And the Empress too. Once, all of them, so giving, so willing, now ... He breathed hard, looked beyond the gently bobbing longship to the distant shore opposite and wondered if life would always play out this way. In the far north, a princess waited, and with her the promise of a new chapter in a life already full. To be king, his destiny fulfilled. Beside him a woman of grace, passion and beauty. A woman to bear him children. To ensure his line: King of the Norse. Father of greatness.

Something moved at his shoulder and he turned to see Ulf gnawing on a piece of coarse brown bread. "You should eat something," Hardrada's faithful companion said between mouthsful.

"I don't feel much like eating."

"Why not? Everything is well. We have all the treasure. Byzantium is far behind us. What troubles you?"

Hardrada shrugged, turning again to the grey, cold river. "I'm feeling morose, that's all, wondering if I have made a mistake."

"How so?" Ulf finished his bread, wiped his hands on his jerkin, and sighed. "Listen, we did what we could for the Greeks. We've done well. *You've* done well. You have enough money now to buy up the Kievian Rus and ensure your journey to the throne of Norway. You can't regret any of it, Harald. Everything you've done has been for this moment. Seize it. Take what is yours. By right, not by force." He gripped Hardrada's arm. "No regrets, old friend. This isn't like you and it troubles me to see you this way. So, come on, share some wine and let's put Byzantium behind us – literally."

"You're right," said Hardrada, sounding heavy and resigned. "I thought … I don't know, I thought that perhaps I could find happiness."

"*Happiness*? Dear Christ, what the hell is that? We're Vikings. We find happiness in the bottom of a wine jug and at the point of our swords. Nowhere else, old friend."

A footstep behind them, followed by a low voice, "Except home."

Both turned as Haldor approached. Regaining some his former strength, the eldest of the three companions still walked with a slight limp, one hand forever clamped to his side. He stepped up alongside the others and breathed in the fresh salty air. "The smell of the north," he said. "I never dared believe we would turn our faces home. I wished it, of course, but I didn't want to tempt fate by saying so. You two," he grinned, without turning in their direction, "you seemed so hell-bent on adventure and money, but for me it was nothing more than an interval, a pause before I went back. And now that we are, I feel somewhat melancholy."

"You sound like a fucking philosopher," spat Ulf.

"Oh, and you don't? I heard what you said, all that about having no regrets. But we do, don't we? All three of us. And I am wondering if, when we return home, more regrets will follow."

"You truly think that?" asked Hardrada.

"Perhaps. We have been away for a long time. You were seventeen when you left Norway, Harald. Much has changed."

"I didn't leave. I fled. As well you know. Fled." He blew out a breath before closing his eyes, allowing the smell of the river to waft over him. Haldor's words spelled out the truth. The water promised dreams of the north, for at its end stood Kiev, and the next phase of the adventure. "You think the people will judge my actions as that of a coward?"

Ulf snorted, "Christ, Harald. A coward? You had no choice. Death, or escape. Yaroslav took you in, and he schooled you, and now you go back to help him. Debts paid. No one will judge you, you can depend on it."

"Regrets you said," Hardrada held Haldor's gaze. "You most of all, old friend. You have never held back from telling me the truth. So tell me now. Do I make a mistake in going back? Will the people accept me, or will they forever eye me with suspicion and fear?"

"The people will accept a king who treats them with fairness, who defends them against enemies, and fills their bellies with food. Nothing much else matters."

"So what I did? Running away?"

Ulf slammed down his fist. "Harald, you've got to stop thinking like this and—"

Hardrada cut off Ulf's words with a raised hand. "Haldor? Tell me, in truth. Will the people follow me?"

"You fled because the alternative was certain death. And many who lived then are now dead. They will see you as the returning star, to lead them forward. The great Viking age may have passed, but you Harald, you will restore it. Of that I have no doubt."

The silence stretched out, Haldor's words drifting out across the glade, to mingle with the encroaching trees and settle within the leaves, whilst all three men stood and allowed their own thoughts to cloud and become distilled.

When at last Hardrada's shoulders dropped and he turned to go, Ulf caught him by the arm. "Harald," he said, "I've followed you for many years, since we were both young. We have lived and fought as brothers and I will follow you to the ends of the earth if need be. Whatever you decide to do, I will be here."

"My good friend," said Hardada quietly, then nodded at Haldor. "Both of you. I would never have achieved any of it without you."

Haldor looked grim. "Harald. I too, as Ulf, have followed you, but..." He shook his head. "I've thought long and hard since we spoke in the hospital in Constantinople. And you, you have tried so hard to dissuade me, but I am old, old and weary. I cannot go to Kiev."

"I thought you might have changed your mind," muttered Hardada, not daring to hold Haldor's eyes.

"No. Decisions. Like we said."

For a moment, it was as if the world had ground to a halt. Not a breath of wind, not a bird's song. Only the stillness of that place, and Haldor's words burning deep.

"You can't leave us, Hal," said Ulf at last. "You're one of us. You cannot turn away now, not when Harald needs you so much!"

"No, Ulf," said Hardrada. He smiled. "Hal, I always hoped, once your wounds healed, you might stand alongside me again, but ... I understand and accept your wishes."

"Do you?"

"Aye. I do. You wish to return home, as we too wish. But your home is not with us, and to ensure your safe journey, I give you as much as needed, to send you home with all speed."

Haldor's voice quaked, raw with emotion, "Are you sure, my friend? I would not ask for much."

"Aye." Hardada nodded. "With Zoe returning the rest of my booty, I have more than enough to lay my claim to the throne of Norway. I will give you as much as you need to sail to Iceland and go home. It is the least I can do."

Haldor reeled backwards, eyes filling up, the tears threatening to fall. "Harald, I cannot ask you to—"

"I know you would never ask, old friend. It is my gift to you. When we reach the far north, you take a ship, and a crew, and make your way back to your island home." His smile grew broader. "I knew this day would come. Your wounds have healed well enough, but your heart and soul, Hal, they are no longer bound with mine. I release you." He reached out his hand and took Haldor's, gripped it firmly. "Go with God, Haldor, and with all my blessings."

They embraced then and Ulf looked on, agog. Hardrada saw it in his friend's face, his incomprehension and when he stepped back, it was to Ulf that he now spoke. "But you, you will stay by my side and together we will make Norway the greatest kingdom in all the world. I have dreams, Ulf, dreams of greatness. We have such deeds to perform, such adventures. We will become legends, Ulf. Men will tell the stories of what we do for centuries to come. They will write poems and sing songs and for as long as the sun rises, the world will remember."

"They already sing songs," said Haldor. "Your exploits, the legend that is Harald Hardrada, the whole world knows who you are and what you have done."

"I have done much, it is true. I would have been nothing if it were not for both of you."

"We are minor players," said Haldor. "Arriving as you did, in Constantinople, a young man, still stinging from the wounds you bore. It was you who recovered and made yourself into someone great."

"I do not know it all," said Ulf. "Before we met, Harald, who you were, what brought you to Byzantium? It is a story of myth and legend, but neither of us knows the truth of it. Not the whole truth."

Hardrada nodded. "Well, whilst we wait here and the men dry themselves, and we eat and drink, I will tell you."

"All of it? How you came to be here?"

"Aye," said Hardrada. "It is a tale I have never spoken of, but now," he smiled at Haldor, "now perhaps is the best time to tell it, before you go your separate way, old friend."

With that, he put his arms around the shoulders of his two companions and guided them towards the camp fires of the Varangians and told them the story of who he was, what his roots were and how he became known as Harald Hardrada.

One

The great wooden gates swung open. Ancient hinges groaned in complaint, and the riders came through into the square, the sheep-rustler stumbling behind, tethered to the lead animal by a coarse rope, secured around his neck, pulled tight. The captors moved at a steady pace astride worn out ponies, nevertheless the man battled to keep upright, his wrists bound before him. He struggled to maintain his footing, wild eyes darting from side to side, aware of the animosity of those pressing in from all sides. People pushed and strained for a better view, edging in ever closer. The hunters raised their horsewhips, forcing the crowd to give way, sending them two or three steps backwards. A guard closed the gates and drew down the bar. Children laughed, old women bayed. The air of expectation grew.

When the men reached the centre of the yard, they reined in their mounts, the lead rider easing himself down from the saddle. He stretched, grimacing as he bent his back, and fired a look at the nearest peasant. "Fetch me wine."

The youth ran off without another word.

"Sanda!"

The voice boomed through the yard and for a moment, the place became as the grave. Sanda, the King's personal *bryti*, or steward, looked towards the great hall and the man who leaned over the first-storey balustrade. A huge, swollen man, unkempt beard hanging in tattered ribbons to his bare chest, and he shook the rail with rage. His brows bristled with barely contained fury. "There were two of them."

Sanda turned and nodded towards his companions, who swung from their ponies and flanked the captive, seizing him around the biceps.

"They ran like rabbits." Sanda spat into the dirt, aware of the crowd pressing in, anxious to see justice served. He frowned at the man above him. "We caught them at Blesnoc Ford, where this craven oaf threw up his hands and cried for his mother. The other made a fight of it." He shrugged. "He died for his efforts."

"I hope he died badly."

"I slit open his gizzard and watched him die. He took a long time about it and screamed a good deal."

This seemed to please the big man. "Fetch the oxen," he said, whirled away and disappeared into the depths of the great hall, shouting out for wine.

Sanda stood and watched the man's receding back for a moment before turning to the crowd. He glared at them. "You heard our lord, find oxen and bring them. *Now!*" He became aware of someone at his shoulder and about to lash out when he recognised the youth he had sent to find wine. Sanda eyed the trembling hand clutching an animal-skin gourd, took it without a word and raised it to his lips. The wine tasted sour and strong and he closed his eyes and took a moment to lose himself in the warmth that spread through him.

All too soon, the clamour of the crowd brought him back to the present. He dragged the back of his hand across his mouth and fixed the youth with a hard stare. "Ever seen a man die, boy?"

The youth shook his head, his mouth trembling, unable to form any words.

Sanda sighed, pushed the stopper into the gourd and thrust it back into the youth's hand. "You may need that after it is done." He strode away, shouldering through the assembled peasants. He had no wish to witness his lord's retribution.

7

He positioned himself well to the rear. Despite his view being some-what obscured, he knew what followed. When the lord appeared from the great hall, the peasants hushed, many bowing, none wishing to catch his look. He ignored them all, marched to the captive, gripped him by the cheeks and squeezed. "Damn you, but you'll know what it means to steal from me." He swung around, making a great dramatic sweep of his arms. "As will you all. Learn your lessons this day, and see my justice for what it is."

Sanda leaned back against the lean-to close by and folded his arms. *If the man knew the meaning of justice, then he should feed these rabid dogs, show some leadership, some care.* He hawked and spat at his feet. His own homestead barely sustained his family and the winters grew harder each passing promised year, the sun weaker. Turnips meant to feed cows were now used for soup. Traders had grain, declaring they had secured agreements with lands to the east, but nothing ever came of it. The truth of the matter was the realm had no money, the coffers bare. Distant lands were not charities, they demanded hard cash, and when there was none, the grain dwindled away and the people starved. Unrest grew; more and more took to stealing, like the two poor bastards who had run off with the king's sheep. Three sheep: one butchered and devoured on the way, the others lost, taken by wolves no doubt. And now the remaining rustler about to be torn apart by oxen while the people cheered. For a few pitiful moments, the ache in their guts forgotten, they would look upon the spectacle as great sport and the youngest learn how to harden their hearts. The old might turn away with seasoned indifference, having witnessed such scenes many times before. Times were hard and cruel, but nothing was as cruel as the king's rule.

Loud shouts of encouragement rose over the constant rumble of the crowd. Sanda didn't need to look to know the oxen had arrived, that the rustler's hands were being lashed to halters around the huge animals' necks. Soon would come the sound of the lash, the oxen urged to move, each in an opposite direction, and they would tear the man apart. The crowd would cheer and the king would have his justice.

He waited. And waited.

A stirring began in the crowd, barely audible at first, but growing louder; voices, raised not in amusement, but in anxiety. Sanda pushed himself from the lean-to and forced his way forward.

The king lay in the dirt, on his back, teeth clamped together, eyes screwed up, his entire body rigid with agony. Sanda quickly looked around. The men with the oxen stood aghast, the captive hung limp but unhurt, mouth drooling as he whimpered, barely able to believe what had happened.

And what had happened? Sanda got down next to his king and did not know what to do. The man's body was in spasm, legs and arms out straight, trembling, sweat sprouting from his brow and upper lip. "He fell." Sanda turned to the owner of the voice; Sven, one of the men who had helped hunt down the rustler. "One moment he was standing, telling us to ready the beasts, and then he fell."

Sanda scanned the crowd, searching their faces, looking for a sign. "An assassin?"

"No. Look at him. There is no wound. No arrow, no knife. He fell, and that is the end of it."

Sanda scratched at his beard. "Falling-down sickness? But, he showed no signs, no ... " He shook his head and stood up, hands on hips, at a loss what to do, or even think. This was beyond his knowing. Battlefield wounds were one thing, the spurt of blood, the screams of pain, but this was unlike anything he had ever witnessed.

Silence settled, feet shuffled. And someone moved through the crowd. Sanda lowered his head as the figure drew closer. "My queen," he said.

Queen Asta of Westfold; a striking woman, taller than most, her limbs long and slender, her face unblemished by the harsh Norwegian winter. Dressed in a long flowing robe of saffron yellow flecked with gold thread, her hair tied back and secured by a band of delicate white flowers, as small as fingernails, she glided to a halt and gazed down at her husband. No concern crossed her features, the merest downturn of her mouth the only sign of emotion. "He complained of pains in the night," was all she said, her voice even and controlled.

"What shall we do with him?" Sanda studied his king, the still rigid body, as if frozen solid, the pain ingrained around the eyes and mouth, the skin drawn tight.

"Let him die." Her head came up, eyes holding Sanda's with cruel indifference. "And when he's dead, send me word and we will bury him." She nodded to the rustler, who hung like a rag between the two waiting oxen, their breath steaming in the growing cold. "And see to that base-born thief whilst you're at it."

"My lady?"

"Release him."

Her voice, resolute and strong, carried over the crowd and people responded with gasps, some heartfelt cries, and a few guffaws of disbelief.

"You mean to let him go?" Sanda had to force himself not to raise his voice as the anger developed inside him. "But he stole the king's sheep, my lady. He has to be punished." The king's justice may be cruel, but it was justice. The people deserved nothing less.

He went to speak, to voice his protest, but she held up a hand and stopped him. "Do not presume I know nothing of justice, *bryti* Sanda." She smiled and Sanda felt a trickle of ice run through him. "Once my husband is in his burial pit, lay that wretch next to the king … and bury him alive."

Two

The wind lashed at Olaf's face, sea spray stinging his eyes, drenching his hair. Feet planted firmly apart, he held onto the great, single mast as the longship ploughed through the surging swell, heading for home. His men, Viking raiders, sat huddled up against their oars, no longer needed with the wind so powerful. They had followed him, as they always did, with great enthusiasm, their blood lust up, the promise of booty, women, slaves all the enticement they needed. Now, with thoughts of hearth fires so close, their eyes shone with a new type of expectation. Home. The welcome embraces of loved ones, the drinking and feasting in the great hall.

Olaf twisted around and peered towards the second ship struggling a quarter of a *mil* behind. On board were the captives and other meagre pickings taken from a desolate island in the North Sea, not far from the coast of what the Romans called Hibernia. There were many other names Olaf could give that mournful place. Shithole was the one which sprang most readily to mind. Half a dozen goats, three scrawny youths and an old crone who spat venom every time she opened her toothless mouth. Olaf sighed. The hero returns. Damn them all.

The tillerman steered the ship into the waiting bay, villagers already running along the jetty to greet them. Children jumped and skipped with joy, women wrung their hands in expectation and old Brün, the herdsman stood silent and grim, the folds of his long robes lashed around his legs by the wind, his hair a wild fury. As the ship came alongside the wooden dock, and the crew secured it with coarse mooring ropes, Olaf's eyes locked with the old man's and what he saw he did not like. He vaulted over the side and hit the water with a grunt, waded ashore, shaking himself as he edged through the press of well-wishers.

"What is it?" he asked above the boiling mass of raised voices, all eager to know what had befallen the crew on their latest raiding party.

Brün's face remained impassive. His duty had been to head the village in Olaf's absence, a task he always fulfilled with vigour, carrying out the wishes of his chief with unflinching devotion. He rarely showed emotion, even when things went badly, but now the look in his eyes gave a hint of just such an occurrence. For a moment, he held his chief's gaze, then flinched, the mask falling. "Your father."

Crew members shuffled past, the captives herded before them, others bringing the goats. A small boy played tag with two girls, and a buxom woman held onto her husband's hands and danced around him, laughing with unbounded joy. Olaf barely gave them a glance. "He's dead?"

The old *hirdman's* features betrayed the truth, words not needed. Olaf sighed. He knew his father ailed with some sickness, complaining as he often did of pains in his chest and arm. Olaf dismissed it all as the cantankerous mutterings of the aged, always finding fault in everything, the way they all did. Moaning about life, how things were not as good as they once were in this hard, harsh world. Perhaps Olaf should have listened, paid heed to the man's groans, prepared himself for what he knew was bound to happen. *I wanted my life to continue, to cross the seas and raid, and I closed my ears, and my mind to it, to the truth. He was dying, or grievous sick, and now, with his death, I am king. And king of what? A ramshackle collection of crumbling villages, and discontented people, the great days gone?*

"Your mother has sent word," continued Brün, voice low, tremulous. "She awaits your return at Westfold." He dropped to his knees, head bowed low. Many of the still disembarking crew stopped what they were doing, the others strewn along the beach also growing silent. All eyes turned to watch and listen, see what was happening. Brün, with his head bowed, cried out, "To you, my lord king, I pledge my service and my life. Hail the new, right born King of Westfold!"

A ripple of chatter ran through the gathered people as the aged headsman's words struck home. At first stunned, they slowly, one by one, fell to their knees to join with the headsman in declaring their allegiance to the new king. "Hail Olaf," they cried as one, "King of Westfold!"

Olaf stood, struck dumb, unable to think or move. Yes, he was the king now, for good or ill. Fate had played its hand and he knew, at that moment, that his Viking ways would have to come to an end. No longer could he sail to distant lands, feel his heart surging with the promise of booty, and rejoice in the terror he brought to those foreign shores. A king must rule, and care for his people. His place was here, in this land he called home.

He placed his hand on Brün's head. "Arise, my noble lord. And to all of you," he raised his voice, swinging around to face the silent assembly kneeling in the sand. "I give you my oath – to serve you with all my strength, and bestow all my love upon you, my people, my kingdom!"

A great roar erupted from the collective mouths. Some drew swords and raised them skywards, others clasped their hands together, some even cried. Olaf stood and dragged in a breath, offering up a silent prayer, '*God help me, and aid me in doing what is right.*'

* * *

What was right was that Olaf should travel to Westfold, 'As soon as you can, my grace,' being Brün's advice. But Olaf required time to think. He sat in his chair in the hall, staring at the floor, continuing to struggle with the news and the implications of what it all meant. He'd known this moment would come. His destiny was to be king, to stand in his father's stead, to pass judgements, give council, lead his people, but he never expected it so soon. Now, with the day drawing on, the burden of responsibility growing strong and heavy, he refused to take food and water, and gazed into the distance. No one approached. He preferred it that way and so he sat, mind blank, until the night came.

He did not sleep. When dawn rose grey across the horizon, he stirred and ordered his horse to be saddled. A nervous stable hand informed him there were no horses available in the village, nor had there been for many years. He took the news in silence, stepped out into the cold of the day and looked to the heavens. *God help me.*

Within the hour, accompanied by a retinue of two score chosen warriors, he set off across the wild, windswept landscape, crossing the few miles to the capital on a shaggy pony that someone had hastily readied for him. Swathed in thick furs, snow flurries spattered his face, but he cared not. He was king now, and kings did not flinch from the vagaries of the weather, no matter how harsh.

In the short space of time since he landed at Winterfeld, so much had changed, his life upturned, his past nothing more than a flickering dream. No longer the lord of a scattering of village dwellings, as king his responsibilities were great. He had much to do, and he was under no illusion of the difficulties facing him. For too long his father, King Harald, had allowed control to lapse, giving free reign to petty chieftains to swagger and argue amongst themselves over who owned what piece of muddy dirt. The land ran brown with shit, and crops withered in the ground whilst spiteful, jealous men squabbled and farted their days away. And all the while, the great king festered in his hall, surrounded by simpering sycophants, stinking of sweat and ale-ridden filth. Olaf knew it all, and he hated every thought. But the mantle laid upon him, for good or ill, was his now and his mind was clear. There would be struggles ahead, obstacles to overcome and minds to meld to his will. He was under no illusions as to the difficulties facing him, given the resistance of his countrymen to controversial ideas.

Five years or more ago, Olaf had woken from a dream, eyes wide with terror, the images still burning across his mind. Through a seething black furnace of blazing shields, axes, swords and Viking helmets, a man strode towards him, a man like no other he had ever seen. Slim and tall, dressed in simple peasant's garb, the face of an angel with ice-blue eyes piercing into his very soul. And a smile, so warm, so mild. When the man reached forward with a hand and pressed it against Olaf's heart, the fires died to reveal amongst the smoking ruin, a single cross.

The cross of Christ.

Olaf converted to Christianity that same day, trekking over the empty land to the coast. He took a skiff across the isthmus and landed on an island he knew well. A journey of half a day, to a Dane-held promontory and a tiny wooden church perched perilously on the cliff edge. Throwing himself to the ground, arms spread out in supplication, he announced his wish to serve God. The monks, awestruck for several moments, recovered their wits, tended to him and baptised him.

And now he must do the same for this pagan land. Christianity had made inroads, but wandering monks and priests were still set upon and many murdered, their bodies stripped and thrown into ditches. The old gods held sway over much of the kingdom, and every other village had a *hirdma,* a powerful dignitary who would lift his voice to Odin and damn the 'eastern effete whoremongers' who brought their creed to the far north. It was a creed, Olaf knew, that had flourished in Rome and continued in far-off Byzantium. Even those erstwhile cousins in France, the so-called Normans proclaimed the Christ as the one, true God. The message, given by saints and disciples, was powerful and irresistible. Olaf had no intention of allowing it to be ignored in his own, frozen land.

The imposing walls of Westfold stood as solid and as intimidating as he always remembered. Thick timber ramparts as high as the largest trees in the surrounding forests, a vast enclave and a sign to all that here was a seat of power. Flanking the main gate, reached by a draw-bridge that, when lowered, spanned a deep, steep-sided ditch, were two immense black towers, bristling with guards, the twin dragon pennants fluttering in the breeze. Olaf reined in his mount and leaned forward. So, they had yet to lower his father's banner, no doubt be-lieving Olaf would retain the device that had served his family for at least three generations. He screwed up his mouth, the knot in his guts twisting tighter. To replace it with the cross of Christ would be the least difficult of his obstacles to overcome. That particular pleasure would be in how to present his ideas to his mother, the queen.

Still some distance away, the teeth-clenching sound of grinding, groaning ropes and pulleys filled the air as the drawbridge came down with controlled slowness. It hit the far side of the ditch with a resounding thud, throwing up puffs of snow and ice. Olaf kicked the pony's flanks and eased forward as the great double-doors yawned open, warriors already assembling in the bailey. They lined up in two opposite ranks to form a corridor for the new king to parade through. Over the drawbridge he came, the steady clump of his pony's steps across the creaking boards giving the impression of a confidence Olaf did not feel. He dipped his head as he passed through the doors and almost baulked when he saw the throng pressing up against the lines of soldiers. It seemed as if the entire population of his realm had come to witness his inaugural visit as king. People waved, cheered and laughed, happy faces upturned towards him, all filled with expectation and hope. Dogs barked and children laughed. A festive atmosphere, so unlike anything he had known before. He maintained his stiff-backed pose, eyes set straight ahead, jawline hard as stone, although he so longed to turn, acknowledge their greetings, smile back and thank them. He swallowed the urge, and continued on an unerring line towards the figures standing at the end of the avenue of spears.

Queen Asta folded her arms, face impassive. She wore a simple sky-blue gown, her head covered with a white mourning shawl. Next to her, Standa, looking serious, dressed in his finest clothes and well-oiled byrnie, holding his helmet in one hand and leaning on his axe with the other. Neither flickered as Olaf pulled up before them and swung down from his saddle.

Falling to one knee, Standa proclaimed, "Greetings, Lord and King of Westfold," and bowed his head. In the background, voices cheered.

Asta's eyes narrowed. "Greetings Olaf. How was your raid?"

Olaf sucked in his lips and ignored the barb. "How is your mourning, Mother?"

The queen shrugged. "He was old and had been sickly for months. I trust you are not going to blub."

"I've done enough blubbing. Why did you bury him with such haste?"

Before she could answer, Standa rose, his face full of concern, and motioned for Olaf to move into the Great Hall. "My lord, perhaps we could continue inside?"

Olaf turned to his retinue drawn up behind him. "Get yourself some refreshment, lads. And to you all," he threw out his arms in a show of collective embracing, "I greet you, my people! May God's love shine upon you all."

A murmur meandered through the gathering, some people cheering in response, others too shocked to say anything. Olaf spun on his heels and strode into the hall.

The door closed with a loud, heavy thud, shutting out the sounds of the crowd. Olaf stood, looked around the huge, cavernous space, and breathed in the pervading aroma of stale beer and sweat. At the far end a fire roared in the grate, the trestle tables ready for the celebratory feast. Along the walls, set high up, shields adorned with numerous motifs identifying the various chieftains and *hirdmen* who would attend later. Olaf let his eyes scan over them, recognising most but not all. When he came to the two at the very far end, he paused. Hanging on opposite walls, they were identical and each accompanied by crossed, gold-tipped spears. The prancing bear of Sigurd Syr, ruler of Ringerike and the most powerful Earl in the land. If anyone were to confront Olaf and contest his desire to see Christianity established across Norway, it would be Sigurd Syr.

"I'm not sure if that was wise, my lord."

Olaf frowned, craning his neck as Standa approached. "There's no point in hiding my intentions, Standa." He looked again at Syr's emblems, which many considered magical, and sighed. "When do they all arrive?"

Asta moved passed him, her gown sweeping across a floor recently covered with fresh straw. "They are already here." She stopped and measured him with a hard stare. "They couldn't wait to proclaim their loyalty to the new king."

"Whilst the old one is barely interred? Without my having the chance to see him for one last time? I'm saddened by that, Mother."

"You've seen him many times, so save your feigned sorrow Olaf for those who do not know you as well as I."

He bristled, straightened his back and returned her gaze. "I'm not the man I was."

"Really? So what has changed you, pray tell? Your new-found faith in a god that no one can see, who demands you feast on his flesh and drink his blood? I am not the only one who has misgivings about what you have become, Olaf."

"I see the main table has not yet been set," said Olaf, ignoring her remarks. "Who will sit with me, Mother? Besides you, I mean."

She glared, "Damn your arrogant hide! You'll not bend this kingdom to your ways, Olaf. You will bring nothing but strife and disorder to this land if you continue with your plans to embrace what is not the Norse way. Think well before you make any more proclamations." She swirled round, the conversation ended, and strode off towards the rear of the hall and the exit to her private chambers.

Standa blew out a long breath, laid his great axe on one of the tables and leaned on his hands. He shook his head. "My lord, I need to talk to you."

"No more about my beliefs, Standa. I've had enough of trying to justify myself to—"

"Forgive me, but it is not that." Another breath, longer again this time. "It is something of much graver importance, I fear."

Olaf frowned. "Graver?" He clapped Standa on the shoulder. "What can be graver than my wish to lead my people towards the true faith, eh? It won't be easy and there will many who will oppose me." He flickered his eyes across Syr's shields. "But it is something I have to do, for the sake of all our souls."

"Of more pressing importance, then. It cannot wait."

"You've always been a good and faithful friend of mine, Standa. If what you have to say is causing you pain, then perhaps you should simply tell it?"

"Aye." Standa stood up straight and turned to face his king. "But I fear that what I have to say will cause you nothing but heartbreak and ... perhaps even rage."

Olaf leaned back against the table edge closest to him. "Then take a deep breath and tell me, old friend."

Standa closed his eyes briefly before saying, in a low, quaking voice, "So be it.

Three

The first snows had not yet fallen, but it was bitingly cold and the man in the coarse green cloak shivered uncontrollably as he tramped up to the lonely, dilapidated hovel and banged on the door. After a moment, the rotting timbers creaked open and the old crone, face in deep shadow beneath the enormous cowl covering her head, jutted out her chin, cackled, and waved him inside.

Rivulets of damp ran down the walls, and a thick pall of smoke clung to the rafters. A meagre fire spluttered in the grate, giving off the merest hint of warmth. The man in the coarse green cloak went down on his haunches and rubbed his hands in front of the last few embers. He coughed constantly.

"Drink this," she said, handing him a chipped cup filled with steaming, black liquid. He sniffed it, screwed up his face. "It will help take away the cold."

He raised the brew to his lips, took a tentative sip and, surprised at how good it tasted, he drank it down.

Almost at once a warm glow spread out from his stomach, bringing not only warmth but a kind of elation. A lightening of his spirits. He rocked back, peering into the fire, feeling safe, secure, as if he were home again in the bosom of his loving family. His eyes grew heavy and he surrendered to the delicious sensations enveloping him.

* * *

She sat him in a stiff-backed chair, removed his boots and massaged his feet. His head lolled on his chest and he moaned in a faraway voice. She smiled, her nimble fingers sliding upwards beneath his loosened breeches, over his shins to his thighs. His head tilted backwards, mouth open, a long, low groan coming from deep within.

"You will see whatever you wish to see," she said softly, almost to herself. "And I will use you as I see fit."

She put her hands under his armpits and lifted him with ease. Emaciated, he was as light as a child. She laid him down on her truckle bed and removed his clothing. She stood back, imagining how firm and strong his young body would be once he healed. Her nails raked across his torso and he squirmed beneath her. The skin appeared grey, the sickness within him close to victory. He barely stirred as she examined his manhood. It promised much. Then, with more haste, she went to the stove, returning with a bowl of hot water, and bathed him with a sopping rag. She splashed sweet-smelling ointments over his flesh, bringing new life to his limbs, a vibrancy to his skin. She spooned one of her many potions into his mouth, holding his nose, forcing him to swallow. After several tiny convulsions, he grew quiet once more, his breathing regular and shallower. He slept.

When at last he woke, his eyes clear, skin glowing, she crossed to where she prepared her meals. "There are beans," she said and without waiting for an answer, ladled lumps of clotted green goo into a wooden bowl. She moved back across the room, shoved the bowl across the table and waddled away again to the corner, where a great iron pot bubbled on a bright flame.

He gathered the blanket around him, took up a chair and set himself down to eat, using the same spoon as the crone had served the food. He munched noisily and she studied him over her shoulder and made a contemptuous clucking noise with her tongue. "Have you the payment?"

He grunted, licking his lips as the last mouthful disappeared down his throat. He motioned to his coat draped over the back of another chair. She took hold of it and passed it over. From inside his cloak he produced a small leather purse and tossed it onto the table. She hefted the purse and gave what might have passed for a smile and returned to her endeavours.

The man coughed up a globule of bloody phlegm and spat it out onto the earthen floor. He studied the red, frothing bubble and shuddered.

"You'll catch your death if you go out again," the crone said, sniffing at her brew through nostrils, which sounded as if stuffed with dried mucous. "Best stay here for the night. It'll make no difference to the poison if you wait another day. Or several."

She came over and held out her hand. He eyed the limb, confused. The skin here was smooth, firm, not like an old woman's at all. He turned his gaze to her face, her features concealed within the dark shadows of the cowl she forever wore. Shrugging off his confusion, he groped inside his cloak. He brought out a sheathed dagger, the scabbard of red, cracked leather, the tip strengthened with metal, but it was past its best. Not so the blade. When the crone took it from him and slowly drew it out, she gasped, marvelling at how the weapon sparkled even in the gloom of that stinking hovel. She held it up, squinting as she ran her eyes over the superb craftsmanship, the keen edge, the promise of a sharp, swift death.

"A wonderful thing," she whispered in awe, turning the dagger this way and that. "How did you come by it?"

"Did you undress me?"

The question wrong-footed her for a moment. She looked around, as if the answer lay somewhere in the room. She sniggered. "I bathed you. You had a fever."

He frowned, averting his eyes. "Has it gone?"

"Time will tell. You have travelled far, as they always seem to do."

"They?"

"Men, like you." She ran her eyes over the blade once more. "But none has ever had a weapon like this. Where did it come from?"

"A trader from the east sold it to me. He told me it was Arabian." A sudden bout of coughing seized him and he doubled up, body heaving and groaning as he hacked up another mouthful of catarrh and spat it into the ground.

"You're sick," she said needlessly, and slid the blade back into the sheath. "If you don't rest here, your mission will be doomed before it even begins."

"Mission?" He glared at her. "What do you know of it?"

She tilted her head, noting his attempted intimidation, but given his current condition he was no more of a threat to her than a whimpering newborn. She clicked her tongue and threw the dagger onto the table top. "As much as I need to, and a damned sight less than you suspect." She put her hands on her solid hips and leaned forward, "I could brew up some spiced wine, that'll do you good. Laced with cinnamon, a few herbs to ease that chest of yours?"

Stifling another cough, he turned from her gaze and fingered the dagger. "It will work, won't it?" He shook his head. "The poison. It must be swift, I might only get one chance."

She straightened her back, as much as she was able. Living in constant humidity had swollen her joints, made her old before her time. His mention of the east brought back distant memories, of a time when she had dreams and desires, a yearning to go far, far away, feel the warmth of the sun on her face, to lie on silken cushions and feel the love of a good man's hands roaming her body. But the only 'good' thing about Rance had been his premature death. A deceitful, worthless man, he had wooed her with promises of travel, of a merchant ship, of long nights beneath his urgent loins. She soon realised all of it was a fabrication, that all he wanted was her skill at concocting potions, and the chance to sell them and make as much as he could before he abandoned her to the cruel, cold winds of the Norse. None of it worked out. After their third or fourth coupling, and the frustration she always felt, he went out into the ice and snow, caught a chill and died. No one mourned. No one cared. But being alone aged her, made her hard and unfeeling. It had been that way for twenty long and bitter years.

"When you apply the liquid to the blade, allow it to dry and become invisible again. It will remain potent for a little over a year. As long as you do not expose it to daylight. That is the key." She reached over and patted his arm. "Stay. I will care for you, rid you of your sickness."

His eyes glazed over, and she could see the resistance leaving his body as his shoulders slumped and his chin fell onto his chest. "I must travel to the coast, from where I came. Time is running, and I must do what I have to do before the winter snows take hold."

She squeezed his arm. "It'll take but a few days. I have ointments and creams that will warm you, rid you of your ills ... In mind as well as body."

"I have no ills in my mind," he said, but his voice betrayed his uncertainty.

"And I have other things too." She squeezed his arm tighter, and she was pleased that he made no effort to move away. "I have potions that will make you more *alive* than you have ever dreamed possible."

He raised his head. "What do you mean?"

I have him, she thought to herself in triumph, sensing her heartbeat quickening, the warmth spreading through her body. She was older, wiser since Rance's betrayal. But not old. She may have the appearance of a crone for she had laboured long in appearing as one. Her body, beneath the folds of her coarse garments, remained firm, and she still yearned for companionship. A man such as this, young, eager, could give her the companionship she yearned for, keep her safe and, with her potions, well satisfied. "I mean why don't you rest? Sleep? I will make you the wine, and you will see. Don't fight it." Another squeeze. "I will serve you well."

He went to say something, but then, without warning, the blood drained from his face and he jackknifed forward, his head hitting the table with an ugly sounding slap. She felt for a pulse under his chin and gave a long sigh of relief when she found it. Then, she sat back and thought about lifting him into the bed again. He was light, but still something of a burden. Not for the first time she wished she had the knowledge to concoct a potion that would give her physical strength.

Four

A serf fumbled and dithered with the hauberk, adjusting and readjusting whilst Sigurd Syr stood with a horn of ale in hand and tapped his feet with impatience. Finally he could take it no longer and he shoved the serf away with a curse, "I'll do it my damned self!" He threw the ale away, the horn clattering against the far wall, and struggled with the leather straps. The serf, sitting on the floor, whimpered and struggled to his feet just as the door flew open and Queen Asta strode in. She dismissed the serf with a glance and he ran out at a sprint, grateful to be free of his master's rage.

"What are you doing?"

"What does it look like," he breathed, grunting as he tried to get his hands around the side of the chain mail.

Asta clicked her tongue and stepped forward, swatting his hands away, and gave the leather a fearful tug. He gasped. "Quiet, you fool! All you need to do is lose some weight."

He gritted his teeth and sucked in his gut. Another tug and the straps were done. The Queen stepped back and admired her handiwork, and Sigurd Syr. "Not bad for a roly-poly pudding."

She laughed, and he did too, opening his arms and embracing her. After a moment, he pushed her back and let his eyes take in her loveliness. Her mouth drew him in and he kissed her, long and passionately, tasting the sweetness of her lips; honeydew and apples. Under his half-coat, his member pressed hard against his breeches and she laughed, cupped her hand around him and gave him a playful squeeze. "I have to have you," he said in her ear, his voice thick with lust.

"And so you shall." She kissed him again and then it was her turn to push him away. "But not at this moment, you great boar!" He laughed but soon ceased as her eyes levelled him with a new cold, seriousness. "Olaf is here."

Sigurd's shoulders dropped and he pulled a face. "So soon? He must have flown on an eagle, damn him."

"No. He's simply anxious to sit on his dead father's throne ... before you do."

"Damn his hide." Sigurd whirled away and strode over to the table and a waiting flagon of ale. He looked around for the horn, saw it and decided to drink from the flagon instead. The ale ran down through his beard and he smacked his lips loudly when he was done, and slammed the flagon back down on the table top. "What have you told him?"

"The truth."

"About—?" He stopped when he saw her face, that mischievous glint in her ice-blue eyes. "No, you haven't, have you?"

"I told him his father had dropped dead from a seizure. That is all ... for now."

Sigurd lifted the flagon and took another, much slower drink this time. "What do you think he will do when he discovers the truth?"

"Go into a rage, as he always has. In that regard he is as much like his father as summer heat is to the sun."

"Or a foul stench is to a pool of piss." He drank.

"How eloquent you are, my love."

He dragged the back of his hand across his mouth and stared at the floor for a long time. "I've heard things, Asta. Whilst back at Ringerike, news reached me of Olaf's desire for Norway to be wholly Christian." He shook his head. "Such a path can only lead to disaster, to the break-up of the country, even war. The northern lands will never give up the old gods and it is folly to try to force them."

"All the more reason why you should take the lead, my love." She glided forward, her finger running under the collar of the heavy hauberk. The chain links were well oiled, the metal shining. He stank of ale and sweat and she loved it. She put her cheek against his chest and almost swooned as he put his great arm around her. So unlike Harald, her late husband, in every conceivable way. Lusty and strong, his body that of a great rutting elk. The first time he had come to her bed she believed he would kill her, so ardent his advances, so urgent his desire to couple. As he lifted her and thrust manfully into her, all such notions disappeared and she knew that at long last she had found a man to savour.

He put his bearded chin on the crown of her head. "When the time is right, fear not."

"But when? I had hoped you would strike him on his journey from the coast."

"As I said, he took me by surprise. Besides, I believe he will do much of it for us. All this talk about a new faith, the people won't accept it. Nor the Earls. You'll see. Before long, Olaf will have slit his own throat without us even raising a dagger."

"And if there isn't an uprising? What if he seduces them with that oily tongue of his, with promises of bread and safety? No doubt there are many who will follow him, probably more than you would believe. The promise of eternal life, of salvation. It's a powerful lure, my love. You had best not underestimate this new faith, this new god."

"It'll fizzle away, Asta. The old gods will prevail, as they have for a thousand years or more."

"But what if they don't? What if the people want something new, something as unlike the old ways as you can imagine? What then?"

"Then we find another way."

She pulled back her head and stared at him. "What sort of 'other way'?"

He grinned, took her by her slim shoulders and was about to kiss her when he stopped and frowned, body tensing, alert. Gently, he moved her to the side, winked, pressed his finger to his lips, and drifted over to the door. With a sudden lunge he tore it open, grabbed the serf lurking outside by the throat and yanked him inside. He threw the boy to the ground and kicked the door shut with the sole of his boot.

"What is the meaning of this?" Asta was furious, her eyes wild, lips drawn back across her teeth, hissing like a wild cat preparing to strike.

"Mistress, *please!*" The boy squirmed around on the ground, both hands up in supplication, the tears streaming down his face and a developing patch of damp spreading across the crotch of his breeches.

Sigurd stepped over him, face black with rage. He yanked the boy's head back by the hair and glared down at him. "Who sent you to spy on me, boy."

"No one, my lord, *I swear it.*"

"Then what were you doing listening outside the door," demanded Asta, her fists bunched, her whole body shaking. "Was it my son who sent you? King Olaf?"

"*Impossible,*" spat Sigurd, "this whelp has been with me for six moons." He tugged the hair tighter and the serf yelped. "Tell me who sent you." In a blur, Sigurd drew out an evil looking dagger, its blade black, dented and jagged. "Or I'll slice open your throat and feed you to the crows."

"Dear God, no!"

At that moment the boy soiled himself and Sigurd stepped back, gagging, clamping his hand to his nose and mouth. "You dirty bloody bastard!"

"*Wait!*" Asta flew forward and got down next to him, ignoring the vile smell. She gripped the boy by the cheeks. "What did you say?"

He looked at her without understanding, his eyes filled with tears, body quaking, the terror conquering him.

The Queen looked up at Sigurd, lips pressed together, voice hard when she spoke. "You understand now, Sigurd? How difficult this is going to be?"

He frowned, cocked his head to one side. "What are you talking about, woman?"

"This ... *viper*," she threw the serf's head away and stood up, careful not to step in the piss and shit that seeped out of the boy's breeches, "is a Christian."

Sigurd gaped. "Don't be so bloody stupid! He can't be."

"Well, he is. Aren't you?" She gave him a sharp kick in the ribs with the toe of her shoe. He cried out, clutched his side and nodded, muttering something incomprehensible. "He said 'Dear God, no'. Didn't you hear him? A Christian, in your own household. They're everywhere, Sigurd. And if you don't act, they'll take over everything."

He gaped at her and stumbled over to the table and the flagon of ale, swore when he found it was empty and sent it flying away with a swipe of his hand. He hung his head low and mumbled, without turning, "Then we have no choice, do we?" He straightened his back and turned. "He'll have to die."

Five

The thick smell of smouldering wood invaded his nostrils and he spluttered, opened his eyes and tried to focus. For a moment, panic gripped him, the memory of where he was vague, images blurry, nothing defined. Smoke from the burning logs in the grate filled the room, stinging his eyes. He rubbed away the grit and the tears with his fists and sat up. He was naked, the bedclothes thrown back revealing his body, and his groin smeared with a sort of grease, a grease that burned but not in any way unpleasant. In fact, as he grew more aware of his surroundings, sensations developing across his lower abdomen, a comforting warmth, a tingling through his member which grew into something quite delicious.

He fell back on the bed, groaning as his erection stuck out like a post, pulsing with intensity. Sweat broke out on his upper lip, his heart thumped, his throat tight. He reached down with his hand and caressed himself and gasped at what he found. Never had he been so hard, never so full.

Someone moved in the gloom. A figure, small, making tiny, mewing noises. Soft hands fluttered across his hard manhood, cupping him with the palm, then teasing him with fingers so light, so delicate he almost cried out. Soon came a warmth, moist, soft, enveloping his engorged sex and he realised at once what was happening but he didn't care. He gave himself up to the sensations, lifted up his hips to give his silent seducer greater access. He wanted to scream, to surrender, to feel the rush of orgasm. Before he could, however, the figure straddled him, eased him into something more luscious than he had ever known. He was lost as that sweet flesh gripped him, moved with urgent thrusts and all too soon he was coming, coming with such heat and ferocity he believed he would die. He cried out, seizing the figure's hips, and drove himself deep, erupting in wild convulsions of passion.

He collapsed back on the bed, breathless, awash with sweat. The figure slipped from him, pausing only to plant a soft kiss on his lips before darkness came and sleep overcame him.

* * *

A thick fur draped over his body when he awoke the second time and the smoke had gone. Despite the cover, a sharp coldness clawed at his flesh and when he sat up he saw the door gaping open, the snow drifts beyond, and the ice-blue sky. Morning. He put his face in his hands and rubbed himself vigorously. The dream had been so real, so vivid he felt almost ashamed as the images returned to his mind. In all his life, such sensations had never visited themselves upon him, so why now. He had known women, not many, but enough. None had brought him to such a height of satisfaction as the one in his dream. His fever must have been great indeed.

He looked around. The tiny, cluttered hovel was empty. A fire crackled in the grate, a blackened pot simmered over the flames. Next to it a rickety table, close to collapse, covered with various jars, bottles and horn cups, and more black pots. The smell of potions, herbs and spices clung everywhere, but the dreadful smoke had gone, and he thanked the gods for it. He swung his legs over the side of the bed, and realised he was still naked. As in the dream.

Something seized him. A chill, deep inside his bowels, freezing his joints but focusing his mind. He dared to glance down and saw his limp manhood. And the remnants of a grease or cream.

He leaped to his feet, desperate to find his clothes, a thousand thoughts tumbling through his mind, confusion, fear, dread. He snapped his head this way and that, threw over chairs and boxes, clumps of straw, old clothes, the clutter of a lifetime. He had to find his clothes, he had to get out of here. He was in the clutches of a sorceress, a witch.

"You shouldn't be out of your bed."

He whirled around, forgetting his nakedness, and glared at the woman as she struggled through the door with a great bundle of firewood. With an effort, she crossed to the fire and threw down the wood, wiped her hands on the front of her gown, and looked at him smiling. "You seem better, but you should be in bed. The fever still lingers."

"What did you do to me?"

She cackled, shaking her head as she bent down and began to sort out the firewood into different sizes. "Nothing that you didn't want yourself."

His mouth fell open and he looked at her, not daring to believe that his dream could be real. But, no matter how hard he tried to convince himself otherwise, he knew the truth of what had happened. She had covered him in some ointment, to bring him to hardness, to a level of excitement previously unknown. And he hadn't resisted. Couldn't resist. The ointment had done its work, and he had coupled with her, and now here she was again, grinning at him, knowing he had enjoyed it, knowing it was indeed what he had wanted.

He looked at her, swathed as she was in thick clothing, a gown, undergarments, shawl, each layer padded to give some protection against the extreme cold. Cold that dug deep, set his teeth to chatter. All at once he realised how cold he was, his flesh exposed and, without another thought, he jumped back into bed and drew the fur up around his throat, his body shivering.

She waddled over to him, a cup of steaming liquid in her hand. "Drink this. Sweet, spiced wine. It will warm you, give you strength."

From beneath his blanket, his eyes glared. "How could you do this to me? Ensnare me like this. Where are my clothes, damn you?"

"Drink." Her voice was soft, gentle. She brought the cup closer and the delicious aroma set his mouth to salivate. He took her hand in both of his and drank, closing his eyes as the warmth seeped through him, spreading out from his belly and into his groin. He put his head back and closed his eyes.

"What have you done to me? Bewitched me with your potions and your …" Her hand slipped under the fur and found his cock. He wanted to push her away, to tell her to stop … or did he? The touch of her hand, the movement of her fingers, the rich glow of the wine. He groaned and surrendered, despising himself for his weakness, but loving what she was doing.

She stepped back and tugged away at her clothing, the many layers that covered her dropping one by one. He watched, mesmerised. As her last undergarment fell to the ground, he gazed at her body and saw that she was not a crone at all, but a woman of middle years, stomach hard, breasts pert, and waist and hips slim, round and soft.

"I'm going to love you like no one else has ever done," she said, moving closer, "and you are going to stay, and keep me warm through the winter."

She came to him, and his arms draped around the soft giving flesh and he no longer wished to resist, and could not resist as her mouth closed with his. The need to again experience her became all-consuming.

* * *

Later they lay side by side on the floor, having evacuated the bed as their hectic lovemaking splintered the frame and rendered it useless. Three times, he had coupled with her, and now he felt raw and spent, but glowing with a whole series of wondrous sensations. He had his arm under her head whilst his other hand toyed with the nipple of her left breast. She nuzzled into him and moaned softly.

"What am I to do?" he said in a low, frightened voice.

"Do?" She did not stir, her lips pressed against his throat. "You will live here, with me. My potions will bring fire to your manhood, and you will never—"

"No, I meant about my task, the one set for me. I have to complete it or it will be me that becomes the hunted one."

"They will never find you here."

"I did. I sought you out."

"Yes, but it took you months, and that was in autumn, not now in the cold of winter. No one will come looking for you, and when the spring thaw comes, then you can complete this *task* of yours. Your knife will still be potent, even then."

"But what if everything has changed? What if my employer is himself dead, what then?"

"Then you will no longer have to see the thing through, will you? You can return to me, and we will live our lives here. Together."

"So, you think I should still see it through?"

"Yes. But after the winter, after we have kept one another close."

Her hand wandered down to his crotch, but this time he gripped her, pulled up her arm and snarled, "Damn you, woman. Do you never *stop*?"

"Do you want me to," she asked, her voice playful. She nipped at his earlobe and he let her hand drop. "I thought not," she breathed, and slowly crept her fingers over his stomach and down to his twitching manhood.

"This potion," he said, eyes closed tight, tongue so big in his mouth he could barely speak with the desire which conquered him once more. "What in the name of God is it?"

She giggled and draped a leg over his. "Something which will keep us happy."

And happy he was as she slid over him and drowned him in her flesh.

Six

They assembled in the Great Hall later that day, all of the jarls and haulds from across the realm. Pristine in oiled hauberks, polished helms and well-scrubbed faces, they stood in serried ranks, straight of back and hard of gaze. Behind them, set high upon the walls, torches spluttered giving off a dull, red glow. In the hearth, a huge fire roared, serfs forever running backwards and forwards, feeding the flames with thick, blackened logs. The tables laden with platters of roast boar, elk, salmon and pigeon, accompanied by full flagons of mead and ale, some so full they spilled over the rim and splattered the tabletop. No one spoke, but an air of anticipation filled the thick air, everyone waiting for the entrance of their new king.

In the antechamber, Queen Asta put the finishing touches to her eldest son's regalia, repositioning his embroidered cloak of emerald green, edged with gold. The eagle feathered helmet lay waiting, and she stepped back, gave him an approving nod, sweeping a last strand of golden hair from his face before turning and leaving the room.

Olaf let out a long breath and closed his eyes, trying to still his pounding heart, quieten the quivering in his guts.

Sanda picked up the king's sword belt and fastened it around Olaf's waist. He passed over the helmet and inclined his head slightly. "Lord, will you now grant me a moment to speak?"

"Damn it, Sanda, you're like a bloody wolf with a rabbit 'twixt its jaws."

"I wouldn't ask if it were not important, my lord."

"Spit it out then, before I shit my fucking pants."

Sanda dragged in a breath, his eyes still locked to the ground. "It concerns the queen, my lord."

Olaf reached across for the horn of ale on the table and drank it down. "Tell it."

"I am certain your lord father was unaware, but his wife – the Queen, she ..." He brought his eyes up to lock with his old friend's. "She had taken lovers, my lord."

Olaf blinked, then bellowed like a rutting deer. "Is that *it*, Sanda? By all the gold in Rome, I'm not such a fool to not realise my mother had—"

"There is more, lord. Her nightly movements were well known, and she made no efforts to conceal them, slipping out from the rooms she shared with your father, to take her pleasures elsewhere."

"Then what of it? I've heard all this, Sanda. For years I've had her watched. I know all about her *nightly movements* as you so graciously call them. My father married her when she was fourteen, and I was in her belly then. No one can expect any woman, least of all a woman like my mother, to stay with a decrepit old man like Harald. I may not like it, but I can't blame her. Now, if that is the end of it, I'm late." He poured another mouthful of ale and swallowed it down. Smacking his lips he went to turn away. "The sweet earls of Norway await their king."

"What you may not know," said Sanda hurriedly, "is the name of the man she shared her pleasures with."

The king-to-be sighed loudly. "Earl Gissurdson, so I'm told. Hakon Eriksson and haulda Freign. No doubt others."

"Sigurd Syr."

Olaf stopped, eyes staring straight ahead. He wanted to move. To walk through the antechamber door and stride down between those ranks of waiting Norwegian chieftains, to meet their stares full on, to sit upon the royal throne, drink and eat, belch and fart, and guffaw with the best of them. But somehow he couldn't. His legs refused to work and he teetered, reached out for the table's edge and held on whilst the thumping in his head grew so loud he thought his skull would crack open.

Sanda rushed around to face him, placing his palms on Olaf's chest. "Lord, forgive me. I know your spies worked hard, but Syr's worked harder. He is rich and powerful, as well as dangerous. Money buys silence, and with that silence comes a grudging acceptance."

Olaf's lips moved but no sound came from his mouth.

Sanda pushed on, relentless in his desire for the truth. "Lord, there is more."

"More?" Olaf shook his head, lost, unable to understand. *Very well, Syr may have paid everyone, but to know nothing of this.* The most powerful Earl in the land, the one man who could thwart his plans, to block his every move. *He was his mother's lover?* He slumped in a chair and gazed into the distance.

"Your mother ..." Sanda's breath came in short jabs. "Your mother the queen gave birth to two boys, my lord. Twins. She had them in secret and they lodge in Syr's hall, wet-nurses seeing to their needs, guarded night and day by—"

"Children? She's had children by him?" Olaf's fist came slamming down on the table, so hard it sent the empty drinking horn crashing to the hard ground, "No, by Christ. No!"

Sanda stepped back, straight and determined. "It is true, my lord. There can be no doubting it. You have brothers, my lord."

A tiny whimper, like the sound of a strangled bird, came from the back of Olaf's throat as a single tear spilled from his eye and rolled down his cheek.

"Lord," Sanda drew closer, getting down on his knees, and he held the king's hand in both of his. "I am your closest friend, and your oldest, and you know my love for you is beyond doubt, so what I say now I say in earnest. You must act, Lord, act before it is too late." Olaf stared at him with glazed eyes. "Sigurd Syr will object to your desire to make Norway Christian. He has said so himself, both privately and publicly many times. And he has many allies. Many." He squeezed Olaf's great paw. "If you act now, this very night, we can spirit him away, gut his hide and send him on a raft to Trondheim, as if brigands waylaid him. No one will know, this much I swear. Such an act will avert war, and you can secure your realm with not one drop of Viking blood."

Silence hung heavy and ominous in the room. A few last burning twigs sputtered in the grate and, beyond the door, someone pounded on a table demanding ale.

"I ... I never suspected," Olaf began, his voice that of a chastened child, all of his former confidence and strength replaced by shock, even disbelief. "Twins you say?"

"Aye, lord."

"Their names?"

"My lord?"

"Their names, damn you. What are their names?"

"Guthorn and Halfden. Guthorn is the eldest by a few moments, springing from his mother's womb first."

"My father did not know?"

"Not an inkling, lord."

"Then I thank God for that." He turned his gaze to Sanda's hands, which still held his own, and pulled himself away. "I thank you, Sanda. I know this could not have been easy for you."

Sanda smiled, but it was clear the sadness cut deep for his old friend and he remained on his knees as Olaf stood, brushing away an imaginary piece of fluff from his hauberk. "How many know the truth?"

"Of the children?" Sanda shrugged. "A handful. But no one here."

"How did you ... how did you discover it?"

Sanda drew in a great breath as he got to his feet. "I saw them. One night. I had long suspected Gissurdson and Freign were nothing more than playthings and this night I learnt the truth. Sigurd Syr came too often to Westfold, and never stayed long. I followed her this night and saw them." He shook his head. "I'm not proud of it, my lord."

"And then what, you watched her belly swelling?"

The words struck him like slaps and he winced, averting his eyes. "She concealed it well, from those who did not know. She even took to dressing herself, leaving her maids outside of her rooms. To anyone with eyes, it was clear. She had not shared your father's bed for long, so nobody even questioned her. Except myself. When she announced she had business to attend to in Ringerike, I knew her time had come."

Blowing out his cheeks, Olaf adjusted his belt and picked up his helmet, rimmed with beaten gold, great silver eagles wings emblazoned on either side, the eye slots circled with gems. A king's helm.

"Lord, we must move against Sigurd Syr before he can—"

Olaf held up his hand. "Enough, Sanda. Enough." He gave a grudging smile and clamped his hand down on his friend's shoulder. "Not now. Now, I must act the king. *Act,* you understand? Even if this news grieves me, cuts deep, I have my role to play. And I have to convince them all that I am still the strong, and ignorant Olaf Haraldsson. I'll not let them see me as a whimpering cuckold, Sanda, even if that is what they all suspect."

"You're *not* a cuckold, lord. It was your father who—" He clamped his mouth and eyes shut, realising what he was about to say. But Olaf ignored him, squeezed the man's shoulder and moved to the door. "I'm sorry, lord."

"I feel it was me, Sanda." He pushed the helmet down over his head, positioning it with a few jerks before he was satisfied with the fit. "I feel as if my own wife had been violated by that pagan ingrate. And for that reason, more than any other, I'm going to take great pleasure in killing the bastard."

Seven

The hall resonated with the sound of laughter, like great roaring waves, from the assembled mouths, accompanied by the clash of goblets coming together in drunken revelry. Fists pounded on table tops, chins dribbled with grease, men stood on chairs and showed their backsides, farted and belched. Some fought with fists and feet, kicking and punching their way over the floor whilst onlookers urged them on with chanting.

As Olaf entered they bent their knees and lowered their heads and roared as one, 'Hail, King of Westfold!', and then their swords and spears and axes had been collected and taken outside. As the drink flowed, and tongues grew loose, violence was always a probability. Olaf remembered his great uncle's wedding feast, how some had kept daggers. He remembered the killing. Since then, all weapons had been banned from such gatherings. It was a sensible precaution, but it didn't prevent men locking together with their hands, pulling each other to the dirt. And it didn't prevent the blood.

Olaf sat at the head table, raised on a dais, with his mother to one side and Sanda on the other. He watched, aloof, having barely touched his wine. A serving wench had brought his slabs of roast boar but he pushed it away, and his eyes roamed the room and he wondered how many of them knew the truth.

All the lords of the land were here, to proclaim him their king. In two days, his father's crown placed on his head, he'd take the vows.

Old vows, ancient and incorruptible, sworn at the Great Assembly Hall at Haugar. His father, Harald Grenske, had been part of the Fairhair dynasty, his illustrious forefather, another Harald and bearer of the dynasty's surname, being the first great king to introduce Christianity to the northern lands. But subsequent rulers had had little appetite for the new religion, and soon pagan rituals crept back into daily life.

Olaf's father was one of those whose enthusiasm had waned. Under his rule the petty kingdoms had begun to wander back to the old gods, whilst he lusted after other women and allowed his wife, Asta, to couple with other men.

Olaf closed his eyes and squirmed at the thought of it. There was so much to do and the task would not be easy. He opened his eyes and scanned the press of wild, drunken men around the hall, the stink of sweat and ale hanging like a great pall over them all. How was he to lead them back to the path of righteousness without blood-letting, violence, death? His daily prayers for guidance had received no answers, not yet.

"My lord!"

Olaf blinked and snapped his head around to find a tall, youthful looking man dressed in a sable tunic and red breeches standing before him. The man's hair was cut short and he wore no beard, something rarely seen in the Kingdom of Westfold.

The man bowed low from the waist, "I thought it a suitable moment to introduce myself." He had to shout above the din, but there was no denying the cultured tones of his voice, and the unusual accent he possessed.

"And who might you be, sir?"

The young man straightened and grinned. "My name is Robert Gieves, my lord. I am Emissary from the great Duke of Normandy, Richard the Good, sent to bring you his grace's greetings and best wishes for a peaceful and benevolent reign, praise be to God." He bowed again, with a great flourish of his hand.

Olaf gazed at the man, wide-eyed, unblinking. Richard the Good was the greatest champion of Christian belief in Western Europe. To have such a man as ally and friend could well be the greatest coronation gift imaginable. With such support, Olaf could sweep away the old practices of this country in one campaigning season. He leant forward, grinning broadly. "Come, sit with me, Robert Gieves, and tell me more of his grace, and how faith in Christ binds his land." On his travels, Olaf had learnt much of the great Duke, his establishing of monasteries, his church building, his encouragement of the arts and learning. A wise and successful ruler in a hard land.

Without being asked, Sanda stood and beckoned for the young Norman to sit in his chair. Gieves assented with his head and did so, whilst Sanda shuffled away to find another seat. From the other side, Queen Asta leaned forward, a lopsided grin on her face, much the worse for wine, having insisted the beverage be served for she had no taste for ale or mead. Olaf groaned inwardly. Her face flushed, strands of hair poked out from her headband, she made too much of running her tongue over her lips as she eyed the young man with obvious interest. "And who is this charming gentleman?"

"Gentleman in truth, my lady," said Olaf maintaining the proper etiquette despite wanting to bind her mouth shut with a piece of strong cloth. "He is Duke Richard's emissary, from Normandy."

Gieves bowed his head again. He placed his hand over of his goblet as a serving wench attempted to pour ale a for him and smiled his gracious refusal.

"Normandy?" Asta leaned even further forward, right across Olaf who was forced to press himself back against his seat. "I've never been to Normandy. Always wanted to. Heard much about it, of course. As we are of the same blood, it seems only right that we should journey there. Don't you think, dearest son?"

Olaf scowled at her, saw that look on her face, those eyes slightly out of focus, the mocking leer. "Indeed," he muttered.

"Yes!" She slapped her palm down upon the table and laughed. "A regal procession, don't you think? A progress through your new lands, my son, and on through Denmark, the Lowlands of Flanders, and Normandy. What a thing that would be. Wouldn't you agree ... " She frowned and sat up straight, her right index finger waggling in the general direction of the emissary. "You haven't told me your name."

"Robert Gieves, my lady."

She smiled. "Robert? Nice name Robert. Why have you not had any sons called Robert, my dear?" She leaned towards Olaf, and there was spittle on her bottom lip. She gripped his leg at the top of the knee. "In fact, why haven't you had any sons at all? Eh? Why is that, my darling boy?" She grinned, raised up her wine cup and drained it. "Your father wasn't much for sons. Wasn't much for anything, truth be told." She gave a short laugh. "After he got himself involved with that awful woman ... What was her name? Stigurd?"

"Sigrid." said Olaf, who pressed finger and thumb into the corners of his eyes, praying to be anywhere else but here at this moment.

"Yes. That's it. Sigrid. He had to concoct some ridiculous story about him being burned alive in some hall she owned, because he was too *ardent*. There's a laugh — ardent! Only Harald could come up with something so ludicrous. The fact that he couldn't get it up and she sent him away feeling like a weasel was pointedly ignored. Stupid man." She leaned across for the wine jug, but her fingers were just out of reach. She swore and collapsed back in her chair. "I'm tired," she said.

"You should go to bed, Mother."

She narrowed her eyes and studied him for a moment. "Yes, you'd like that I dare say. And you," she pointed her finger at Grieves once again, "would you desire me to go to bed?"

Olaf sucked in a breath, sensing the young Norman's discomfort. He dared not turn to the man, see his cheeks reddening. Instead he kept his face to the front, watched men drink and eat, exchange remarks and stories, heard them bellow.

"All right, dearest boy," said the Queen, shoving her seat backwards and climbing to her feet. "I'm going." She brought up both hands and yelled, "Feast well, my lords!"

Nobody acknowledged her and she spun around with a great swirl of her flowing gown, leaving the dais at the rear, two handmaidens taking her by the elbows and guiding her out of the Great Hall.

When she had gone, Sanda returned and took her place, giving Olaf a quick look before he settled down and tore into a piece of roast pigeon.

Olaf smiled. "Apologies for my mother, she is somewhat the worse for drink."

"It's understandable," the young emissary said, picking up some slivers of pork from the salver before him, "on a night such as this, who can blame anyone for celebrating?" He slipped the pork into his mouth and munched it down, juices running out the sides of his mouth. He licked his lips and took up another piece. "My lord the Duke is most happy to learn of your ascendancy, my grace. It is no secret that many rulers throughout Europe have grown uneasy at what has been happening in the far north. The King of France himself has openly stated he dreads the thought of the Norse returning to the yesteryears of plunder and conquest, all of it fuelled by beliefs in Asgard, Valhalla and the wrath of Odin."

Olaf frowned. "You know much about our pagan beliefs, Robert Gieves."

"Only what I've heard. I've never undergone any formal study, but yes, I know a little." He swallowed the meat and licked at his fingers before continuing, "My lord the Duke is anxious to learn of your plans, your grace. Most importantly of all, he wishes to know how you intend to proceed with the conversion of your subjects. Your father was not the most *devout* of rulers."

"Are you from Normandy, sir, *or Rome*?" Gieves smiled. "Do not doubt my determination. I am not so foolish as to believe it will be easy, but neither do I have any intentions of shying away from what has to be done." He took a breath and rested his head against the back of his chair. "But you're right. My father was lax in his duties. A Christian man himself, he cared not what others believed and perhaps it was that which maintained the peace for so long. Who knows?" He picked up a goblet of ale and studied it. "He was a dullard, apathetic, enjoying the trappings of being king without performing any of the tasks which were his duty to undertake. Others did that for him, or so he believed.

A great pile of clerks and scribes who, for the most part, went through the motions of government but who sat on their arses and played dice, whored and drank." He threw back the ale in one and gasped. "I'll not go down that route, Robert Gieves. You can reassure your masters, there will be no return to the Viking ways whilst I sit on the throne."

"*Masters?* Your grace, I serve the Duke of Normandy who—"

"You serve the wishes of Holy Mother Church, Robert Gieves. Not that I'm against those, of course, but it would have been courteous of you to mention the Pope by name."

Gieves let his mouth open, but then smiled. "You're a wise man, your grace. A *modern* man, I would add. One who has looked into the future and realises that the past, no matter how glorious, must be put away. Paganism has no place in Europe, not now."

"I know that, and that is what I propose to do." He raised another cup of ale to his mouth.

"Yes, and my lord the Duke wishes to deliver to you a thousand horse, to aid you in your endeavours."

Olaf coughed and almost choked on his drink, sending a spray of ale across the table. Those who saw it in the pack of revellers roared with laughter, raised their goblets, and cheered.

The king waved them away with a grin and wiped his mouth with the back of his hand. "A thousand horse? Dear God, is he serious?"

Gieves spread out his hands. "Of course. If your grace will grant us safe haven, my lord will send the men by ships to your port within the month. Before the snows come and the ice begins to harden."

"I'll need more than a month to ready my men. Best if he sends them by spring. We cannot campaign through winter."

"You expect a campaign? My lord is of the belief that as soon as any of your pagan earls set eyes upon Norman cavalry, they will throw down their arms and surrender their souls to Christ."

"He could be right, but even so ..." He chewed on his lips, dragging in portions of his beard, tasting the salt and the spilt ale. "I'm not sure. You lord has no understanding of our winters. They are hard and cruel. I would beg of him to consider spring."

"He is impatient, your grace. And so is God."

* * *

Olaf stood in his bedroom, the shutters open, and he stared out into the night. The sky, blue-black, was clear, the stars like so many precious gems twinkling in the frosty air. Nothing moved, the occasional hooting owl the only sound to break the stillness. *A thousand horse. Dear Christ, such a force would send dread through the souls of heathen folk. To couple them with his own huscarles, now there would be an army. It would mean changes in tactics, and the logistics of maintaining all those animals a serious headache. Especially in winter. Damn winter, and damn the snow. And damn Harald for dying.*

He closed his eyes and breathed in the good, clean air. "Dear Christ, give me the strength," he said softly. He needed strength if he was to see his chosen path through to the end. But Christ was good, and would answer his prayers. Olaf knew that now. Not with miracles or detached voices in the night, but by deeds and actions. Ask, and the Lord replied. Olaf had asked, and the reply had come in Duke Richard's promise of one thousand horse. No more doubts, not any longer. Only the certain fact that what had to be done would be done.

And now was the time to do it.

Eight

The procession wended its way across the open plain, a great snake stretching behind the lead ponies, Olaf astride the lead one, swathed in a thick blanket, huddled against the cold. His retinue behind consisted of his personal guard, servants, grooms, cooks and maids. Queen Asta sat inside a covered wagon, kitted out with soft cushions and fine drapes in an effort to make it as courtly and as comfortable as possible. The journey to Haugar, the seat for the *Haugathing,* the establishing and proclamation of a new king, was not a long one. But in this intense cold, with the wind howling across the fields to pinch and bite at exposed flesh, it seemed farther than any of Olaf's Viking raids. He squeezed his lips tight together, pulled his blanket closer, and tried to empty his mind of any thoughts, least of all the ones from his past. He was a king now, and a Christian one. The past was done, dead and buried. What he had done he had done in ignorance. Five years ago, a boy of nineteen, he had raided, pillaged and raped with the best of them. Not any longer. His last raid, a paltry affair, had proved to him that such excesses had to end. Even if his father had lived, it is doubtful whether Olaf would have continued the life as a raider. The old Viking ways no longer held such sway over him. Much remained to be done if he were to rein in his vengeful spirit, he knew that. God may forgive him. That is what he prayed for. Forgiveness. But Viking blood coursed through his veins. Not everything about the old life could be put away so neatly and calmly.

At last, the thin wisp of grey smoke that drifted up through the trees told them all that Haugar was close. A cry went up from the scouts and Olaf pulled up his pony and raised his head. The farm was huge, a vast sprawling estate given over to cereal crops and some cattle. But it was the buildings which took everyone's breath away. Three great barns larger in size than any great hall in the whole of Norway, set around the huge, solid looking central building, with its towers and fortified walls. More a castle than a farm, it was not the possession of any single earl or lord, but the great meeting place of Westfold. Here kings were crowned, proclamations set. Its prominence over all other seats of government, clear to see from miles around.

Olaf had never laid eyes on the place before, his father's rule well established by the time Olaf was born. Harald had reigned since the death of his own father. At eleven years of age he had ascended the throne, nursed and guided by a succession of powerful earls who schooled him in the ways of government. But Harald had showed little inclination to do what was right and took much greater pleasure in creating a series of mythical stories concerning his life, employing court poets and writers to embroider and embellish. One such story told of him being burned alive by a lover, whilst Asta, his queen and wife, gave birth to their son Olaf. Here, at Hauger, Harald had sat in judgement and received the fealty of the rich and powerful most of whom were in two minds over their king's nature. Did he believe in the tales written about him, or could he be an even-handed and just ruler?

The mysterious deaths of anyone who voiced doubts seem to prove this was not the case.

Olaf kicked his mount and slowly slipped over the slight rise and continued towards the great farm, a buzz of anticipation accompanying him from his entourage. His father may have been full of fanciful fictions, and his rule may have been oppressive and severe, but Olaf had sworn before God, and himself, that he would do what was right. To bring the love of Christ to these disaffected, leaderless people, to steer them towards the bosom of Holy Mother Church. That was his destiny, and it was to begin this day, in this hallowed place, where ancient kings had sat and received the pledges of allegiance from landowners, both great and small. Now it was to be Olaf's turn and it would be interesting to see which of them would bend their knee.

A hand took the reins and brought his pony to a halt. "My lord," said the old man who looked up and grinned, showing a wide, blackened gap where his teeth should be. "It fills my heart with joy to see you so well."

Olaf grunted and swung down from the saddle, and immediately rubbed his backside through the many layers of clothing meant to protect him from the harsh weather. "How can you stand to live here, Svein?"

"It's beautiful in the summer." The old man chuckled to himself, and gave the pony over to a stable boy who led the wretched animal away. All around, the remainder of the procession drifted into the wide courtyard and dismounted, stamping their feet, and blowing hot breath into their hands. Svein raised an eyebrow. "You've brought many soldiers, Olaf."

Svein was so old he had overseen the coronation of Olaf's own father, some twenty-four years previously. Many said he had been in service during the time when the Danes held sway over Norway and Bluetooth ruled. Olaf did not know if this were true or not, but Svein seemed older than the hills, his face dried up and criss-crossed with myriad creases, his eyes rheumy and weeping, hair white and sparse. Despite the years, it was clear he retained his wits.

"Are you expecting trouble?"

"I'm expecting resistance."

"Ah?" Svein looked at the king-to-be.

"There are those who will not accept my desires to bring the true faith to this land, and unite it under God."

"I fear you may be right. Your father was a good Christian, so to your grandfather. But they never did what you wish to do, my lord. Convert the entire land."

Olaf's breath streamed out of his mouth and nose. "My father a good Christian? Is that what you believe, old man?" He shook his head. "My father was a whorer and drunkard, you know it as well as I."

"But he was respected, Olaf. Feared."

"But not loved."

"A king cannot be loved by all."

"No." Olaf rolled his shoulders and cast off the blanket, folding it over his arm. "But God can. And God will be."

They crossed the yard together, their boots sinking into the soft black mud that oozed with animal manure and set off a dreadful stink. Closing his mind to it as best he could, the king-to-be stomped into the vast hall where already the gathering of earls, lords, landowners and various lesser vassals mingled. The murmuring gradually died away as Olaf stood in the entrance, framed by the light from without, an impressive figure encased in fur robes and thick leather jerkin, face ruddy with the journey.

He took a moment to scan the faces of the many who bent from the waist, and those who merely lowered their heads. He noted the ones who did the latter and shouldered his way through the press towards the far end of the hall. There, set upon a raised platform, sat the throne. A simple affair, wide and squat, unpadded and made from hard, seasoned oak. Black with age, no one knew how old it was, lending more power to its air of mystery, myth and magic. There were some who still held the ancient belief of Odin having built himself and given as a present to the very first kings in the dark days, before the Norse set forth upon the seas, and the world was grim and barely without form.

As he ran his hand over one of the smooth, worn arms Olaf himself could not say if such tales were untrue. There was a resonance about it, a power that seeped out from the heart of the wood, ancient and strong. He may have embraced the Christian God, but his spirit was born of an age before such beliefs were accepted, or even known. Perhaps Odin still resided in Asgard, awaiting the return of his warriors to begin again the dominance of the world.

Svein's voice broke through his thoughts, but as the old man made the proclamations and the great lords pressed closer to swear their allegiance, Olaf sank into a sort of dream. He was faintly aware of shouts and cheers, of other men in robes, of something sweet smelling dribbling over his head, of gestures and grins, of his mother kissing him on the cheek, of a golden crown perched high above him.

The fog lifted, his mind clearing and the glint of gold brought with it a sudden realisation that this was the moment when he would truly become king. Everything came into focus and he saw the faces, sensed the anticipation, the awe. He looked into the eyes of a priest whom he did not know and held his breath as the words came floating out of the man's mouth. "By the grace of God, I crown you King Olaf Haraldsson, Ruler of Westfold and Lord of the Norse. May He bring you long life, wisdom and grace." The crown came down and pressed over Olaf's hair. The priest stepped back making the sign of the cross and Olaf felt his mouth grow slack and his eyes widen. His heartbeat pounded in his throat, making him feel queasy and he gripped the arms of the throne and held on as Svein swung around and threw up his arms towards the assembly. "God save King Olaf!"

As one, the gathered throng echoed the salutation, immediately followed by a chorus of cheers, raised clenched fists, wild stamping of feet. The hall reverberated with the clamour and Olaf stared in amazement that so many were proclaiming him as their liege lord.

Slowly, bit by bit, calm settled over them, even Olaf, slumped back in the throne, relaxed and allowed his breathing to settle. He wiped the sweat from his face, stared at his palm and saw that it still shook.

"You are well, your Grace?"

He looked up. Svein leaned over him, the old man's face creased with concern.

Olaf grunted, squeezed the man's arm, and said in little more than a whisper, "I'm fine. Just tell me, is that it?" Svein frowned, not comprehending the question. "The ceremony? It is concluded?"

Svein stood upright. "Not quite, your Grace. You must receive the fealty of your subjects. Earls from across the land have come to pledge their allegiance." He turned to the assembly and Olaf leaned passed him and surveyed the mass of eager faces. "You must accept them all."

"*All?* But there must be over a hundred!"

"There are two hundred and twenty-seven, My Grace." Svein looked again at the king and smiled. "It shouldn't take more than the rest of the day."

But as Svein stepped away and informed the gathering that the acts of swearing allegiance would now begin, no one moved. Some shuffled their feet, others grunted, but no one took the step forward. And as Olaf waited, he experienced a terrible grip of cold terror which squeezed around his throat relentlessly. What was happening, why did none of them move? Was this the moment when all of his plans, his ideals came crashing down around him? His great idea of bringing the love of God to the ignorant masses, smashed before it had even begun? He knew some would resist, but everyone?

The mutterings grew less as one by one the great earls and lords moved apart, creating a pathway for one man who stood at the far end of the hall. Silent, aloof, his long, yet thinning black hair falling like a curtain to his shoulders, a limp moustache and a trimmed beard, dark eyes penetrating the gloom. Beside him, sentinels, two enormous guards, leaned on ceremonial axes, gold-bladed, and their hauberks glinted even in that dull and somewhat drab hall.

At last the man stepped forward, with exaggerated slowness, and with every step his features came more into focus. Olaf knew who he was and his pulse soared with every soft tread of the man's progress.

Sigurd Syr stood silent and straight, eyes unblinking, holding the King's stare with an arrogance that made Olaf feel he should turn away. But he held the gaze, and fought against wiping away the new trails of sweat that rolled down across his temples and mingled with his beard.

"My liege, and king," said Syr quietly and bent his waist before dropping to his knee. With his head facing the ground he said in a clear voice, "I pledge you my service, and my undying loyalty. God save you, lord king Olaf!"

For a moment Olaf thought he would faint, such was the level of heat that rose up to his face. But all of that was forgotten as the assembly roared out their cries and when Syr stood he was smiling.

Nine

The morning had turned bleaker, the rain pouring down in sheets, angling across the open fields to hammer against the exposed sides of the tiny hovel. Bartholemy pushed back the bedclothes and sat up, already shivering with cold. Beside him, the slight impression of where she had lain and he touched it and felt it was not warm. He looked around, suddenly afraid, expecting to see her beside the fire, or in the corner preparing beans. She was nowhere, the gaping emptiness of the room seeming to mock his fear as his stomach lurched. He stood up, not fully understanding why her absence brought with it such anxiety. Was her hold over him already so strong? It was true she possessed his every waking thought, his desire for her boundlessness, but this was something more. Separated, without a word, the unknowing crushing him, he found a flagon of wine and finished it. It did little to calm him.

He gathered the meagre bedclothes about him and, shivering, shuffled over to the door and pulled it open. The hinges screamed and a blast of cold air hit him like a blow, almost toppling him backwards. He braced himself against the door-frame, and peered out into the grey world around him.

White clouds hung heavy and low amongst the branches of the trees, cloaking the forest in an impenetrable shroud. Rain dripped from every branch, soaking the ground beneath, turning it into a black quagmire. It must have been pouring down for hours, but he had slept so deeply he had not noticed. They had coupled again last night, her love-making growing ever more eager and adventurous; insatiable she was, demanding he performed whenever she commanded, and she commanded him lots. When he could not, she applied the mysterious cream to his limp member, and he sprang forward, ardour inflamed, rock hard within a blink of an eye. Then she would slide over him and he would scream out his lust, desperate to ejaculate, to ease some of the heat.

Now he stood, exhausted. She had brought him to the peak at least four times and his manhood throbbed. He had examined it a few days previously and he found the skin reddened and sore to the touch. He hadn't told her, preferring to grit his teeth and bear the agony as she rode him. Perhaps she had begun to guess. Already he had noticed the mood swings, how, if he could only manage one coupling, she became moody, surly and ill-tempered, crashing around in the hovel, muttering foul language.

The winter would be harsh, she told him. And when it had passed, and the sun returned, he could go. But go where? To honour his vow, carry out his instructions for which he had already been well paid? What if he could not, what if his intended victim were lying dead in a ditch? His employer's instruction had been implicit regarding the deadly deed – until completed, under no circumstances was he to make any attempts at contact. But circumstances had changed. Brief directions, scrawled on a piece of parchment, brought him to this place and this woman, but who could have envisaged what would transpire.

If his employer knew, so much as suspected such impropriety, or if the assassination failed, his own death would soon follow.

Such thoughts ran through Bartholemy's head but now, alone and afraid, they grew larger and far more terrifying.

Where *was* she?

He slammed the door shut and went over to the few, pathetic embers in the grate, all that was left of the fire she must have made before her departure, and rubbed his hands before them. He looked around for more logs, but there were none save some pieces of kindling which he chose to ignore. He spread his palms forward, and tried to absorb what little warmth there was, closing his eyes. He rocked himself backwards and forwards, trying to keep his mind from thoughts of her, and, failing miserably, curled himself up into a tight ball and dreamed of her body.

He must have dozed off, for when he awoke, he was on his side, the blanket having slipped, leaving his body raw with cold. Cursing, he sat up, saw that the fire was long dead, and rubbed himself briskly, trying to bring some life back to his bones. He gathered up the blanket, went to stand and cried out. His left leg had gone to sleep, and the rush of the tingles and lack of feeling almost sent him crashing back down to the earthen floor. He hopped over to the door and leaned against the frame, stooping to knead his leg with both hands. The blanket dropped from his shoulders and he cursed again, went to pick it up just as the door burst open.

The door struck him high on the forehead with a sickening clunking sound, propelling him backwards, lights flashing before his eyes. Unbalanced, shocked and confused, he hit the ground with a jolt, the air rushing out of him. All he saw was her face looming large before his eyes, concern written in every line, and her mouth moving, forming words. But he didn't understand and he didn't care, all he wanted was to drift away.

When he awoke for the third time that day, she was still there, but this time on her knees, close to the bed, dabbing his throat and chest with a cold, damp cloth. She smiled and leaned forward to kiss him lightly on the lips. He groaned, smacked dry lips and mumbled, "Where have you been?"

She moved the cloth from his throat to his forehead. When she applied some pressure a jolt of pain brought tears to his eyes and she instantly withdrew the cloth and held his hand, "I am so sorry, my love. I had no idea you would be behind the door!" She grinned, and then laughed. "It's your own damn fault."

Her laugh proved infectious but each time he tried, another stab of pain cut him short, and he winced. Before long, however, his head ceased to spin and when he sat up there was no stabbing across his eyebrows. She patted his hand and stood up. "It is easing?" He nodded and she grinned and turned to go over to the fire. Already it was alight and she stooped down and turned a spoon in a great black pot. "When I took you to your bed, I noticed your flesh."

She had his back to him so he could not see her expression, but her voice sounded flat, without emotion. Nevertheless there was something, an edge to it, and when he sat up anxiety seized him. Her temper could be ferocious, and her demands ever constant. "My flesh?"

"Yes," she turned, and her eyes stared back as black as the pot she stirred. "The flesh of your cock." She stood up and he gripped the sides of the bed, preparing himself for the whiplash tongue, even the strike from the back of her hand. "Why did you not tell me?"

He gaped at her, not knowing how to respond, feeling small and fearful, a tiny animal caught with nowhere to run. He managed a shrug, knowing he must have appeared pathetic. "I was worried."

"Worried?" She frowned, "Worried, or ashamed?"

"I ... I do not know ... Forgive me."

"Forgive you?" A grin spread across her face. "Forgive you for what? For not telling me?" She clicked her tongue. "You have much to learn my sweet. I am not so terrible that you cannot be honest with me."

"No, it is not that, it is—"

"Yes. I know. You feel ashamed. But you needn't." She glided over to him, dropped to her knees again, and reached underneath the blanket to find his manhood. He gasped as she gently held it in her palm. "You are a wondrous lover, my love. But I, I cannot be satisfied, and I need more than you can give. You try, but it is never enough."

"Please, I ..." Panic overcame him. What was she saying, that she had grown weary of him, that his attempts at coupling, of giving her pleasure were simply not proving adequate?

"Shush, my love." She leaned across and kissed him. "Do not be afeared. I am not about to give you up for some other. No. But you should have told me. My potions are many and varied, and I have made a soothing balm that will ease your discomfort and bring the power back to your cock." She rocked back on her heels. "You will enjoy the sensation, my love. I promise."

He fell back down amongst the blankets and she moved back to the pot and gave it a few more stirs. "This is soup, my love. So do not worry about the heat." She laughed. "I shall apply the balm after we have eaten." She busied herself with ladling hot steaming broth into two wooden bowls. She had bread too, which she tore in half and laid one serving on the old table, and brought the other over to him.

Bartholemy sat up and watched as she blew over a spoonful of broth, and then placed it against his lips for him to drink. He took it into his mouth, and the taste exploded in his mouth, over his tongue before he swallowed it down, the warmth spreading across his stomach. He sighed, closed his eyes, and accepted more mouthfuls. Before long, he was munching down on the bread, the meal over far too quickly and he swung his legs out of bed and realised all of his strength had returned.

She sat at the table, taking her soup with careful slowness, savouring the flavour. She smiled as he sat opposite her.

"So, where did you go?"

Taking a piece of bread, she ran it around the inside of the bowl to mop up the last few droplets of soup, popped it into her mouth and studied him. When she had finished, she wiped her mouth with the back of her hand. "I needed to go to the village and pick up some food. But it rained so hard I had to seek shelter in a tavern." She leaned forward and gripped his forearm. "Such news I heard, Bartholemy. Such news!"

"Tell me," she said, his hand clamping over hers, eager to listen.

"There is a new king. His name is Olaf, and he is Christian. You understand what that is, Bartholemy?"

"I think so. Some eastern thing, I understand. They say the English are Christian, Normans too."

"Yes. They are cannibals, partaking of human flesh."

"Nothing surprises me about the English."

She nodded in agreement. "I overheard the menfolk saying he had been crowned, to great acclaim, at Haugar. That a Christian priest dressed in a black gown, a great crow, poured oil over his head and that all the great landowners bowed down and given their oath to him."

"*All* of them?" His astonishment was palpable. He would never have believed it possible that the land would turn so readily to this alien creed. He put more sway in the power of the earth, wind and rain than he would ever do for a God that demanded the eating of human flesh. Or so he heard. It was an abomination. "That cannot be so. All ..."

"Well, that is the interesting part, my love. Not all. Svein Hákonarson refused to bend his knee. Indeed, he did not even attend, sending his bodyguard to tell the king of his master's refusal. Olaf grew angry and rose to his feet, and the guard informed him that his master mustered a great fleet out of Trøndelag and gathered other forces to join with him."

So it is war?"

"It would seem that way." She turned in her seat and reached behind her, picking up a stone jar, which she put on the table. She poured out two cupsful of dark, rich wine. "The menfolk told me that Olaf grew white with rage, pounded his throne with his fists, and called Hákonarson a rebel and a traitor, and that his head would grace the entrance to the royal estate of Sæheimr."

"So Olaf was surprised at Earl Hákonarson's refusal?"

"Have you listened to nothing I have said? Of course he was surprised. Furious he was." She nudged a cup of wine towards him and watched as he drank. "No one could be surprised, given Olaf's blind stupidity. We are people of the forests, not of some distant magician who no longer lives. It is only a wonder that others did not throng to the so-called rebel call."

"So what shall become of us all?"

"Nothing shall become of us, my love. We are safe here, no one ever comes to visit the old crone and her witch's brews!" She laughed, bunching up her shoulders and returning to the old, shrivelled woman he had first laid eyes on. She cackled.

"Please don't do that."

She relaxed, her features growing smooth once more, her back becoming straight, her eyes lustrous, mouth full and ruby red. He stared, amazed at the transformation. "The old woman is what will keep us safe, my lovely. If people suspected that I may not be such a hideous old crone, they would come and seek me out. Men, my beloved. Men with fire in their bellies and iron in their cocks." She sat up, taking him by surprise, and she laughed. "Which reminds me, I must attend you."

She came to him, leading him back to the bed by the elbow. There she laid him down, unhitching his breeches, cooing softly as she produced a tiny pot. She plunged two fingers inside and, a moment later, brought them out, covered with a thick goo, yellow and sweet smelling. He watched, mesmerised, and she smiled, "You will feel so much better after this, my love." Without hesitation, she began to apply the cream and instantly the pain left him, replaced by a gentle warmth, so comforting it felt like a thick, sheepskin blanket. His eyes grew heavy and he thought he might fall into a dream. Her soft voice came to him as if from a long way away, "When you awake, my lovely, I shall show how much you have improved."

Ten

One of the large anterooms, furnished with a bed, some chairs and a table, glowed with warmth. A fire burned in the hearth and candles guttered in the corners, giving off a feeble yet comforting light. Nevertheless, it did nothing to improve Olaf's mood. Two day's previously he had received pledges of service from men throughout the Norse. Even Sigurd Syr, his contemptuous sneer forever planted across his thin face, had bent his knee. Not so Earl Hákonarson, whose man had stood as solid as an oak and appeared to relish what he had to say. Announcing to everyone present that his lord and master would never bow down to a weak and loathsome god. A god that proclaimed forgiveness as the true way; instead he would rid the land of any such profanities and show the people, through the might of his swords, that only Odin, his brothers and sons, were the rightful gods of Norway.

He could still hear the murmurings as the man strode from the hall, whispered voices of agreement. Olaf knew many would flock to Hákonarson's call; the response needed to be swift and massive. He could not afford to wait for the Duke of Normandy's men. Action had to be immediate.

The door opened and he turned. It was quiet now in the hall, almost all of the earls having returned to their homesteads so he was surprised to see Sigurd Syr standing in the doorway, sword at his hip.

"May I enter, my lord?"

Olaf felt a tiny tremor along his spine, wondering how Syr had got passed the guards without being announced. This may not be the Royal Court, but as king he demanded, and expected, a degree of respect and obediance. Syr's influence and power were well known; rich too. Perhaps even the guards were in his pay?

"Please, take some wine."

Syr lowered his head a little, closed the door and moved to the tablet and watched his king serving the wine.

"My servants are in bed," said Olaf, "and I am surprised to find that you are not. Perhaps my guards are also asleep at their posts?"

Syr raised the wine and took a sip. The corners of his mouth curled downwards. "I've never been fond of wine."

"Ale perhaps? Or mead?"

"Neither. I'm not what you would call a great drinker."

Olaf bristled at the thinly disguised barb. After the ceremony, Olaf had become much the worse for drink and could not remember much about what happened in the latter part of the evening. He awoke late the following day, with a head full of straw, and received an endless stream of hauldas and lesser landowners, all anxious to learn of his plans for taxation. No mention of religion, or war. Olaf had listened, his scribes beside him, and dreamt of home and a huge roaring fire.

The only lightness to the day occurred when a minor earl called Niels Nielsson presented his daughter. 'Simply out of politeness my grace, as you may have noticed Ingrid from afar and wished to meet her?' He had not noticed her, but he wished he had; one glance at her loveliness may have made the drabness of the day so much more bearable. A young girl of perhaps sixteen, dressed in a long flowing ivory gown, bordered at the cuffs and collar with a motif of green, interwoven vines, long hair cascading down to her bare shoulders. A face like alabaster and eyes that smoked grey, beguiling and captivating, drawing him in.

His voice was thick when he asked, "And what is your name, child?"

"Ingrid."

Of course, what else could it be? He smiled, motioned for her to sit, and they talked and laughed whilst her father ushered the scribes and pages from the room to leave the king and his daughter alone together.

"My king?"

Olaf snapped his head up, blinking rapidly as he realised with a jolt where he was. He forced a laugh. "I'm sorry, Earl Syr, I was thinking of …" He grinned. "Please, sit down. Tell me what brings you to my room so late."

Syr seemed vexed, screwed up the corner of his mouth and sat down, pushing the wine away from him. Olaf took up the Earl's barely touched drink and threw it down his own throat.

"Are you having trouble sleeping, my grace?"

Olaf scowled, shoulders tensing. "Why do you say that?"

"Merely that the hour is late, and your light burned so brightly." He smiled in the direction of the weak, struggling flame of the candles. "I thought perhaps the actions of Sveinn Hákonarson had caused you to feel uneasy."

"Uneasy? Why should the actions of a pagan numbskull cause me any unease?" He sat down. "He has some support, but not enough. His days are numbered, and the people know that. A strong belief in God and the Church will guide us to victory, Earl Syr, do not concern yourself over that."

He chuckled. "No, no, my grace. It is not that which concerns me. Rather, the fact that Hákonarson does not act alone. News has reached me that he is gathering many to his banner, including the great Erling Skjalgsson, Hakon Eriksson and Thore Hund. Their combined forces would outnumber yours, my grace, in any clash of arms."

Olaf seethed and pressed himself forward, looming across the table. "That may well be true, but what you fail to mention are the allies I have, Earl Syr."

"Not many."

"What? Are you mad? Over two hundred earls and lords have just pledged their allegiance to me. I have more support than Hákonarson could ever imagine, and I'll crush him like the insect that he is."

"Most of those earls and jarls are weak, ineffective, able to muster no more than a dozen huscarles. Your Norman friends will not arrive before the end of the month, and already Hákonarson's fleet is amassing in his home port. He could sail within days."

Olaf's voice was ice when he spoke, "How do you know about my so-called 'Norman friends'?

Syr shrugged. "I know many things, my grace. I know that almost all those earls who swore allegiance to you only did so because they believed taxes would come down, and that you would enter into trade agreements to ensure more grain. King Harald, your late and illustrious father, was not the most diligent of men when it came to ruling his people. He preferred the taste of good food and wine rather concerning himself with the welfare of his subjects." He smiled, and nonchalantly ran his forefinger around the rim of his wine cup. "I doubt if any of them will stand with you in any fight against Hákonarson."

"I could raise three thousand men within the week," spluttered Olaf, and he struggled to stop his hand from shaking as he poured himself more wine. Syr's words tore into him, ripping away his self-confidence. No, the Normans would not be here soon enough, and his own forces were meagre, mostly untrained levies. If the earls did not rise to his call, then his reign could be ended before it had barely begun.

"Hákonarson and Hund have almost sixty ships between them, and together with Skjalgsson can muster a force of well over four thousand, half of which could be huscarles." He reversed the direction of his finger, his smile growing thinner. "It may have been more sensible to have judged the reaction of your subjects before you made any announcements about converting them all to Christianity, my grace."

Olaf ground his teeth, threw away his wine and got to his feet. He swung away, knocking over his chair and went over to the window where he fumed, gazing out into the night. Feeling the sharpness of the air and wishing he could run out towards the trees and lose himself amongst the undergrowth, never to come back. Make his way north, perhaps east to Sweden. Find employment on a merchant ship, travel the Baltic Sea.

"What in the name of Christ am I supposed to do?" He turned around and looked at Syr in the half-light, slumped in his chair, looking so at ease, so apathetic. It was all a game to him, of course. He had nothing to lose, perhaps everything to gain. So where was all this leading? Olaf went back to the table and leaned forward on his knuckles. "Tell me, what *can* I do?"

"I have great landholdings, your grace, as well you know. My family has built up considerable farms through the east, and we are rich and powerful and have many trusted and faithful friends. We are not of royal blood, but we have certain ... *connections.*" He smiled. "I can muster more than enough men to smash the upstart Hákonarson and all of his measly allies, and I have some doubts over Jarl Eriksson. I think I can persuade him to come to our side. Together, we could meet him in the open sea, break his back before he lands, and send him and his dreams of kingship to the bottom. And we can do all of that without a single Norman ever setting foot on our soil. Hákonarson has played his hand too early, hoping to catch you ill-prepared. But he has underestimated my oath of service to you, my grace. His blindness will lead to his doom."

Olaf stood up very slowly and nodded, already preparing himself for the man's demands. He knew that nothing would ever be given freely; there would always be a price to pay for the loyalty of men such as Sigurd Syr. So he took in a breath and held it for a moment, restoring some of his former calmness. "So, tell me Earl Syr, what would you want in return for this welcome and *timely* show of friendship?"

Without any hesitation, Syr's smile grew even broader and he said, "The hand of your mother in marriage."

Eleven

Four men crouched over a worn and ageing table, which creaked alarmingly should any weight be put upon it. Outside the wind howled, and so the men huddled close, wrapped in thick layers of fur and sheepskin, trying to keep warm. The room itself gloomy, with only the light from a fire in the hearth and some torches burning feebly from sconces mounted on the walls to help them to pick out the details of the map one of the men had rolled out. But the lines on the large piece of vellum were faded and difficult to read, so they leaned closer, and the table groaned in protest.

"If we set sail in the early spring, I think we will be able to catch him before he has had time to prepare his own fleet."

"Spring? You mean to wait that long?"

"We have no choice! The winter is already upon us, and the seas are treacherous at this time of year. We must wait."

They peered closer still at the details of the map, the mountains, rivers and forests that separated their homelands from that of Westland. The largest of the men, a hulking, gruff individual, raked his fingers through his ragged beard. "I can see no other course. Besides, the wait shall give us more time to train our men."

"More time to train? We outnumber him at least three to one." This talker slammed his fist down hard on the table, which almost gave way, and he stood upright, face twisted in rage. "By the gods, I say we force march against him *now*, before he has time for anything! He will not be expecting an attack, not at this time of the year, and we will crush him before he even opens his eyes to the possibility!"

"But our men are too green; they have little experience of battle, and Olaf's huscarles are tough and dependable fighters."

"Bah! Our numbers will overwhelm them. How many has he?"

"Perhaps two hundred."

The man hawked and spat on the earthen floor. "Two hundred! We will wash over them as the sea does the rocks. They will not stand, I guarantee it."

"And like rocks his huscarles will stand, and you will turn as the tide always does."

The man's eyes simmered with anger, lips curling back over his teeth. "My men will *not* turn! They will prevail, with me at their head, and they will show you all that we are not craven."

"No one mentioned anything about you, or your men, being craven, Earl Girrurdsson."

"The words may not have been aired, haulda Freign, but it is clear what was meant." Gisurdsson stabbed his finger at the man who had dared to hint at such a thought. "Perhaps that is why you are so eager to join battle at sea, so you can stay huddled down behind the keelson?"

Freign gasped, then instantly took hold of the hilt of his sword, "Damn your eyes, I'll kill you for that!"

"No," yelled the huge one, gripping Freign by the bicep and pushing him backwards. "We swore an oath, to fight together and rid our land of the curse of Christianity! Would you destroy our plans even before they have begun?" He glared, still holding Freign, and turned his malevolent gaze at Girrurdsson. "Listen well. I bow to your passion and understand your desire to attack now, but it would be foolish and disastrous. Our men are not ready. They are farmers, and they shall break at the first wielding of Olaf's axe!" He released Freign, who staggered back, clutching at his arm. "We must meet him at sea, where we will have every advantage."

"But if we overcome him *now*, think of what that will mean!"

The other two men exchanged looks and Freign said in a voice of ice, "I still say we should follow Sveinn's lead, and wait until spring."

Girrurdsson shook, veins throbbing in his neck, close to losing control. "Do you think Olaf will be sitting quiet and warm in his hall as the snow falls, do you? He'll be making his plans, preparing *his* men. He will not sit idle, and as he grows strong we will grow weak." He came forward and leaned down hard on the table, his fists bunched. "I tell you now, if we wait he will win. And when he wins, he'll take our lands, and our people, down into the very bowels of hell. You and me too."

"We meet him at sea, in the spring."

"Then you're a damn fool!" He swivelled his head to cast his malevolent glare over the others. "Damn you all. I'll not wait, I'll march now and when Olaf lies dead with his craven host about him, I will send you word to come and pay homage to the new Lord of Westfold."

Before any of them could speak, Girrurdson tore open the door and plunged out into the raging gale.

Freign had to put his shoulder against the door to close it and when he had, he leaned his forehead against the timber for a moment and let out a deep sigh. "What if he wins?"

"He won't," said the big man, and looked at his companion in the corner who had remained silent throughout the exchange.

"Aye," Freign turned around, fear in his eyes, "but what if he *does*?"

The man in the corner stepped forward, the light from the burning torch beside him sending curious strands of red and yellow across his face lending him an eerie, preternatural expression. "Lord Sveinn Hákonarson has spoken, and what he says will come to pass. Girrurdsson will fail."

Freign appeared unmoved. "How can you be sure? He has a strong host, and if he overcomes Olaf then everything we have worked and planned for will be doomed, and it will be Girrurdsson who sits on the throne, not either of you."

Hákonarson flexed his massive arms and turned to the fire, rubbing his hands before the flames. "There is sense in what you say, Freign. I cannot dispute it."

"Then what can we do?" Freign's voice quivered, panic tinged with terror. "It'll be my head that Girrurdsson will first decorate the city walls of Westfold. And then yours." He narrowed his eyes towards the one in the corner. "Perhaps even yours."

The man cackled at that. "Freign, you need to calm yourself. Go back to your hall and lie with your wife, drink wine, sleep through the winter. When you awake, all will be well."

"How can you say that? There are no guarantees, even though Olaf's huscarles are the finest, they are *too few*."

"Then we shall have to help him."

Freign leaned back, his mouth agog. For a moment, struck dumb, glinting flecks of ruby red reflected from the fire played with his eyes, amplifying his confusion. "Help him?"

The man nodded. "By helping him now, we weaken him for later. Girrurdsson, if he acts, has given us the means to victory, my dear friends."

"Yes," said Hákonarson, holding out the palms of his hands to the fire, "you speak well, as always. Olaf will counter this threat, overcome Girrurdsson with your help, and in so doing put his future trust in you, a trust which will disappear like the snows of winter in the spring sunshine when we launch our seaborne attack." He clapped his hands together, his face alight with a ruddy glow from the fire, and exultation from within. "By Odin's beard, I can almost taste the victory already!" He stepped forward and clamped a huge paw on the other's shoulder. "You'll have the whole winter to strengthen his trust in you, my friend. And you know how best to do that, do you not?"

"Aye," said the other, the smile thin, "I'll marry his mother before the year is out and put a son in her belly."

"And we shall proclaim a new King of Westfold." And with that Hákonarson lifted the man's arm and shouted, "Hail to the right-born king, Lord Sigurd Syr!"

And they drank to their plan well into the night.

Twelve

The days grew shorter and colder and Olaf would stand on the battlements of his great Royal Estate at Sæheimr and await news of his enemy's approach. And each day the news failed to arrive until, at last, he began to doubt the words of his father-to-be. On the eleventh morning since his return from the proclamation ceremony, as he sat in the Great Hall and listened to the bleating of an old man whose wife had run off with his sons to build a new farm of their own, a commotion without stirred him. He stood up and strode out, ignoring the old man, who fell to his knees and wept.

Outside the snow drifted down, the stillness of the air in sharp contrast to the grim faces of the group of riders who clattered into the yard, their skin almost blue with cold. The lead man jumped from his mount and strode forward. Swathed in thick furs, a cloth scarf wrapped around his mouth, at first Olaf did not recognise him, until he came up close and bowed. "My king."

It was Sanda and Olaf hugged him, clapped him on the back, and motioned to stewards to help the other riders. "Give them hot broth and see to their every need." He pushed Sanda away with both hands, held him by the shoulders, and beamed. "Thank God you're here, my friend. I had fears. So long without any word. Come inside, and warm yourself."

"There is little time for that, your grace."

Olaf frowned, fearful now. "Then tell me, but inside before you freeze where you stand."

The old man was still weeping as Olaf returned inside with his friend. He cuffed the man on the back of the head. "Stop your snivelling, fool. Go back to your farm, and feed your cattle. Winter may well kill you all."

"But your grace, how am I to tend to anything without my sons? I am old and the cold is too much for my feeble bones."

"Where is your farm?"

The old man turned and took in Sanda, who appeared like a bear before him. "No more than twenty leagues to the west."

"Then you'd best stay here. Your farm is already lost."

Sanda walked past the old man, whose face crumpled and Olaf cocked his head and narrowed his eyes. "What in the name of God does that mean, Sanda?"

"It means, your grace, your enemies have taken to the field. We ranged far, to the north and to the west, and everywhere we went we found the discontent of the people. They bemoan your father's misrule, and wish for some signs that the future would be better. As they do not believe any will be forthcoming, many homesteads have fallen in with Thore Hund and Sveinn Hákonarson, both champions of the old ways. Their host is moving, your grace, and we had to fall back as elements threatened to overrun us."

Olaf put his knuckles into his mouth and slumped down into his great chair. He stared sightlessly into the distance whilst the others in the hall looked on, no one daring to speak. Others drifted into the hall, several visiting earls, but no one dared hardly breathe, sensing the air of despair that hung over everything.

"Not even a month into my reign and already they rally against me."

Sanda glanced down at the old man, still weeping, and dismissed him with a curt snap of his head towards the door. Then he turned to the captains of the royal bodyguard who stood against the far wall. "Muster the men, send out the call. Prepare the huscarles of the king."

As the officers rushed off to prepare, Sanda went over to the king and went down on his knee before him. "Your grace, a body of perhaps a thousand are making their way across the frozen waste to attack you. We have but a hundred men here at Sæheimr. We must withdraw to a place of safety."

The king allowed his fist to drop to his knee. "Send word to Sigurd Syr. We will hold here until his men arrive."

Sanda's mouth fell open. He rocked back, his face white. "Syr? You cannot trust him, your grace! The man has designs on your throne. If he knows you are in danger, he will allow you to fall, then move in afterwards to proclaim himself as king!"

Olaf shook his head. "No. He will not."

"You cannot trust him. The man is a devil, a treacherous, dishonest—"

"Hush, dear friend." Olaf smiled and placed a hand on Sanda's shoulder. "You should not speak so disrespectfully about my father."

* * *

Three days later, the forces clashed in the open grassland beyond the walls of the Royal Estate. Olaf stood on a slight rise, his huscarles arrayed on either side, his standard held tall and straight behind him, emblazoned with the cross of Christ. As the enemy forces emerged from the thick forests around them, Olaf sucked in his breath at the size of their host. An endless stream of men, bristling with spears and shields, emerged from the pines and Olaf believed they would never stop coming. Spear butts slammed against shields, and voices chanted in guttural rage, 'Onward, onward, farmers onward!'

Olaf drew in a deep breath. "Who leads these men? Is it Skjalgsson?"

"Your dear friend, Earl Gisurdsson."

Olaf threw Sanda a glare. "My mother's lover? Or should I say, *one* of them? How many turn against me?" He squeezed his eyes shut for a moment, then slapped a fist into his palm. "Well, by the love of Christ, let them all come! They'll all fall. And Gisurdsson shall be the first.

He'll no longer have the memory of my mother's affections to keep him warm at night. Not after this day is done."

It was Sanda's turn to release a long sigh. "We are but one hundred and eighty, your grace. Sigurd Syr has not brought his men."

"Not yet he hasn't." Olaf slowly drew his sword, as the air grew louder with the sound of the enemy's chanting. "But I have faith in the Lord, my old friend. He shall not fail us." He threw his sword hand high into the air and screamed, "For the love of Westfold. For the love of Christ!"

His huscarles, and the hurriedly assembled levies raised their axes, brandishing them as they echoed their king's cry. And then the enemy broke into a charge and rushed across the open ground, voices raised in their battle-cry. At their head ran Earl Gisurdsson, his swinging axe setting him apart from almost all the rest.

Because the rest were unarmoured farmers and peasants. As they pounded over the snow, their progress impeded by the thick covering of the winter fall, Olaf counted the huscarles in the enemy host. He could see no more than twelve. Gisurdsson's own bodyguard, the only ones in mail and helmets. The remainder had little in the way of weaponry. Most had spears, some farming tools, but none wore any armour, not even pot-helms.

Olaf breathed hard through his nose, and looked to the rear of his position on the ridge. Thirty men stood behind, all of them archers, arrows already knocked and ready. "Prepare to fire, lads." They raised their bows as one and Olaf returned to watching the foe struggle forward, every step of every man sinking into the deep snow. They laboured, many stumbled. Even Gisurdsson had lost much of his momentum.

"Faith, my king?"

Olaf grinned at his old friend, and winked. "Aye, Sanda. *Faith.*"

He waited until the enemy were less than a hundred paces away from his dispositions then he dropped his sword arm. The arrows released as one, thirty darts forming a small cloud which coursed across the sky before curving downward from the top of their trajectory to fall upon Gisurdsson's men.

* * *

Later, scribes and poets would write about the great victory of the Christian King Olaf, the first of his reign, but they made it sound far more glorious than it truly was. As those first arrows struck, the enemy broke, a swathe of men, unused to battle and death, turning on their heels and running for the safety of the forests. Another wave of arrows, and a third, impressed upon those who remained that this would not be as easy as Gisurdsson had promised.

Some were brave enough to gain the ridge, and Olaf's huscarles swung their axes, cleaving heads, parting bodies from shoulder to breastbones, blood and brains and guts spewing out across the snow. Screams replaced the chanting, and farmers fell like the wheat they had once harvested in their fields. They were not fighting men, and their spirit left them together with their lives, and they threw down their weapons and fled, the route total.

Olaf held his men on the ridge, despite many urging him to pursue. But he held out his arms and his men remained in their formation and they watched as the enemy struggled through the snow, fighting desperately to make the relative safety of the treeline.

It was then that Sigurd Syr's force emerged from beyond the opposite rise, hitting the retreating remnants in the flank. The slaughter was dreadful and Olaf turned from the field, his jawline set solid, and he tramped back to his Hall without a word.

* * *

Sanda sat with him before the fire, both men staring into the flames, neither having the courage to speak. A steward brought wine and they drank in silence. The time stretched on, without importance. The victory done. Nothing remained to be said.

When the double doors burst open and a great blast of cold air hit them on the back, Sanda turned first, and Olaf heard his old friend's troubled sigh. The king closed his eyes, not wishing to face his so-called ally, who had arrived so very late. "Is it Syr?"

"It is, your grace."

"A great victory, my king!" cried Syr, and he stomped across the hall towards the others.

There were a half dozen spearmen in the Hall, and Olaf sensed them stiffening, and when Sansa's inhalation was full of shock, he knew something was not quite right. He turned in his chair.

Despite the half-light of the many candles and the blaze of the fire, Olaf clearly saw the details. Syr stood, legs planted apart, his face and beard speckled with blood, his hauberk appearing rusty because of it, and his hands ... his hands. In the left he held his great battle-axe, but in the right the reason for his look of sheer ecstasy.

"A prize for my lord the king," said Syr with a flash of teeth, and he threw the trophy from his hand. It bounced across the floor and rolled until it finally came to rest at Olaf's feet, who looked down at it and nodded.

It was Earl Gisurdsson's head.

Thirteen

Ice and snow still clung to the landscape, a frozen blanket, impenetrable, endless. The thaw was weeks, perhaps months away. Bartholemy woke and stared towards the ceiling. Thin wisps of smoke clung to the cross beams, holding his attention and he studied them, fascinated by how they swirled and drifted but never appeared to dissipate totally. The room needed air. For too long they had shuffled about in the confines of the place, huddled in thick animal pelts, the fire roaring, the woman sometimes venturing outside. Despite his requests, she would not allow him to accompany her. Her eyes would narrow, her hand gripping him by the collar, "You stay here, my lovely. I do not want anyone to know you are here." *Anyone?* The ramshackle small holding nestled in a small valley, surrounded by thick woodland. Nobody ventured close. And with the winter, there was even less danger of a stranger stumbling upon them. Only the mad, the foolish or the lost would come this way.

But one day, somebody did.

It was the morning whilst Bartholemy lay on the bed, following the smoke trails, that a noise beyond the walls caught his attention.

He sat bolt upright, aware instantly she was not inside. Another visit to wherever it was she went. She often returned with wood, or supplies. A few scraps of dried meat, some barley or maize. Rarely, at this time of year, did she bring vegetables, perhaps a turnip or two. Winter stores were growing low, she told him. The nearest village lay

77

wrapped in snow. Times were hard, the cold biting deep, the worst in living memory.

Bartholemy waited, holding his breath. He listened to the soft footfalls, the crunching of hard, impacted snow as the person moved. It was the tread of someone unsure, testing the ground, biding their time. A stranger.

Twisting around on the bed, Bartholemy scanned the room. Slung across the back of a rickety chair was his shoulder bag. Inside, his knife, daubed with the poison she'd brewed. Beyond, close to the far wall, cooking pots stacked haphazardly, carving knives, a cleaver. In the fire, spluttering and spitting, an iron poker, resting against the smouldering logs. He made his choice, and crossed to the fire.

Even as his fingers curled around the handle, he realised he'd made too much noise, the floorboards groaning like an old man crying out in alarm. The door burst open and the stranger came in, a great bull of a man, caught Bartholemy's arm, jerked it violently up his back. Bartholemy squealed, snapped his elbow backwards into the man's guts, heard him grunt, expelling air, and the grip broke.

Gasping, Bartholemy whirled around, the poker in his hand. Ignoring the pain in his other arm, he brought the improvised weapon down upon the stranger's head with all the force he could manage.

But the stranger was no indolent buffoon. His own sword rasped from its scabbard, blocked the ferocious blow, turned the glowing poker and snapped the pommel of his sword into Bartholemy's face, sending him crashing back against the far wall, blood erupting from his nose. He slid to the ground, the poker falling from numbed fingers.

He gagged, pressed one hand against his face, the blood warm, seeping from shattered nostrils. Through a red mist of pain, he saw the shape of the man looming over him, went to stand and dropped back as the point of the stranger's sword pressed against his throat. "Move and you die."

Bartholemy did not move, save for the simple act of slumping against the wall, defeated.

"Where are the others?"

Bartholemy, his breathing ragged, coming in short, sharp gasps, shook his head. "I live alone."

"Liar!"

The sword pressed harder, the metal about to penetrate flesh, and Bartholemy bleated, throwing up his hands, "All right! Please, I beg you."

"Tell me, you bastard, or I'll run you through."

"There is only one other. A woman."

The pain in Bartholemy's face gave way to a deep, burning throb. He dabbed at his nose, the blood flow slowing, and studied the great hulk standing over him. Swathed in a woollen coat, thick leggings and animal skin boots, cross belts at his chest, hand-axe and dagger to his right, scabbard on his left hip, his face drawn, blue with cold, eyes red with the fire of battle fury. A wild shock of black hair, frozen stiff, tinged with clumps of ice, now dripped and slowly turned wet and heavy as the heat from the room did its work and thawed him out.

He rocked back and studied Bartholemy for himself. "A woman?"

Bartholemy nodded, went to sit up and again the sword thrust forward, forcing him back once more.

"Where is she?"

"Here."

The sound of her voice startled both men. She came upon them like a shadow, silent, her slight frame slipping through the door unheard. The stranger whirled on his heels, already the sword arm coming up, and she landed against him, a knife in both hands driving forward, burying deep into his chest. She grunted with the effort, the sharp blade cutting through the thick sheepskin, into the flesh.

Bartholemy rose to his feet, sweeping up the poker, and cracking it across the man's skull. He yelped, fell to his knees, the sword clattering to the ground. His great paws gripped the woman's hips and she struggled, desperate to free herself, holding onto the knife, pushing it ever deeper. Not pausing in his desire to see this giant dispatched, Bartholemy cast away the poker, took up the sword and prepared to strike.

The man's strength was frightening. He lifted the woman in his great paws and turned holding her close to his chest, his eyes boring into Bartholemy's. She struggled in his grip, limbs flaying, caught in the trap, unable to break free. "Drop it, or I'll break her back." To give truth to his words, he squeezed. Her back arched, mouth opened, no scream, simply the contorted, twisted expression of despair.

He was crushing the very life out of her.

Bartholemy didn't wait. He dropped the sword, brought up both hands, surrendering to the man's phenomenal strength.

The stranger grinned, relaxed his hold and she fell, gasping for breath. He looked down to the knife, buried almost to the hilt. "She's a wildcat," he said, took a firm grip of the handle, and slowly drew it from the thick padding of his clothing. Bartholemy gaped. As the blade came free, a tiny trickle of blood glistened on the tip. The blade had barely broken flesh.

"First time I can say I am glad of the cold." As he spoke, blood dripped from the corner of his mouth, and when his eyes came up to hold Bartholemy's gaze, something passed across them. A question, bemusement, confusion, mixed and his hand, which snaked towards the back of his skull, trembled. He spluttered, face growing even whiter than before.

"Kill him," she said as she lay on the ground, breathing becoming easier.

Bartholemy, engrossed by the spectacle before him, had not the strength to move and watched as the brute rolled backwards, legs giving way. He crashed against the table, almost smashed it, and hit the ground with the blood leaking from the terrible blow Bartholemy had delivered. He lay still.

She climbed to her feet, rubbing her chest. "We have to finish him," she croaked, reaching for her knife.

"Wait," he said, kneeling beside her, hand folding over hers. "We do not know who he is. Perhaps there are others."

"What are you saying, we should tend to him, as I did for you?"

He held her gaze for a moment, then looked away. "When he recovers, we will interrogate him. If he is part of a band of raiders, we need to know where the others are. He might be a scout."

"There are no others."

"But he may have moved ahead of them, searching out for a place to stay. Food." He looked down at the fallen giant, chest rattling with laboured breath. "If he doesn't return to them, they may well come here too. All of them."

"If we tend to him, that will take time and they will come anyway." She pulled her hand away from his. "Besides, I watched him. There are no others. He is alone."

"You can't know that."

She grinned. "I know. I haven't lived here all these years without being able to tell the signs."

"I still think we should question him."

"And I still think you're a fool," and her face hardened, eyes black, cold, lifeless coals, and she cocked her arm and plunged the dagger deep into the man's throat. He gurgled, spluttered and thrashed about, despite his unconscious state, and she held on, the blood bubbling over her fist until he grew quiet and limp as a wet rag.

Horrified, Bartholemy stepped back, hand pressed against his face, feeling the bones pulsing, the swelling developing across his nose, cheek and under his eyes. "By the gods, what sort of a woman are you?"

"The kind that survives," she said, standing up, wiping the blade across the tails of her thick garment. She smiled at him, stepping up close, her hand delving under his pants. "Don't tell me it doesn't thrill you."

He almost swooned as her fingers found him, hot fingers, laced with blood. "How can you ..."

"It excites me, the taking of lives," she said, her tongue darting like a snake's. She craned her neck, reached to him, and gently licked the swelling on his face. "I will make a balm, ease the pain. Then we shall couple, with him lying there, watching us."

His tongue thick in his mouth, Bartholemy could not answer. Instead, he allowed her fingers to do their work, overwhelmed at the thought of what was to come.

* * *

They struggled and strained to drag the body out into the snow, heaving him around the back of the hovel, creating a trail through the white, with the blood stark and black.

"The ground is too hard to dig a grave," she said, breathing hard, hands on hips leaning forward. "We'll cover him over. Wait for the thaw, then put him away, out of sight forever."

"It'll attract wolves, desperate for food."

"So much the better," she grinned.

Bartholemy wiped his brow, careful not to brush his hand against the swelling. Despite his efforts, he hissed when he caught the edge of the bruising and she rushed to him, hands on his, cooing gently, "Let me tend to you." She smiled.

He saw her eyes, soft and gentle now, the mask of fury replaced by a face as lovely as any he had known. "Why do you disguise yourself as an old hag?"

It was a question he had long meant to ask, up until this moment fearing her wrath. "It is a long story," she said, resting her forehead against his chest. "I'll tell you. Later."

She took his hand and led him back to the house, their feet sinking into the snow. He went without complaint, the stirring in his loins overcoming everything. But as he followed, he cast his eyes over the dead stranger's body, and the mounds beyond. He frowned. Rarely had he ventured outside, and never to this area. They could be flurries of snow, compacted, turned to ice. Or something else.

And as he studied the shapes, imagination gave way to certainty. The mounds were not piles of snow and ice. They were graves.

Fourteen

Men, for the most part, filled the hall, their laughter loud, laced with drink. The priest did not approve, standing a little way off, clutching the bible in front of him, doing his best not to catch the mocking stares of the drunken crowd.

"You must allow them their merriment, Father," said Olaf sidling up beside him, clamping the priest on the shoulder. "They are nothing but children, happy to be here, to celebrate their lord's moment of happiness."

"Is that what you call this?"

He turned down the corners of his mouth and Olaf smiled. "Father, the old ways die hard. Sigurd is a good Christian, but he is mindful that many here are not, so he allows them this brief period to celebrate in the time-honoured way. Do not think any less of him because of it."

"And you, Olaf? Do you think any less of him?"

"I am happy my mother is happy, Father. In a few days, Sigurd and I shall journey north and set in place the reforms, which will transform our land into one of piety and faith. He will prove a powerful ally." The priest nodded, but remained silent. Olaf sighed, growing impatient. "Father, nothing will deter me. These men, they drink, they curse, but they are the backbone of this country. You must trust me to do what needs to be done in my own way. The Holy Father sees it so." He reached inside his tunic and brought out the message he had received some days before. He held it up. "You've read this, you know I have the blessing of Rome. What you see here is no threat to my plans to make all of Norway Christian."

"And you are certain Sigurd Syr is the man to assist you?"

"There is none as powerful as he, in the whole land, Father. There will be many who will resist, and the far north is where the old beliefs linger, tenaciously. It will be no easy task, but with Sigurd Syr's help, I will succeed."

"Very well. If you trust him, then I shall also, but I cannot pretend I approve of all this drunken revelry."

"No one would expect you to, Father." Olaf gripped the priest's arm, "Just don't spoil it for any of them. They're a rowdy lot at the best of times."

A great roar came up from the far side of the hall and Olaf squinted, trying to make out what had caused such an eruption of noise. The smoke from the byres running along the centre of the massive room made it hard to see more than ten steps, so he left the priest behind and, shouldered his way through the gathered throng. As he pushed closer, he managed to catch sight of his mother in her crimson wedding dress and Sigurd Syr in a white, green-edged tunic, sword at his hip, wooden goblet raised in his hand. "To us all, our future happiness and the strength of our good land!"

Voices lifted loud, charged tankards and goblets were downed, and Olaf saw his mother, brimming with joy, and his heart swelled. For all his talk with Father Ersted, he bore no love for Sigurd Syr. The man troubled him, his actions more so and he doubted the man's faith in Christ. He could not shift the unease he felt whenever he was in the man's presence, and yet here he was, married to his own mother. And his mother's eyes blazed with love. How could he deny her these moments? So he put his doubts and concerns aside, stepped up onto the dais and threw his arms around Syr, who responded by crushing him to his chest, pounding Olaf's back with his arms.

* * *

They walked through the comparative quiet of the square, a few dogs barking somewhere in the distance, the only sound to disturb them. Olaf held her by the hand and mounted the nearest set of steps which led to the ramparts. There they both stood, looking out across the endless, rolling plain, bordered to the east by the distant wall of black trees stretching as far as the eye could see.

"This is your land now," she said, not turning her eyes from the view. "Sigurd has bent his knee. No one will question you, not now."

"I pray it is so, Mother. I have much to do."

Asta turned her face towards her son. "And yet, I hear the mistrust in your voice, Olaf. You have the opportunity to bring the people of Norway together, as one. That is something your father could never do."

"Because of Sigurd."

She pulled in a sharp breath, stretching her back. "He loves me and pays you homage. Proof enough of his fealty, would you not say?"

"Perhaps."

She bit down on her bottom lip. "You are an obstinate brute, Olaf! What more proof do you need?" Her breathing eased. "I love him, Olaf. So should you."

"You did not love my father."

"I *served* him, and I bore you – his child, his successor."

"Aye. And you have borne Sigurd children, Mother." She gaped at him. "I know much of what happened."

"What you need to know is why."

"No. I do not need any of that. I wish to move on, put my energy into what I have to do."

"But will you forgive him?"

"Sigurd?" He peered into the distance. "Time will tell."

"But isn't forgiveness one your abiding principles?"

He snapped his head around, his time to glare. "*My* principles? Dear Christ, Mother, is his pagan heart already infecting your own?"

"Do not say that. Sigurd is—"

"Sigurd Syr is whoever he wishes to be, and he will *say* and *do* whatever is required in order for him to fulfil his ambitions. Including allying himself to me."

"How can you stand there and speak such venom?"

"Because it is true. I welcome his support, his fealty, but that does not mean I shall lower my guard."

"You cannot believe he would ever do anything to harm you?"

"As king I must always be prepared … for any eventuality."

"Then you are a fool, Olaf. Sigurd is my husband, he is no threat to you."

She whirled around and stomped off, the wooden ramparts shaking with the pounding of each angry step she took. Olaf stood and watched her go, wondering if she really knew the heart of her newlywed lover.

For his part, Olaf believed he knew what lay brooding deep in the pit of Sigurd's being, the venom building – his only concern being when and how the viper might strike.

Fifteen

Although used to her unannounced absences, the memory of the stranger's sudden attack made Bartholemy cautious and prepared, arming himself with the cleaver, placing a pitchfork in the corner. Already awake as she slid out from beneath the covers that morning, he waited until she swathed herself in thick, coarse clothing and left the warmth of the hovel. He crossed to the door, peered through the gap in the frame, and spied her trudging over the rolling fields, patches of snow still clinging tenaciously to the turf. The spring thaw had begun some two weeks previously, yet she continued with her demands that he should remain locked away. 'It is not yet time,' she would say, repeating the phrase every morning and every night, before snaking her hands across his loins, urging him to couple.

He turned from the door, wondering, not for the first time, if her visits to the unnamed village were really to gather supplies. Perhaps, as he guessed, she had a lover there, for she often told him how unsatisfied she was despite his most ardent endeavours. Whatever the truth, he no longer cared. His life had become one continuous bout of eating, sleeping and fornicating. Little else broke up the tedium. He enjoyed her body, right enough, but always the thought of fulfilling his task sprang forward and, as the snows receded, he grew anxious, desirous to break free and do what was required.

She had mentioned, only a few days previously, how when the ground turned soft, he should bury the dead stranger. Today might be as good a day as any, so he struggled into a sheepskin, tied it tight, and ventured outside.

The air struck him sharply across the exposed skin of his face and hands, and he lurched backwards, sucking in his breath. Winter remained, the cold like the jabs from a blade. He wrapped his arms around himself and tramped towards the rear of the hovel.

The wolves had done what he suspected, gnawing away at the body, tearing it open and feasting on the more tender morsels before the winter air froze the flesh and made it inedible.

The man's lifeless eyes gazed out from a face of putrid green, daring Bartholemy to draw closer. He did not, instead he sucked in his breath and looked across the fields. The black wall of woodland stretching across the rise caused him to imagine a whole mass of armed, murderous strangers emerging from the depths and he shuddered. He skirted around the corpse and went towards the mounds he had noticed some weeks before. No longer covered in snow, he studied their outlines, estimating the size and acknowledging they were very likely graves. Unconsciously, he prodded one with his foot, found it frozen solid and returned to the hovel, a little deflated.

He slumped down on the bed. Soon he would have to leave and she would have to understand. There was no choice. Hiding out here for the winter was one thing, but to absent himself from the world was not an option. Perhaps, after his hands were bloodied, he could return, take up with her again. He would have money then, enough gold to find somewhere more comfortable, less remote. She might approve of that, the chance of an easier life surely as good a reason as any to leave behind this ramshackle hovel.

Something stirred outside and he instinctively reached for the cleaver in his belt. As he rose to his feet, the door inched open and she stepped inside, struggling with a large bundle. She glared at him, "Well help me, for the love of the gods!"

He ran over to her, relieving her of the sack. It was heavy and he grunted with the effort of lifting it. Flinging it onto the bed, it clanged loudly and he stepped back, rubbing his hands. "What is inside that thing?"

"Tools, pots, some flour. I needed replacements." She went over to the fire, warming her hands. "I had some difficulty."

"Difficulty?" He frowned, glanced over to the open door and moved over to push it shut. "What do you mean?"

"Someone took a shine to me, is what I mean." She cackled. "They saw my hands. Stupid things, hands. The one part you can't fake."

"I don't understand. What is wrong with your hands?"

"Nothing. And that's the problem." She turned around, presenting the backs of her hands to him. They appeared smooth, fingers well tapered, elegant and slim. "Not the gnarled claws of an old hag, which is what I pretend to be."

"So what happened?"

She shrugged. "We got to talking, then he invited me outside." He sucked in his breath. "What's the matter? Jealous?"

"A little."

"Good." She grinned, throwing back her cowl. Her cheeks were glowing, either with the exertion of her journey, or something else. "I like my men to be jealous. Proves you care."

"You know I care."

"Yes, well ... We rutted outside, behind the blacksmith's shop. Couldn't get enough of me." She grinned, stepped forward, and scurried her fingers, spider-like, over his chest. "He made me *groan*, Bartholemy. You understand my meaning?"

"I think so."

"You *think* so? Let me tell you, he was like a bull. And, what's more, after he'd finished with me, he told me he wanted me again."

Bartholemy barely managed to shake his head. "You ... You didn't agree?"

"Of course I agreed." Her fingers stopped at his collar, tugging gently at the twine keeping his shirt together. "I told you. You don't give me enough, no matter how many times I apply the potion."

He squeezed his eyes shut, gripped her fingers and wrenched her away from him. "Damn your eyes," he snapped, glaring down at her. "To think I sat here, dreaming of making a life with you."

"You can't."

He blinked. "What does that mean, *I can't*?"

"What I say." She tore herself free from his grip. "He is coming here tomorrow. You have to leave."

His mouth fell open, too shocked to speak. He fell onto the bed, breathing laboured, unable to overcome the developing panic looming up from deep within. "Leave? But where am I supposed to go?"

"To Ringerike." He gaped at her and her grin grew wider. "I not only received a damned good fucking, I learnt some news too. News which is of more than passing interest to you."

He gazed at her, waiting, breath held.

"Sigurd Syr is married. To King Olaf's mother." She leaned forward, gripping him by the collar again. "So, you see, your opportunity presents itself. The die is cast. And you, my sweet, poor, inadequate you, you must leave." She let him go and stepped back, hands on hips, thrusting her pelvis forward. "Of course, you don't have to go until morning. So … What say you? One last night of pleasure? You won't have it this good ever again, my little friend."

But Bartholemy was no longer listening. The red veil had descended. With Sigurd Syr married, revelling in Ringerike, a better opportunity may not present itself again for quite some time. Her words were true. Best for him to leave, strike hard and sure at the least expected moment. He smiled. "You're right."

"Of course I am." She turned, rummaging through the few remaining root vegetables she had managed to keep back. "I'll make us a stew, and then we can lay together, all through the night."

He stepped up behind her, snaking his arms around her slim waist, feeling the swell of her buttocks beneath her thick robe. His erection sprang forward and he pressed his lips to her neck. "Please. Come with me."

She giggled, her hand dropping to his crotch. "I cannot. This man, he ruts like an elk." She turned in his arms, kissed him lightly, her eyes smouldering with desire. "Bartholemy, you are a sweet boy, but that is all you can ever be."

"But I love you."

"No," she pressed her finger over his lips. "No, you don't. You *think* you do. When we first met, you needed the potions I prepared, because you thought of me as an old, dried up hag. Now, you see me as I truly am."

"You said your potions would only make me see what I wanted to believe."

Her eyes narrowed, "Bartholemy. Your desire for me is real."

"Yes, yes it is. But I wonder how much potion you administer. In my food, my wine. Perhaps you have addled my brains."

"Aye, but not your cock, eh?" She gripped his manhood and squeezed. He winced, moaned and she laughed. "I have an idea, my sweet. Listen. Go to Ringerike, fulfil your duty, and return."

He frowned, "But what of this new man, this rutting elk?"

She laughed, throwing back her head. "By the gods, Bartholemy, but you can be stupid at times. *Yes,* I shall have him, and he shall satisfy me without any question ... You shall live in the barn, or at least the barn we shall build with the profits of your killing! And when he is spent, I shall come and visit you. Not every night, of course. But once in a while. Enough to keep you sweet. What do you say to my little plan?"

"I say it sounds wonderful." And he kissed her, his tongue plunging into her mouth. He gripped her buttocks, lifted her onto the side table and pulled away her clothing. She was laughing uproariously, her whole body rocking, as he plunged into her, desperate to relieve himself of the burning need raging through him.

And when he was spent and collapsed breathless to the floor, her laughter continued, louder than ever.

* * *

At first light, he rose, drank water, and gathered together his few meagre belongings. She studied him from the bed, breasts exposed, her skin shimmering in the half light. "How long will you be?"

He looked at her over his shoulder. "I cannot say. A week, a month. As long as it takes."

"Well," she stretched her arms high above her head, interlacing her fingers, purring like a cat. "I'll be here. Take care, my sweet boy. I would not wish any harm to befall you."

"None shall. I am good at what I do."

"Indeed? Well, let us hope your skill at murder is better than your skill at lovemaking. You light the embers, Barthelemy, but cannot extinguish the fire."

"Why do you delight in humiliating me?"

"Because you deserve it. You know, it might be a good idea if you waited for a while, meet my bull, watch him perform. You might learn something."

"What is his name?"

"Ranulf."

Bartholemy chuckled, "An apt name for a bull."

"So, you'll stay?"

"I think not." He gathered his bundle, hoisted it over his shoulder and stepped to the door.

"It will be worth it."

He paused and looked back at her. For a moment, his loins stirred, the sight of her, her breasts full, perfectly formed, the waist flat and hard. "I hope he is."

She licked her lips. "Oh, believe me, he will be."

At that moment his hand almost pulled out the cleaver. He saw it in his mind, running it through step by step. The feel of the heavy blade striking through her grinning mouth, the teeth and bone shattering, the scream as the blood spurted. But he held himself back. The revenge he had formulated would prove infinitely more satisfying.

Without another word, he tore open the door and went out into the biting cold, head down, muffled in a sheepskin coat, blanket and head scarf. The only sound her laughter, cackling like a crone, and again he wondered just how much of her potion remained in his body.

* * *

The time passed as slow as snails trailing across the ground. He sat under the shade of the trees, gnawing at slivers of dried meat, drinking of the mead he carried in a goatskin gourd. He put his head back against the trunk and wondered how much longer he should wait. Perhaps all of it was just another of her fabrications, conjured up by the same twisted mind that concocted her many potions. He would not be surprised if it were so.

But then, just as his eyes closed, came the unmistakeable sound of approaching footsteps, tramping through the woodland. Bartholemy shook himself and got to his feet, readjusting his clothing, hefting the cleaver and waited, his breathing shallow.

The man, Ranulf, indeed was a bull, his powerful shoulders straining against the voluminous cloak wrapped around him. He made no attempt to mask his approach, unaware of Bartholemy or anyone else who may be lurking in the undergrowth. His breath steamed from a mouth surrounded by coarse black hair, moustache and beard matted together, wild hair draping downwards to join it, giving him a terrifying appearance. Sudden images snapped across Bartholmey's mind, of this giant mounting her, pressing her against the blacksmith's wall, as she flayed about in his huge paws, moaning and crying out for all the world to hear.

He moved in behind the lumbering oaf, as silent as the night, none of his skills deserting him, the cleaver in his hand. But this was not his chosen weapon of despatch. Rather, the dagger, the deadly poison hardened to a dull gleam. He slipped it from its sheath, moved closer, and struck.

The blade sliced across the nape of the man's neck. Ranulf stopped, clamping a hand to the wound, and swung around, roaring out his defiance, hand already reaching for his sword.

Bartholmey skipped out of range, nimble-footed, light as air. Ranulf gawped at him, went to speak, then pulled back his hand and peered at his fingertips. "Who by Odin's beard are you to…" He frowned at the blood on his fingers, cocked his head, the slightest trembling flittering across his lips. "Wha…" Tiny bubbles of white spittle formed on his mouth. He gazed into Barthelemy's eyes, bewilderment overcoming every other emotion. His eyes rolled and he fell, like a tree, straight and rigid, to land flat on his face, the blood oozing like thick, black oil from his mouth.

Bartholemy waited, not daring to breathe or believe what had happened. He studied the blade, the tiny dabs of blood, but otherwise unchanged. It worked. By all the gods, *it worked*!

Sixteen

The news, when it came, struck Olaf like an axe in his side, almost toppling him. Teetering over to his throne, Olaf collapsed into it, a shaking hand reaching out for wine. One huscarle pressed a wooden goblet into his king's hand, whilst a second looked on. The bearer of the news. Grim-faced. Silent.

Stepping out from the shadows, the priest, Father Ersted, hands swallowed up by the deep sleeves of his habit, levelled his gaze towards the messenger; a man whose face ran with sweat, whose clothing and mail shirt were encrusted with dust and dirt. A man who had ridden hard from a considerable distance.

"You have seen this for yourself?"

The huscarle's eyes grew dark as he turned to the man of Christ. "Aye, I saw them. I saw the ships beach, the huscarles and hirdmen streaming ashore. I watched and heard the trumpets blare as Cnut strode before them, arms outstretched, as if embracing the land."

"How many men?"

The messenger turned to his king. Olaf, slumped in his throne, stared towards the ground, rolling the goblet between his palms.

"Maybe ten thousand."

"Ships? How many ships?"

"They covered the horizon, sire. More than I have ever seen before."

Olaf nodded and sat back, eyes closed, the goblet slipping from his fingers. No one moved as it hit the ground and rolled away. "Damn him. To come at this time. Damn him."

There was no anger in his voice, rather a low, deep tone of acceptance.

"Such a host can mean only one thing," breathed Father Ersted, "subjugation of your lands."

"Aye. He craves all of the Norse. Sweden included. Not content with England, he wishes to bring us all under his kingship."

"There were English with him," said the messenger. "I recognised their banners. English and Danes."

"Then a formidable force indeed." Olaf brought his hands down resoundingly on his knees and stood up. "We must send news to Anund Jacob, and also to Sigurd Syr. We must assemble as many men as we can, to thwart this tyrant before he manages to gain a strong foothold in our land."

"The King of Sweden is always resolute," said the priest.

"Aye, for he knows Cnut covets his lands also. But together," he slammed his right fist into his left palm, "we will crush him. You," he pointed to the messenger, "you have done well. Go and rest, take some nourishment. You," he nodded to the other huscarle, "take a horse and ride to Earl Syr's seat at Ringerike. By my command, he is to send ships and men. Our land is in peril and we cannot delay."

The huscarle slammed his chest with a solid fist and strode out. A few moments later, the messenger bowed his head in assent, turned and trudged out, leaving Olaf and the priest alone.

"So this is what it comes to," said Olaf. "That my lands must look towards Syr for their continued existence."

"You have no reason to doubt him, Olaf. In the past he has always come to your aid. Look how he crushed Gisurdsson."

"Aye. I have often thought of that day. Perhaps Gisurdsson was an obstacle to Syr's ambitions."

"Why do you torture yourself with such thoughts. Everywhere you look you see enemies, conspirators, pagan assassins."

"I'll not deny I am forever watchful. I would be foolish not to be. But with Syr, it is something more. I feel certain that one day he will show his hand. Perhaps the day is drawing close. If he were to ally himself to Cnut or, worse still, stand idly by whilst I am destroyed and then sweep away these Danish dogs, he then would be proclaimed king. The Thing would not hesitate in electing him, especially at a time of such danger."

"You honestly think such an odorous chain of events is possible?"

"As possible as any other."

Ersted did not seem convinced as he screwed up his mouth. "I will pray for us, sire. For the whole of Norway, for Sigurd Syr, Queen Asta, all the sons and daughters of this noble land. But mainly for you, my king. For wisdom, insight, and victory."

Olaf grinned and gripped the priest's arm. "Aye, victory. That more than anything."

"You will move, perhaps to Nidaros, and engage the enemy?"

"No. I shall seal myself up here, and wait for Syr. We shall then assemble a war fleet and smash those bastards to the four winds."

"And if Syr does not come?"

Olaf's feature grew dark. "Then I shall sail to meet them myself."

Seventeen

Standing on the prow of Sigurd Syr's great longship, the only ship the Earl of Ringerike had sent, with one foot propped up next to the ornately carved dragon stempost, Olaf closed his eyes in the face of the harsh wind. His whole body struggled to maintain his position, but he was determined not to move. With every lull in the gale he took the chance to look out across the slate grey sea, the waves chopping up in a mad maelstrom, crashing into the sides of the boat, rocking it from side to side as if it were a child's plaything. Olaf had faced worse storms than this, but never had he rowed in such conditions towards a foe determined to see him sink to the bottom.

He cast his eye on either side, and a surge of pride in seeing the other ships, with the men grouped together, braced for conflict, proved far stronger than any wind. He struggled to bite back the tears. These men were sailing to engage in battle *for him*. For his beliefs. For God.

"*There!*"

He spun, the raucous voice of the ship's captain almost lost beneath the roar of the wind. Olaf followed the man's outstretched finger and he narrowed his eyes, desperate to see the sign. His heart pounded, and he gripped the stempost with both hands and leaned as far forward as he dared.

And then he saw them, like black wraiths floating above the sea, shadows from the bowels of hell itself. An endless spread of ships, with the wind behind them, their speed dreadful to behold.

He became aware too of something else, perhaps more terrifying still. The howling rage of the wind grew, the storm turning to a tempest, the sea boiling, waves swelling large and dangerous, smashing against the ships, sending out great clouds of spray.

It happened so quickly, some of the accompanying crews taken unawares; he watched with dread as one or two capsized. Perhaps more would follow. He could not be sure as rain lashed down, creating a terrible, hazardous curtain. He could no longer wait.

"Give the signal," shouted Olaf and the captain immediately turned to one of his men, who brought up a bow, with two arrows already prepared. Another armoured man set a light to the tightly woven hemp around the points and the noxious smelling mixture instantly burst into flame, despite the rain. The archer lifted the bow and drew back the string, grimacing as he did so, and sent them off into the murky sky at a steep angle.

Olaf watched the two arrows in their arcing flight, relieved to see the orange-yellow flames burning so fiercely in the greyness pressing around them. Confident every ship's captain would respond as they said they would in the pre-battle planning all had attended that very morning. As he turned once more to the sea, he saw the ships break off into two squadrons, creating wedge formations designed to smash through the enemy, splitting the larger force arrayed before him. No storm could prevent what God had brought to pass. Unbelievers and sinners both would perish this day, and Olaf's desire to bring conformity and faith to this lost land fulfilled. He grinned in the rain.

* * *

The sea boiled, as if every god had joined with Thor to brew up the depths, scattering the careful formation and set doubts inside Thore Hund's mind. Doubts which would not shift, no matter how much he tried.

He stood, clinging to the prow, a hand raised to ward off the worst of the spray, and peered into the driving rain, trying to get a glimpse of the enemy. They had to be there. Scouts along the shoreline had brought the news: Olaf had assembled, his fleet edging closer. And then came the storm, from nowhere. A storm that must be crashing against the ships of Olaf's fleet too. Christian God, or any other, surely could not prevent this tempest from wreaking havoc.

Someone screamed close by, the wind snatching away the words. Hund turned and scowled. The man staggered forward, bent forward against the gale, gripping ropes so tightly the flesh broke, blood seeped.

"Ships, my lord." He managed to gesture wildly over to the west.

Hund grunted, peered into the distance. He thought he saw something, a faint glow of orange streaking across the sky, but he could not be certain. The rain obscured everything now, even those ghostly, indistinct shapes, dipping in and out between streaks of grey and black. Were they ships, or rocks? Could they be Olaf's battle array, or perhaps an ally's? Only time could tell.

"We turn about," he roared. "No one knows who they are. We turn about and wait until they are closer."

The man nodded his head, able to discern the orders about the noise of the storm. He went stumbling back to the rear, put his lips to the ear of the pilot, and the ship groaned and creaked in objection to being turned.

Orders always took time. With no way to transmit commands to the other ships, each would have to follow the lead of Hund's. Every second would bring the ghost ships closer. By the time they had all moved away, their identity would be known.

And then, the wind died, as suddenly as it had begun.

Hund held his breath, hardly daring to believe. There was no discernible pause between storm and calm, only a blink of time. The wind dropped, the rain ceased, the lapping of the sea a memory of its churning, the remaining evidence of what had been.

"By the gods, we have him."

Hund reacted to the voice of his lieutenant, a brawny individual called Eldred, whose orange-red hair, cut desperately close to his head, gave him the look of a human firebrand, his skin so white against the brightness of the flames topping his head.

"He moves forward like a blind man," continued Eldred, still having to shout as oars hit the water, men grunted, and sails billowed, the wind continuing to ring through the rigging.

"He sees us and speeds to his death," growled Hund. "Well," he slapped his hands together, rubbing them with glee, "We turn fully about, as if we are afeared and, as planned, we lure him into our trap."

"It will end this day, his hopes and wishes."

"Aye. And, by the gods, his life too!"

* * *

"They're turning!"

Olaf strained forward, unable to believe what he witnessed. The ships of Thore Hund were in disarray, some turning to the east, others to the west, still more remaining on their original course. He laughed, throwing his head skywards, "Dear Christ, we have him!"

Orders barked out across the many decks, rowers responding, doubling their efforts. Each ship mustered forty warriors, the larger vessels sixty. When they were within proximity of the enemy, arrows and javelins would block out the meagre sunlight, grappling hooks would hurtle across and clatter amongst the decks of the foe. As ships pranged against each other, the warriors would surge forward, each crew desperate to overcome the other. In the mad, wild clash of arms, men would die in great spurts of blood, but Olaf's men would prevail. There could be no doubting that. Olaf knew it, his faith unshakable.

The thrill of battle, the expectancy of victory overshadowed caution. The fleet ploughed on, eating up the distance between their ships and Hund's. Caught in their desperation to turn, as soon as they closed, Olaf's men would bring such a slaughter that none would survive. "Forward lads," roared Olaf, a hand projected forward as if he alone had the power to guide them, omnipotent, victory assured.

He could pick out the details of the enemy now, the faces of the crew, red with strain. Somewhere amongst them was Thore Hund himself and Olaf ran his eyes over the enemy ships, trying to pick out the flagship. If he could close with it, bring Hund to combat, then perhaps the inevitable slaughter could be averted.

But it was impossible. In the confusion of turning ships, some clattered together, oars becoming locked, and nowhere could the leader's banner be seen. Lost amongst the chaos, perhaps even Hund himself did not know which way to turn. Olaf laughed, forgetting for a moment the precepts of the Christian Church, lapsing instead to the age-old Viking traditions of revenge, honour, the killing of enemies. Alive with the promise of blood, he hefted his axe and waited for the ships to run up alongside each other and for battle to be joined.

The sagas spoke of this terrible day in prose as bleak and as despairing as the battle itself. With Olaf so close to victory, too late came the cries of alarm. Already sucked in, too late to turnabout, Olaf could only watch in dread as the second fleet of enemy ships bore down upon his Christian host. A headland masked them from view. Blind in his pursuit of victory, the net tightening, he had little hope of averting disaster.

He saw the proud flagship of Sveinn Hákonarson leading the enemy forward and Sveinn himself, without a helmet, eyes ablaze with the light of certain victory. The same light that had played around Olaf's own, now extinguished, replaced with disbelief and dread. Caught in the trap, there was no way out, no room to manoeuvre, his last hope remaining in the fortitude and fighting prowess of his men. Even so, with heart sinking, he realised numbers were against him. Where his warriors found success against Hund's men, Sveinn's fell upon them from the rear and skill and strength meant nothing in the confusion and clash of arms.

Olaf's men fought with all the honour and bravery they possessed, the slaughter dreadful. Olaf, himself awash with the blood of his enemies, cut great swathes through his opponents, blocking, parrying, cutting through flesh and bone. He found Hund in the mad mêlée, craved a path towards him, and closed at last with the man who had brought him to this moment. As ships rocked alarmingly in the seething fury of water and death, Olaf locked weapons. Hund, armed with sword and shield, fought gamely, but such was the fury of the king, he staggered backwards, stumbled over fallen comrades. The axe bit into his side and he loosed a great wail which seemed to freeze everyone's hearts. For a brief pause, battle ceased and all eyes turned to see the great Jarl crumbled, eyes not daring to believe in his defeat. And Olaf's axe swung, cut through the neck, and cleaved the head.

But it was not enough. Sveinn remained, urging his men on. Hundreds of them, swarming like beetles across decks, smiting the forces of King Olaf.

"We have to break free," someone shouted in Olaf's ears. With the flame of battle roaring through his body, Olaf had no thoughts for retreat. If retreat it could be. For as he looked, he saw the force of the enemy host and knew, in that moment, defeat was imminent. He looked at his lieutenant, himself covered in blood and brains, mouth open, hair lashed over his face, unable to disguise the hopeless look in his eyes. He gripped Olaf's arm, "We make for ships on the flank and we break away." He brandished a huge, curling horn. "Give the order, Lord."

Olaf stared. The raging mass of combat all around, and despite the lieutenant's words, the sense they made, something stopped him from giving the order to allow the awful bleat of the horn to cut through the clamour of death. "We must alert our warriors of the need to withdraw," screamed the lieutenant.

"What is your name?" asked Olaf, raising his voice as the first stirrings of wind promised a return of the storm.

"Magnus Grenskeson."

"And from where do you hail, Magnus Grenskeson?"

"My Lord, you need to sound the retreat, otherwise we are all—"

"From *where* do you hail?"

"Ringerike, Lord."

"Then the halls will ring of your exploits this day, Magnus, for look you there!"

The king gripped the man's shoulder and turned him to face the far west. And when he looked and recognised the sight for what it was, his voice cried out, "For the love of Christ, we are saved!"

For it was so. Even now, with Hákonarson's forces pressing home their advantage, the many ships of Sigurd Syr's fleet, stretching across the horizon, bore down upon the chaos, bringing with them the certainty of victory. Caught in a trap of his own making, too late Hákonarson realised his terrible plight. As he stood and stared, an anonymous warrior plunged his spear into the great Jarl's back as around him men fought and died.

The day drew on and Syr's men overwhelmed the opposition, huscarles from Olaf's ranks joining in to bring victory to their king. It was Palm Sunday and Olaf dropped to his knees and gave thanks to God, and to Sigurd Syr, the man who probably saved his life.

Eighteen

Great cheering and celebration greeted Olaf, astride his pony, as he entered Ringerike at the head of his victorious army. People pressed in from all sides, arms and voices raised, all of them laughing and shouting his name. He smiled and waved in return, elated at the reception, assured this was the beginning of a new and successful journey, to bring the love of Christ to his people.

At the far end of the great courtyard, guards held the reins and he jumped down, arms aloft, basking in the adoration of the crowd. But as he scanned the faces, the grin froze on his face. He saw them, every last one, turn away and raise up their voices even higher as Sigurd Syr came through the great double doors of the citadel. Not for him a pony, but a prancing, powerfully muscled charger. No doubt a Norman stallion, trained for battle, defiant and proud, head held high, with Syr nodding, smug and aloof.

Olaf seethed inside, but dared not show his anger. This man had changed the course of the battle, but his arrogance, his smirking, conceited face brought Olaf nothing but disdain. Sigurd Syr chose the right side, but did it for himself, and for himself alone. As the king locked eyes with the hero of the moment, something passed between them. Not a grudging respect, more an acceptance of the loathing they held for one another. For the moment, they needed one another's support, but Olaf could not help wondering for how long it would remain so.

"Is he not a man unlike any other?"

Olaf snapped his head around to find his mother, face flushed, hands clamped together in prayer. Her lips moved, mouthing something which Olaf could not catch, but it was clear from her expression she was enamoured, no doubt chomping at the bit to have Syr in her bed.

She turned to her son. "I have prepared for you a great banquet, my son. You, and you alone, are now King of Norway. Sveinn Hákonarson is dead, and the other jarls and earls will bow down to your banner." He gazed across the seething mass of people, still jumping with joy, Sigurd Syr in the middle, face awash with elation. "But without Sigurd, none of it would have come to pass. You must reward him, my son." Her eyes narrowed as she looked at him once more. "In the time-honoured way."

"I know where my duty lies, mother."

"Aye, I believe you do. But..." She leaned forward, pressing a finger against his chest, "try to show some appreciation, eh? Take the scowl off your face and give thanks for having such a powerful and faithful servant."

Without a word, Olaf spun away and strode into the great hall.

The fires were lit and servants busied themselves with brushing away the last remaining patches of debris and dust whilst others laid down fresh straw and rush matting around the raised dais at the far end. Torches burned and all around a soft, warm glow radiated from every side. Soon the space would fill up with the sound of raucous laughter, eating and drinking; the great feast to welcome back the victors.

The victors.

Olaf cast his mind back to the dying moments of battle and wondered how things would be if Magnus had led him away at the head of a rout. Who might be feasting now in this great hall? Syr and Hákonarson? Olaf could see them, heads thrown back, lapping up the adoration. He shook his head. He must speak to Sanda, seek out his counsel, his hatred for Syr well known. Perhaps if he had listened to his old friend before now, the situation could be so very different. For now, Syr was the second most powerful man in the land. He delivered his promises ... and, he was not a Christian. Olaf knew it for certain. How to unseat him, bring him down from his lofty position?

The door creaked open and Olaf turned to see Magnus standing in the space between the doors, a timid child waiting for permission to enter. Olaf beamed, relieved to see someone whom he could trust.

"Sire." Magnus crept forward, subdued, eyes averted. Beyond, the cries of jubilation continued unabated but when Magnus eased the door closed nothing but indistinct rumblings were heard.

Olaf strode forward, clamped his hands on the man's shoulders. "What a day, eh? The people are so happy, free from fear, anxiety and..." He stopped and frowned, noting his lieutenant's mood, dark, troubled. "What is it, Magnus? What is wrong?"

The man shook his head, unable to hold back his emotions, and he sobbed as his voice faltered and broke. He turned away, face in hands. "Dear God, sire. Such news."

Olaf gaped, body stiffening, wondering what could be so awful to bring him such grief. "Is it another attack, more enemies bearing down on us?"

"No, sire." He pulled in a rattling breath and slowly turned. "Behind the stables, sire. I was tending to your mount, together with mine and as I and two servants took to brushing down the ponies, we saw him, in the far corner, half covered with bales of straw."

Olaf tilted his head, not fully grasping the man's words. "Saw him? Saw *who*, for pity's sake?"

"Sanda, my liege. Dead. His throat cut."

* * *

The feast lasted for three days.

When the food ran out, warriors and earls slept between bouts of drinking. Olaf slumbered in his throne, took to his bed on two occasions, and when awake watched Syr strutting between the files of men, receiving their praise, their thanks. It seemed to the king that the man never ceased, he alone not needing sleep, the adoration of others bringing him energy and endless stamina. At one point, Olaf pulled Magnus aside, eager to learn more of Sanda's death.

"I have spoken to as many as I could, sire," said the lieutenant in whispered tones, shooting the occasional glance towards Syr and his retainers, who seemed to be everywhere. "So far, my investigations have revealed nothing. The last time anyone saw him alive was on the day of your departure, after you had charged him with defending the citadel lest you failed to return."

"I remember it well," said Olaf, biting his lip, "How he begged me to take him, to have him stand at my side, to avenge the shame of Nidaros. But he was my most trusted friend. No one was better able to defend my interests."

"Everyone knew that, sire. Especially your enemies."

Olaf, shaking his head, looked away. "We shall never find any witnesses. Even if somebody saw or heard anything, they would not dare come forward. We can only surmise..."

From the far depths of the hall, Syr's laughter rang around the rafters, joined by those still conscious.

"Aye," said Magnus, his voice thick with barely contained anger, "we may not have the proof, but we both know who is responsible."

Olaf's breath came long and steady. He slapped his lieutenant's arm and crossed over to the dais, stood before his throne and brought up a horn of ale, pausing with it in front of his mouth. "Friends, the feast draws to its close," he waved away the few groans of disappointment, "but before we part, I have one last, final duty to undertake. Lord Syr, step forward."

Mutterings of anticipation accompanied Syr as he moved forward, grinning to his followers, shrugging his shoulders as if not understanding what any of this meant. As he approached the dais, he looked towards Olaf, who raised the horn higher still and, without being told, dropped to one knee.

"Lord Sigurd Syr, in appreciation and thanks for the service you have given this land, and your king, I grant you the ownership of Sveinn Hákonarson's estates, the stewardship of Ringerike and title of Admiral of the Royal Fleet. To you is charged the rebuilding of our ships, lost in battle and the defence of our eastern borders." He raised the horn to his lips and the remaining throng cried out a loud cheer, before quaffing more ale. Olaf looked down at Syr, whose eyes brimmed with tears. The king smiled. "Furthermore, by the grace of God, I bestow upon your children, if the Lord sees it fit that I die without issue, the right to rule as my heirs, to bring peace and security to my realm. I shall summon, in three months hence, a *Thing* of the governing body, and lay down these promises in law. For it is right and just that the whole world knows the esteem to which we hold this great, heroic man." He stretched out his hand, lifted Syr to his feet, and raised his arm with his own. "Lord Sigurd Syr!"

And a cheer exploded so loudly, the walls of the hall shook and dust fell like snow from the roof.

"Thank you, my lord."

Olaf smiled, "Thank *you*." He clasped his hand around Syr's forearm, held it firm. "If only my loyal friend Standa were here to witness this, eh?" His eyes narrowed, waiting. But Syr showed no reaction, his steely expression never changing. "Loyalty and truth are virtues to be celebrated, Sigurd. And trust."

"Aye, sire. And you can trust me, with your life."

Olaf's mouth creased into something resembling a smile and he slapped Syr's arm and gave him a gentle prod towards his adoring companions.

From his slightly raised vantage point, Olaf studied how Syr took the proffered hands of his men, returned their grins, and saw how nobody turned their faces to the dais. He turned and was about to make his way to his chambers when Magnus stepped out from the shadows. "Forgive me, sire."

"I know what you're going to say," said Olaf, studying his lieutenant's grave features. "As king I have many duties to perform, not all of them palatable."

"Are they duties you fulfil, or a game you play, sire? How can you bestow such gifts upon that murderous dog's head?"

"Magnus, you and Standa are so alike. You do not understand the intricacies of rule. I have raised Syr so high that when he falls, the whole world will hear his cry of despair. Never underestimate me." He glanced back towards Syr and his followers, cracking horns together, punching the air, slapping each other's backs. "No one should ever underestimate me."

"And what of Standa, sire?"

Olaf nodded, mood turning darker. "Aye. My dear friend. On the morrow, prepare a funeral. A funeral for a Viking, for Standa was not of my faith."

"My lord?"

Olaf laughed at the startled expression gripping his lieutenant's face. "Don't look so shocked, Magnus. I know the hearts of men. Standa loved me, but he did not embrace the true faith. He tried, God bless him, but his old beliefs held sway, and he deserves to pass into eternity as a lover of Odin. I owe him that much."

Nineteen

Olaf watched the burning longship from afar, arms crossed, standing on the balcony of the great hall to watch his old friend drift out into the bay on his last journey. Detached by distance, he allowed the tears to run down his face unchecked, detached in body, but linked by memory. Standa, murdered, the crime demanded revenge. He clenched his fist and swore he would find a way.

Over the course of the next weeks, Olaf sat in the hall and received the fealty of those remaining landowners who had yet to bend their knee. He went through the motions, smiling or scowling when needs must. At the end of every long day, he would retire to his chambers and fall onto his bed, stare sightlessly towards the rafters, until eventually sleep overcame him. Another day dawned, another charade.

On one dismal morning, as he prepared himself for the daily grind, news arrived that his mother wished to see him. Initially reluctant, eventually he decided a journey across the wastes to Ringerike would relieve the tedium of rule, so he shouted out his orders and prepared for the journey.

The great thaw had begun. The trees dripped, a dismal lament for the promise of sun was so far away most believed it would never come. Memories had dulled when it came to thoughts of summer, the winter having proved harsh, harsher than anyone could remember. Spring was a far-off notion and, as he tramped across the plain, his pony downcast, head lowered, Olaf soaked up the gloom of his surroundings and the despondency of his entourage. Huscarles grumbled, servants dragged feet, retainers and free men refused to smile. The air of depression hung heavy like a yoke across everyone's shoulders.

After more than a week, they gained the heights, which looked down to the sprawl of Ringerike, ancestral home of Sigurd Syr, its walls strong, black, and silent. Within the enclave, many buildings, both large and small, were squeezed together, separated by pathways of running mud mixed with dung. In the centre, the great hall, with its lofty keep, soaring amidst the smoke of a hundred fires hanging thick over the roofs. Olaf signalled for the entourage to continue as he held back. Magnus plodded up beside him.

"Forgive me, my lord, but you seem troubled."

Olaf pulled down the corners of his mouth, "It is unusual for my mother to summon me. It bodes ill, I fear."

"We have had no further reports of rebellions, Lord. The northern frontiers appear secure, and soon the Normans will deliver their promise of men."

"It's been a long time coming."

"Aye. Perhaps they wished to wait for the outcome of Nesjar."

"It wouldn't surprise me. The Normans always play everything close to their mailed chests."

"You believe they would have allied themselves to Earl Sveinn, if his ships had overcome our own?"

"They'd ally themselves to a turd if it suited them."

Magnus laughed, saw the glare in his king's eyes, and grew serious once more. "All the more reason to thank Earl Syr for his timely intervention."

"You think so?"

"I don't quite understand your meaning, Lord. Are you saying—"

"I'm *saying* our Lord Syr is also a man who plays his game with an astuteness that would surprise any one of us."

"But not you, Lord?"

Now it was Olay's turn to laugh, although his was nothing more than a low chuckle. "I've lived most of my life surrounded by deception and double-dealings. I've learned to recognise it. And Sanda's death has done nothing to change my way of thinking."

"Lord?"

Olaf reached across and patted the neck of Magnus's pony. "Let us wait and see what my mother has to say, shall we?"

But as they followed the rest of the entourage through the main gates of the citadel, it became clear the shroud of gloom settling over the many roofs was mirrored in the grim, downcast expressions of the people. Winding their way towards the huge Great Hall, Olaf acknowledged one or two bows from onlookers, but overall their air of depression and sadness brought nothing but consternation to him. He shifted awkwardly in his saddle and when he dismounted, he averted his gaze and made straight for the entrance, Magnus close behind.

In the centre of the hall the great elongated cooking fires stood silent, and most of the torches too were lifeless. Lost in the darkness, on the raised dais a figure sat huddled, a single candle guttering next to it. As Olaf approached, the figure stirred and Olaf gasped when he recognised his mother.

She had aged, more wizened and bent than he remembered only weeks before, her face drawn and deeply etched with lines of worry. Or were they lines of grief? Certainly her eyes, when they looked up to hold his own, were black rimmed, tearful. He stepped closer, dropped to his knees and took her hand. "Mother. What in the name of God is happening here? Why are the people so forlorn, so filled with despair? And this," he twisted, spreading his free arm in a wide arc, "where are your Earls, your bondi? Why is everything so depressed?"

"My husband, Olaf."

"Sigurd? What of him." He shook his head, bringing his other hand to join the first. He squeezed hers tightly. "What has happened?"

"He is dead."

Magnus, standing a few paces behind, gasped and Olaf, as if struck by a blow, remained motionless, gaping, unblinking.

For some moments no other sound disturbed the awful silence.

When, at last, Olaf recovered some of his senses, he shifted position, drawing closer to his mother to sit at her feet. Still holding her hand, he gazed into her face. "I don't understand."

"It's quite simple, or are you more of a dullard than even I suspected?"

"Mother, for the love of God, I—"

"Do not speak to me of your god, Olaf." She tore herself free from his hold, and turned her face away, cramming a fist into her mouth. She bit down on her knuckles, squeezing her eyes shut as tears sprouted and fell unchecked.

Olaf stood and backed away, turning to see Magnus looking dumbstruck. "Fetch me Gyrrth Hennersson, master of the Queen's household. I'll make sense of what has happened, as God is my witness." Magnus bowed his head and raced outside. Olaf swung around and strode up to his mother once again. He put one foot on the second strep, and leaned forward on his knee. "Mother. Tell me."

She dragged in a breath, dropped her hand, and turned to him. She appeared as if every vestige of youth and joy had perished, replaced by a tired sickness, cheeks hollow, eyes rheumy, lifeless. "Tell you? Is it not obvious, haven't you ears to hear? He's *dead*. How many other ways do you want me to say it?"

"But how? I mean, he was fit, active, strong. I saw him less than a month ago, after our victory at Nesjar, the victory he helped secure."

She leaned forward and gripped him by the collar. Her voice hissed through gritted teeth, "Aye, he helped. And when he journeyed to the Uplands, to Hadaland to give council over some dispute to do with land, he was assassinated."

Olaf's jaw dropped. He stared, aghast, the blood draining from his face. At once dizzy, he staggered backwards, pushing the simple fur cap he wore off his head, clutching at his skull, unable to comprehend anything she said.

"You heard me correctly, Olaf," she continued, her face twisting with anguish, and something else. Fury. "They found him, lying in a privy. You have the picture, in your head? *In a privy*! Lord Sigurd Syr, the greatest nobleman alive, dead amongst his own shit." She stood up. Gone was the frailty, the withered coldness of her flesh. Instead, here was a woman emboldened by anger, her face blazing red, eyes afire. "They found a cut on his arm. A single stripe, made by a blade. Not enough to kill him, they said. So why had he died? Eh, I ask you that, my imperious son. How could a single slice of a knife, made on a part of his body that would otherwise have proved no more troublesome than a scratch, kill such a man as he?" Olaf gaped, shaking his head. She came down the steps towards him, every step slow and measured. "Poison."

Olaf went to speak, but her hand flashed out, quicker than the strike of a hawk, and her fingers gripped and twisted the top of his tunic. "Sigurd Syr, the *great* Lord of Ringerike, my husband, father of my children, poisoned. And you, you weasel, you ordered it."

The king's eyes opened wider than seemed possible. "*I ordered it?* How in the name of God can you believe such a thing?"

"Because I know *you*, Olaf. You agents were there, in Hadaland." She pushed him away, glared for a moment, then whirled round and returned to her chair.

"My agents ... I have no agents, mother. This is nothing more than cruel hearsay."

"Liar," she spat, drawing herself up into a tight ball, just as he had found her when he first arrived. "Why else would they be there, eh? Answer me that? To avenge your friend, Standa? Isn't that why you had my husband murdered, because you suspected him of complicity in Standa's death?"

"The venom that springs from your mouth is ... Mother," he threw out his hands, "I did not plot Lord Syr's death, not for *any* reason. Who are these 'agents' of whom you speak?"

"Don't attempt to cajole me with your treacle-covered tongue and your feigned shock, Olaf. I bore you, do not forget that. I *know* what you are capable of."

"No, this is wrong. I swear to you, on the blood of Christ, I had no knowledge of any of this."

"Leave your piety where it belongs. In the walls of your church. I'll not listen to it here."

Olaf went to speak further, but before he could, Magnus burst into the hall, accompanied by others, clumping across the compacted earth floor of the Hall. Olaf turned. Three brutish looking individuals, two wearing helmets, the third with ropes of yellow hair lashed across his face. They all stopped and bowed.

"Gyrrth." Olaf stepped towards the yellow-haired huscarle, who stiffened at his king's proximity. "Is it true?"

"Aye, my king. Sigurd Syr is dead. Poisoned."

Olaf pulled in a breath, looked from one warrior to the next. "And you were with him?"

"Every moment. Save one. He died—"

"I know where he died," said Olaf, holding up his hand to cut off Gyrrth's words. "My mother has spoken of agents. Did you question anyone, seize any suspects?"

"We made inquiries and discovered there were strangers. And some folk spoke of Lord Syr pushing past a bunch of customers in the market square. We were there, sire. We saw him, but we witnessed no attack. We had no cause, at that point, to suspect any wrongdoing. Only later, after we found the body, did we realise it, but by then it was too late. We called out the Watch, mustered what warriors we could, closed the gates and made a good and thorough search. But it was not successful. The strangers had fled."

"So they were responsible?"

"Almost certainly."

"And you know from where these strangers came? Were they foreigners?" Gyrrth looked over Olaf's shoulder towards the Queen, and nodded once. "So tell me," continued Olaf, "who or what were they?"

Gyrrth held his king's stare. "They were Normans, sire."

Twenty

Bartholemy tethered his pony to the hitching rail outside the cluster of black-timbered buildings, stomped his feet to bring some life into them, and went through the door.

The blast of heat from the fire caused him to halt, turn his head and wait for a moment. He pushed the door closed and took in his surroundings.

A wide room, trestle tables assembled close to opposite walls, a few weary travellers stooped over bowls of steaming broth. Smoke trailed from the blazing fire to the roof before it travelled across to the vent in the far corner, but not before it left behind the residue of various smells; dung, turf and peat. Windows were shuttered, to keep out as much cold as possible, and torches hung from sconces set high on the walls, whilst tallow candles guttered, giving off a feeble, stinking flame. The tang of sweat hung heavily, catching the back of Bartholemy's throat. He'd been on the road for two days, his clothes damp, body stiff with cold. Hunger gnawed away at him and the sight and smell of the broth caused his guts to rumble and groan. He shivered and went over to the fire, ignoring the curious looks from the others.

A door opened and a woman came out, holding a large tray festooned with hunks of bread and goblets frothing with ale. Behind, a large, dangerous looking individual, bald, ponderous belly sagging over pants secured too tightly with twine. His pained expression spoke of a lifetime battling against his large appetites, and losing.

"You need a room?"

Bartholemy, in the act of shrugging off his sopping wet sheepskin coat, glanced up from the fire. "I'm meeting with friends. I will only be here for a few hours. Maybe some food?" He nodded across to the men who continued to slurp loudly over their bowls. "Broth would do very well."

The man grunted, whilst the woman went over to the eaters and served them the bread and ale. She wiped her hands on her greasy apron and shuffled through the door.

"Friends you say? It will be dark soon. If you wish a room, I have one remaining, otherwise it's the barn out back. It's dry, but stinks like a dog's fart."

Bartholemy shrugged, holding up his coat before the flames, the steam billowing from its fibres in a wispy, continuous cloud.

"You have no need to wait, friend."

Both Bartholemy and the proprietor turned to the owner of the voice, one of the men slurping soup. He sat up, throwing back his cloak. "Join us, Bartholemy, and tell us what you know."

Before moving, Bartholemy checked the other corners, wary of being set upon. None of the other customers moved. Two in the far corner, big men, merchants by the look of them. On a table next to the counter, an older man, feet splayed out, dozing in his chair. No one had the look of a warrior. Nevertheless, Bartholemy took his time, readjusted his waistband, brushing the hilt of his sheathed dagger, and went to join the one who called him.

The man licked his lips, patting the corners of his mouth with his sleeve. "My name is Françoise."

"Your real name?"

The man smiled. "Sit, Bartholemy, and relax. You're amongst friends."

With a non-committal grunt, Bartholemy did so, studying the others, noting their chainmail, their heavy cloaks, the swords out of sight, but evidently in close range.

The proprietor hovered close and settled a bowl of broth on the table. Bartholemy nodded his thanks and attacked the steaming liquid with gusto.

The others watched him in silence.

"You've travelled far."

Bartholemy eyed the man called Françoise under his brows. "Far enough."

"Who are the friends you wait for?"

"Maybe you."

Françoise grinned. "Aye. Maybe us. Hungry and tired, you seem a man on a mission."

"Surely you know what it was."

"*Was*? So, it is completed."

Bartholemy tore a piece of bread from the accompanying half-loaf, and ran it around the bowl, soaking up the dregs of the soup. He munched it down, smacked his lips, and sat back. "Let us end this game."

"Is that what you call it?" It was one of the others, a square-shouldered man with a ruddy complexion, muscles bristling under his hauberk. Small piggish eyes blazed with latent anger. "This is far from being a game."

"Soften your temper, Pierre," interjected Françoise, his voice soft. "Bartholemy is tired. Perhaps he needs some rest, to settle his mind, consider his words."

"The task is done," said Bartholemy, avoiding eye contact with Pierre. "You can pay me the balance."

"We know it is done," said Pierre, leaning forward, "we almost lost our lives getting away. Know anything about that?"

"I don't like your tone," said Bartholemy, turning to face his accuser. "You imply I betrayed you?"

"How else would they know where to look?"

"Perhaps you sat in some sordid brothel, boasting of what was to befall the great Sigurd Syr?"

"Watch your mouth," snapped Françoise, eyes flashing towards the other customers. "Too many ears are close, and some might be agents of your esteemed victim."

"News cannot travel so fast."

"No, unless they had prior knowledge."

Again Bartholemy studied Pierre. "Say it clear. You accuse me of betrayal? For what purpose?"

"Double payment."

"You are a stupid man if you think I would murder our revered friend and hope to survive the vengeance of his followers."

"He had enemies everywhere. Most notably Olaf."

"Olaf would not dare conspire to murder his own mother's husband."

"You are naive if you believe that."

Bartholemy shook his head in despair and turned to Françoise. "Do you agree with this?"

"I don't know. They certainly knew where to look, Bartholemy. We barely had time to get out of the gates before they were closed."

"But you managed to escape, didn't you?" Pierre leaned further forward, half-rising out of his chair. "Tell us how you managed that?"

"I was long gone before they discovered the body."

Then how did you know he was dead?"

"Because no one, king or serf, survives." He cocked his head. "Are you telling me he is not dead?"

"He is dead, true enough," said Francoise. "We simply need to know where your loyalty lies, nothing more."

"You employed me. I have done as instructed."

"You took your own sweet time in fulfilling your task," continued Pierre, his voice thick with threat.

"I was indisposed. As soon as I learned the moment was right, I struck."

"And then, as if by magic, everything followed so quickly."

"When I decide the time has come, I act. I judge the best time and place. No one has ever complained before."

"You think highly of yourself."

"And rightly so. He's dead. The job is done." He turned once again to Françoise. "I want my money."

"Not until we know we can trust you."

Bartholemy sighed. "It works both ways. How do I know you haven't lured me here to kill me?"

"If that was our plan," sneered Pierre, "you'd already be face down in the dirt."

"Now who thinks highly of them themselves?"

"You think I couldn't crush you, like the insect you are?"

"I think you're full of bluster and horse shit."

Pierre erupted in a mad, furious rush, his right hand streaking out to grip Bartholemy by the throat and squeeze the life out of him. But Bartholemy was no longer in his seat. He moved, in a graceful flowing action. Dashing away Pierre's arm with his right hand, twisting the man's wrist, using his forward momentum to press him down onto the table top, whilst his left came around in a blur, the dagger materialising out of thin air, the blade within a hair's breadth of the brutish man's throat.

"One tiny nick and you will be in hell, my friend."

Françoise kicked back his chair, hand reaching for the hilt of his sword. And as he did, a leather purse, heavy with coin, flopped down next to Pierre's sweating head. Bartholemy looked across at the third stranger, who raised his head for the first time and glowered. "I am Emissary of his Highness, King Robert of Normandy. You have done well, Bartholemy. Let this wretch go and breathe easily. I have another task for you to complete." He nodded towards the purse. "There is the balance, with a lot more besides."

Bartholemy's eyes moved from the emissary to the purse, and back again. Behind him, the serving door burst open and the proprietor rushed in, bellowing, "I'll have no trouble here! Get out the lot of you."

"Calm down," said Françoise, sheathing his half-drawn sword. "There is no trouble here."

Bartholemy looked to the owner and gave him a cursory nod, releasing Pierre's wrist and stepping back, the dagger still in his hand, ready.

Pierre fell back, nursing his wrist, rubbing it with his other hand, his face red, sweat sprouting from every pore. "I'll kill you."

"No, you won't," said the emissary. "Bring more ale, landlord. We're all in need of a drink. Françoise, take this imbecile outside, before I forget my manners and cut off his head."

"Aye, my lord."

Françoise grabbed Pierre by the collar and hauled him to his feet. As they went out, Pierre growled, shooting a venomous look towards Bartholemy, who watched him until he was out of the door.

"My apologies, Bartholemy. We had to be certain."

Bartholmey allowed himself to relax. He slipped the dagger back into its sheath and sat down. The proprietor brought ale and Bartholemy drank, waiting.

"Things will change dramatically now," said the emissary, not touching his drink. "No one can foresee what King Olaf's reaction will be. He may do nothing, he may launch an investigation."

"Or others may take the opportunity and strike. I don't care." Olaf reached out towards the purse. Before he could take it, the emissary's hand closed around the assassin's with surprising speed.

"Precisely. Which is why I want you to strike fast and sure."

"Another killing?"

"Why else would you be here? With such a payment."

He withdrew his hand, allowing Bartholemy to weight the purse in his own. He turned down the corners of his mouth, not needing to open it up and count out the coins to know a healthy amount waited inside.

"Fast and sure."

"As you deem fit, Bartholemy. But time is pressing."

"Then you had best tell me who it is."

The emissary smiled. "I think you probably already know."

But the emissary informed him anyway.

Twenty-One

Funeral

The crowd pressed along the sides of the great square of Ringerike, silent and respectful. The funeral cortège passed by, flanked by guards, resplendent in oiled hauberks, and pulled by a pair of white geldings draped in opulent blankets of ruby red, hemmed with gold thread. The only sound was the slight creaking of the wheels rumbling across the ground. Behind, head lowered, Ásta walked with a measured step, proud and undaunted. She looked every inch a queen, regal and majestic, her gown of simple, shimmering ivory. A long way behind, not wishing to divert attention from his mother and her grief, Olaf walked, Magnus by his side together with a further honour guard of royal huscarles, axes sloped on shoulders, helmeted and in full armour. In living memory, none of Ringerike had witnessed such a grand procession.

Not far beyond the walls of the citadel, at a chosen point set upon a slight hillside, the cortege stopped and the body, open to the elements, lifted down. The burial site waited, a simple affair, without decoration save for a wooden cross to indicate this last resting place of Sigurd Syr.

As Ásta stood, the priests performed the funeral rites, lamenting the death of such a great man, but the priest reassured those present, his voice rising high. "Even now he is taking up his place in heaven. This was the promise given by Christ to those who believe. There should be none who cast doubt upon such a certainty."

"Two very different funerals, sire," said Magnus, standing close to his King's shoulder. "And very different responses." He nodded towards the gathered onlookers who stood some way off, some silent, most shuffling uneasily at the Christian words reverberating across the open ground.

"Syr was a committed Christian," said Olaf, standing bolt upright, "It is good the people witness this. It gives them courage, strengthens their faith."

"Aye, sire. That it does."

The priests called for people to lower their heads in prayer as the guards eased the body of their earl into the ground.

As the amens were uttered, Olaf made the sign of the cross and pulled Magnus aside. "How are your investigations, my friend?"

"I have uncovered much, sire. There are many amongst your subjects who have grave misgivings about Lord Syr's manner of death."

"They suspect my hand in it?"

Magnus released his breath slowly. "Aye, sire. They mumble their accusations in taverns and the marketplace. Many reject it, but others are convinced."

"And Gyrrth?"

"Always there, sire. Looming large."

"Once you have the evidence, have him taken into custody. But you must have proof, Magnus. I'll not move against him until his guilt is assured."

"It is difficult, sire. He has a loyal guard, inherited from Lord Syr's household. The two of them were close."

"Close enough for Gyrrth to grow jealous and murderous."

"To be open to promises, sire. From our erstwhile friends, the Normans."

Olaf pursed his lips, stiffening as his mother drew close. Already the crowd were moving up to the graveside, to pay their last respects, throw flowers into the open grave, some silently offering prayers to the old gods.

Ásta stopped and looked towards her son. There was the slightest hint of wetness under her eyes, but other than that, she remained stoic. "I shall retire to my private apartments after the funeral feast. My presence will be brief and from that point, I do not wish to be disturbed."

"It is your right to mourn, Mother, in whatever manner you see fit."

Her face darkened, jaw tightening, eyes narrowing. "And it would suit you well too, eh, my loyal and obedient son?"

Olaf reeled from her barbed words, "Mother, for the love of God. On such a day—"

"On such a day, I thank God I now know the depths to which you sink, Olaf. My husband was a just and honourable man, and you took him from me."

"Mother, your grief blinds you—"

"No, on the contrary, it has focused my mind. I am not alone in my suspicions, as well you know." She turned her accusatory glare towards Magnus, "And whilst you delve as deep as you can, my own agents seek out the truth. Be warned. When the truth is uncovered the repercussions will be swift and *final*."

She whirled around and strode off, her guards struggling to keep up.

The two men watched her, stunned by what she had said.

"I shall pay my own respects at Sigurd's graveside," said Olaf. "You'd best accelerate your investigations, my friend. We cannot afford to delay any longer."

"I shall leave you some men, sire."

"No need." Olaf glanced across to the mingling crowd, deep in reverence as they huddled together at Syr's grave. "This is a melancholy day. I do not wish to intrude on people's grief. I'll merely pay my respects and return to the Hall for the feast within the hour."

"At your command, sire." Magnus punched his chest, swung about and strode off, in the same direction as Ásta, but at a comfortable distance behind.

From amongst the crowd, a solitary figure stepped aside, watchful, hands hidden beneath the folds of his heavy cloak. He studied King

Olaf easing his way between the gathered mourners. Olaf wore a full hauberk, which fell to his knees, and covered his arms down to the elbows. Beneath was a thick leather jerkin, at his side a sword, hanging from a black baldric. He did not wear a helmet, allowing his long hair to fall to his shoulders, the slight breeze of the morning playing with the ends, flicking them across his thin, serious mouth. Not many of the crowd seemed to notice him as they shuffled around the open pit of the grave, gazing down at their dead lord, some throwing flower petals to cover the body. Olaf closed his eyes and mumbled something, probably a prayer. The watcher gauged the distance, wondered if this would be the time. But the crowd was deep. If any spotted or suspected what had happened, the net would closed tight. So he waited, stepped back, considered his options.

Olaf squeezed through and tramped across the field, heading back to the citadel of Ringerike. After a few moments, as the crowd broke up, the silent stranger pulled his cloak tight around his throat, and fell in behind his king.

* * *

The Great Hall was thick with the smell of wood-smoke and baking fish. In the great long fires which ran the length of the hall, the cooks laboured hard and fast over the spluttering flames, preparing the many courses of the funeral feast. Already the room was filling up as the many earls and lesser nobles took up their positions, at first solemn and serious but gradually, as ale was distributed, tongues loosened and laughter crackled through the smoke.

Olaf found his mother sitting in deep concentration on her chair of honour, set upon a raised dais, chin in her hand, staring towards the floor. A large, mangy-looking dog sniffed at her feet, licked around her ankles. She did not stir. Olaf shooed the animal away and sat down beside her, frowning. "Mother?"

She did not look up, eyes unblinking, deep in thought.

He called for ale and the servants ran to fetch a goblet. Men continued to come through the great double doors and the clamour of voices grew. Servants struggled to set down the many benches and trestle tables, trenchers arrayed across the top, blunt-edged knives and flagons arranged hurriedly in readiness for the feast. Laughter rang out and from somewhere in a far corner, one man took up a song. Olaf listened, picking out the words. An old poem of honour, battle and love, set to a tune he did not recognise. And Sigurd Syr's name featuring large in every stanza.

Olaf caught sight of Magnus, shouldering his way through the press of gathering warriors. The man's eyes roamed from side to side, wary. He seemed on edge and Olaf gestured for him to approach. The king eased forward as Magnus stepped up to him, pressing his mouth close to his lord's ear.

"Gyrrth has left the citadel, my lord."

Olaf winced at the news. "You cannot follow him?"

Magnus shook his head, his face taking on a pained expression. "He left before the burial, sire. Riding hard on well-prepared mounts. With him were a good twenty or so huscarles. He went north, but that is as much as I know."

Olaf threw himself back in the chair, bringing his fist down hard on the armrest. "Damn his heart. The man is guilty enough, conspiring against me, and probably Sigurd too."

"I suspect his hand was stained with Standa's blood also, sire."

Olaf's eyes glowed with rage. "This is not the work of some petty jarl from the provinces, Magnus. I see another's hand in this."

"It is plain to see, sire."

"Gather the evidence, Magnus. Do not cease. If you can find anyone who might tell us a name, then we will have good cause to act."

"You mean to use force of arms, sir?"

Olaf almost laughed at Magnus's incredulity. "Not war, my friend. Merely retribution. Do what you can, but have some ale first."

Magnus lowered his head and swung away, moving over to a group of huscarles, joining in with their laughter. Olaf watched for a moment, before his attention was taken by a slight figure moving through the jabbering assembly. By the slightness of its frame, Olaf judged the person to be a woman, and as she approached and dropped to her knees, holding out her hands in supplication, Olaf saw it was true. Her arms were slim and smooth, the fingers of her hands tapering to well-formed nails. Her face, however, swallowed up by the cavernous expanse of her hood, remained a mystery.

"I bring you a message, my lord king."

Olaf frowned, unconsciously dropping his hand to his sword hilt. Close by, his guards bristled. He held up his hand to ward them off. "What message?"

"Your life is in danger."

Olaf narrowed his eyes, looked around him, aware his guards had wandered off, reassured. He looked again at the woman. Her hands trembled, but her voice did not. A strange, throaty utterance. Strained, but not fearful. Who was she? "How did you get in here? Who are you?" An inexplicable dread gripped him and he stood up, reaching out to take hold of the woman's cowl, tear it away to reveal her face.

"*Sire!*"

He swung round, alarmed, reaching for his sword as the owner of the voice strode towards him. Or did it? He gazed into the crowd towards the direction from which the figure emerged. But there was no one there. He took a step down from the dais. Had he imagined it, or...

Light-headed, he pressed his finger and thumb into his eyes as a swirl of grey mist descended, confusion spreading through every fibre of his being. Giddy with bewilderment and uncertainty, he staggered backwards towards his chair, stumbling and fell on his backside.

From out of the swirling gloom, strong hands grabbed him, hauling him to his feet, anxious voices crying out, "Sire, are you sick? Are you injured? Are you..."

He fell into his chair and gazed to where the woman sat with her hands stretched out. There was no one there now.

"Your father dropped down in much the same manner."

Olaf blinked a few times, shook his head and turned to his mother who, throughout, remained in her transfixed state. "What?"

"Your father died from the falling-down sickness. Perhaps you have inherited it?"

"Sire?"

Olaf turned, half expecting another mysterious apparition. Instead, what greeted him was a tall earl from the northern realms.

"We await your address, my king."

And it was true. The Great Hall had become quiet, the men milling around, goblets charged, faces expectant. Olaf felt his throat, forced a swallow. Something wasn't right about any of this, and he struggled to focus on his surroundings. Voice sounded strangely hollow, as if uttered in a cave. And as figures and furniture seemed to retreat into a black fog, by the door stood the woman, proud and straight, her hood at last thrown back. He gasped. Her face was stunningly beautiful, wild, raven hair framing a pale, finely chiselled face, with full red lips and wide, lustrous eyes. "Take care, my king. Take care."

She slipped out of the doors and Olaf, agog, gazed into nothing, dimly aware of distant voices, growing more frantic, insistent.

A great roar of onrushing air brought him out of his trance with a start and he snapped his head towards the jarl who still stood, mouth open. He thrust out his arms. "Sire? Are you unwell?"

"Unwell?"

"Sire, your address. The feast must begin, to honour Lord Sigurd."

"*Lord Sigurd...*" A memory stirred, of a death, perhaps two ... Sigurd.

"My husband," said Ásta, rising from her chair, her voice strong, ringing out across the throng, "Lord Sigurd Syr was a great and noble man. Defender of the northern realms, his feats sung of in halls throughout the land. The sagas have yet to be written of his exploits and his greatness." She threw a wild glance towards her son, King Olaf who sat, sprawled in his chair. "And he served our King well, right to the end, smiting his enemies and bringing peace and security to this land." She stepped down to the nearby jarl, ripped the goblet from his hand, and raised it high above her head. "To Lord Syr, hero of Ringerike, and saviour of our realm!"

A great cry of, "*Lord Sigurd Syr!*" boomed around the hall, and mouths opened, and ale drunk.

"And now, my lords, earls and jarls, we feast!"

Another roar, and the entire place erupted into a wild, mad chorus of upraised voices, of laughter, backslapping, pounding of goblets on tables, and eating. Eating of every type of dish, of fish, meats, fowl, eels. And as they feasted, Olaf stared, lost in the unease which rolled around his insides, turning his stomach to mush and setting off such a pounding in his head he believed at any moment his skull would burst.

But it didn't.

In time, his eyes glazed, dimly aware of the noise, of people moving, of musicians and jugglers performing. Of laughter, raucous and seemingly unending until, that is, Ásta motioned for some nearby servants to draw closer. She said something and they bowed and hurried away.

"Olaf," she said in a loud voice.

The king looked askance, not bothering to draw himself upright. The goblet in his hand was at an angle, his body heavy, drained. His other hand propped up his head, which lolled. His mouth barely moved and he frowned towards his mother, "Yes? What do you want?"

She ignored him, spreading her arms wide like wings, "Good people of Ringerike," she smiled. "Friends. We have mourned, we have remembered, and we have laid to rest our good and noble lord. Now, let us rejoice in his memory and the fruit of what he has left for us all to enjoy!" Olaf sat up, intrigued. She clapped her hands. All eyes turned to the far end of the Great Hall as the doors creaked open. Two fully-armoured guards stood and, with the light behind them, casting them in silhouettes, a shimmering yellow halo surrounding them, three small figures entered.

Olaf threw down the last of his ale, dropped the goblet to the floor and rubbed his eyes. "What is this?"

The three figures moved forward and as his eyes grew accustomed, Olaf recognised them as three boys, two quite tall, the third much younger. However, this third boy appeared different, more aloof, his features stern whilst the others smiled, gawping, somewhat embarrassed by the attention of so many important personages.

"These are Sigurd's sons," declared Ásta, stepping down from the dais to ruffle the hair of the two eldest. She hesitated for a moment before reaching out to do the same again to the third. But this boy swayed out of reach, his eyes locked on Olaf, cold, indifferent.

"If I am not mistaken," said Olaf, pressing down on the arms of his chair to lever himself upright. "These are my half-brothers."

"That they are," said Ásta, stepping aside.

The king came down the creaking steps and, towering over the three boys, leaned forward, his face twisting into a scowl. "I'll not have them here. Look at *them*! Weedy, unfit. They dare to smile at their king?"

The two older children cowered, stepping away. Only the third, the youngest stood rooted to the spot.

"Are you not afraid of me, boy?"

The boy tilted his head and the faintest of smiles creased the corners of his mouth. "The only man I ever feared was my father. And he, as you know, is dead."

An audible gasp ran around the room. Men, hardened by battle, looked to each other in alarm.

"What did you say?"

The boy's mouth parted in a wide grin and then, before anyone could move, his hand shot out to seize Olaf's beard and gave it a violent tug.

An awful silence, followed swiftly by gasps of disbelief, which turned to groans. Some laughed, most held their breath.

For a moment it appeared Olaf might go into a sort of seizure. His face reddened, eyes watered and he jerked himself free of the boy's grip, clutching at his beard and stared hard into the boy's face.

Ásta rushed forward, creating a barrier between the king and the other two, who cowered behind her. She held up her hand, "Olaf," she said, her voice uncertain, tremulous, "he is merely a child, he does not understand who—"

Olaf held up his hand, never moving from the boy's unblinking stare. "Silence. This whelp has more courage than most of the men in this room." He ignored the raised mutterings, "*Silence*, I said." He leaned forward, moving his face so close to the boy's, their noses almost touched. "What is your name, lad?"

"Harald."

"Harald. A good name. Strong. Like you. Like your father. Harald Sigurdsson. I think you will grow up to be a great and vengeful warrior. What say you to that?"

"I say when I discover who murdered my father, I will indeed have my revenge."

Some of the gathered earls cried out in agreement. Olaf grinned. "By the Lord our Father, lad, you have grit. How old are you?"

"Five summers."

"*Five...?*" Olaf stood back, tearing his gaze from the boy to consider his mother. "And the other two?"

"This is Halfden," said Ásta, pulling the first of the other boys from behind her traces. "He is seven, and this," she strained to grab hold of the third boy's coat. She put her arm around him, calming him as he quaked and blubbed, "this is Guthorm. He is also seven, but is the eldest of my boys."

"Well," said Olaf, rubbing his hands together, not wishing at this point to let his mother know the boys were not a secret to him, "do not be afeared, lads. It was nothing more than a jape. I'm not half so terrible as I appear." He laughed, turning once more to Harald. "If I am not blessed with sons of my own, it may be that one day you will rule this land for yourselves. What do you say to that, Harald Sigurdsson?"

"I say if my destiny decrees, it shall be so."

Olaf pursed his lips. "You impress more and more with every word you utter." He stepped back to his chair and sat, studying each of them in turn. The boys still entwined in their mother's arms, continued to tremble. "Tell me, Guthorm, if it came to pass that one day you would be a great and powerful lord, what would you most desire?"

Without hesitation, Guthorm took in a deep breath and said, "Cornfields."

"Cornfields? And why would you want those, eh?"

"To feed my people, my lord."

"Ah," Olaf nodded, lips pressed together, impressed. "A noble sentiment, to care for one's own. And you, Halfdan, what would you do?"

"Cattle," cried the lad, standing stiff, shoulders thrown back, chin jutting out. "I too would care, but I would give my people meat to eat, to strengthen their bodies and make them more able to work and serve me."

Again Olaf nodded. "Well, here we have something more. Single-minded in spirit. That is good, Halfden." When at last he turned to Harald the king leaned forward and, as if to remind himself of the boy's previous reaction, covered his lower jaw and beard with his hand. "And you? What would you desire?"

"Huscarles."

Those close by cheered, raising up their goblets to drink to the boy's reply. But Olaf silenced them with his arm, raised high. "And how many warriors would you require, my lad?"

"As many as needed to eat up all of Halfdan's cattle, and all of Guthorm's corn, ground into bread for my coronation feast."

Olaf threw up his other arm and roared with laughter, the assembly joining in with great bellows of rejoicing. "By all the saints, mother, you've prepared this one well. A warrior born, that's what he is."

"That is why I named him Harald. Ruler of warriors." She swung round to face the throng, "And, one day, ruler of all the Norse!"

* * *

In the far corner, the man who stood at Sigurd's graveside, shifted position, finished his ale, and pushed his way through the press of drunken warriors. No one paid him any mind, too engrossed in their own excesses to notice him. Swathed in his black cloak, he appeared like a shadow, but his journey towards the king, quaffing ale, was direct and determined. As he drew closer, he slipped the dagger from its sheath. All it required was a single strike, a mere slice through the flesh for the poison to do its worse. Sigurd had not even noticed until he fell to his knees in the privy, gasping for breath. Nothing had saved him. Nothing would save Olaf.

Bartholemy stepped closer. A huge huscarle noticed him, went to move, and the dagger streaked through the thick, stifling air. The man gasped, clutching at his hand, not daring to believe such a thing had happened. He turned disbelieving eyes to the shadowy figure, saw the blade, and prepared to draw his sword and smite the impertinent turd with a single strike. As he moved, he gagged, throat closing up, unable to take in another breath. He clutched at his throat, his eyes boiling in his head, toppling backwards to land across a nearby trestle. His companions roared with laughter, pushed him over onto the floor and continued with their drinking.

Bartholemy flung back his cloak and took another step. There stood Olaf, the great and faithful king, head thrown to stare at the ceiling, laughing heartedly as the small gathering of children as their mother looked on, gibbering together like the gaggle of geese that they were. *Well, damn them to their hell. I might even finish them all, have an end to it, and allow the Normans to ride straight through this rotten, stinking land.*

He drew back his arm, preparing to strike.

A pain, like a searing hot lance, exploded in the small of his back. He went to move, not understanding what it was, and the pain increased, a powerful thrust of something needle-sharp, plunging deep into his body. Frantic, he attempted to take hold of whatever it was, and again it went deeper, accompanied by something else. Something new. And terrifying.

Her voice, soothing, a mere whisper, floated into his ear as it used to, calming, sensual, captivating. "You should have stayed with me, my lovely."

"Oh, Christ."

"Yes, my lovely. I can see more than you know, being the witch that I am." She grinned. "Prepare to meet him."

One final press and the tip of the blade punctured through his flesh and clothes. Bartholemy looked down at the point of the offending blade protruding through his body, saw the blood and knew death had come to claim him.

* * *

Those sober enough to react, swarmed around the dying assassin, sagging on the blade, the woman behind with her arm across his chest, supporting him, not allowing the blade to withdraw. She held on until Bartholemy went limp, his weight causing him to slide from the deadly weapon's embrace and he crumpled to the steps of the dais, a lifeless heap.

Huscarles seized the woman by the arms, one of them bringing his sword around to rest it against her neck. Others knelt down next to the dead man, his eyes wide with disbelief.

Olaf, at first frozen with surprise, managed to find the strength to turn and look at her. In that exchange, he saw so much and understood who this man, this would-be assassin, was. "Let her be," he said, voice no more than a croak.

"Sire?" The man with the sword gaped towards his king. Behind him, Ásta gathered her children to her bosom, protective as always. Everywhere, men drew swords, shouting, no one knowing what had transpired. Someone, with enough sense, ordered the doors closed.

"Let her go."

With great reluctance, the men acquiesced and slowly the atmosphere settled, swords returning to sheaths, collective sighs echoing in the stillness.

Olaf went to her, lifting her chin with his hand. "I should have listened."

"Aye. You should."

He nodded towards the body. "You know him?"

"I did. Long ago. But that part of me is dead now also." She turned and smiled at Harald. "Take care, little one. Learn from what you have seen this day." And she brought the cowl over her head and slowly inched her way towards the door.

"Who was she?" asked Ásta, moving up close behind Olaf, who watched the woman as she slipped through the doors and disappeared into the early evening.

"My saviour," he said and he stepped over to his chair, flopped down into it and closed his eyes, sleep suddenly closing in all around him.

Twenty-Two

The Dneiper River, 1042

They stood on the banks of the river, watching the men loading supplies, and nobody spoke.

A light breeze ran across the water, the far bank festooned with trees of every kind, rolling hills capturing the eye, taking thoughts, hopes and dreams on a journey of far away. Haldor, limbs still stiff from his injuries, was the first to recover. He knelt down by the river's edge, scooped up a handful of water, and let it trickle between his fingertips. He watched the merchantmen scratching their calculations on pieces of parchment, and he smiled. "Look at them. Their only concern is for profit. They grab at any opportunity to make a quick a *tetarteron*, regardless of how. They've come all this way, stumbled upon us, and leap at the chance. I hate merchants."

"You think they followed us?" asked Ulf, stretching out his legs, cramped up after sitting and listening to Hardrada for so long.

"I doubt it. If they had, there would be more of them. Soldiers, too."

"You reckon they've decided to let you escape unscathed, Harald?"

Hardrada remained as a rock, staring into the distance, eyes clouded over with the memories. "I sometimes wonder how my life would have been different if my father had not died the way he did."

"We can all ponder on such things," said Haldor, tugging out a stalk from the bank and putting it into the water to watch the current play around it. "Life throws up its choices and we make them, often without thinking. I sometimes think we have little choice anyway. I remember speaking to one of the many mystics who passed through Mikelgard. He told me it was better to simply let life take you on its course, to not think too much, but rather ride with the current, not against it." He picked up the stalk and peered at it. "A little like this stick. If I throw it, it does not fight and where it goes no one decides, save the river."

"Such things have no choices," said Hardrada, eyes remaining fixed ahead. "Plants and animals do what they do, actions dictated not by themselves but by nature, instinct. That stick has no say in what you do to it, whether you throw it into the river or not. We are the ones who have choices, for right or wrong. That is what makes us who we are." He shook his head. "I remember my mother calling us together to tell us the news, of how my father had been 'taken from us all'. She stood like a piece of granite, but I could feel her pain. My brothers wailed but I did not. I turned to the window and stared out across the fields and I swore I would make them pay. One day, I would take up my sword and have my revenge. I barely knew him and nowadays the memory of him is so vague I can no longer remember what he looked like. But I remember the anger, which gripped me the day mother came and spoke of his murder. It's with me still. I doubt it will ever leave."

"But your father's death was not your choice. Others were responsible, without your knowledge. You had no say in what happened and yet, your life was determined by it. You cannot punish yourself for things over which you had no control."

"I'm not punishing myself," said Hardrada, "but I do often wonder if he had lived, how different things might have been. Would I even be standing here, having travelled across half the world? Having seen the glories of Byzantium, loved the most beautiful woman who ever took a breath, and lost her in a moment's recklessness."

"Perhaps you would have stayed in the north," said Ulf, sitting up, scratching his chin, "stuck inside an old stinking hall, surrounded by ale and salted meat. You'd be fat and sad and you'd rail against the whole world because you had not known adventure, or the love of a good woman."

"In a strange sort of way, that is almost what I did do. Olaf spent his days criss-crossing the land, from the southern coast to the northern wastes, taking with him the Word of God, whilst I languished in my mother's household, doing my utmost not to grow soft, unlike my brothers who belched and farted their way through life. I do not know why I trained with the remnants of my father's huscarles, but thank God I did. I crawl into bed, battered and bruised, and the following day I'd drag myself up and go through it all again. I honed my skills, hardened my muscles – and my heart – and readied myself for what I felt certain would come. For I was not deaf to the gossip and the rumours. Talk of unease and mistrust at Olaf's desire to bring Christianity to the whole land. I'm not even certain my mother agreed. I never saw her pray, that is for sure."

Haldor stood up and eyed his friend with interest. "Yet they buried Sigurd in a Christian grave."

"Aye, they did that. I remember years later, perhaps when I was around twelve summers, I went to stand beside his tomb. It was not long after Magnus died, Olaf's faithful retainer. They put him in the ground with little ceremony. He was always kind to me, so I stood and said some words. When the few who mourned wandered away, I went over to my father's grave. It was clear to me it had been tampered with, many years before."

"Tampered with?" asked Ulf. "What do you mean by that?"

"I mean he was no longer there. When I confronted my mother with my thoughts, all she did was shrug. She knew, you see. She had given the order to take him from that Christian site and give him a Viking burial."

"You can't be certain of that," said Haldor, clearly appalled at this revelation.

"I know it," said Hardrada, slamming his fist solidly against his chest, "in here. There were many who were prepared to fight against the Christian way, and my mother was one of them, though she never once did anything to provoke suspicion. But whilst Olaf put all of his energy into building churches and installing priests, forces gathered against him. Not all of them pagan, not by any means, but all jealous of his position and determined to overthrow him. He grew complacent, ignorant perhaps, of the threat building against him. But when he struck, he struck with the fire and strength of the old Vikings, all piety and Christian virtues forgotten. When the kings of the Upplands conspired against him, he showed his mettle, putting out the eyes of Rorek, one of the five traitors. And Swedish incursions fared no better. Olaf hanged any who crossed his borders, leaving them for the crows, a warning to those who might believe him soft and weak."

"And yet he was overthrown," muttered Haldor, drawing closer to his friend. "I do not know much of his story, but I do know he was forced to flee, to the court of Yaroslav, King of the Rus, in Kiev."

"*Kiev*?" blurted Ulf. "Isn't that where we're going now, for you to take up with the girl you left behind?"

"I didn't leave her behind," said Hardrada, a flash of anger crossing his face. It soon fell away. "I came away to win enough treasure in order to satisfy her father. Who was I but a wounded, landless ruffian with no prospects, eh? Not the most promising match for Yaroslav's daughter, that's for sure. So I went south, to Mikelgard, to seek my fortune. You know the rest."

"But I don't," said Ulf. "When we met, you were already a warrior, forged in battle. I know nothing of how you came to be the man you are now."

"Then I'll tell it," said Hardrada, sitting down on the grass with a sigh. "I'll tell it all."

Twenty-Three

Europe, 1028

They dragged the whimpering and bloody youth through the double doors of the Great Hall and threw him at the feet of King Olaf.

"We found this wretch, boasting of the money he'd earned," one of the burly huscarles towering over the grovelling youth said.

Olaf growled, shifting in his throne. He eased his great bulk forward and, taking a mouthful of ale from his flagon, cackled. "Another bribe from the wily Canute, no doubt."

"He showers his money on any who might voice doubts concerning your highness's legitimacy, sire."

"Aye, well, he's a mealy-mouthed bastard who has designs on my throne. But he'll not have it." Olaf pushed himself to his feet, took a step and stumbled. The huscarles rushed to his side, catching him by the arms. He swayed backwards, ripping himself free of their grip. Ale slopped from the flagon and he collapsed into the great chair again, pressing his fingers into his eyes. "Get him out of my sight."

"But what shall we do with him, sire?"

"I don't care." Olaf drained the flagon and hurled it aside.

"Sire, he has besmirched your good name in alehouses throughout the Vek. His complaints of your harsh treatment towards him, of how you seized lands granted to him by his stepfather, have rung loud throughout the capital. Many have listened and many give credence to his grievances by voicing their support. Sire," the huscarle dropped to his knee and threw out his hands, "you have to act against such disrespect. Give the order and we shall strip him naked and hang him from the walls, so all can see the consequence for those who would dare to undermine your rule."

A figure emerged from the shadows, swathed in a voluminous heavy robe of deep blue, trimmed with ermine. The huscarles tensed at his approach, stepping away, bending from the waist. "Lord Sigvat, a warden of the north. Damn," muttered the first warrior.

Sigvat glanced down to the youth, sprawled across the bottom steps of the dais. "Why did you beat him?"

The huscarles went to speak, then stopped, exchanging bemused expressions with one another. "Lord?"

"There was no need to treat him this way." Sigvat stopped down, smoothing away the youth's lank hair to reveal a face bruised and battered. "You did this in full view of everyone, I'll warrant."

"What would you have us do, lord?" demanded the second warrior, face growing red. "You have heard how he—"

"All I have *heard* are your accusations. There is no proof."

"You have the proof of our words, by God."

Sigvat snapped his face up to the two men, whose expressions had turned dark and dangerous. "I think you should go."

"And what of him?"

"Leave him with me, so I can speak with him and ascertain what his grievances are."

"But we know his grievances," spat the first, taking a step towards the still kneeling Sigvat. "You cannot allow the treason he uttered to go unpunished."

"You dishonour us if that is your desire."

"And we will not allow such disrespect to—"

"Enough," said Olaf, through his hand, which remained covering his face. "I'm weary of such bickering."

"But sire, you have been wronged. You cannot allow such things to go unpunished!"

"Damn your eyes, Karlson," snapped Olaf, forming a fist and slamming it down on the arm of his throne. "You'll not lecture me on what I should and should not do!"

"Forgive me, sire," said Karlson, ashen-faced, "it was not my intention to—"

"*Enough*, I said. Take this bastard out and do as you suggest. I'll not suffer the likes of him in my presence any longer. Root out any others who share his traitorous views and trouble me no more with such trivialities." He stood up and, as if reinvigorated, strode down the steps, crossing to the huge hall to the far side where he helped himself to more ale. With the moans of the stricken youth ringing out, Olaf drank and did not watch. When Sigvat came up beside him, the king remained as if in ignorance to the cries and the sounds of fists and boots striking flesh. Only when the doors slammed shut did he release a long breath and turn to the man facing him.

"You judge me, Sigvat. I can see it in every line of your face."

"No, sire. I do not judge, but I am saddened." Sigvat held his king's gaze. "You know who the youth is?"

"I don't care, but I'll tell you this. *Never* disrespect my huscarles in my presence again. They are my most trusted servants and their loyalty is essential to my continuance as king of this blighted land."

"It's a land which is deserting you by the day, sire. The more cruel your punishments, the more their resentment towards you grows. The boy is the stepson of Jarl Kalv Arnason. By executing him, you've instigated a blood feud which will rip this nation apart. Olaf." He reached out and gently took his king by the arm, "I've composed so many poems about your life, your achievements. Your *faith*, Olaf. Where is your Christian charity when you deal with your subjects in such a violent, unfeeling way? For the love of Christ, I beseech you to retract, to forgive, and by so doing rebuild the trust and love of your people."

"I need their loyalty, Sigvat. Times have changed. Whilst I was in the north, the people in the south grew restless, turning their eyes towards my enemies."

"You mean Cnut?"

Olaf paled, turning away and when he reached out to hold onto the wall, his hands trembled. "God is punishing me, for not being strong enough, for not doing his work. I tried, in everything I have done, to bring the true faith to this land. But I'm dealing with beliefs so ancient, so *ingrained* that success, even temporary, has not been achieved. Only here, in my homeland of the Vik do the people turn their eyes to God. I should have done more, I should have worked harder. And now my enemies come and sow their seeds of discord, paying for obedience. Cnut's coffers are bulging and he will do whatever it takes to expand his lands." He dragged in a breath, his forehead resting against the wooden panels of the wall. "I know you believe me cruel, Sigvat, but I am like the good shepherd, keeping his flock together in the face of a growing storm. Sometimes I have to assert force, so that those in my care can hear my voice above the tempest and take note of what I say. For there is a storm coming, Sigvat, the most violent that has ever crossed this land, and at its head is Cnut."

* * *

Less than two weeks later, news reached Olaf's capital of Sæheimr, news which was grim in the extreme. Cnut's fleet, freshly arrived from England, made its way north along the Norwegian coast and everywhere it stopped, not only did it receive supplies, but the support of the people. Chieftains, both great and small, were called to a *thing* at Nidaros to proclaim Cnut as king of Norway, and those who so swore were rewarded with money and land.

"They flock to his banner," said Sigvat, standing in the darkened hall as Olaf sat with his face in his hands, immobile, the news of Cnut's progress striking him hard. "Jarls who once gave their fealty to you, now cross to him. Harkon Eriksson, whose holding at Lade bulges with warriors, swears death to you and to your family."

"My family?" Olaf frowned, "Dear God, how has it come to this, that the whole world rallies against me? Have I truly erred so badly?"

"It is not you have erred, sire, more it is the manner in which you attempted to bring your subjects to the Cross." Sigvat stepped forward,

"Sire, you still have a loyal following, men of stout heart and unshakeable faith. Perhaps, by mustering such men of proven worth, you may present to Cnut such a force as he will reconsider, perhaps negotiate."

"Negotiate? He has invaded my lands, damn it! There'll be no negotiation. Call together the headsmen and summon a levy. We'll do what he least expects, and strike north, catch his force in the rear before he can swell his ranks still further." He squeezed his fist tight. "I'll become the champion of Christ, for all the world to see, and they will tremble at my sight!"

* * *

They caught Cnut's rearguard not far from where Sigurd Syr had saved Olaf all those years before at Nesjar. Falling upon the enemy camp at night, Olaf's men gave no quarter, hacking through the enemy ranks as most of them lay sleeping. With little chance to gather arms and armour, the slaughter proved great and one-sided, defenders dying, unable to retaliate. As the groans of the dying rang out like the peals of bells proclaiming Armageddon, Olaf grinned, triumphant, teeth shining white in a gargoyle face. In the glow of the campfires, he stood, feet planted apart, an unbending tree of wrath, receiving the submission of the few survivors.

Thrown at the king's feet, the enemy leader, Jarl Erling, one of the most powerful of the northern landowners, knelt on hands and knees, panting, a trail of blood dripping from his broken mouth.

Olaf studied him for a long time. With the last of the enemy despatched, the only sound now – the crackle of burning wood – lent the scene a strange, malevolent air. "The fires of hell," muttered Olaf, almost to himself. He lifted his voice and boomed, "You wronged me, Erling. You took bribes from Cnut, false promises of land, and you hoped to profit from my fall. Did I so wrong you?"

Erling barely moved. A huscarle stepped up and slammed his boot into the jarl's side. Erling shrieked, fell over, squirming in the dirt. "Forgiveness, sire," he spluttered.

"Where is Cnut?"

Erling grew still, as if the very name of the great King of England and Denmark swept away the pain of his body, replacing it with dread. He sat up, face aglow from the nearby fires, black slug trails of blood glistening on his cheeks. "Sire, Cnut's host is huge. Jarls from all across the northern and western lands have rushed to his banner. His fleet straddles the horizon and his soldiers—"

Olaf rushed forward, hauling the quivering jarl to his feet by the throat. "Where?"

"North," whimpered Erling, becoming limp in the king's grip. "Close to Stad."

Olaf threw Erling to the ground. "Then that is where we sail. Make ready," he roared and swung around on his heels.

"And what do we do with him, sire?"

Olaf levelled his gaze towards the solid-looking huscarle who, axe in hand, stood over Erling, expectant and eager.

"As you see fit," said Olaf.

Even before the king moved, the huscarle seized Erlson by the hair and cut through the jarl's neck with a great strike from his axe. The blade cut through sinew and bone down to the breast bone, opening up Erling's torso like meat on the butcher's slab.

Olaf hawked and spat before he turned away and strode through the night towards his waiting ships.

* * *

They came like a great black wave, from every direction, the water between the ships invisible, cutting through the raging squall, which sprang from nowhere. Cnut's banners trailed in the wind, drawing eyes towards the great man's vessel, whilst around him rowed men from all across Norway, disaffected men, angry, thirsty for revenge. Men such as Hakon Eriksson, Kalv Arnason, and the sons of the slain Jarl Erling. And Olaf gripped the dragon-headed stempost of his flagship and knew all was lost. He lowered his face as wind and rain lashed across his exposed flesh and stumbled between warriors battling with their oars to the pilot gripping the steerboard.

"Turn about," screamed Olaf above the spray and crash of the churning sea down. The pilot frowned. "We cannot prevail. Turn about."

Olaf's meagre fleet beached, the men scuttled towards the dry land, taking whatever they could with them. The king stood, bracing himself before the gale, wrapping his cloak about him, but never once turning his face from the open sea and the innumerable ships bearing down on his position with relentless fury.

Amongst those who slipped and struggled was his son, Magnus. He'd pleaded to stand beside his father and now, watching the youngster wading through the foaming water, he regretted not leaving him behind with his mother, Queen Astrid.

Lifting his axe arm as a form of standard, Olaf strode away from the shoreline towards the relative safety of the nearby treeline. Here he gathered his loyal retinue together, waiting patiently until soaking wet and bedraggled warriors and bondi grew silent. He addressed them in a voice strong and proud.

"I'll not bandy words with you all. All is lost, that much is evident. The forces arrayed before us are too great in number. There is no shame in retreat, for it affords us the opportunity to regroup and rebuild. Towards this end, those of you who wish can return to your homes, with my blessing. Any who stay, I must tell you, the journey will be long and hard. We will travel east, over the mountains to Gudbrandsdalen, where my queen awaits together with Bishop Grimkjell. I'll not abandon my land until I am assured that the love of Christ will remain in those churches we have sanctified. Grimkjell is the man I entrust with this task whilst we move further east, across Oppland to seek refuge under the protection of my friends in Sweden." He held up his arms as grumblings grew, disbelief descending on those assembled to hear the king's words. "I will return, have no doubts. The Lord will find a way, so put your faith in Him and together, our destiny will be fulfilled."

They roared their support, some falling to their knees, others openly weeping. Olaf nodded, basking in their loyalty, went over to his son and put his arm around him. A slight smile brushed his lips in farewell before he turned and slowly tramped through the trees, aware of others joining him, but never pausing to see.

Twenty-Four

Hardrada – 1030

Fate, not design or guidance from God, brought me to the lonely hovel in the clearing. The winter descended harsher than any I had yet experienced. I fled, my mother's words like daggers in my heart. 'You must live, Harald,' she said, gripping me by the shoulders, eyes full of tears, her aged fingers imbued with a strength I never guessed she possessed. 'When they come, they will kill you. They will kill us all.'

She organised provisions, a single pack animal laden down with food and blankets, and when she stood outside the hall, she did not speak. And when I stopped at the rise and looked back to my home, her tiny frame appeared black and forlorn.

I never saw her again.

Accompanied by two trusted huscarles, we left Ringerike and made our way across the blinding wilderness of snow and ice. We took a circular route, in the hope of confusing our pursuers. It was the winter of ten hundred and thirty. My step-brother, King Olaf, had gone south, to the Kingdom of the Rus under the protection of Jaroslav, the Grand Prince. But my thoughts did not tarry long on Olaf's plight. I knew neither if he were dead nor captured. For those first days and weeks, nothing filled my mind save for images of Ásta and what might befall her and my brothers under the blades of Cnut's henchmen.

Sometime during the second week, our food gave out. The mule, which bore our meagre supplies, we butchered and for a little while, we gnawed on its raw flesh. With no means to make a fire, most of the animal proved inedible. Forced to scavenge for whatever we could find, our bellies ached with hunger. The ground, packed solid by the ice, refused to give up whatever bounty lay underneath the snow and game proved scarce. Four days later, one of my companions keeled over and died. Whether it was through starvation, despair or disease, I know not. But he fell and died and I knew then, as I stared into his frozen features, survival truly was in the hands of God.

At one point, we huddled together, my surviving companion and I, sheltering amongst the black, silent trees of the woodland. For how long we remained that way it is difficult to recall, but the weather turned colder, great snowdrifts stacking up between the trunks, blocking our path. We realised this cocoon of ice and snow afforded us a kind of shelter from the worst of the elements, so we drew our blankets tighter and waited for a break in the freezing downpour.

When finally it came, endless days and nights later, my bones were frozen solid, my muscles weak. And when I staggered to my feet, I found I had not the strength to take even a single step. For my companion, however, life's flickering light had already been extinguished.

From somewhere, I dragged up the means to continue. I was a pathetic wretch, wasted, lost to the world. I stumbled blindly to where I believed the woodland might give way to open ground. And when I saw the clearing, I became as one possessed, a sudden surge of energy coursing through me. I pressed on, invigorated, doing my best to run, forever hopeful I would come across something, or someone. Salvation. Food. Warmth.

I saw her as I emerged from the tree line. At first I believed her to be a wraith, a creature of the dark realms I still remembered from the old stories my mother used to tell. Covered in a black, trailing cloak, head hidden beneath a heavy cowl, she gathered wood from a pile next to her hovel. As she did so, she sang a simple song and her voice called to me, soft and sweet.

A thin trickle of smoke drifted skywards. The promise of a fire, let alone the hope for food, forced me on. If she were a wraith or a demon, I no longer cared. I fought my way through the snow, and I cried out to her, to give her warning of my approach. For all I knew there might be others, men perhaps. Not wishing for her companions to rush out and slay me before I experienced whatever sanctuary she could provide, I made my way with painful slowness towards the hovel, my arms stretched out to make it clear I offered no threat.

Tramping and cursing through the snow, with all the grace of an overladen bullock, she snapped her head up in alarm.

For a moment we both stopped, something passing between us. Fear, uncertainty, I know not. She gasped and without a pause, bent herself double as if an invisible weight pressed down across her back, and she croaked in a pitiful voice, "I have nothing here for you. Be gone. I am nothing but a poor, old woman. Be gone!"

As I stood and listened to her pleading, pathetic voice, a strange feeling came over me. A feeling of utter despair. I teetered forward, aware of moving, but with little strength in my legs, as if my entire spirit of preservation drained from me. I pitched into a huge, gaping hole, my face hitting the cruel, cold snow-covered ground, and everything went black.

I next became aware of light. Blinding, boring through my open eyes, penetrating into my brain. Pain mingled with dread as shadows came and went. I did not know where I was, or what was happening to me. Warm hands, a soft, soothing voice, but nothing of any substance. I drifted in and out of consciousness and I no longer cared. If this was the beginning of my journey into the afterlife, as promised by King Olaf and his many priests and bishops, then so be it. A Christian assurance of a new life, without fear or concern. My forefathers promised an eternity of feasting and drinking in the great hall of Valhalla. This seemed infinitely more seductive and I surrendered to it, weak and unsure. My soul was now in a state of flux and I allowed myself to be subjected to whatever fate awaited me. All of the fight deserted me and I slept the sleep of the lost.

But one morning, everything changed. My eyes were able to focus once again and I knew where I was. Not in any heaven, but in this woman's home. Blankets stacked up around me gave me warmth and comfort and I turned and saw her busying herself by the fire, brewing up some sweet-smelling concoction in a large pot. When she came to me, her strong hand holding up my head, she fed me and I took whatever it was she gave.

Each mouthful filled me with new life and new hope. My limbs slowly returned to life, bones, which had once felt as if vicious beasts gnawed away at them to the very marrow, became sturdy and strong. I may have lain there a day or a week, I know not which, but soon the ability to discern and recognise my surroundings increased and I was able, at long last, to sit up on my own and take the spoon in my hand and lift it to my mouth.

She sat and studied me, the hood of her thick, black habit thrown back to reveal a face kind and not as old as I first suspected. But a face of experience and, from the way her eyes shimmered with liquid blue, one of loveliness.

Often she would leave her hovel, sometimes for only a short while to collect wood, other times for longer periods. I never asked her where she went, but I often took the chance to ease myself out of the bed and force myself to pace around the cramped hovel, to re-educate my limbs, gradually reawakening the ability to walk as well as think. This proved difficult, the roof so low and I stooped and scurried around like a beetle. I longed to go outside and stretch my limbs, but I knew my body, not sufficiently recovered from the cold, remained weak with muscle and sinew compacted, bones aching.

The day I managed to make myself a kind of stew was when everything changed. I stood next to the fire, slicing scraps of turnip into a pot, together with a few beans and a mountain of herbs. Having settled the concoction over the fire, I rocked back on my heels to admire my handiwork and became aware of being alone. This in itself was nothing unusual; many times she left me sleeping on the bed whilst she attended to her business, whatever that might be. But something about the atmosphere caused me to stop. The air changed, charged with a crackling tension, which reminded me of the morning I left my mother's homestead. It was as if unseen eyes studied me, shadowy figures awaiting their chance to leap out and strike. I sat and listened, mouth open, all my senses alert. My eyes settled on my sword, which stood propped up next to the door. It must have been weeks, perhaps months since I last drew it and my skills were no doubt rusty. They thought of engaging in training and practise had not entered my head, until now.

I stood. The floorboards groaned and I waited. Without there was no sound at all, save for the gentle fluttering of snow as it whispered down in a constant stream. I chanced to peer through the single window. The shutters closed, as they always were, the latch in position, gave me a moment to reconsider. Should I open them, I wondered, and look out into the world, to see where she might be. Perhaps this was one of her sojourns to the nearest village, from where she would buy whatever she could, and trade some of the potions she was forever brewing up. Caution prevented me from taking this course, so I slowly crossed the room. As my hand curled around the hilt of my sword, I heard it.

The neigh of a horse.

I froze, my body colder than at any time since I tramped through the snow and came upon this place. Locked rigid with fear, I forced myself to slide the sword from the scabbard. I stared at the blade, wondering if I had the strength, even the desire to wield it. Whoever was outside, they would be armed men, well trained. I knew that much. No doubt they had picked up my trail, found the bodies of my companions, followed me to this lonely spot. And now they had the woman who had saved my life. Whoever they were, they must be stopped.

I held my breath, steadying myself, conjuring up the meagre remnants of courage that remained in the darkest recesses of my body. Tearing open the door, I rushed outside, the battle cry coming out of my throat sounding shrill and tremulous.

There were three of them. Great hulking brutes. One of them had her around the throat, holding her tight. Her feet, lifted from the ground, kicked and danced, whilst his thick arm covered her mouth. Her eyes blazed when she saw me.

The first of them, in a flowing cloak covering mail hauberk, came at me as something possessed, screaming, the sword singing through the cold air. I saw his livid eyes underneath the helm, the nasal guard lending him a brutal disguise, and I knew his only thought was for my death. With teeth bared, he swung the sword and I met it with my own. The massive blow almost knocked me down. My knees buckled, arm ringing with pain from the shock of the strike. I recovered, made to dodge and weave as he attempted to deliver the killing blow. The snow, thick underfoot, hindered my movements. But what it did for me, it also did for my attacker. A lumbering beast, he struck for the umpteenth time, grunting with the effort as his frustration grew. I swayed to my right and as his blade struck air, I lunged, the point of my blade puncturing through his mail. He gasped and without a pause I struck a second time, swinging across his unprotected legs, the blade cutting him below the knee. He squawked, toppled and fell, splats of blood hitting the snow, turning it pink. But I had no time to admire my victory. I turned to meet the second man as he attacked. My sword met his, but this time luck deserted me and the sheer power and ferocity of his strike broke my sword in two. I gasped in disbelief, starring in cold terror at the shattered remnant of my blade before lifting my face to meet the hate-filled stare of my opponent.

He stopped, glowering, breath smoking from his mouth, a mouth filled with glistening, blackened teeth bared in a maniacal grin of victory. I looked beyond him to the woman, still struggling in the third man's arms, and in that moment our eyes locked together and I recognised who she was.

"Remember who you are, Harald."

The brute before me frowned, snapped a glance back to her, and I took the chance and smashed into him, putting all my weight into his gut. We crashed into the snow, floundering like a pair of stricken oxen. His sword left his hand and I struggled to gain some advantage over him. I was not as muscle-bound then as I am now, but my height always gave me an advantage, and I trapped his squirming body in my arms, swinging my knee into his groin, two or three times. He howled, his frame growing limp for a moment, and I pushed the jagged piece of what remained of my sword under his corselet with all my might, the cruel edge cutting through the bulk of his belly, hot blood boiling over my fist. He writhed, squealing, and it was as if my strike brought him renewed vigour, no doubt borne out of desperation and the realisation death had found him and not me.

His paws found my throat and he squeezed. Dear God how he squeezed.

We rolled over, my knee jabbing upwards again and again, but his desire to blank out my life gave him an irresistible, frightening strength. I gripped his wrists, leaving the stump of my sword buried in his flesh, but no matter how much I pulled and wrenched, his grip remained firm. I gagged under his grip as he pressed his weight on me, pinning me, pushing me further into the thick blanket of snow that covered everything. My eyes rolled, the world blurring before me, white heat searing into my brain. Nothing mattered to me except for those cruel fingers, crushing my throat, blocking out my ability to breathe. I floundered, growing weaker, and felt as if I were drifting, rudderless, lost in an eternal sea of greyness. I heard him grunting with the effort and I knew it was the last sound I would ever hear. Looking into his eyes, a strange kind of peace descended and I surrendered, sinking ever deeper into that grey void.

With consciousness and life almost gone, from somewhere the pressure eased. The weight left me and I became vaguely aware of shadows moving around the edges of my eyes, mumblings of disbelief, alarm. I gasped, the air hitting the back of my throat like a razor. I was free of him. I knew not how and I was not about to consider the reasons.

Desperate now, I rolled onto my knees, staring down into the white ground. I took up handfuls of snow, washing them over my face, breathing ever more deeply, not daring to believe I had survived.

A body thumped down next to me and I snapped my head around to see the man who, only moments before, crushed my larynx with his fingers of steel. His eyes were wide and unseeing, a stream of bloody saliva trailing from his quivering lips. I scrambled around, forcing out a cry, my throat rough and sore, unable to give out more than a strained shriek.

She stood there, the cowl thrown back from her face, revealing eyes alive with a burning intensity. In her hand, she held a blade, and it shone with a thin film of brown, like a sort of glaze, and along the edge tiny splatters of blood. Next to her, the man who had held her, a look of total disbelief on his face, his body contorted in an aspect of indescribable agony, hands reaching out, fingers curled into rigid claws.

I pushed myself backwards across the snow, believing whatever dreadful powers she possessed would soon be visited upon me. Whimpering like a child, I swung away as she came up next to me. But instead of the cruel strike of her blade, her warm hands came to my face and turned me to her. I settled on her lips. She was not old, as she would make herself out to be, but middle-aged, her features striking, finely chiselled, with high cheekbones, thin nose, and full, smouldering lips. As her eyes held mine, I became drawn to her mouth and I spoke in little more of a croak, "You saved me."

"Aye, I did."

And her mouth folded over my own and all my fear, pain and confusion disappeared.

Twenty-Five

In the confusion of the struggle, the first attacker had cut me across the arm. Now, lying in the safety of the hovel, the pain creased me up. She lowered me gently to the bed and stripped away my jerkin, and within moments applied a soothing balm over the angry looking slice across my right bicep.

Her fingers were like the touch of angels and I almost swooned beneath her as the pain eased and I became like one floating.

"By the gods you are well made, Harald."

My eyes snapped open and I caught her wrist, for her words brought a different pain to me, not to my body, but to my soul. "By the gods?"

She smiled, "You need something for your throat," and she went to move away. But I held her tight, pulled her back to me. She frowned. "Don't tell me you are fearful of my beliefs? You have always known I am not Christian."

"The old gods are long dead," I croaked.

"Are they? Who says so, your White Christ?" Her fingers curled around my own and her face loomed close. "I'll teach you, if you wish. I'll teach you all the things you need to know for your journey through life."

"I *know you*," I rasped. "You came to Olaf's Hall, and I saw you slay the stranger with the knife."

"You cannot remember such a thing – that was many years ago."

"I remember it as if it were yesterday. I saw your face, and I have kept it with me all these years."

"Have you?" Her lips curled upwards into a smile as her hand fell to my crotch. "If you were a man, Harald, I'd teach you other things."

I dashed away her hand. "Who in the name of God are you? *What* are you?"

"I am many things, Harald Sigurdsson. Some call me witch, some soothsayer. I've lived my life out here alone for many years, abandoned at fourteen by a man who I thought of as my father. I never knew if he was, but soon other men came, and they raped me, here in this very room. There were four of them, perhaps more, and I knew there would be others. So I disguised myself as a hag, and I took to bending my back, screwing up my face, until I believed I was who I wished to be. A twisted, freakish old woman. Soon men stayed away and in my self-imposed solitude, I experimented with things I found in the forest. I brewed potions and created ointments. I took them to the markets and over the years, I became renowned for the power of my medicines. Men came to me to put fire into their belly, to renew their lost ardour. Women came for ointments to smooth their wrinkled brows, and when they were sick, I gave them potions and powders that cured them. And then, one day, two men came and asked if I could make them a poison." She stepped away, my grip having grown slack and I watched her shuffle across to the table where she kept her array of ingredients. "I was not sure at first what I could do. The skills I developed always took me in the direction of curing, not killing. But nevertheless, the challenge spurred me. I created something so potent, so deadly I do believe it has any equal." She turned, the dagger in her hand, the same smear of brown glaze taking all of my attention. "This is what I used on those hounds outside. A single cut is all that is required. No one can survive. It acts within seconds, cutting off the ability to breathe, and they die in agony." She smiled, a most dreadful sight given the horror of her words. "A foreigner visited me. He spoke with a curious accent, but he had enough of our language to tell me someone else would visit me, an assassin charged with murdering a great and renowned leader of men and I must prepare a blade with enough poison to kill an ox."

"Who was this leader of men, were you told?"

"My only instructions were to prepare the blade, I was not privy to the victim's name. But I knew who it was, Harald. I always knew."

I frowned, holding my breath, wondering if I dared to ask the simple question and receive an answer, which might crush me. I asked nevertheless, "Who was it?"

She replied without hesitation, "Your father. Sigurd Syr."

* * *

She took to bathing me as I said on the edge of the bed, lost in thought. My eyes remained locked on the dagger, set down on the small table, its edge gleaming with the poison I now knew had destroyed my father.

"Who killed him?"

"You need not trouble yourself with such things, not now. What's done is done."

She dipped a cloth into a basin, filled with heated water, wringing it out before applying it to my body. "I need to know," I said, my voice fragile, not yet recovered from the attacker's assault.

She sighed. "What good would it do?"

"It would give me a peace of mind."

A short cackle. She tilted back my head and washed around my throat, gentle, luxurious strokes. The power she possessed to bring calm and vigour to the body, breathtaking. Divine.

"If revenge is in your heart, Harald, put it away. There is nothing you can do now."

"Revenge is the Viking way. I may have sounded shocked by your fealty to the old gods, but I am not yet fully Christianised. The killing of my enemies is in my bones."

"You cannot kill that which is already dead, Harald."

I jerked my head forward and took hold of her hand. "He is dead?"

"The time you saw me in Olaf's Hall. The man with the blade, the one sent to murder your king, was the very same. Bartholemy. He was a Fleming and an assassin. I killed him, Harald." She tore her wrist from my grip and her eyes brimmed with tears. I saw her face crease with despair and she whirled away, pressing the cloth against her face, a muffled groan emitting from deep inside. Keeping her back to me, she spoke with enormous effort, her voice splintered with emotion, tears punctuating every word. "He came here and he stayed. And we … we grew close. Closer than I ever could have imagined. I had known men, of course. I allowed some to lay with me, but Bartholemy … Without my even realising it, he captured my heart. When the time came for him to leave, I was out of control. I went to the nearest town, became friendly with another and I invited him here. I wanted to punish Bartholemy, you see, cause him to consider his life without me." She expelled a long breath, sniffed and turned. She had stopped crying, but her lips continued to tremble. "He didn't love me. I knew it. When he left, he murdered the man who was due to come here. No one else has ever come. Except you, Harald." She came to me in two strides, cupping my face in both hands. "He was given the task of murdering your father, with a blade smeared in my poison. If anyone is responsible, it is me."

"But you killed him."

"Aye. I did. My sense of injured pride, or a broken heart. I know not which. But I sought him out, learned of his whereabouts and discovered by the very subtlest of means, just what his next mission was. To kill Olaf."

"But … this series of assassinations … I do not understand. Everybody believed Olaf was responsible for my father's death. Even my mother."

"Yes. Which is precisely what the real culprits wanted. They wish to sow discord, even civil war amongst the Norse. When this did not transpire, the decided to remove Olaf from the mix, allow Cnut to seize control and work with him in assuring security for their own, blighted realm. As it was, Cnut was able to achieve such a situation without the king's death. So, in the end, the plan succeeded, albeit not in the way planned."

I gently pushed her hands away. "Who?"

"It would be best for you not to know. Not yet. You are still a boy, Harald. There is nothing you can do."

"I won't always be a boy. Tell me who it was who ordered the deaths of my father, and of Olaf."

Her eyes narrowed. "Robert Gieves, the emissary of the Norman court in Rouen."

The news struck me like a slap. The Normans, they spread their contagion like a cancer. Always striving to bring discord, fear, death. And to think their ancestors were of the same blood as my own. I hissed, "By the blood of Christ, I swear I'll kill that bastard."

"You are not ready for such an endeavour, Harald."

"I killed a man this day. There will much blood on my hands before I leave this life."

"You killed him not by design, Harald. And he almost killed you. If I had not put my poisoned blade across his throat..." She shook her head, smiling. "Your promise is clear, but you require training. I know someone. His name is Arnulf Matersson. I have a purse of good, gold coin," she swung around, going to the table to rummage around the various pots and phials she used to create her concoctions. She came back with a leather purse, drawn closed. She jangled it in her palm. "He'll teach you, Harald."

"I know how to fight."

"Not so you will triumph, my sweet. Your skills need to be honed, developed. This man is a swordsman of the highest renown, as his father was before him. Give him this payment and tell him who you are. I have spoken to him already and he knows you will come."

"You sought him out on one of your journeys to the market."

"I did." She smiled and came up to me. She pressed the purse into my hand. "If only you were already a man, we could have such a life."

"Such a life..."

"You are already so impressive ... Dear God, the very thought of you..."

She allowed her head to fall back, her eyes closed.

"But you killed my father," I said. And I put the stump of my sword blade into her and buried it up to the hilt.

She did not gasp or groan. Rather, she appeared to accept my killing blow like a long-awaited friend. A smile crossed her face and she brought her face towards mine, her eyes alive with a perverse sort of glee. "Oh, Harald," she said, and her body went limp. I caught her around the waist, thrusting deeper, and she sighed, the blood frothing from her mouth. I lowered her gently to the ground, keeping the blade inside, and I felt the life oozing from her.

I lay upon her for a long time.

Twenty-Six

With panniers packed with whatever provisions I could muster, I made my way to the town indicated to me by the dead woman. I'd left the bodies of the brutes sent to kill me for the wolves, but her at least I put in the ground. I took the horses and plodded across the open fields. Everywhere white, as constant as a sea, nothing to guide me save for the position of the weak sun struggling to burn through the thick clouds, and by night whatever stars I managed to find. But I lost my way more than once and at one point was forced to butcher one of the horses. Unlike when I first set upon my journey, I now had flint and steel to make a fire, so my feast was wholesome and I survived, despite the numbing cold.

The town nestled beneath the mountain range of the Dovre, some miles south of Gaulardal. I crossed a narrow river, frozen solid, and wended my way through the gorge, seeing the smoke trailing up from the huddle of houses which made up the town. A fortified wall enclosed these buildings, with two or three wooden towers guarding the gate, blackened with tar, from which fluttered large, grey banners. I reined in my horse and studied the homestead for some moments. Olaf had come here, almost ten years before, forcing the people to take up the cross. Those who refused, he put to the sword. I knew if I revealed my identify, my throat would be slit within a few hours. So I pulled up my hood, drew the collar tight, and took on the aspect I learned from the woman. To not only appear as an old man, but to become one. If I believed it, so would others.

And the trick worked.

The guards at the gate gave me nothing more than a passing glance, and I dismounted as I came into the town square. People mingled around, most of them swathed in several layers of thick clothing, noses pinched red with the cold, eyes bleary and distant. Nobody paid me any mind. I found lodgings in a dismal inn, nestling between a farrier and a tanner in a grim side street. The stench from the tannery was enough to keep most people away, and that was what I wanted. If men had been sent to hunt me down, I was sure they would not be the only ones. Cnut or the Normans, either one wished me dead. No doubt the rest of my family had fallen under the assassins' blades. Having sworn vengeance against Robert Gieves, I was more than content to broaden my desires to spill the blood of any who dared cross me.

At the farrier's I learned of a horse trader who I visited later the same day. He proved a sallow-faced individual who refused to make eye contact, but he gave me a good price for one of the horses, without asking any questions. The horse was a fine animal, well looked after, and something of a rarity in Norway at that time. I was surprised he did not ask where I acquired it, but remained impassive myself, not wishing to give too much away. I left feeling a little uneasy, despite the bulge of the coins in my purse.

Later in the evening, as I sat and took the meagre gruel offered to me by the innkeeper, I noted amongst the many huddled inside the three men in the corner. They glanced over to me now and then before exchanging words with each other, and cackles of laughter. I stretched out my legs, unease spreading through me. No one else gave me so much as a glance. Clearly, the three knew who I was, or had been informed of my sale of the horse and, with suspicions aroused, planned to relieve me of my money.

I called to the innkeeper for ale and, as he stooped to take away my empty plate, I caught him by a chunky forearm and pulled him closer. "You have a rear entrance?"

If he understood my meaning, there was no indication save for a slight frown. I put a coin into his palm and released him. "For my bed and the meal." I stood up, towering over him. The men in the corner stirred and I made my move, pushing past the innkeeper to the rear room.

A portly woman with a great shock of white hair sweated over a cooking pot. She eyed me angrily as I entered, her mouth cracked open to reveal a slack, toothless gash. "You want more, you'll pay for it."

"I want the way out."

She straightened herself, planting her fists on her ample hips and cackled, "By the gods, but you're a big lad. Have you paid what's due?"

"I have."

"Then it's through there." She pointed a crooked digit towards a grey, threadbare blanket covering a gap in the wall.

I went through it as the men behind me erupted into the tiny kitchen. I heard her screech, pondered over turning to face them, but decided today was not the best day to risk death from the hands of cutthroats. The memory of my last encounter with killers still rumbled in my mind, plus the painful fact I would not be alive if it weren't for the woman's intervention. So I ran, vaulting the rickety, rotting fence, which encompassed the small yard. I raced through a series of courtyards, herb gardens, and wet, sodden clods of earth, until I skidded into the town square. The snow had not fallen since my arrival, but ice lay thick on the ground. It was treacherous underfoot and I flailed around like a drunkard, balance deserting me. I crashed down hard onto my backside, feeling like an oaf, listening to the many guffaws from the people all around. I cursed them all and managed to stand again, turning to see my pursuers closing in fast.

I looked around for another exit. Surely they would not assail me in open view? Nevertheless, I drew the sword I had taken from one of the dead men back at the hovel, and backed away, hoping to find other means of escape.

They closed around me, slow but determined, their faces alive with slobbering, leering lips. Drunk they might be, but I needed no further evidence of their violent intent as they threw back their cloaks and slid out broad-bladed knives of Saxon design. The Scramasax.

I baulked at the sight of those cruel knives, turned and ran, feet sliding out from under me. I scrambled forward, sometimes cracking my knees against the hard earth, sometimes managing two or three strides before falling again. Desperation forced me to continue, plus the knowledge those looming up behind me would experience the same wild dance of pursuit.

I made the first side street. Here, the cramped confinement of the passage had made the ice thaw, and I managed to put more distance between myself and the men. Or so I believed. Their voices barked with anger and frustration, growing louder. I chanced a quick look and there they were, bearing down on me like furies, their cloaks trailing behind them, weapons glinting in the weak, evening sunlight.

And as I turned my head forward again, to continue with my flight, my heart lurched, and awful dread seized me, bringing me up to a sharp stop.

The passageway was a dead end.

Twenty-Seven

Looking back to my youth, the way I am now, it is difficult to recognise the youth I once was. How craven, how lacking in physical courage. True, when I blundered out into the snow from the hovel, I formulated no plan of action, acting purely on instinct. I had no time to think. If I had, I may well have remained inside, trembling in a corner, hoping against hope those men would go away. In that dark, cramped alleyway, the peril I found myself in pressed in all around, as if the very walls of the squat buildings themselves were about to crush me. I had time to think, to allow the awful reality of my situation to worm into my very soul. I turned to face them; three brutes, grinning like devils, coiled ready to pounce, their vicious blades giving the promise of a cruel and bloody death.

I held the stare of the undoubted leader, a pace or two ahead of his companions. He was almost as wide as the passageway itself. His grin widened as he spoke, a grating sound, betraying how out of breath he was after the chase, "We want your money, you rat-faced bastard."

Here was a chance, I thought to myself, to hit them before they recovered their energy. A fanciful thought, one which I dismissed almost immediately as I tried to lift my sword arm. But strength deserted me, replaced by freezing dread. Shame mingled with fear and I took a step backwards, holding up my free hand. "I have it," I croaked.

"Give it to us and we'll not cut your throat."

In that instant I knew he lied. Men such as these not only robbed, they butchered too. My life would end in this filthy place, down in the slush, a meal for the vermin that scurried along the edges of the walls. If I could summon up the desire, invigorate my bones, and at least dispatch one of them, the leader himself perhaps. I'd watched my mother's huscarles in the training yard, noted how they screamed before attacking. They said it gave them strength, pushed away the fear. I didn't understand back then, how could huscarles have fear? They all told me the same – fear is what gives you the courage to strike. There is no alternative, for your enemy wishes only your death. So, best to strike first and strike true. Death comes to us all, but it is the manner in which we die which is all important.

The manner.

To be remembered in battle, to have the halls ringing with voices singing out your name, that was the true Viking way. Not to die like this, caught in a trap, withering like an aged, cowardly thing of no substance, no spirit. By God in heaven, I'd not allow myself to fade in people's memory, nor have any think of me as the one who rolled over and wept.

So I screamed, raising my sword arm aloft, and charged at the leader.

He moved like a young girl, nimble and quick, twisting as I bore down on him, blocking my arm with his own, catching me around the throat and flipping me into the dirt over his outstretched leg. I landed with a grunt, my sword slapping into the mud. I groped for it, but a foot came down over the blade and I looked up to see another grinning down at me, triumph glinting in his wild eyes.

I rolled over, sodden, and slammed myself against the far wall.

"Silly mistake," said the leader, tossing the knife from one hand to the next. He was a couple of paces away. The others came up to his right shoulder, blocking my escape route. There were no more chances. I had thrown the dice and lost.

Pushing myself against the wall, I straightened to my full height and stared directly into the leader's face. I saw no pity there, no hope of quarter.

He thrust out a hand, palm upwards. "The money."

As if of their own mind, my fingers crept under my jerkin to where I kept the purse concealed underneath, tied to my waistband.

"Is there some trouble here?"

We all stopped at the sound of this intrusion.

I looked down to the entrance and there, a dark shadow in the dwindling light of evening, stood a man. Not big or imposing in any way. An ordinary man, or at least so I thought.

My attackers must have thought the same. All three swung about and I could hear the threat in the leader's voice as he growled, "This is no business of yours, stranger. Be gone, unless you wish to feel the edge of my blade." He brought up the knife, to give weight to his words.

I stared in disbelief as I saw the stranger stepping closer. "No need for such unpleasantries, friend. Let the boy go. He has nothing you need."

"He has *everything* we need, you bastard. Now piss off before you find yourself eating dirt."

The stranger chuckled, taking another step. I felt my attackers tense. This would not end well, but at least the situation may be given the good grace to reclaim some pride. I glanced down and saw my sword. I might make a grab for it and launch another, more considered attack. Unless the stranger decided to make his retreat, of course. Any sensible person would do such a thing.

But he did not.

"Come now, friend," he said, in that easy, relaxed tone of his. "Let him go. We can then all retire to our beds and rest easy. Tomorrow is another day."

"Aye, and it's one you'll not see. Nor this bastard," he jerked his thumb in my direction. "I'll tell you again, piss off. This is no concern of yours."

"Oh, but it is," he said and I noted the change in his voice and I watched him, not daring to believe what I saw.

He moved as if liquid, flowing with a sublime ease, the sword materialising in his hand as if conjured up by magic. He dipped low, his blade arcing through the air, slicing across the midriff of the first, coming around in a huge sweeping blow to cut through the neck of the second. All the while he came forward, dipping, dodging, not allowing his opponents time to strike or parry. And even the leader, who had thrown me as if a child, had little chance. He tried to close with this phantom, but as he struck with his knife, his quarry was no longer there. In a blur, the stranger came around his opponent's flank, driving the point of the sword deep into the leader's side. The man let out a great groan and bent down, clutching at his ribs as the blood welled over his fingers. His knees went from under him. The sword streaked like a flash of silver to cut through the leader's neck in one smooth, devastating blow, lopping off the head as one might remove an ear of wheat.

My eyes bulging in disbelief, I saw the leader's headless form drop to its knees and fall to the ground, whilst the head rolled and stared towards the darkening sky, its eyes wide with surprise.

What had this taken but a few seconds? Never in all my life had I seen such contained, effortless aggression. Expertise, deadly and devastating. I turned my gaze from the dead to my saviour and watched him cleaning his blade on the leader's cloak before standing straight once more, returning the weapon to its scabbard held against his side. He pulled over his cloak to conceal it again, and he smiled. "You'll be Harald Sigurdsson. I know of nobody else as tall as you."

I gaped at him.

"Don't worry, my friend. Eleanor told me to expect you."

I shook my head, my senses reeling after the explosion of violence and I managed to mutter, "Eleanor?"

"Aye, the one who pretends to be an old hag. I'll miss her." He took a step towards me and gripped my arm. "We must not tarry. No doubt somebody will have alerted the guards, although I suspect one or two of them were in on this little play." He glanced down the passageway to where it opened out into the square. It was a black space now, the sun well down below the horizon. Night would soon cover everything. "We'll make our way to my home before the curfew locks us all in."

He went to move but, with some meagre scrap of strength, I reached out and touched him. "But, how did you know?"

He grinned, teeth shining bright in his hard, chiselled face. "I've watched you since the moment you arrived, lad."

"I thank you, for what you have done."

"You're a big lad," he said, chuckling, "but ungainly. I'll teach you how to harness your strength, and wield that sword with more skill than you could imagine. Eleanor paid me well to do so and I'll not forsake her. I'm guessing she is already dead?"

I winced at his remark, pressing my head against the wall, mouth open, breathing proving more difficult. How could he know such things? I shook my head, not knowing how to respond, the fear rising again.

"She told me it would be so, that men would come, to take your life as well as hers. That if you managed to survive, you would make your way here. She had the gift of prophesy, amongst other things." Again, a small laugh. "She paid me well, by Christ. I'll not forget her, I can tell you that much. Nor shall I find any other like her." He leaned forward, close to my ear, "It'll be my honour to repay her with this duty she has given me. Best we hurry now, my lad. Leave your things at the inn, you have no use of them now." He leaned back, and kicked at my fallen sword at his feet. "And this sorry lump of iron you can do without also." He stooped and picked it up, eyes roaming along the blade. "Norman. Or French. Either way it's good for a half dozen blows at most before it shatters. I'll furnish you with a blade about which poems have been written." He tossed the sword back into the mud and swung about. "Come on, lad. We have a great deal to do over the next days and weeks." He glanced back at me, "We must prepare you for greatness, Harald Sigurdsson."

Twenty-Eight

Matersson refused payment, saying Eleanor had already given him far more than any gold coin ever could. Over the course of the next weeks, I stayed at his farm, a smallholding half a day's ride from the town. Every day we would train. He taught me to fight with sword and axe, how to defend myself with a shield or without. He punished every mistake I made, my body soon becoming a saga of cuts and bruises. I grew to hate him, the daily regime of exercises, moves, parries and ripostes relentless, without end. He told me to focus my hatred, and give iron to my limbs. Anger must be controlled, the desire to win all-important. So I strove to better him, to give him a taste of what he gave to me every day of my pitiful life.

Of course, no matter how hard I tried, he always answered every assault with a new trick. His mastery of the sword was beyond anything I have ever since encountered. He bounced me around the yard as if I were a fledgling, laughing contemptuously, prodding, slapping, kicking. The more strength I put into my attacks, the more fluid he became, using my strength against me, unbalancing me, tripping into the dirt day after day.

"Do not strive, Harald," he would say, "become as one with the blade. Let it be your guide, your master."

I tried. Dear God, how I tried, but I could never better him.

And then came the day when I vented my anger in a way which went beyond the rules of swordplay. My control and skill were beyond anything I could have dared hope, but nothing I did could break through his defence, until one morning my patience snapped. I rounded on him, hurling away my sword, grabbing hold of his arms, lifting him off the ground as if he were a babe. I butted him full in the face and followed through with an elbow strike across his jaw, which almost tore off his head. As he fell to his knees, I swept up his sword and put the point against his throat.

He brought his head up and when I saw the look of total, complete despair on his face, I reeled backwards, horrified at what I had done. Seeing him defeated, the shame of it creasing up his features, such sorrow coursed through me I believed I was close to swooning. I had done the most despicable thing, throwing my honour and everything he taught me away, in a mad rush of frustration and hatred. And yet, what had he done to cause such resentment, such loathing? He had taught me how to fight, to survive, to win. Was this how I repaid the hours of instruction, the constant pummelling of muscles and bone, the development of the means to greatness? The tears rolled down his cheeks and, horrified, all ill-feeling left my body in a sudden rush. I lowered the sword, not knowing what to do.

He hit me.

Hard, between the legs.

The blood surged through me, overwhelming nausea, blinding, stabbing pain. Everything coming at once in one huge wave and I creased over, clutching at my groin, the sword clattering to the ground, and I retched and gasped, sucking in breath, eyes squeezed shut. The world swirled around me, nothing making sense, and I was aware of nothing but the agony pulsing through my lower body. I fell, curling up into a tight ball, whimpering as from somewhere far away came his voice, mocking, chiding me, the blade of my sword resting across my neck. "Never hesitate, Harald. For to hesitate is to die, as you have just done."

I heard him tramping away, the sound of his laughter cutting through the thick mist of pain which wrapped itself around me. It did not dissipate for many moments.

When I finally found the strength to lift myself upright, I dragged the back of my hand across my face, sniffed loudly, and looked around. I was alone. Some way off was my sword, discarded. The sword I should have ended Matersson's life with, but I'd failed this most crucial of all tests. I'd bettered him, but had ended up in the dirt nevertheless. Lesson learned, it was one I would not forget. Defeat for me was never to be an option again.

Over the next period of training, attitudes changed. Matersson was wary now, despite his prowess continuing to be as awe-inspiring as it ever was. I honed my own, probing for weaknesses relentlessly, without finding any. No chinks, no opportunities. But this proved the most telling of all lessons. For in my attempts, I learned patience and when the final morning came, without him able to land a killing blow, he stopped, breathing hard, and he studied me with a new expression. One of respect.

"You're ready, Harald," he said, putting his sword away. He approached. I remained tense, expecting a sudden renewed assault. Instead, he clamped his hand around my arm and squeezed. "By God, lad, your strength is phenomenal. Your resolve too." He smiled, "There is nothing more I can give you. The world is your tutor now."

Later that day he helped me pack my few, meagre belongings. The horse I took from the men at Eleanor's once again became my means of travel. I swung myself into the saddle and regarded him. A slightly built man of almost unquenchable strength and finesse. A man who, in any other circumstance, I would be proud to call friend. "I'll not forget you, or what you have given me."

"What I gave you was to recognise your strengths, Harald. Your skill was always there, deep inside you. I showed you how to bring it to the fore, nothing more." He took my proffered hand and clasped it with the steel of his fingers. "God keep you, lad. Temper your hatred and remember, be patient, for greatness is not something that comes to many of us, but you, you have unbounded reserves of it. When next I hear your name, it will be from the mouths of minstrels and poets."

He stepped back, gave my horse's rump a firm slap, and watched me as I rode out of his training yard and into my future.

* * *

Winter was giving way to the first hints of spring. Snow no longer fell and my journey proved far easier than when I had first left my mother's homestead. This now was the destination I sought. I pushed myself, and my horse, to the very limits of our endurance, catching brief moments of rest amongst clumps of undergrowth, pieces of woodland, or even abandoned buildings, dilapidated by age and bad weather. All the food I possessed I gave to the horse so by the time I reached the homestead, every part of me ached with hunger.

I dismounted in front of the entrance, a chill wind cutting across the surrounding fields. Peasants toiled amongst the mud, black crows circling overhead, and I saw the distant flash of heavy mattocks breaking through the top soil. Soon the time would be near for planting, of making ready for the summer harvest. The roll of the year, with the hope of a full belly spurred on the workers. For winters were long, long and cruel. I stamped the earth with my boot, aware of the ice remaining solid and enduring just below the surface. For men to spend their days, breaking limbs to bring life back to the unforgiving earth, nothing could give me greater pain or despair. The limited ambition of so many, struggling for a few meagre scraps, is this really what God had in mind for them? Would their true reward be found in heaven, and if not, what then was the purpose of life other than to seek fortune and fame? To be a peasant, born to know nothing of the world other than the limits of eyesight, how could such an existence be called life? I was Harald Sigurdsson, my destiny awaited me. Whatever it was, I swore then to give my people, whoever they were, a purpose, a reason to live.

Putting my depressing thoughts to one side, I led my horse into the yard and took a moment to take in my surroundings. I'd grown up there, running between the outbuildings, wrestling with others, catching frogs, chasing chickens. Distant memories, tinged with regret. For childhood had ended, innocence replaced by cold, unbending hatred for those who had destroyed everything I knew. And in every downcast face I now saw, every broken building, every piece of barren soil, I recognised the bloody hand of Cnut. All was despair, downtrodden, bereft of hope. The peasants scraped in the fields, and the children no longer laughed. Joy replaced by anguish.

I bit down the tears brewing up from within. This was not what I had hoped to find. I searched for some sign, some glimmer of memory to help me recognise this place as the one I once knew. But there was nothing. I tied my horse to a nearby post and went towards what had once been my mother's home.

She was a lady of repute. Formidable and beautiful. Men fell in love with her, and many found moments of tenderness in her arms. I knew the stories, had listened to the whispering of crones as they gossiped, and realised some at least must be true. My mother, the firebrand Ásta, took lovers like others picked fruit from the bowl, but when my father came to her bed, she changed. Ever faithful to him she nevertheless remained married to the old king, Olaf's father. Hypocritical perhaps, but love changes us all. And my mother loved Sigurd Syr.

Her unchanging love delivered death to her door. I saw it plain, standing there in the old entrance, the roof collapsed, open to the sky. I kicked my way through the smashed remnants of a life, overturned chairs, shattered tables, pots, pans, crockery hurled around, smashed into every corner. Dust covered everything like a shroud and as I went through what once had been the hall, floorboards groaned alarmingly, close to splintering. Nobody had maintained the fabric of this building. Perhaps nobody cared.

I stepped back into the yard. By now, news of my arrival must have reached the men in the fields as a gathering of them stood at the far gate, eying me nervously. They gripped their farming tools, but none seemed able to make a move towards me, perhaps suspicious of who I might be. The hood of my cloak masked my face, and I had grown since I fled from this household only a matter of months ago. I decided to bring some lightness to the developing tension. I spread out my arms and smiled. " Please, do not be alarmed. I am a simple traveller, looking for somewhere to rest."

They exchanged looks, shuffling nervously. One or two mumbled words, none of which I managed to catch, but their inference was clear. Fear seeped from every pore of their bodies.

"If you're looking for any of the House of Sigurd, not one remains," said one of them, a bent and wizened man with white wisps of hair sprouting above his ears. Perhaps the elder, he appeared to possess more courage than the others, who remained fidgeting, shuffling their weight from one foot to the other.

"They're dead," yelled a woman who, having cowered behind the menfolk, now pushed her way to the front. She stood brazen, jaw jutting forward, openly antagonistic. "You hear what I say, your companions have done for them all." She turned to the men, "Done for all of us!"

The men took up the challenge in her words, lifting their voices in anger, brandishing their collective pitchforks, mattocks and hoes.

As the clamour grew, both in volume and severity, I threw back my hood and waited, meeting their burning eyes, and shouted above the din, "No assassin here, you blind fools! I am Harald, son of Sigurd and my blighted mother, Ásta." The cries died down, replaced by gasps of disbelief. Then one of them laughed, and I walked towards them, arms still spread. "I have come to reclaim what is mine, and to seek out the devils who have done all of us so much harm."

They pressed forward, faces split into wide grins of relief and joy. All save the woman, who remained as a statue, unmoving. Her eyes locked onto mine and I saw the brooding anger there. I pushed through the assembly, smiling as they clapped me on the shoulders and pumped my hands. Some bowed their heads, some even kissed my fingers. But all the while she stood rooted and waited until I was within a breath of her.

"They came, not long after you left," she said, her voice low, sharp as a blade. As she spoke, the others around me grew quiet. "They cut through us as if we were nothing, none of us able to stand. The few warriors who remained offered some resistance, but even they were overwhelmed." Her hand came up like a withered, blackened twig, a finger pointing over to the ruined hall. "They burst inside, ransacking everything, and when they found our lady, they stripped and dishonoured her." I averted my eyes, tears springing, and it was if a thousand darts struck every portion of my frame. Unable to bear her withering glare, I tried to turn, but she held onto me, forcing me to listen. "And they butchered your brothers, Harald Sigurdsson. Here, in the open yard for us all to witness. 'Never forget,' they said, 'who your rightful king is!' Then they went, unmolested, arrogant, confident no punishment would ever befall them." Her eyes narrowed. "What will you do, Harald Sigurdsson? Will you run away for a second time?"

My throat, gripped tighter than even the assassin at Eleanor's hovel had managed, closed. I could not speak. Turning from her scorn, I tramped over to my mother's hall again, threw myself onto the floor and there, amongst the ruin of my family, I wept until I could weep no more.

Twenty-Nine

Word spread of my return. Soon men came from the outlying villages, some of whom I recognised as companions to Olaf. They presented themselves to me and I was in awe of them, how they went down on bended knee and called me jarl. I was my father's son, older than my fifteen years, and despite the many uncertainties assailing me, their trust brought me great resolve.

As the months past, men, far wiser than me, came to offer advice and encouragement. I listened to them all, eager to learn the extent of the unrest throughout the land. Many continued to be loyal to Olaf, but many more had turned from him, through either fear or bribery, and given fealty to Cnut. His shadow, reaching everywhere, spread a shroud of fear and uncertainty over everything and everyone. And another name, one spoken with more venom than even that of Cnut, came to my ears more than once. Jarl Hakon Eriksson, whose fleet had overwhelmed Olaf's all those months ago. He now ruled this land, so to him I vented all of my hatred and I vowed, before all those assembled to hear me speak, his blood would wash over my avenging sword blade.

At the summer solstice, we did the best we could, this sorry bunch of downtrodden and masterless farmers, to belatedly celebrate the sacrifice Lord Jesus Christ on the cross. As I was not with them at Easter, and none had wished to feast at the accepted time. Now, with the sun growing higher in the sky, we gathered together in the remnants of my mother's hall. Once more cheerful voices filled the rafters, a roof hastily repaired, and as we drank and ate whatever meagre scraps we managed to gather, news came of Olaf's return.

He rode in on a blown nag towards the end of the third day of our feast, and presented himself to me without ceremony. I listened to this messenger, a man who had travelled from the east, bedraggled and starving. Only when he finished speaking did I give him leave to eat. As I watched him cramming bread and stewed vegetables into his ever-open mouth, I considered the implications of what he told us. Olaf, together with a retinue of warriors from King Onund of Sweden, marched across the borderlands, calling men to his banner, intent on taking back his crown.

"We must join him," I said, peering at the ground, knowing destiny would bring us all to the battlefield. For although discontent over the cruel rule of Cnut and his cronies, opposition to Olaf and his attempts to force Christianity upon the land remained strong.

"Other news arrives," said the messenger, wiping his mouth with his sleeve, "As I travelled, I have learned much, Lord Harald. Men, summoned from the far north, gather across Trondelag under jarl Harkon's banner to oppose King Olaf's attempt to regain his throne. Men such as Thore Hund and Kalv Arnason, powerful jarls, whose lands are rich. They have openly declared their desire to put Olaf's head on a stake.

"Have they, by God?"

"Aye. And even now jarl Hakon assembles his fleet, to cut off Olaf's retreat to Ringerike and the Vik."

"Then we raise a general levy," I said, rising to my feet. "This is the moment we have long looked for, to give aid to our Lord Olaf, and banish forever those who would dare strip him of his birthright."

"The king does not know of your position," said the messenger. "I shall go to him, inform him of your support. Where should I tell him to meet you, lord Harald?"

I looked across the many faces turned expectantly towards me. These were miserable men, leaderless, fearful of the future, tortured by the memory of what Harkon visited upon them so very recently.

Not one offered me any suggestion until, at last, the same resourceful woman from before stepped forward. If I had a thousand men with her resolve, I thought, victory would be assured.

"We should meet at Stiklestad," she said. "It is three days' march from here, and a good base from which to strike out against Arnason and his men before he meets with Harkon, trapping Olaf between them."

"You know much," I said, "for a farmer's wife."

"I am nothing of the sort," she said, bristling with indignation. "My father was one of Lord Sigurd's huscarles. He taught me well how to use both the sword and the axe. I am a shield-maiden, Lord Harald, and I shall stand and fight with you to avenge the blood spilled by the cur Harkon and his like."

"By Christ, so you shall," I said, drawing my sword, raising it towards the ceiling. "We march to Stikelstad!"

* * *

The force, which tramped across the Upplands towards the coast was not the host I wished for. At the head of a long, strung-out line of ragged spear-wielding farmers, my unease grew. When faced with the skill and resourcefulness of powerful jarls such as Arnason and Hakon, I wondered how well they would fare. They were keen enough now, with the moorlands quiet and peaceful, but against the sustained charge of armed warriors, my doubts and fears grew with every step.

Word reached me from various scouts; Olaf was making good progress, although his call for men brought no further additions to his army, despite promises of land and booty. It seemed Cnut's tendrils reached far, and fear of his wrath towards any who broke with him proved much the greater enticement. Nevertheless, he commanded upwards of three thousand, with his kinsman Dag Kingston promising a further thousand.

"The King crosses the Kjolen Mountains," said the last of the scouts, reaching my retinue one day out from Stiklestad.

"Then we are close," I said, casting my eyes over the rolling landscape, empty of any living thing save clumps of scrub and bits of purple heather. "With any luck we shall gather our forces together before our enemies fully assemble."

"There is good news to go with that, my lord."

"Good news? By Christ I could do with some. What is it?"

"Jarl Hakon is dead, drowned."

I gaped at the scout, unable to believe his words. In one moment I felt elation at the cur's death, but in the other a great swell of disappointment at not having the joy of hewing the bastard's head. I shook my head, struggling to keep my temper, curling my hand into a fist around my mount's reins. "Damn him. Even in this, my hope for vengeance, I am thwarted. Drowned you say?"

"Aye, his flagship smashed against the rocks in an unexpected storm. Leadership of Cnut's force has passed to Arnasson."

"Then I'll cleave his head in Hakon's stead. It makes no difference to me." I grinned. "Tell my brother we shall meet a day's hence."

The rider galloped away and I gave orders for us to make camp and rest well before the following day brought us all to our destiny.

* * *

We met on the hillside overlooking the valley where the cluster of farm buildings at Stiklestad lay. I saw his approach from afar, his banners trailing in the wind, the sun glinting from his silver byrnie. He looked every inch the great king I knew him as. When last I had seen him, I was nothing but a boy. Much had changed since I tugged at his beard and as he drew closer I noted how much he too had changed. Grown portly and grey, the weight of worry pressed heavily upon him, and when he slid from his saddle, he groaned as if every joint ached. But when he saw me and grinned, his old self returned and I recognised the spirit of greatness which continued to burn in his features. I ran to him and we embraced. I felt the strength in his arms and I knew all would be well.

"By God, Harald, you have grown." It was true. I towered over him, as I did most men. His neck strained as he looked up at me. "I had some foolish idea of placing you at the rear, fearful you may not be yet ready to face battle."

"Have no fears on that, my lord king. I've trained hard since last we met."

"Aye well, I gave battle at fourteen in England. We're much the same, you and I. Our mother's strength runs through us both."

"They murdered her."

"So I have heard. And Hakon is dead, so I understand."

"Aye, God rot his soul. But Arnason lives, and Hund. Bastards both. I'll split their guts and stuff their cocks in their mouths before they die."

Grinning, he put his arm around my waist and led me towards his camp, where already the fires were being set and the cooking pots prepared. "We'll feast and talk, brother. I want to hear all about you, what you have done, where you have been. You're a boy no longer, I can see that. You're a man, and I'll warrant a great one as you shall prove when we meet with our foe."

And the following day, at first light, meet them we did.

Thirty

Olaf arraigned his men in three battle formations, strung out across the hillside to make as good a use of the high ground as possible. He harboured fears the superior forces drawn up before him might attempt an outflanking manoeuvre. For vast our enemies were, assembled below us, spears bristling, banners held aloft. They filled the valley like a vast, grey lake, perhaps ten thousand or more, and my stomach lurched at the sight of them.

"Fear not," said Olaf, sensing my alarm. He peered at me from behind the ringed eye-guards of his burnished bronze helm and grinned. "My plan is simple. We shall strike hard and sure into their centre, forcing them back upon their second line. As the wings of their force close in, Dag shall come out of the north and deliver the killing blow."

I looked around me. Way to the left, the Swedes stood solid, here in the centre Olaf's huscarles, and to my right, the men I had brought to this place. Dag's contingent was nowhere.

"Don't be alarmed, Harald. All will be well. Dag will come."

He drew his gold-hilted sword, Neite, a weapon made by the finest swordsmiths of Germania, far to the south. He kissed the blade. "The Lord is with us," he said and gave the signal. From between the ranks of warriors, bannermen strode forward, holding rough-hewn versions of Christ's cross, and minstrels sang songs of heroes and their escapades of long ago. This curious mix of old and new stirred up my courage, filling me with renewed desire to join with my enemies and bring them to their knees. It was emotion shared by all around me, as spears and axes rattled against shields, the clamour of voices growing as one, a thunderous, rumbling noise that made the very ground shake.

We poured down the slope, our battle cries filling the air, and smashed into the enemy front, sending a shock-wave through their ranks. Already many of them were breaking, terrified at our determination. We may have been less in number, but our resolve proved greater, and we hacked and hewed our way forward.

Within the mad, confused fight, I saw Olaf smiting opponents with his great sword, the grin set on his face, eyes wild with bloodlust. It raced through me also and I soon found myself in a sort of dream state, swinging my blade. Every lesson Matersson taught proving its worth as I dipped and swerved, parrying, slashing, cutting through flesh and bone, the blood of the dead spurting over my chest and face. I cared not and laughed as I fought.

In this mad confusion of screaming and dying, the sound of axe and sword clattering against shields, I did not at first realise what was happening farther from where I fought. We seemed to be pressing ever deeper into the ranks of the enemy, men breaking like waves upon the rocky shoreline, falling back, cries of despair and terror spewing from their throats. But, just as the sea always does, they came back, mercilessly. Their second ranks pressed forward, soon clear their superiority in numbers was beginning to tell. A bondi thrust at me with a spear, and I cleaved it in two and put my elbow into his face and saw him fall. But beyond him, so many more men, axes raised, shields locked together and, amongst them, Kalv Arnason.

I saw him, the bastard. His cloak was bright red, his hair a mane of brown, streaked with grey. He wore no helmet, contemptuous of his foes, and I saw him, transfixed, cutting his way through my hirdmen. They fell back, stumbling and falling, some casting away their weapons to flee.

Around me the mad struggle continued, men blowing out their breath, the stench of sweat and fear all-pervading. In that moment, standing in a gap with the dead heaped around me, I surveyed everything as if from a distance. Men struggling, hand-to-hand, falling to the earth to wrestle in the blood-drenched ground. Others wandering with arms missing, great cuts across their faces, or crawling through pools of their own blood, legs hacked through. A hundred wild faces, black with dread, some turned skywards, hands reaching out to implore God to save them, others on their knees sobbing, calling for their mothers or wives. I watched it all, never believing such horrors were possible. I believed battle to be a noble thing, an opportunity to become renowned and feared as a true warrior, a Viking of old. The pagan desire to die in battle, brave to the last, and meet with my ancestors in the halls of Valhalla coursed through my veins as strong as it ever was. The White Christ promised everlasting life, but never spoke of heroes. My longing was to be known as such, to have songs sung about my feats, but here, in that butchering ground, I recognised nothing noble or heroic about any of it. Every sense assailed by the presence of death, the stink of fear. This was not what the sagas promised.

And yet, the elation grew. A youth rushed me, bringing me out of my reverie. Holding a two-handed axe, his intent clear, I went with his charge, and cut through him with all my strength, almost chopping him in two. He writhed on the ground, intestines spilling out around him like boiling snakes. And others surged forward and I cut and stabbed, and all my loathing of battle left in that instant.

From the corner of my eye I saw Olaf summoning his bannerman to join him. A brute of a huscarle called Thord, he rammed the point deep into the ground just as an enemy bondi ran him through with a spear. He held onto the shaft of the banner and died there, whilst Olaf fought on. And as I watched, I knew. Our numbers were thinning and all around us, the enemy seemed to swell.

A scalding pain ripped through my back, and I threw out my arms and fell, overcome with the searing heat of burning coals. I swung around and saw him, my nemesis. Arnason, head thrown back, laughing loud, his sword dripping with my blood. The bastard had come from behind and I, deep in thought, had taken his strike between my shoulder blades. I felt the blood running hot down my back and I fell to my knees, waiting for the final thrust of his sword.

But the blow never came. Dag Ringsson burst against the enemy flank, splitting it, and Arnason let out a great wail of despair, wielded his sword like a standard, rallying his forces before it was too late.

I took the chance to drag myself away and realised my sword had fallen. I cared not. My body trembled, locked in agony, the sword cut perhaps not deep thanks to my leather jerkin, but deep enough. I found an outcrop of rock and propped myself against it, and let my mouth hang open, sucking in breaths.

Not so far from me, amidst the continuing mêlée, and drawn to him by his banner fluttering high and proud, I saw Olaf fighting on as, around him, his kinsmen fell. I longed to summon up the strength to stand by his side, but when I attempted to rise, my legs gave way beneath me. I fell back against the boulders, crying out with the sudden shock of pain. My mind in disarray, a horrible sickness rose up from my gut. I bent forward and vomited, retching like a stricken, squealing pig. And then, as I struggled to fight down my rising panic, the most appalling blanket of darkness fell over that blighted field.

An awful moan ripped through the ranks of the fighting men, and five thousand faces turned skywards, myself amongst them. I witnessed the sun change, no longer shining, but blacked out, and a cold stillness fell over us all. For several, terrifying moments, the world came to a shuddering halt, no one daring to believe such a thing possible. What terrible portent did this phenomenon bring? Was it the twilight of Olaf's reign, or the destruction of his enemies? I stood, aghast, everything else forgotten as I gazed at the strange black disc in the sky, a white halo wrapped around its edge. And I knew, at that moment, what it all meant. God's terrible visage of rage, glaring down upon us, forsaking Olaf and everyone who stood with him. For it must be God, the halo said as much.

I stood, the pain ignored, and although I swayed a little, I gritted my teeth and summoned the strength to remain as a rock. For if God deserted us, what hope was there for victory. Better to withdraw, lick our wounds, and plan for a future assault. We had sinned, grown vain and haughty. When was the last time I had bended my knee and prayed? I could not remember. And Olaf? For all his fine words of bringing Christianity to this land, his failure was acute. The old gods still held sway across the northern and western lands. Our Lord's displeasure was here to see, his wrath dreadful as now He turned His face away from us and abandoned us to the strength of our enemies.

The light returned in a sudden, unexpected burst, the darkness driven back, and in that piercing blast of sunshine, I saw Olaf, brandishing his sword. With the sun returned, the fight broke out again, all across the field, and men resumed their struggles. A huge, wild-looking beast rushed into Olaf. I say 'beast', for it was clad in a thick hide from some animal. So thick, its wearer appeared resistant to any blow. He closed with Olaf, and the king's sword hewed the man's shoulder, but still he came on. He swung a hand axe, cutting into Olaf's thigh, and my stomach turned over.

The fates had turned.

God had left us.

Olaf hacked and stabbed, felling two more warriors, but the one in the thick animal hide, sprang forward, the point of his spear sinking into the king's stomach. I screamed out my brother's name, staggering forward with my hands held out before me. I neither knew what I could do, nor did I care. He was my blood and my king, so I forced myself to stumble on, desperate to come to his aid.

But I was too late and too weak. Within a few strides, I collapsed to my knees, my back engulfed with pain. I squeezed my eyes shut, trying to block everything out, but when I opened my eyes again, the sight before me brought nothing but despair.

Olaf stumbled back, clutching at his gut, blood oozing from his fingers. He looked down in disbelief, his sword falling to the ground. He no longer had the strength, life spilling from him. And then, from between the press of desperate, exhausted men, Arnason strode forward and brought down his blade against my brother's neck. The one in the hide threw back the hood and I recognised Thore Hund. He laughed, put the spear into Olaf's gut and rammed the point all the way down to the shaft. Olaf threw out his arms wide and slid to the ground, his helmet slipping from his head to show eyes wide and white.

Dead.

Silence fell over the struggle. Men, from both sides, paused and stared. The omen of the blacked out sun had proved true. Olaf, slain. Arnason lifted the king half off the ground by the hair and roared his battle cry. Those close by shook their spears and swords towards heaven, and cried out in great cheers of victory. I watched, blubbering like an infant, and as useless. Abandoned, defeated, there was nothing else for me to do but stand and die, so I rummaged around the blood-soaked ground for a weapon. Anything would suffice. Tattered mind, unfocused, bleary eyes, all conspired to turn me into a hapless, pathetic flapping child, sprawling around in the mud, unable to raise myself. My heartbeat pulsed through the wound in my back and I snarled and gnashed in a mad attempt to haul from within me the means to force my muscles to work. But they would not, and I collapsed onto my back and cursed all the gods that had ever looked down upon us for making me such a weakling, such a failure.

A hand gripped my shoulder. The moment was upon me, the cold embrace of death. I could do nothing, unable even to lift up my arm to ward off the killing blow. But instead of the hard, burning thrust of a blade, a face loomed close. "All is lost, Harald," he said, "and we must withdraw. I swore to Olaf I'd see you safe, and by God I'll not renege on my word now."

He turned away, shouting over the continuing battle. Despite Olaf's fall, our brave men fought on, slaying as many of the enemy as they could before deserting the field.

"You can walk?"

I frowned, struggling to recognise him. He seemed to sense my confusion, and he gripped my shoulder. "I am Dag Ringsson." He jerked his head to his right, where stood a giant. A man as tall as myself. "This is your dead king's surviving bodyguard. Rognvald. He'll carry you to safety."

"I'll not go."

"Yes, you shall, Harald. Your fate is not to die here, not this day."

With that, Rognvald stooped down and lifted me as if I were a baby. He threw me over his shoulder and carried me away.

Bucking and jarring upon the man's shoulder as he strode across the land, scenes of death flashed all around me. Upturned faces, cries of despair, the slash of blades, the sound of the axe against wooden shields. Recurring images of a battle begun with such hope, ended with the death of our king.

I did not struggle, allowing my saviour to take me from that place of death. Only when we reached the comparative safety of dense woodland did he put me down beside a tree. I gasped as he tore away my jerkin, his fingers prodding at the wound across my back.

"It's bad," he said, voice flat, without emotion.

"Am I going to die?"

"Perhaps."

He pushed me against the tree and, crouching down on his haunches, took off his helmet and wiped the sweat from his brow. "I know of a village, to the north," he said. "We might make it before Arnason closes in, but you need tending to and I have not the means."

"You've done enough, by saving me. I'll not forget it."

"You may, if you die."

"Then I'd best not."

He laughed and I looked to the sky and far off, above the trees, I caught a glimpse of the sun and wondered why our Lord God had deserted us.

It is a question I have never found the answer to.

Thirty-One

The Dneiper, 1042

They set sail, their ship laden with provisions, the crew grim, straining at their oars. Ulf and Haldor sat as silent as stone, Harada's words smothering them in a dark shroud of despair. Hardrada himself, peering across the broad waters of the river, eyes locked to the distance, dared not meet their eyes. He had laid bare his soul, revealing more than he wished. Over the years an aura of invincibility followed him, one which he promoted, indeed revelled in. Perhaps now his friends might look upon him through different eyes? At Stiklestad, all those years ago, he had failed when Olaf needed him most. He was weak, craven, his soul corrupted by blind hatred. *Did not the Lord teach to turn away from violence, to forgive?*

He gripped the stempost, peering down into the murky depths of the Dneiper, ever more conscious of his failings. He was not a Christian, could never aspire to be. And God knew it, turning away from both him and Olaf, leaving them to their doom. With Dag Ringsson's intervention, and his rescue by Rognvald, Hardrada recovered, grew stronger, straighter, more resolved than ever to smite his enemies. And yet now, here he stood, travelling north to an uncertain future, with Arnason long from his thoughts. The recount of his time in Norway brought all those old hatreds back to the surface. To find Arnason, to stare into his face and watch him die. What a joy that would be.

"Harald?"

The unexpected voice caused Hardrada to jump, and he swung around, a hand reaching for his sword out of instinct. When he saw Haldor's concerned face, he relaxed.

"You're blaming yourself for his death."

Hardrada blinked a few times, shoulders sagging, and he looked out across the river once again. "Aye, I do. I should have been at his side."

"But nothing you could have done, or tried to do, would have changed his fate."

"Fate. Destiny. My destiny was to watch him die, knowing there was nothing I could do."

"But that was not your fault. You were wounded."

No reply came. For a few moments, the only sound was the rhythmical movement of the oars, cutting through the river. "You know, I never shed a tear. Through all these years, not one." Hardrada shook his head, and sat down. Haldor joined him, leaning forward, looking fixedly into his eyes. "To be honest, it was only with the retelling my mind turned to him. But now ... " He put his head back, allowing the breeze to play around with his hair. "I had forgotten how my heart burns over that cur, Arnason. Now, everything has come back. The need for revenge, the guilt."

"Guilt? No, Harald, there is no guilt on your shoulders."

"Of course there is. There is guilt on all our shoulders. God deserted us that day, Hal, because of our arrogance. We turned our hearts from Him, and our reward was to suffer catastrophic defeat." He shifted position, turning his head to face his friend. "We listened to Olaf's priests and bishops, telling us how our lives, no matter how hard and uncertain, would lead us into the heavenly kingdom. All we needed to do was repent, to seek out forgiveness, and strive to turn away from the old ways. Ways of revenge, of killing. The Viking way. But we failed. The past holds us in its grip, never letting us go. I am not a Christian, Hal. I've spilled too much blood."

"Who can say they are wholly Christian? You think the Byzantines punish themselves the way you do? They give great service to

God, do they not? With their magnificent churches, their chants and their prayers, the icons glowing with gold which cover every wall … Remember when we stood on the balcony of the Hagia Sofia, and scratched our names on the balustrade?"

"Aye, I remember it well." Hardrada chuckled. "Whilst below us, the patriarch conducted his service, beseeching them all to confess their sins, turn away from avarice and debauchery. And we all knew he was the biggest sinner of the lot. A hypocrite without equal."

"And you believe he lies awake at night, begging God for forgiveness?"

"He might. I know I don't." He chuckled, "He may even be dead for all I know."

"All of Byzantium is shrouded in a veil of hypocrisy. They do what they need to do in order to survive, and if that means turning their backs on their religion, they do it without conscience. You should do the same."

"I thought I had." Hardrada put a finger and thumb into the corners of his eyes. "All these years I've hardly thought about it. Olaf. They revere him as a saint now, did you know that?" He dropped his hand and sighed. "They said his blood restored the wounded at Stiklestad. I know it never restored mine."

"Did you try?"

"Aye. Rognvald told me when he lifted up the king, his blood washed over his arms, and his wounds healed. So he smeared some of it on me."

"And it worked?"

A grim smile. "No. We went through the forest, travelled for days until we came across a farm. By then I was in a fever. I cannot remember much of what happened, only that Olaf's blood did not help."

"So what did?"

"The farmer's wife. She kept me well, cleaned my wounds, applied a poultice. Some two weeks later, we left and crossed the plains on ponies until we reached the land of Sweden. From there, we journeyed to the very place where Olaf himself had sought out sanctuary two years before. The realm of the Grand Prince Jaroslav."

Thirty-Two

Novgorod, 1031

The port teemed with activity, and as Harald stepped ashore, he was assailed by a score or more different tongues. Traders from the far south and east, men with sallow skins and others, wild men who paraded themselves in thick padded coats made from reindeer skins. At these, Harald stopped and stared whilst Rognvald conversed with a swarthy group close to the quayside.

"We are in luck," said Rognvald, drawing close. "My son is close and I've paid some Poles to ride down towards Novgorod and give news of our arrival." He leaned closer, "Are you well, Harald?"

"These men, in their coats, I've seen their like before. At Stiklestad."

"Ah, you mean Thore Hund? Aye, he wore a coat much the same. It is said they are imbued with magic, to make them weapon proof."

"It was he who delivered the first killing strike against Olaf."

"Harald," Rognvald clamped his hand on the youth's shoulder, "you shall have your revenge, but you must learn patience. These men are Chuds, renowned warriors, seeking service with Prince Jaroslav. It seems he is recruiting men from all across the Steppes to mount a campaign. Varangians, too. If we are fortunate, we might ourselves become more than useful to the Prince." He smiled. "You acquitted yourself well at Stiklestad, Harald. With my son Eilif's help, you could find yourself on the road to riches. And revenge."

They pushed their way through the throng, leaving behind the smell of fish and oiled animal skins, to scattering of buildings beyond. Large warehouses, boat-builders' yards, and taverns. At one such place, they settled down at a rickety table and ordered broth and ale. They ate and drank in silence, both keeping their eyes averted despite the curious, lingering glances from the many gathered inside.

Harald shifted uneasily in his seat, becoming more and more conscious of the looks. After some minutes, he could stand it no longer, pushed his bowl away and glared over at Rognvald. "I don't want to stay here. You see them, staring. I'm damned if I'll take their insolence."

Rognvald paused with his wooden spoon raised to his mouth. "You'll sit and ignore them. We're travellers, passing through. That is all."

"But it's as if they know who we are."

"They might," Rognvald shrugged, sipped his spoon clean and put it down, "but if we start a fight, they'll know it for sure. We stay quiet and wait."

"Then I do it outside."

Rognvald shrugged. "Suit yourself." He grinned and reached over for Harald's bowl. "I'll finish yours seeing as you've lost your appetite."

Harald sneered and stood up, pushing his chair back so violently it toppled over onto the floor. Everyone stopped and even those who had not noticed him before now did so. His sheer size gave him away, and many of the men gathered there huddled up closer and gabbled with one another.

Smouldering, Harald stormed out into the daylight. He stood in the doorway, wincing as the sun struck his eyes. The tavern was gloomy, so he forced himself to take a moment to adjust to his surroundings before moving on. Ready, he focused on the three men standing there, some ten feet or so from him, fully armoured in bronze helmets and leather corselets. The one in the middle was grinning.

"You must be Sigurdsson. They said you were tall, but I had no idea just how big you really were."

Harald frowned, hand dropping to his sword. "That name means nothing to me."

"Sigurdsson? Well, it should," said the young soldier in the middle, taking a step forward. He was broadly built, muscles straining against his armour, and yellow hair sprouted from beneath his helmet. As he moved, the leather corselet creaked. "It was your father's name. The great and sadly lamented Sigurd Syr. You do him a disservice by not acknowledging him."

"And you had best watch your mouth, lest you wish to end your life here, in this pox-ridden place."

The young man smiled. "Ah, now there it is … that famous anger precedes you, Harald. You wear it like a cloak and you'd best take care, lest it reveals you for who you truly are." He took another step and Harald's grip on the hilt of his sword grew tighter. "Stay your hand, Harald. I'm not here to berate you, but to escort you to Novgorod. I believe my father is inside?"

Harald gawped and turned as the door to the tavern screeched open on its rusty hinges. There, filling the entrance, stood Rognvald, goblet of ale in one hand, open-mouthed, laughing, "Dear Christ, Eilif – I thought you'd never come!"

"*Eilif*?" Harald shook his head, turning again to the young man now moving closer. "Why didn't you say so?"

Eilif came up the steps, and slapped Harald on the arm, "It wouldn't have been such fun!" He moved past the giant Norseman and fell into his father's arms, ale slopping down his back unnoticed. Rognvald almost lifted him off his feet.

"I've missed you, lad."

"Aye, and I you, father." Eilif managed to push himself away from Rognvald's bear-like embrace. "News has travelled fast of what befell you all at Stiklestad. I'll not lie to you, there were not many who believed you still lived." He swivelled around to face Harald. "Nor you. Many thought you dead from your wounds."

"I almost was."

"Well, I'm glad to see you still breathing. I hope we can be friends, Harald. I'm as anxious as you to see your brother's death avenged."

"Not only my brother. Our mother also, murdered at the hands of Cnut."

Eilif nodded, the smile fading from his lips. "You've lost much, and there's the truth of it. But the Viking way is one of revenge, Harald. And revenge you shall have, but first it is to the service of the Grand Prince that you must place yourself. For he has great need of the likes of you, strong and able warriors. His army swells with Varangians and he much respects the prowess of the Norse in battle. You will be made most welcome, especially as Olaf was such a good and close friend."

So they gathered their belongings, loaded up their mounts, and set out towards Novgorod where Harald found himself amongst the swell of the dispossessed and the desperate. Men who were willing to fight and die if need be to gain a few gold coins. The mercenary camp of the Varangians.

Known to be hardened drinkers, the barrack rooms of the Varangians stank of stale sweat and ale, and Harald held his breath when he first shuffled inside, to find himself a bunk. He took his time, taking shallow breaths, adjusting his senses to the thick fug of the interior. A dark, miserable place, his bed was made from rickety, rough-hewn timber and padded with moss and turf, dank and alive with rummaging creatures. He decided to settle himself on the earth floor and when the doors burst open to throw over him a blinding shaft of light, he heard the voices of derision, the cat-calls of the cruel.

"Well, well, what have we here?"

Harald squinted up towards a large hulking individual, fat face gaping, hands on hips, thrusting his pelvis forward.

"Arsehole," said another, kicking away at Harald's bedroll. "What's this, eh? Home comforts?"

With laughter ringing, Harald ignored them, gathered up his blanket again, and placed it on the ground, smoothing it into the closest approximation of comfort he could achieve. Exhausted, the journey from the north on the back of a waddling, clumsy pony without sleep, his eyes were heavy, gritty and he had no desire to engage in arguments. He curled himself up into a tight ball and closed his eyes.

They laughed and chattered well into the night, drinking incessantly, and the Varangians ignored him. Until morning dawned, when someone planted a solid boot into his ribs.

Springing up, Harald glared at the wild-haired ingrate laughing before him. "Move your fucking, arse. It's late, and we are assembling in the yard."

He strode off and Harald gathered up his sword belt, fastening it as he went. The light hit him as he went through the door and he paused, rubbing his eyes, and stumbled down the steps into the training ground where already men practised their swordsmanship.

"Sigurdsson?"

The voice sounded like the crack of a whip and Harald instinctively jumped, muscles taut and eyes wide, focusing on a large individual who stood, studying him, some paces away.

"My name is Bolli Bollason, and I'm charged with licking you into shape, boy. So move your lanky arse over to those training posts and let's see what you can do."

Harald turned to peer across the yard to where a number of wooden manikins were placed, each with numerous solid arms jutting out from the sides. Men already practised attack moves, swords clanging against the arms, practising thrusts and strikes. In the distance, other men fought against each other, some with swords, others with axes, the grunts and cries mixing with the ring of metal on metal.

"Did you hear what I said?"

The man was up close now, twice as wide as Harald, but significantly shorter. "I heard you."

"Then do as you're told," snapped Bollason. "I've heard a lot about you and not much of it good."

"Aye, that's what we've heard too, Bolli."

Harald turned to find a gathering bunch of perspiring warriors pressing in around him, no doubt intent on throwing him a few more barbed comments. He sighed, homing in on the one who seemed to be the gang's spokesperson, the one who had taunted him the previous night. "What have you heard?"

The man laughed, looking at his friends for support, who gave it willingly, all of them cackling like farmyard birds. Harald would have told them so, if he wasn't aware of the crackling tension. These men wanted a fight. He was hungry, still tired, and a long way from home. And they were big, mean. Common sense should have told him to remain quiet.

"You're connected, in some way, to poor old King Olaf."

"I am his half-brother."

The man tilted his head, still grinning, "Ah, is that what you are? Makes you next in line to the throne, does it?"

The others rumbled and cackled. This was developing into something of a show, a sorely needed entertainment. Some of them slapped the big man on the back, encouraging him. He didn't disappoint, and bowed low from the waist, sweeping his arm around in a great, theatrical arc. "Your Majesty!"

Harald blew out his cheeks and looked at Bollason, who stood some way off, eyes sharp, waiting. "Is this part of your training regime, Master Bollason?"

Bollason shrugged, remaining silent.

"Tell us how you came here, Your Majesty," continued the thug with the big gash for a mouth, "how you managed to escape from the clutches of your enemies?"

"Aye," said another, "we heard Olaf died a terrible death at Stiklestad. And all of his faithful retainers fell with him."

"Indeed it is so – many of them did," said Harald, voice low, straining to keep the emotion from his words. "I was there."

The thug gaped and a stunned silence rocked the small group. "*You were there?*" He scanned his companions and they mirrored his dismissive, doubting look. "Really? And what did you do there, lad?"

"I fought and was wounded."

"You…" The thug shook his head. "Well, well. Who'd have believed it. A young lad like you. What are you, eighteen summers?"

"Sixteen."

The thug rocked backwards, "This grows even more wondrous. How come you didn't die in that field, lad, eh? Alongside your brother?"

"Before I was able, I was struck down."

"Ah," the man nodded, lips pressing hard together, "Yes … struck down. Explains a lot."

"You don't believe me?"

The man held up both hands, "Never let it be said I doubted the word of such a young warrior."

Without a pause, Harald pulled up the front of his jerkin to reveal the livid red scar, which ran across his side. Some of the men mumbled their appreciation, but the thug, leaning close to study the wound with interest, merely pulled a face. "How did you get that, lad?"

"I told you," said Harald, stuffing his shirt back into his breeches. "At Stiklestad, as I tried to reach Olaf, I was cut and fell. Rognvald helped me make good my escape."

More mutterings. Someone whispered, "Eilif's father," and the thug looked suitably impressed. But by now, Harald's anger bubbled to the surface, common sense disappearing fast.

"I like not your assertions," he said, his hand falling to the hilt of his sword.

The thug frowned. "Oh, have I offended you? Why so, because I voice some doubt over a young boy fighting in the front ranks of a battle? Natural, lad, not meant to dishonour you."

"Don't rile Bjorn Urldesson," said someone close by. "Just take it in good humour, Harald Sigurdsson."

Harald shook his head, "I couldn't give a good fuck who he is," he hissed, his eyes never leaving Urldesson's. "You have a point to make, then you make it plain, or keep your fat mouth shut."

"All right," said Bollason, stepping between them quickly, holding up his hands, "enough of this. Bjorn, go back to practise." Jabbing Harald in the chest with a meaty index finger, he said, "And you get over to those posts and let's see what you can do."

"I'll show you what I can do," returned Harald, jutting his chin towards Urldesson, who had yet to move, "by killing that bastard."

The group gave a collective gasp and, beyond Bollason's shoulder, Harald saw Urldesson grow tense, his hand dropping to his sheathed sword.

"You're a surly bastard," spat Bollason, pushing Harald away, "and when I tell you to do something, you do it. You understand?"

"I understand enough."

"Don't fucking rile me, you shit," said Bollason through gritted teeth. "You've got a lot of persuading to do, and your fucking arrogance hasn't got you off to a good start. These men here are seasoned fighters and they've never run from a battle."

"And neither have I."

Bollason's eyes grew wide, his voice taking on a mocking tone as he trilled, "Is that so? Then why the fuck aren't you dead, like your upstart of a brother?"

Harald swung his fist, but it was ill-judged and Bollason dodged it with ease and dropped Harald with a hefty knee straight into his guts.

As the big Norseman groaned on the ground, gasping for breath, the others broke out into fits of laughter, Urldesson's the loudest. And as Harald climbed to his feet, his hand was already drawing his knife. "You'll pay for that," he rasped.

"No," said Bollason, "you'll swallow it down and from now on you are humble and contrite."

"Like a little girl," said Urldesson, rounding on his comrades, urging them to continue their braying, mocking laughter.

"*Enough,*" shouted Bollason and the men instantly became silent. He stepped towards Harald, took his knife hand and guided it towards the scabbard. Harald winced, surprised at the man's strength. Bollason's face loomed close. "Grand Prince Yaroslav is mustering an army, to go east to fight the Poles. He has placed me in charge of you and all you bastards and I'll not have you killing one another *before* we come to battle with our enemies. I need every last one of you, fit and ready, to fight for our Prince, you understand me." He pushed Harald away, swung around and measured each of the now silent group of thugs with a cold stare. They lowered their heads, each and every one, and when he came to Urldesson, Bollasson's voice grew cold. "You cease from jibes and insults, you hear me?" Urldesson nodded. "And you," he said, turning again to Harald. "I've told you to show us what you can do. So do it. If both of you are still alive after the campaign, you can sort out your differences. Until then, you fight as a unit, and you fight *for* each other, not against each other. You understand?"

"Aye."

"And the next time you throw a punch at me, you better make sure it lands, or I'll break your pathetic little neck, you understand *that*?" Hardrada's face fell and he nodded, without speaking. "Then get the fuck over there and start swinging that sword of yours."

And when he did, the other watched and they saw how Harald moved, the strength in his blows, his perfect balance. Impressed, one or two looked askance at Urldesson, who ignored them, chewing at his bottom lip.

In the barrack room much later, after supper and a good bout of drinking, Harald sat on his bed, running a whetstone over his blade. He did not look up as a fellow warrior sat down beside him. "Ignore him," he said. "The man's a turd."

Harald stopped, holding up his blade to study the edge. "I'll kill him when this fight is over. And that's a pledge. You can tell him from me."

"I'll tell him nothing. I can't stand the bastard. He's a Dane, and he hates us."

"Us?" Harald turned to look at this newcomer, who sat on his bed, and sounded sincere.

"Aye. I'm an Icelander. I was at Stiklestad too."

Harald frowned, trying to recognise the man next to him. He wore his hair short, beard trimmed, eyes smouldering and dark. "You were there?"

"Aye. And I saw you, but not how you fell. I think by then we all knew the day was lost."

"You saw Olaf die?"

The man shook his head. "We were on the far wing. Our first knowledge was when the shield wall adjacent to mine gave way and broke. With the enemy streaming in all around us, the cry went up that Olaf was dead. So we withdrew, fought our way to the woodlands, and from there some of us made the journey south." He gripped Harald's leg, just above the knee. "I knew your father, too, Harald. There are many here who know of you, so do not think we are all of the same ilk as Urldesson or that bastard Bollason. I hope you do kill Urldesson, truth be known, if a Pole doesn't cleave his head first. It would be fun to watch." His eyes narrowed. "But watch out for Bollason. Urldesson is like a child compared with him."

"Thank you for the warning." Harald rubbed his midriff, the memory of Bollason's knee smarting more than the blow itself. "I'll do my best to heed it."

The man grinned and stood up, stretching and yawning.

"What is your name?"

The man looked down at Harald and winked. "My name is Ulf. And I hope we can be friends."

"If we survive, then let it be so."

He thrust out his hand and Ulf took it. "Aye. *If* we survive."

Thirty-Three

In the pulsing heat of the summer, men laboured under the weight of chainmail and helmet, long columns of warriors tramping across the endless plain, sending up clouds of dust, surrounded by flies. Harald marched with his eyes fixed to the ground, keeping his mind neutral, whilst around him others shuffled and wheezed. They had moved for the best part of a week now, uncertain when the end would come. Scouts roamed far ahead, rarely sending back news. The enemy, reluctant to engage, remained elusive. Discontent grew, and in camp during the evening, disgruntled Varangians spoke of home or the chance to travel south, to the fabled city of Miklagard, where it was known good money was paid to fighting men. Harald listened, silent, a little away from the main groups. Urledsson, a man who had made his disdain for Harald clear at every opportunity, was ever present, seeming to command a great deal of respect from his companions who laughed at every joke and applauded every soliloquy. When he shot a glance Harald's way, the young Norseman turned, not wishing to provoke another confrontation. Time was on his side, all he need to do was wait.

On the twelfth day, riders came thundering towards the columns, flapping arms wildly, struggling to keep their mounts under control. Commanders barked out orders and the men ground to a halt, exchanging puzzled looks, muttering their opinions. Harald squinted down the lines and saw a horsemen turning about. He came trotting along the flanks of the warriors, reigning in next to Harald. He pushed back his helmet and revealed himself as Eisif.

"Well, Harald Sigurdsson, it seems we have them. They are trapped in a narrow pass."

"Of whom do we speak?"

"Poles and Pechenegs." Eisif leaned over his saddle and spat into the dirt. "Bastards. Harald, you will ride with me?"

Harald looked around at the men close by, their disgruntled looks, expressions of distaste. Amongst them, Urledsson, a smirk crossing his sweating face. Eisif may not have knowledge of the man's hatred for Harald, so best not to enlighten him now. So Harald shook his head slightly, "I'll stay with the men."

"You've experience of mountains, Harald." Eisif gestured away to the far distance where a smudge of black could be seen running across the horizon. "I need you to take a group of mounted men and outflank the enemy, hit them where they least expect. We don't want to meet them in open ground, as the Pecheneg bow is deadly. You will gather your men and descend upon them at nightfall. You can stay with your men, Harald, and you'll fight with them too." He grinned. "Just don't get yourself killed."

* * *

They struck out from the main column, heading west in a long arc. Around two hundred, riding fast on squat, thick-set ponies. Soon, they left the rest of the army far behind and by the time they reached the foot of the mountain range, there was no sight of Varangians or the Kievian Rus army.

Leaving the ponies with their handlers, the small force scaled the mountainside, flattening themselves against the rock like insects. With axes and shields strapped to their backs, they used both free hands to climb. Harald, in the forefront, gritting his teeth, felt his heart beat pound in his temples; not through exhaustion, but from the sheer expectation of combat. This would be the first chance he'd had since Stiklegard to vent his hatred. He cared not these Poles or Pechenegs had never caused him harm. All he wanted was to feel his blade sink into human flesh, hear the cries of the fallen, and have their hot blood wash over his face. He licked his lips, pushing himself upwards, eager for battle.

At the top he slithered worm-like over the broken ground until he reached the rim and peered down into the valley below. Rock gave way to more gentle rolling hills, but beyond these ... Harald gasped.

A thousand camp fires, as numerous as the stars in the sky, revealed the vastness of the enemy host. Harald rubbed his face, unsure what to do next. As more men joined him, he noted their moans of disbelief. Below were thousands, and here, on this elevated vantage point, the Varangians numbered less than two hundred.

"By all the gods," said a man slithering up beside him, "there must be ten thousand of those dogs."

Harald twisted his head to squint at his companion. He saw, with some relief, it was Ulf. "You shouldn't speak of the old gods, Ulf. There are some here who would denounce you."

"Pah," he hawked and spat, "all these gods are the same to me. None helps us when we most need it. Look at them," he pointed towards the enemy camp, "do you think they give their trust in a god they cannot see? No, the only thing we need trust in is the strength of our arm, and the sharpness of our blade. When do we attack?"

"I'm not sure if it is wise. I wonder if Eisif knew the numbers we face?"

"Well, we can't go back now. So, what do we do?"

"Aye," came a voice out of the darkness, "what do we do?"

Harald bristled as Urledsson crawled up closer. "We wait for the signal, then we move down the sides and hit them whilst they sleep."

"Dear Christ," said Urledsson, giving a sharp laugh, "who dreamed up this pretty plan, *you*?"

"Eisif."

"And why did he entrust the leadership of us to you, eh?"

"He knows I will not fail. His father has ensured him—"

"His *father*? His father saw you fail before, Sigurdsson. At Stikle-gard. He carried you off, made you safe. What for, I wonder?"

"You know the reason. I am Olaf's brother. It is my destiny to rule the Norse."

"Well, I don't buy into all of that, Sigurdsson. I've seen no evidence of this promise, this *destiny* you talk so much about. All I've seen you do is knock around a few wooden posts in the training ground. There are more able men amongst us who should lead and Eisif will have much explaining to do to the Grand Prince when this endeavour peters out into the shambles it is sure to be."

"Why don't you shut the fuck up," snapped Ulf. "You're a bragging bastard, there's the truth of it. All that ever comes out of your mouth is pure shite."

"Watch your tongue, you bastard, or I'll cut it out."

"Will you, by God?"

"Aye, I shall. You and this child, both. Once this campaign is over, you'll both fall under my blade. I guarantee it."

"So be it," breathed Harald. "Urledsson, you can lead the men down as soon as the signal is given." Both Urledsson and Ulf squeaked in surprise. "What's the matter? Lost your thirst for glory all of a sudden?"

After a long moment, Urledsson finally laughed, "I get it. You want me to have the shame of defeat, rather than yourself. When the blame is doled out, and the Grand Prince learns of our defeat, it will be my head on the block, not yours." He sniggered, rolling away, "Nice try, Sigurdsson, but I'll decline the offer, however gracious it might be."

His chuckling disappeared with him in the darkness and Harald looked across at Ulf, who blew out a long breath and said, "Does he speak true? That was your intention?"

"If Jaroslav had intended the likes of Urledsson to lead this attack, Eisif would have picked him out. He didn't. He chose me." He brought his heavy, two-handed axe from around his shoulders and hefted it in his hands. "I'll not disappoint."

* * *

When the signal came – a burning arrow, from the distant Kievian Rus, sent across the early morning sky – Harald led his men down the incline without hesitation. Many paths criss-crossed the rock, but for the most part, men took whatever route their feet took them, so they became a great shadow, fanning out across the hillside, pouring towards their enemy with all the stealth they could muster.

They hit the camp at a run, racing between the canvas tents, despatching the dozing guards as they half rose in disbelief. Some cried out in terror, some managed to loose off the occasional arrow. But by the time most were stumbling out of their camp beds, the Varangians were amongst them, axes wielding in the night, starlight bouncing off the blades as they cut into the bodies of their foes.

Harald found himself alongside Ulf, both of them cutting through the rapidly recovering Poles. Making their way relentlessly towards the command tent, which stood conspicuously in the centre, two huge banners standing either side of the entrance. The great trail of the dragon devices fluttering in the slight breeze, seemed to invite them forward. Harald grinned and knew the truth of it; neither man was prepared to disappoint.

Cries of alarm rang around the camp. Spearmen and bowmen appeared out of the night, eyes alight with fear or hatred, Harald had no time to discern which. He weaved and dodged, hacking arms and bodies, carving his way ever closer to the focus of his rage. Inside the largest tent he would find the enemy commander. Chieftain or king, he cared not which. He could almost taste the man's blood.

An arrow sang past his head and he ducked low, caught sight of the assailant, and charged him, cutting him into the side with one solid chop of his axe. The man fell, writhing, the bow slipping from his hands and Harald picked it up. It was light, smaller than he expected and he wondered about the ignominy of dying in such a way. Shot by an arrow by an unknown enemy. No honour in that, he mused and he hurled the bow away in disgust, leaned over the squirming man beneath him, and put his dagger into his throat.

Something reared up behind him, and even as he turned, he saw the bulk of a Pecheneg looming out of the dark, curved blade raised, white teeth shining bright in a broad, flat face. But the grin turned into a grimace as the man arched his back, dropped his weapon and crumpled to his knees. And there, standing with his sword dripping blood, was Ulf. "Keep your wits, Harald," he said, then was gone, before Harald could offer up any thanks.

He made the command tent at last, just as the forward units of the Kievian Rus hit the camp, horses piling into the confusion, swords ringing out in the clamour of death. He tore back the entrance flap and rushed inside.

Two guards within, taken by surprise, screamed their war cries and charged towards him. Harald took the first attacking blow on the thick shaft of the axe, kicked the brute between the legs, and, in one fluid movement, cut down the second across the side of the neck, almost taking the man's head off with the ferocity of the blow. He stood, admiring his work, then brought his head up to gaze at the far side.

Stepping over the first, writhing guard, Harald approached the bare-chested man standing in front of him. He wore voluminous trousers of the deepest blue, supported by a broad, scarlet sash around his waist. Trails of sweat ran down his body and his breath came in short, laboured pants. He made no movement towards the dagger in his waistband, but instead pushed out his chest and hissed, "Do your worst, damn your heart."

Harald grinned and swung his great axe. At the very last moment, he turned it in his grip, and hit the man square across the temple with the flat end of the weapon, knocking him over with the force of a horse hitting him with both hind legs. He crashed into the corner and, a wild mess of arms and legs, and lay still.

The flap flew open. Harald turned, ready to engage more of the enemy, and relaxed as Eisif strode inside, accompanied by a group of heavily breathing Rus, one of whom put his sword into the doubled up guard on the ground.

"Is he dead?" demanded Eisif, pushing past Harald to stare towards the sprawled out chieftain. "Dear Christ, you've killed him. Why in the name of—"

"I haven't killed him," interjected Harald quickly. "What do you take me for, an idiot? I've knocked him out, is all."

"By God, you frightened me then, Harald." Eisif spun around and clamped the young Norseman by the arms, "Jaroslav will hear of this, and you will know of his great joy. He'll want to meet you. As soon as we have gathered up prisoners and booty, we secure the area and you and I, young friend, will make our way homeward, to Kiev!"

* * *

Dawn filtered through the rising stench of death that clung to the camp like a canker. Harald strode through the devastation and sought out his newfound friend Ulf, who sat by the remnants of a camp fire, cleaning his axe. He smiled as Harald approached and beckoned for him to sit down next to him.

"I'm going south, Harald," he said without preamble.

"South?"

"Aye. Many of us are leaving, traveling to Miklagard. Bollasson is leading us. Why don't you come? You'll find fame and fortune waiting there."

Harald poked at the sputtering embers with a stick, lost in thought for a moment. When he sat back, he regarded Ulf with a half-grin, "I think I will, but not just yet, my friend. I have much to do here. Besides, my place is with the Norse."

"Revenge, you mean?"

"Yes. That is one reason. But I have a duty too, my birthright. I cannot abandon it, however appealing your offer sounds." He threw the stick into the fire and stood up. He thrust out his hand, took Ulf by the arm, and lifted him to his feet. "We shall meet again, I'm sure of it."

"Well," Ulf gripped the young Norseman's hand, "the gods look down on you, Harald. They seem to have their plans already made.

You led us well and your valour is beyond question. I'll tell of it many times."

Harald smiled his thanks, then turned his face away, to look at the many soldiers picking their way through the camp. "You could be right, but at this moment, I have another task to perform. Where's Urladsson?"

"Harald," Ulf's grip grew tighter, "can't you let it go? The man is a formidable warrior."

"He's also an arrogant thug, who cast aspersions on my honour. I'll not suffer such insults, not from any man."

"You'll forgive me if I don't wait around to watch."

Harald met his friend's stare, unflinching. "You doubt the outcome?"

"I think you will be hard-pressed, but ... no, I do not doubt it."

"Then we part as friends." He turned and moved away. As he wended his way through both victors and fallen, he scanned around, desperate to pick out Urladsson amongst the gathered men.

He found him by the horses, propped up against an outcrop of boulders, two others beside him. By now the sun was above the horizon and Harald saw plainly what waited for him.

Urladsson was bleeding profusely from a hideous looking gash, which ran from his left shoulder to his waist. The wound gaped horribly, revealing sliced innards, broken bones and when Harald got down on his haunches and smiled, Urladsson could offer nothing but a slight smirk. "Seems like the Poles have done your work for you, Sigurdsson."

"A pity. I would have enjoyed cleaving your skull."

"Well," he rasped, turning his face away, a thin trail of blood trickling from the corner of his mouth, "no one will ever know. I hear you fought well, like a demon some have said." He looked again towards Harald. "I wronged you. I should not have done so. You are..."

And as Harald watched, a white mist came over Urladsson's eyes and the light, fuelled by arrogance and contempt, left and the man's body sagged and went limp. Dead.

Harald stood and released a long sigh. The gods may well be watching over him, but this was one challenge he longed to have met head on. Fate had been the victor this time and he swung around and tramped off towards where the horses were tethered, not giving one single thought more to the dead Urledsson. The future, Harald knew, would hold many such challenges and force him to face many such curs. He needed to be patient and strong.

And live.

Thirty-Four

Kiev

The court of the Grand Prince Yaroslav bustled with dignitaries from eastern and southern lands. On his arrival at the walled city of Kiev, Harald stabled his horse and, together with Eisif, approached the imposing central citadel with his head held high, expectations soaring. His fighting prowess seemed to have preceded him as many visiting ambassadors and courtiers, lowered their heads as he ducked his head to enter the huge hall. A few bowed, some even smiled. Harald did his best to avert his eyes, but he grew tense, hunched his shoulders, the heat rising to his jawline. "They know of you, Harald. Already news of your assault on the enemy camp has made you something of a legend."

"I did no more than follow your orders."

"Aye, but in the manner of their execution, you were unsurpassed. Yaroslav would wish to honour you himself." Eisif squinted through the huddle of the assembly, "I do not see him yet. When the heralds announce him, we will move forward. But Harald," he gripped the Norseman's arm, "well-respected you might be, but remember where you are. Yaroslav is the greatest ruler in the northeast. You speak only when spoken to."

A memory stirred in Harald's mind, of Olaf chiding him, stoking up such anger that Harald struck out and grabbed Olaf's beard, tugging it with all his might. He smiled to himself, shouldering his way through the mass of men, making his way to the left wall, beneath the arrayed shields and weapons, which flanked enormous tapestries depicting scenes from Nordic myth. A mix of old traditions and more modern artistry.

"Where did he acquire such works of art?" he asked, staring up at a magnificent depiction of Roland, raising his horn to his lips as his enemies pressed in all around.

"The court of the French king," said Eisif, admiring the intricately woven piece for himself. "Yaroslav receives dignitaries, even dukes and princess, from as far away as Paris, in the West, and Hadrianapolis in the east. The Byzantines grace him with visits, but as yet have not invited him to the fabled city of Constantinople."

"Some of my companions have set out for there. They say adventure and gold await them."

"Aye, that it might. Varangians serve the emperors of Byzantium, and are paid handsomely for their service."

"Have you never been tempted to go there?"

Eisif considered his answer, putting his tongue between his teeth before he said, at last, "My duty lies here, Harald, with Yaroslav. Well, at least until the time being. My father is preparing to strike out West to a group of islands called the Orkneys. I may go with him, settle, becoming something of a jarl in my own right."

"I never had you down as a farmer, Eisif."

The young man shrugged, "I have met someone, Harald. I have a different approach to life now. I want a future, one not riddled with danger and killing."

"You have met someone?" Harald smiled. "Well, you have chosen your path, but mine remains the same as it ever was – to take up my rightful place as king."

"Yes. And once you have achieved your goal, my friend, you too may well look for a bride."

They exchanged a look, tinged with humour and expectation. Harald shook his head. "I haven't even *begun* to think about such things."

"You've learned much about fighting, Harald, but perhaps not so much about love."

"Dear God, Eisif. *Love*? I have no time for that. No time at all."

"Not yet, maybe, but soon. A king needs a bride, he *needs* sons."

Not wishing Eisif to notice how much this conversation was proving uncomfortable, Harald turned away and scanned the gathering around the wide, high-vaulted hall. "I can pick out many different tongues here. There is Norse, and Greek, but also I warrant some French too. Norman French."

"Aye, there will be Normans here, Harald. They have designs to improve trade with Yaroslav."

"They wish their northern borders secure." A knot tightened in his gut and he sighed loudly, "I still have business to attend to with the Normans. Business which has nothing to do with trade." He recalled the news of his father's death, the assassin who came out of the shadows at Olaf's court. The woman who put paid to the murderer's ambition. The woman he had killed. "I know their hand was in my father's death. It is a debt which needs repaying."

"Well, hold back a little while, my friend. Yaroslav will not take kindly to any confrontations within his court. His ambitions are far-reaching, perhaps even to Miklagard itself." Eisif clapped him on the shoulder, "Ambitions that may include you!"

Harald arched a single eyebrow, but before he could speak, a blast from an assembly of trumpets brought everyone to silence. From the far end of the hall, double doors wheezed open. Two lines of heavily armoured warriors marched out, spears on their shoulders, shields emblazoned with the Christian motif championed by Constantine the Great, bronze lamellar armour seeming to shimmer even in the dark, depressing air of the hall.

And within the centre, Grand Prince Yaroslav. He dressed simply, in a long white robe, trimmed with purple. Around his neck he wore a gold chain, the only allusion to his rank as leader of this burgeoning city.

A herald stepped forward, a squat little man sporting a shock of red hair. He roared, "Lords, earls and jarls, pray silence for his majestic highness, the Grand Prince Yaroslav!"

At one, from every corner of the vast hall, the assembled dignitaries bowed deep from the waist. Harald joined in, but allowed his eyes to remain firmly fixed on the Prince as he stepped onto the dais and settled himself into his ornately decorated chair. The warriors flanked him, ram-rod stiff, spears now point upwards, eyes staring straight ahead.

"My friends, I am blessed to find so many of you here this day. News of our great victory in the east is most welcome and affords us all security. With the threat to our borders now relieved, let us turn our minds to more peaceful pursuits. I will be speaking with as many of you as time allows, and in my council, I shall meet nobles from both Europe and Byzantium. We are on the threshold of a new age, my friends. An era of peace and prosperity. Long may it last!"

An answering roar of appreciation rang out from the mouths of the assembly, accompanied with much pounding of feet on the wooden floorboards.

"We'd best do our utmost to get closer," said Eisif in Harald's ear, and took the young Norseman by the elbow. "Remember, wait until spoken to."

Harald grunted and allowed himself to be steered closer to the great man, who sat like a Roman emperor of old, cradling his chin in his palm as he surveyed the dignitaries, some of whom already were bent down on one knee, addressing the Prince in whispered tones.

As the two Norsemen drew closer, Yaroslav's face brightened and he stood up, throwing out his hands, "Eisif!" He stepped down from the dais, ignoring the men at his feet, and strode forward to embrace the commander of his army in the east. "By God, you did well," he pushed Eisif away, still holding onto his shoulders to stare deeply into his face. "Your father assured me you were the man for the task, and by God you have proved it. A great victory, my friend, and your rewards shall be great also, to mirror your fine achievements." He beamed and then, as he turned to settle on Harald, his gaze grew more serious. "And this, so I believe, is my friend Olaf's brother? Harald Sigurdsson."

Harald lowered his head, "My Prince, it is an honour to serve you."

Yaroslav dropped his hands from Eisif and considered Harald for some moments. "What happened to Olaf was a tragedy, Harald Sigurdsson. I loved him and I should have been with him, but those bastard Pechenegs took all my attention. I hope you can find it in your heart to forgive me."

Harald gaped, "My Prince, I..." He shook his head. "I do not need to forgive you, my Prince. The honour to serve you, I sought nothing more."

"And serve me you have, Harald. News of your success preceded you and brought me great joy. I would speak with you, later this evening, when the feast is done. I have some ideas I wish to discuss." He smiled, "If you are not too drunk, that is."

But drunk he was not.

As the day drew on, and the gathering of men took to their seats in arranged trestle tables brought in by a small army of servants, Harald remained quiet in a corner. He splayed out his legs, the wine goblet in his hand moving to his lips a mere half-dozen times, whilst all around high-born nobility quaffed and ate. Some growing sated too quickly and ending up on the floor, to drool and vomit. At one point, musicians struck up a series of jaunty tunes, using instruments the like of which Harald did not recognise, not by design or the timbre they emitted.

He noted a young girl flitting between the tables, giggling as she went, snatching away bits of food from noblemen's plates. They made playful grabs for her, which she dodged easily, laughing loudly. She moved with an easy grace, one which belied her youthfulness. Still a child, she bore herself as one well used to being at the centre of attention. As she finally approached Harald, her pale blue eyes danced with inquisitiveness. "Are you the one they call 'The Viking'?"

Harald shrugged, "I suppose I must be."

"I'm Ellisif. You've probably heard of me." She sat down with a sigh next to him and stared at his half-full cup of wine. "You're not with the others, and you don't join in with their drinking. Why not?"

Harald looked down into his wine. "I'm meeting with your father, so I need to have my full wits about me."

"So you *do* know who I am!"

"Of course." He smiled. "They say you are going to grow into one the most beautiful princesses in all the world."

"Do they?" She tilted her head in mock coyness. "And what do you think?"

He studied her small, oval face, framed with ropes of golden hair, which fell to her bare shoulders. A silver band circled her head and, around her neck, a thick bejewelled necklace of gold. He smiled at her expectant expression. "I think they did not tell the truth."

Her eyes widened in disbelief, and she spluttered, "W-what did you say?"

He reached out and touched the tip of her nose with his forefinger. "You will not be one, but *the* most beautiful princess in the world!"

She laughed, a peerless, delightful sound of relief and pure joy. "I like you, Viking! But tell me, how did you get to be so tall?"

"I was hung by my neck and arms from a tree when I was younger than you are now. They put weights on my feet and left me there for the best part of a week."

Her mouth fell open, "But who did such horrors? Your family?"

"And friends. But it was not a horror, sweet princess, more of a gift. For now, wherever I go, people stop and stare in awe of me. As they do you, but for very different reasons."

She frowned, "Is that story true, Viking? I may only be ten summers, but I'm not a child. I do *know* when someone is lying."

"It is not a lie, princess, merely an ... *exaggeration.*"

A shadow fell over them both and Harald looked up into the flat face of a fully armoured warrior, eyes narrow and hard. "The Grand Prince will speak with you now, Sigurdsson." He lowered his head as he turned to Ellisif, "With your permission, your grace."

She shrugged, turned to Harald and smiled. "I hope I meet you again, Viking. You're funny, not at all like the rest of them. All they do is drink and fall over, but you … when next you come to my father's court, you will tell me tales of Vikings and more about what happened to you when you were younger. Although I think you are not so very old. Am I right?"

"Seventeen summers, my princess."

"Why, you're not much older than me."

"No, but I *am* older." He stood up, bowed, and nodded towards the warrior. "Lead on. Until the next time, Princess."

She smiled and Harald turned away, following the soldier through the groaning tables towards Grand Prince Yaroslav's private apartments.

Thirty-Five

The Dneiper

"I stayed at the court of Yaroslav until the following spring," said Hardrada as he stood on the banks, watching Ulf organise the crew. Haldor, next to him, sat on a rocky outcrop, his face screwed up in pain. Hardrada studied his old friend, concern eating away at him. The wound the Icelander suffered from Crethus might not ever heal completely. *No doubt he still bled inside*, Hardrada mused. So, he talked, attempting to keep Haldor's thoughts from the pain as the others wrestled with the ship, using ropes and sheer brawn to lift it out of the water.

"We did this on my first journey south," Hardrada continued, settling down beside Haldor. "This river is so treacherous in places, and these hills," he gestured to the opposite bank, where the steep, rocky sides gave way to thick woodland, "they teem with brigands. They assailed us more than once."

"But you survived."

Hardrada grunted, "Aye, we did that. Yaroslav assembled a fair crew, and many men who fought with me against the Pechenegs, and some from Stiklegard, accompanied me. It would have taken more than a few score of craven horse archers to overcome us."

"And Yaroslav's plan was truly to have you as his spy, to report back on the feasibility of an invasion?"

"He was deluded. I sent him a message within the first month of my arrival at Constantinople, a message I assume he received. To assail the walls of Theodosius would take an army greater than any Yaroslav could muster. Besides which, there was Maniakes to contend with. I've fought many battles, but never have I seen a general so consummate in tactical ability."

"If Maniakes were dead, do you believe Yaroslav would launch an invasion now, once you tell him of the situation in the city now? The years have not gone well for Byzantium."

"I believe he will attack. But I'll not join him. I've had a bellyful of Greeks. My destiny lies in the Norse, Hal. I'll not wander south again."

"Wise. Byzantium is doomed. It has grown weak, just as Rome did all those centuries ago. Corruption, negligence, conceit ... all combining to eat away at the foundations, to bring it down. And when it falls, this world will never be the same again."

"You're a prophet, Hal. A prophet of doom, by God."

"No, I've simply used my eyes. You have saved them more than once, Harald. Without you, or the General, I doubt they will stand for very long. Forces greater than the Pechenegs, greater even than the Normans, will pour across the Anatolian plain in an irresistible wave. That is Byzantium's destiny, and we are better off out of it."

"Your plan is still to return to Iceland?"

"It is. My home. As yours is the Norse. Home always calls us back, Harald, no matter how far we wander."

They both looked up as Ulf tramped towards them, breathing hard. He dragged his hand across a face awash with sweat. "We've got her out, now we'll rest before manhandling her along the bank to avoid the rapids. If we're lucky we'll manage it before nightfall." He cast his eyes to the summit of the hillside, which loomed behind his two companions. "Some scouts have reported seeing groups of mounted devils roaming not so very far from here. It might be prudent to send out raiders to intercept them."

"I'll do it," said Hardrada standing. "Send the scouts to me, then give me half a dozen of your best men. We'll keep whoever's out there busy whilst you haul the ship farther up river."

"Best if you remained here, Harald. I'll take the men and—"

"No, my friend," said Hardrada with a grin. "I'm eager for a fight. Besides, I'll lose my patience with the men if they don't work fast enough. You're far better at that sort of thing than I." He peered skyward. "We have some time before dusk. Let us not tarry any longer."

* * *

They picked up the trail on the far side of the hill. Looking down to where men worked to haul the ship across the broken ground, Hardrada cast his mind back to how he too had strained on the ropes. How he had slipped, cracking his shin against the rocks. The memory of the pain, his enforced rest on a truckle-bed, how ashamed he felt whilst his companions struggled to bring the ship finally to Saint Gregory's Island. No, better for him to do what he did best – swing his axe and smite his enemies.

"They've made camp," came a soft voice.

Hardrada turned to the lightly built warrior crouching before him, shield slung on his back, javelins in his hand. "How many?"

"At least eight," said the man, holding up his fingers.

"That's seven," said Hardrada with a grin and cuffed the warrior on the arm. "We'll fan out. I shall take the eastern side, you the west. We keep low and move fast. We must hit them before they manage to get to their horses."

He gave the signal for two men to join him and he set off, darting between the rocky ground, whilst the remaining four scurried away in the opposite direction.

The noise on the many rocks of every size and shape, which sprinkled the ground, forced Hardrada to slow right down, and he and his men slithered over the boulders like snakes. Their progress was painful, full of frustration, and Hardrada, with his teeth set on edge, would have liked nothing better than to charge, axe held aloft, screaming his battle-cry. But if any of the horse-archers managed to escape, the retribution which would follow would prove too great. So stealth was their only course and by the time they reached the Pecheneg camp, the sun was already falling behind the horizon.

From where he crouched, Hardrada had a good view of the camp and, as the distance was short, he could hear the spitting of the wood on the fire. The raiders sat huddled around the blaze, swathed in heavy blankets whilst a little way off were tethered three horses, munching nonchalantly at a few meagre tufts of grass.

One of his companions wriggled closer, whispering, "Why only three horses?"

Hardrada shot the man a glance and frowned. He had no answer. He looked again at the camp. At least eight figures squatted down, warming themselves. "Perhaps we should ask them?"

Before his companion could form a reply, Hardrada was on his feet, dashing over the broken ground that separated himself from the Pechenegs.

He took the first one across the back of the head before any of them could react. As he swung around to lop off a second bandit's skull, he stopped in the action of drawing back his axe, his mouth dropping open.

The other two Norsemen came scampering up, preparing to deliver their death blows, and they too stopped, disbelieving faces turned to their leader.

Hardrada had no answer.

Around the campfire were not men, but heaps of clothing, shaped to look like bodies, from a distance.

Too late, Hardrada realised their predicament and brandishing his axe, shouted, "To cover!"

The first arrow took one of the men through the mouth and he staggered backwards, pitching over the rocks as three more darts sank into his body. Already Hardrada was tumbling, making for shelter. Six men, riding on stocky, swift-moving steppe ponies, came out of the failing sunlight, sending arrows streaking through the air. The second Norse was hit two, three, four times, and he pitched onto his face and lay still.

Hardrada rolled over as an arrow flashed a hand's width from his face.

A horseman thundered by and Hardrada leapt up onto the boulder before him, and launched himself at the rider, taking him around the waist. The three of them, men and horse, clattered to the ground. The pony screamed, legs kicking out, desperate to regain its footing, whilst Hardrada put his dagger into the Pecheneg's throat, took up his bow and rolled over into a sitting position.

The pony's mad scramble to its feet allowed him a moment to loose off an arrow at another rider, hitting him in the side, throwing him from his mount. With no time to admire his success, Hardrada raced to another outcrop of rock, swerving, ducking, dodging arrows as the four remaining horsemen circled and fired.

Cries came out of the rapidly diminishing sunlight. The other group of Norse poured over the rocks. A counter-envelopment. Hardrada grinned, chanced a look and watched the Pechenegs rein in their mounts, which reared up on rear legs, and arrows hit more targets. Hardrada took the opportunity of the lull in their caracole, and shot one of the men in the back.

Hardrada ran forward again, loosing off arrows without any hope of meeting a target. When the quiver was exhausted, he threw it away and watched the other Vikings closing with the Pechenegs just as the two remaining riders emerged and took the Viking group in the rear.

Within a few blinks it was over and Hardrada flattened himself, desperate to still his heaving chest, and wait. This was not the Norse way, and he knew it. He also knew he could not allow any of these brigands to escape to alert more of their band. To be overcome when his goal was so close was not something Hardrada could contemplate, so he lay still, hoping they would think him dead.

Footsteps approached. Hardrada concentrated hard on remaining motionless, holding his breath. But then something heavy and hard pressed into his back, accompanied by a snigger. "You are Hardrada," said a heavily accented voice, "I'd know you anywhere, a giant such as you."

Hardrada sighed, turned his head and squinted up to where the Pecheneg stood over him, grinning. Others loomed up close, holding burning torches made from the camp fire, illuminating the scene with an eerie, orange glow.

"Are you sure it is him?"

"Who else could it be?" The man got down on his haunches and cackled, "The empress of Byzantium will give good money for your return, Norseman." He drew a long, thin-bladed knife and pressed the point under Hardrada's heavily bearded chin. "Or would you rather we killed you right here, right now?"

Thirty-Six

Constantinople

The guards came to attention as Empress Zoe rushed past them, flung open the doors to her private apartment, and hurled her golden tiara into the far corner. She went over to the balcony and closed her eyes, taking deep breaths, attempting to extinguish the many images playing out around inside her head.

From far beyond the orange and lime groves, the sound of the multitude filled the air. Citizens, rejoicing in yet another royal marriage, singing and dancing, many of them already drunk. Secure, at peace, an emperor who promised stability, not wild excess. The days of violence and debauchery were at an end. His marriage to the glorious Zoe proved it.

Or so he said.

Right now Constantine Monomachus, Emperor of New Rome, was in a stately apartment not so very far from where Zoe fumed, sticking his cock inside another woman. Scleriana. Zoe screwed up her eyes. Even the forming of the woman's name brought renewed anger to her throat, and she released a strangled scream, gripping the balustrade so hard, her exquisite fingernails broke.

In truth, she couldn't give a fig for what Monomachus did, but the thought that he might prefer another woman to her was beyond the limits of tolerance. Already the instigator for the death of two emperors, the idea of another assassination festered in her mind. Could she do it, would it even be possible? Monomachus had reinstated the Varangians and their loyalty to the emperor was solid, unflinching. *No, there had to be another way, another path to take.*

Once she would have cultivated powerful allies, men whose own ambitions often blinded them to the truth; they were the manipulated ones. Zoe, her beauty irresistible, fuelled men's desires and she moulded them to her will with the ease of a potter at his wheel. She could make of them what she wished. Except now, all of them were gone. Maniakes and Alexius, both dead. John Orphano, fading away in some monastic enclave in the middle of Anatolia. *There's no one.*

A gentle knock on the door brought her out of her reverie. She swung around, preparing to shoot a mouthful of vitriol towards whoever it was who dared disturb her, when she stopped, blinked, and took another, longer look.

The man who stood before her was an officer of the Varangian Guard, his wide shoulders and broad chest encased in bronze lamellar armour. He wore a bronze helmet with a nasal guard, a black plume streaming from the top, and from beneath the leather inner, white hair hung down around his neck.

He stiffened and bowed deeply. "Forgive me, Serene Highness, but the Emperor has sent me to request your attendance, to join him in his royal apartments."

She moved closer, studying him from head to toe. She smiled. "Is he finished? He's quick, I'll give him that much."

"Highness?" The man frowned at her from under the rim of his helmet.

"It doesn't matter." She circled him, allowing a finger to trail over his shoulders and back. "You are a captain of the guard?"

"The Varangian Guard, yes, Highness."

"Hardrada was such a man. You know him?"

"I *knew* him, Highness."

"Ah." She came to his front again, her gaze never leaving his as he straightened. "You are a Norseman, like him?"

"I am Saxon, Highness. From England."

"England? I do not think I know of that place. It is very far away?"

"Beyond imagining, Highness."

She nodded, her fingers running across the collar of the tunic he wore under the armour. "Tell me, you say you knew Hardrada. Do you mean by that, you think him dead?"

"One of his shops went down in the Horn, Highness. Most people say he drowned."

"Most, yes, but where is the proof?"

The captain turned his mouth down at the corners, "It is possible he survived, but no one has heard anything."

"You are a loyal soldier of New Rome, are you not, Captain?"

"Of course, Highness. I have sworn allegiance to the Emperor, and to your divine self, Highness."

"Good." She stepped back and smiled. "I want you to travel north and find out what you can about him, you understand?"

"Highness?"

"Hardrada. I sent him gold, you see, and the men came back to tell me it had been collected, so he must be alive. I want you to find him, and," she stepped up close again, her hand dropping to his crotch. He flinched and she laughed. "I want you to find him and kill him, and when you do, I shall be your reward. You understand?"

He gulped, breath coming in short, strained gasps, "Highness … I…"

She put her finger on his lips, "Yes, I know. You want an advance." She slipped her hand under his tunic and found the lacing of his breeches. He gasped, louder this time, and she sucked in her breath, her eyes widening as her fingers found his swiftly hardening manhood. "Afterwards, you will go to Constantine and inform him I will attend to his commands when I am good and ready. Then, you shall journey north." She pressed her lips against his. After a moment's hesitation, he responded and she groaned deeply, rolling her fingers over the engorged flesh, which jutted out from under the folds of his armour. She pulled away and, tugging at him, led him to her bed. "But first, we have some business to attend to!"

Thirty-Seven

They tied him to a stake after they hauled him across the scree and rocks, taking him far away from their original camp. He sat and watched them within spitting distance of their fire as they laughed, drank and swallowed down hunks of bread and olives. One of them guffawed and hurled a stone towards Hardrada, who moved his head slightly to dodge the missile. He returned their braying with a snarl.

He slept, as best he could, and in the morning he watched them stretching and yawning, one or two stumbling away to a dip in the ground to defecate. The leader, the one who had first come upon him lying in the dirt the previous day, wandered over to him and smiled.

"Your friends will be looking, but they will not find you." He glanced skyward for a moment, "We will travel in a wide arc, far away from the river. Your friends will think you are dead."

"They won't think that until they find my body."

The man shrugged. "Well, whatever they think, they will not find you. We will ride fast and by this time tomorrow, we will cross the border into Byzantine lands. Then, my friend, you will taste their justice. For I think their queen wants your head."

"How could you know that?"

The man leered, "Oh, you are saying it is not true?"

Hardrada looked away, "I know one thing, *friend*, you'd best kill me. Because if you don't, I'll cut off your balls and stuff them in your stinking mouth before this day is through."

The man laughed, went to turn away, then swung back and landed a heavy kick into Hardrada's side. The giant's breath gushed out of him and he sagged against his bonds, gasping.

"Big words for a big man," snarled the leader before he walked away, chuckling to himself.

Hardrada hung there, biting down the pain, eyes squeezed shut, battling to regain his breath. When he managed to stare down at the ground, everything swirled in front him, colours danced across his line of vision. So he waited, taking his time, until at last, the fire died down from his ribs and he sat up. He put back his head against the stake, took a deep breath, and did his best to work the point of it out of the ground.

He failed, the rope bonds cutting into his wrists.

The raiders ate their breakfast; a few scraps of dried meat and unleavened bread. One of them drank from a goatskin gourd, smacked his lips and eyed Hardrada keenly. He said something to the leader, who waved him away, and he waddled over and thrust the goatskin towards his captive's face. "You want some wine, Viking?"

Hardrada eyed the gourd suspiciously, licking his lips. His throat was as dry as dust and he found it difficult to keep his stomach from rumbling. The man laughed and squatted down. "You have no need to be proud, Viking. Drink." He pulled out the stopper and tilted the gourd into Hardrada's opened mouth. He spluttered, the wine catching the back of his throat. "Not too much, Viking. We don't want you falling off your horse, drunk." After a short pause, to allow Hardrada to recover, the raider put the wine to his mouth again.

A cry went up from the camp and the man turn on his heels to see what the commotion was. Hardrada followed his gaze, peering over to see a heavily set man coming over the ridge on a beautiful roan charger, white hair streaming behind him from beneath his bronze helmet. He reined in his horse and jumped down. The leader of the Pecheneg raiders went over to him, gripping his arm in a friendly greeting, whilst the three others gathered around, all of them jabbering at once.

"Who is that?" asked Hardrada.

The man turned and smiled, "Our payday, my friend. From your queen."

"A Byzantine?"

"Varangian, I think. He came to us not three days ago, to make this plan." He chuckled. "Seems as if it has worked, my friend. He will take you south, and there they will feast on your flesh, those Greeks. I hear they eat human flesh, and there is plenty of that on you."

Hardrada grunted. "More wine, *friend.*"

Sniggering, the raider moved closer to Hardrada and tipped the goatskin to the Viking's mouth. Hardrada strained his neck to take a gulp. The raider shuffled nearer still and then Hardrada struck, swinging his foot up to slam squarely into the man's scrotum.

The man squealed and pitched onto his side, doubled up in agony, clutching at his groin, the gourd forgotten, wine trickling from the open neck.

The other raiders reacted, reaching for their knives and bow and Hardrada watched and waited, not knowing what might transpire.

In the end, what happened took him totally by surprise.

Thirty-Eight

Ulf spotted them on the edge of the cliff, swept up his axe, and roared to his men to get into battle formation.

He raced over the rocks to where Haldor lay, sheltering amongst a smattering of gorse and broken, dried up remnants of trees. "What's all the fuss about?" he asked, raising himself on his elbows.

"Raiders. Not many, but they may be a vanguard. I have to get you into the boat."

Haldor held up his hand, "No, Ulf. I'll be fine here."

"Don't be so damned stubborn, you old bastard! If they break through—"

"If they break through, we're all dead, old friend. Set the shieldwall, and make sure they don't do so."

Ulf bit his lip and exhaled loudly, "You're an old mule, Hal."

"And I'm not going to change now." He grimaced as he sat upright. "No sign of Harald?"

"Not yet."

"Then we can only assume the worst. Perhaps these raiders come to parley."

Ulf twisted around to peer towards the cliffs. "Who can say. But if they've killed him, I'll cleave the heads of every single one of them."

"That's the Ulf I know so well."

Smiling, Ulf stood up. "If I see them coming this way I'll—"

A young warrior ran up next to them, eyes wild, arms gesticulating towards the ship, still straddled across the rocky shoreline. "You have to come, Ulf. You won't believe what's happened."

What had happened was simple, as Ulf discovered when he returned to his men.

Coming down the hillside, nimbly winding their way through the rocks, were two men, one of whom was unmistakeable.

"By all the gods," muttered Ulf, and shot a grin to the other warriors, "He's back, damn his eyes! *Back!*"

They caught one another in a chest-crushing embrace. Ulf, the tears running unchecked down his face, could barely speak. "I thought you were dead, you bastard."

Hardrada shook him by the shoulders, "I may well have been, if it hadn't been for my friend here." He stepped aside, and, putting his arm around the stranger, drew him forward. "This is the man to whom I owe my life."

"Then we all owe him a debt," said Ulf, sniffing and dragging the back of his hand across his nose. "Well met, friend."

The two men gripped one another's hand.

"He took them all, cutting them down as if they were sheaves of wheat," said Hardrada. "Seems like he was sent by Zoe to bring me back ... dead if need be."

"Zoe?" Ulf frowned, "So, she's still smarting over your escape."

"More than that," said the stranger, grinning, "the woman is like something possessed. My only regret is I won't be receiving my reward."

Hardrada laughed, "Dear God, she doesn't change, does she." He gave the man a playful punch on the arm, which almost knocked him sideways. "No need to tell us what she had in mind."

Ulf grunted, "Never had the pleasure."

"Well," said the stranger, "I have and, I tell you this, I've never known anything like it. Still," he shrugged and winked at Hardrada, "I was planning on going home anyway. I may as well tag along with you, since you're going that way."

"Home?" asked Ulf, tilting his head. "And where is that? You're not Norse."

"No, I'm a Saxon. Home is England, to my farm in the south. Things were bad when I left, with that bastard Cnut and his sons laying waste to everything we held dear. But now Edward has been proclaimed king, so I'm going back, to serve him."

"A noble plan," said Hardrada, "but I would have liked to have confronted Cnut myself before the old bastard died. He invaded the lands of my brother, seized the throne for himself and put my family to the sword." He pulled in a deep breath. "But there are others, who still live, who will feel my vengeance when I return."

"England is a place I have never visited," said Ulf as the three men wandered towards the ship. Warriors, the tension leaving their shoulders, returned to the ropes, to haul the great drakkar further up river, to a place beyond the rapids.

"It is a fine land," said the Saxon stranger, "and I have been gone too long. Unless another tragedy strikes which forces me to leave my homeland of Wessex, I doubt I shall ever see Constantinople again."

"You and I both," said Hardrada, with meaning. "Where is Hal?"

"Resting," said Ulf. "I think his wound has opened up again, inside."

"I'll go speak with him," said Hardrada, and strode off.

"Thank you," said Ulf, looking again at the Saxon. "If he had fallen, I doubt any of us would have had the courage to continue. Especially not Hal."

The Saxon shrugged. "None of us is safe yet. Once Zoe realises what has happened, she may send others. Her reach is long."

"Aye. Well, we need to be on alert. But, thank you." He took the man's hand and shook it. "What is your name, friend?"

"Hereward," said the Saxon and together they went to help the others with the ship.

Thirty-Nine

Once returned to the river, the ship made steady progress north. Men watched from the sides, scanning the cliffs on either side, all wary now, some with captured Pecheneg bows, knocked and ready.

Hal, suffering a relapse, lay on a pile of padded blankets under a hastily rigged canopy of animal skins, to shield him from the sun. A thin film of sweat lay over his brow and his breathing was shallow and ragged. Ulf attended to him as best he could, mopping his face with cool water. His worsening condition brought a sense of impending doom to the crew and they threw themselves into their tasks with a new resolve, trying to put away thoughts of Hal dying.

"Tell me about Zoe," said Hardrada, staring out across the waters.

Hereward stood close by, the breeze playing with his long hair. He gave a sharp laugh, "Has there ever been a woman like her, in all the world?"

"I doubt it."

"I have never known such wantonness, as if my entire soul was on fire. I was out of control with desire."

"Ah, my friend. Like the spider, she captured you, feasted on your heart."

"No, my friend. I always knew what her ultimate plan was, but I let her think she had me in her power. That way I could partake of her delights with complete abandon."

"Wise man." Hardrada smiled. "I believed the same, once. But she played me for a fool. All she ever wanted was my money, never my love. She made it known her wrath was boundless when she threw me in prison. She'd caught me with the niece of one of the Byzantine admirals and she became like a mad thing, a berserker if you like!" Hardrada remembered the terrible night when the emperor Michael's Scythians struck, butchering the Varangians in their beds. "They planned it together, Zoe and her loathsome creature, Michael. A double-strike, replacing the Varangians with Scythians, and throwing me and my friends into jail. Zoe could not stomach the idea I had lain with another, so she took her chance and, in the process, hoped to get her hands on my treasure." He chuckled. "But she failed. They all failed. And now, she has another husband I hear?"

"Yes. The Emperor Constantine Monomachus. Although, as is common knowledge, he shares the marital bed with another."

"Already? My God, he didn't waste any time."

"He has always been with this other woman, so they say. They live in some bizarre triptych, scandalising the entire city with their lusts. Monomachus has plans, or so he says, to secure the borders, raise money for more mercenaries, undo the excesses and corruptions of the former Emperor. People may not like him, but they trust him."

"Well, the people always were fickle. As long as their bellies are full they don't give a damn who gives the orders. And what of Maniakes? What has he to say in all of this?"

"The General is dead, Harald."

Hardrada slowly turned, his eyes glazing over as he looked back, memories rearing up inside his mind. "Dead? I thought his position was secure, damn him."

"I dare say he believed it so himself. He led a rebellion, but it was ill-judged and he was defeated in battle against the forces of the Emperor. They tied him on a donkey and paraded him through the city, to be mocked and jeered at." The Saxon shook his head. "No one, certainly not one as great as Maniakes, should be abused in such a way. I am well rid of that place, despite the promise of having Zoe's sweet thighs wrapped around me." He leaned over the side of the ship and spat into the river, "She is a viper, as well you know. I hear it said she danced when news of the General's fate reached her. Such a woman is deadly. A spider, you say … well, more a praying mantis I warrant. The strike, when it comes, lethal and total. I was always fully aware of once she had done with me, she would spit me out, throw me to the wolves perhaps. Who knows.

"She wanted you in her clutches again, her actions fuelled by blind revenge. The perceived wrongness you did to her eats away like a cancer, one she cannot ignore. No doubt my betrayal will fill her with a greater desire to destroy us all. But even her power and influence cannot reach the Norse, or England. Soon we will be safe."

Hardrada went over to where the crew had placed several piles of cargo and he slumped down on top of a crate, put his face in his hands and sat for a long time in silence.

When Ulf stepped up to his friend, Hardrada looked up and stared deep into the man's eyes. "Maniakes is dead."

Ulf blinked, took a moment to digest the news, and shot a glance at Hereward. "It's their death knell."

Hereward nodded. "I believe it might be."

"How is Hal?"

"Better," said Ulf, sitting down beside his friend. "His breathing is more normal, the sweating less. We'll have to watch him, Harald. I forget how old he is, how his body takes longer to heal."

"We're all getting older, Ulf." Hardrada stretched his back. "I feel twice my age. All these damn wounds and broken bones I've accumulated don't help."

"Do you think we'll ever truly get old?"

"God knows. I hope not."

"They say Edward is old before his time," said Hereward. "Life does that, if it is hard."

"Edward?" Ulf frowned.

"England's new king," replied Hereward. "The reason I'm returning. The Danes have gone and Wessex is once again in control. But rumour has it Edward is pious, saintly. He likes not battle and making hard decisions. So, others rule in his name, men of power and influence. Men who have already proved they are duplicitous and untrustworthy. The Godwins, the most powerful family in all the land."

Ulf grunted. "Sounds as if your land is as riven with deceit and greed as Byzantium."

Hereward nodded in agreement, "I believe it is. And, before long, such greed will be its undoing."

"Greed can be a good thing," said Hardrada, staring down at his feet, "if it is channelled, used for the right reasons. To better one's life, and the life of subjects. Corruption, well, that is something else. I soon learned about all of that when I first arrived in Miklagard, some six years ago."

"Stories about you abounded when I arrived myself, Harald." Hereward sat down next to him. "Of how you beat the Normans in Sicily, saved the great city itself."

"Maniakes and I, we did it. Together." He blew out his cheeks. "You could even say we were friends."

"Tell us about it," urged Hereward. "Tell us about your time in the great city. It must be a tale worth telling."

"That it must," said Ulf, leaning forward. "And as you tell it, Harald, I'll fetch us some wine. Good tales need good drink to go with them!"

Forty

Constantinople, 1036

With a crew of just under fifty warriors, and a ship provided by the Grand Prince, Harald made his way down the Dneiper River. They negotiated the rapids as Vikings often did, by hauling their vessel across the land and, when the river grew calmer once more, came to the Black Sea in the early summer of Ten Hundred and Thirty-Six.

Pecheneg raiders accounted for half-a-dozen or so of his companions. Before the month of June was out, the remaining crew managed to sail through the Bosphorus unmolested and there they laid anchor and stood speechless, gawping at the wonders before them.

The great city of Constantinople stood, the teardrops of God having fallen like golden rain upon the ground, to create the burnished, glistening capital of the world. Harald's mouth hung open. Neither he, nor any of his companions had the strength to speak, for nothing had prepared them for this moment. Huge, sprawling across the horizon, the domes of the many churches shining in the sunlight, this was like no other place any of them had seen before. And, covering the approaches to the city, like water-boatmen insects darting this way and that, were ships of every size and shape, bringing the riches of the known world to the bustling markets of this wondrous place.

"Dear God, it is huge," managed a young warrior, who stood trembling beside Harald.

"That it is," said Harald without averting his eyes, "and it is a wondrous thing."

They approached the great harbour of Theodosius and as they raised oars, allowing the longship to glide through the approaches, an imperial escort shadowed them, its decks bristling with armed guards.

Buffeted against the harbour walls, men threw ropes to waiting dock workers, who secured the vessel and Hardrada was the first to step ashore.

Two black-robed men pushed their way through the press of mingling merchants, workers and soldiers thronging the harbour. Hardrada eyed them, noting their badges of office. Some days out from the great city, customs officials had checked their ship at the customs station at Hieron and, after a fleeting scan of the ship's provisions, allowed them through. Now, as these two latest agents of the imperial court approached, Hardrada wondered what further delay awaited them.

The first official raised a singled eyebrow as he checked the bundles of supplies in the centre of the ship. He ran his finger across the lead seal, which the *kommerkiarioi* at Hieron had placed on several bundles, and made a sucking sound with his teeth. "We'll have to open these."

Hardrada glared at the official from the harbour wall. "We've been checked, as you can see from the seal."

""Yes," the official rubbed his chin, glancing at his partner who stood next Hardrada, rapidly entering notes in a large, red covered ledger. He struggled to balance both inkwell and quill as he stabbed away at the thick, stiff pages within the book. He nodded in agreement. "So, if you'd kindly open them up."

"It's only clothes, blankets, some pieces of gold, but only enough to see us through the next few days."

"Nevertheless."

Hardrada looked across at his crew, who stood on the ship, expectant, waiting for orders. Some dropped their hands to their swords.

Hardrada went to speak when a group of bronze-armoured soldiers arrived from out of the surrounding crowd, most of whom had stopped to gaze in anticipation of a good fight.

"What's your business here," barked the officer in charge, the white plume sprouting out of the top of his helmet trailing in the breeze.

"We've come to offer our service to the Varangian Guard," said Hardrada, struggling to maintain self-control. He and his men had laboured for days to reach the promises Constantinople seemed to afford. To be so confronted irked him beyond measure. He put his fists on his hips and held the officer's gaze. "Rumour has it you need men such as we, so here we are. Or would you deny your imperial majesty the opportunity to secure our assistance in his struggle against the Normans?"

The man bristled, "We have more than enough men."

"Aye, perhaps so. But not such as these," he waved his hand over his waiting companions. "We have fought in battles from Norway to the steppes of Poland and have always acquitted ourselves well."

"You will have to accompany me to the official barracks, where you will be thoroughly vetted before being considered for service."

"*Considered?*" Hardrada's temples pulsed with indignation. "We have travelled many leagues from the north to come here, you pompous ass. I demand you allow me an audience with the commander of the Varangian Guard."

"You're in no position to demand anything," said the official in the boat. "So my advice is for you to open up these bundles, then go with this officer to where you will billet until a use can be found for you and your crew." He smiled. "If a use can be found, of course."

Hardrada smiled, "I understand. Perhaps some of our gold coins could smooth our passage into your ranks?"

The official shrugged, "Who can say."

The officer sighed, "Bribery, or attempted bribery, is frowned upon here, Norseman."

"Frowned upon or not, you wouldn't say 'no', would you?" Hardrada waited for the reply, but there was none. The soldier's steely blue eyes remained unblinking. "I thought not."

"You are still required to report at the official barracks. You will then be assigned your units, if you are deemed fit to serve." He turned his gaze to the crew. "Although, by the look of you, I doubt many will pass the initial assessment."

"Do not confuse our ragged appearance with a lack of fighting skill, Greek."

"I'm Persian," the man returned, his eyes narrowing. He sniffed the air, "And you need a bath, Norseman. The stink of herrings clings to you like a second set of clothes."

Hardrada stepped to the man's right side and cracked his elbow under the soldier's chin. Even before he fell, Hardrada and his men had drawn weapons, some of them vaulting onto the harbour walls, preparing to attack the other soldiers.

The official in the ship waved his arms, "Stop this, all of you!"

A fist slammed into his guts and he folded, gasping for air, face turning purple. His companion jumped down onto the deck to come to his aid, ledger, inkwell and quill all forgotten.

The Byzantine soldiers snapped themselves together in a defensive block, spears lowered, shields clattering against their chests, Their commander rolled over and climbed to his feet, wobbling on legs turned to jelly. A nearby soldier supported him by the arms, and he stood, breathing hard, one hand pressed against his mouth where drooled blood from the corner. His helmet lay at his feet, but he ignored it for the moment, keeping hate-filled eyes fixed firmly on Hardrada. "By Christ, you'll pay for this outrage, Norseman."

"No, he won't," came a voice from the crowd.

Hardrada turned his eyes towards the impressive looking officer of the Varangian Guard shouldering his way through the crowd of onlookers. He struck an impressive figure in bronzed lamellar armour and helmet, axe over his shoulder, long hair trailing down his back.

As he drew closer, Hardrada saw the familiar twinkle in the man's eyes and he beamed, "*Ulf*!"

The two men embraced and as the remainder of the crew joined them on the harbour wall, the Byzantine soldiers slinked away, the officer alone remaining.

Ulf held Hardrada at arm's length, "You don't waste your time, do you, eh? Impetuous as ever." He shot a glance towards the Byzantine. "Get yourself back to your station, before I report you to your superiors."

"Report *me*? I was merely doing my duty as a loyal—"

"No, you were trying to feather your own nest, you knave! The Empire has need of such men as these." He grinned towards Hardrada. "This is Harald Sigurdsson, and he comes with references and letters of introduction from the Grand Prince Yaroslav himself." He tilted his head, growing serious. "You could have shown them, Harald, and averted all of this nonsense."

"My lads needed entertaining. Besides, I'm not so sure if my credentials will serve me well. I've heard it say foreigners are not all that welcome in the ranks of his imperial majesty's army, and certainly none of royal blood themselves."

"You think it best to keep your true identity hidden?"

Hardrada shrugged, "Time will tell."

Ulf nodded. "Aye, well, we can talk about all of that back at the barracks, where more entertainment awaits." He stretched up and clamped his arm around the giant Norseman. "We have much drinking to catch up on!"

Forty-One

Amongst the mercenary host, Hardrada's men soon settled down, joining in with the general clamour of laughter, slapping of backs, and the consumption of generous amounts of ale and wine. Hardrada stood apart, drinking slowly, whilst Ulf threaded his way through the carousing press of warriors. Men from a dozen different lands: Norse, English, Normans, men from the wilds of Anatolia, Slavs from the Russian steppe, a smattering of Italians eager to regain the pride of the Roman Empire. Hardrada laughed to himself. So, the Greeks did not like foreigners? They were as fickle as they were devious.

"Some of these men, the *Norse*men, gain promotion into the Varangian Guard."

Hardrada turned to face the man who had sauntered up to him, unheard. Dark-haired, broad-shouldered, intelligent eyes peering out over the rim of his drinking horn. He raised this vessel and took a long draught.

"Varangians are mercenaries, as are all the men here."

"Aye, but not the Guard, and that's where the real riches lie."

Hardrada studied the stranger. "It was my hope to acquire booty in whatever service came my way."

"There are always such opportunities. We must seize them whenever we can, but I believe you would serve the Empire far more effectively as a member of the Guard." He winked, "As your reputation dictates."

"What do you know of my reputation?"

"Much, Harald Sigurdsson. You cannot , nor indeed should you, keep your identity hidden. Already His Imperial Majesty is planning to rid the Aegean of corsairs, who prey upon the islands, seize their treasure, terrorise the population. We have need of men of your calibre, Harald. As leader of your band, you will find yourself in the vanguard of the Empire's strategy to vanquish these pirates from our seas and secure our borders against their incursions."

"Who decides such things? You?"

The stranger chuckled, "No, not I. Like you, I am little more than a captain of men. For now." He went to move away, but Hardrada stopped him with a firm grasp on his arm. The stranger grinned. "We will be comrades, Harald. I hope we will become something more, in time."

"Before that happens, you'll give me your name ... *friend.*"

"Haldor Snorrason, and tomorrow we are to meet with the commander of His Imperial Majesty's endeavour – General Maniakes himself."

The rain beat down as the men assembled on the barrack square the following morning. A buzz of resentment ran through the ranks of warriors, their feet shuffling across the ground, huddled up in cloaks already soaked through. Hardrada stood at the head of his detachment, looking askance at the other captains, water dripping from bronze helms, their eyes staring straight ahead. He recognised Ulf and Haldor, who shot him a knowing smile, and, beyond them, others encased in burnished bronze armour. Twenty-four hours had allowed little time for preparation, but they all seemed capable enough. Arab corsairs were known for their ferocity in battle, but also for their powers of self-survival. When hard pressed, they would always seek to flee in their swift-moving *dhows*. Hardrada wondered how the Byzantines could counter them and thought he might seek out the opinions of the others. But before he took a step, the murmurings of the assembled warriors quietened and he turned his face towards an approaching horseman, resplendent in gleaming cuirass and huge oval shield of azure blue, bearing the Chi-Rho symbol, still so beloved of many Byzantine troops.

However, the most imposing thing about this man was his great size. His prancing white horse carried him well and was, itself, an enormous beast that snorted loudly as the rider reined it in some half dozen paces from the waiting warriors. Hardrada viewed the man keenly, quietly impressed by what he saw. Not many equalled Hardrada for size but, as the man dropped from his saddle, it was clear that here was one to do so.

The officers came to attention, heads lifted despite the rain, and Hardrada unconsciously followed suit, eyes trained ahead.

"We sail at high tide," roared the newcomer before stepping forward to study the ranks before him. "This foul weather will not persist, but will afford us a degree of subterfuge which will act in our favour. You all know to where we sail, and are well aware of how swiftly the Arabs can cross the open sea. My capital ships shall engage them full on, and as those bastards make their escape, the Norsemen amongst you will cut them off in light, highly manoeuvrable *ousiaí*, vessels not unlike your own. We will rid the Greek islands of these scum once and for all."

The men cheered as one, raising their spears and axes aloft, shaking them as if berating the heavy leaden sky for daring to pour down its tempest over them.

And then the man looked to Hardrada and their eyes locked.

He stepped closer, one of the few times the Norseman was able to look another directly in the face.

"I've heard about you, Sigurdsson, and what you did in the harbour."

"If I have offended—"

"If you had, Sigurdsson, your balls would already be floating in the Propontis. I know who you are." As if to put emphasis to his words, he prodded Hardrada hard in the chest with his index finger. "But you'll rein in your haughty ways whilst you're under my command, understand?"

"Your command?"

"I am General George Maniakes. You may think yourself a seasoned warrior, lad, but I am as hard as they come. If you fail me in this your first outing as a serving warrior of the Byzantine Empire, I'll publicly castrate you, and all your dreams will be as this damned, fucking rain – best forgotten. Do you understand me, lad?"

"Aye, General, I do."

"Good." He loomed closer. "You've got royal blood, have you not?" Hardrada nodded. "Then you'll not take kindly to being told what to do. I understand. But what you also need to recognise is that your past is what it is – dead. You're here now and if you wish to keep your position of a commander, you'll obey orders at all times. Am I clear?"

"More than clear."

Maniakes smiled and rocked back on his heels. "Good. But, just as a little assurance, I'm having someone watch over you for a little while." He looked past Hardrada's shoulder and motioned with his chin.

Hardrada frowned, turned and saw him, edging through the ranks. His hands bunched into tight fists and his voice was low and threatening as he said, "I hoped you were dead, Bollason."

"Hello, Harald," said Bolli Bollason. "I'm glad to say I'm not and I'm looking forward to keeping my eye on you, just as I did in the old days."

"*Old* days?" Hardrada sighed and snapped his head again towards Maniakes. "What has he told you?"

"Oh, a great deal. Enough for me to consider you something of a rebel. You have a tendency to do what you think is best and I'll not allow that. So, from now on, you take your orders directly from Bollason."

"Fuck that."

Maniakes shot forward, his hand gripping Hardrada by the front of his jerkin. "Bollason is a commander in the Varangian Guard, Sigurdsson and if you want to *live* and perhaps find a position in the Guard for yourself, you'd do best to follow his lead." He shoved Hardrada from him and took a few steps backwards to address the others. "Get yourself under cover, lads, and wait for orders to assemble. We're going to give those pirates a lesson they'll never forget!"

The men roared again and Maniakes swung up into his saddle and turned his majestic horse away, trotting off into the distance, the rain soon masking him from view.

"If you step out of line," said Bollason, leaning forward to hiss down Hardrada's ear, "I'll flay you alive. And I'll do it with Imperial authority. Now get to your barracks and prepare your men. You're in the lead *ousiai* and it's time to prove your mettle."

Forty-Two

The Byzantines trapped the corsairs in the natural harbour of the small island of Poros, Maniakes's lead ships smashing into the enemy flotilla. One of the dhows made a break for open water. Hardrada, in the bow of his vessel, urged his men to increase their efforts, yelling, "Row, row as if your *lives* were in peril!"

Bollason loomed at his shoulder, spray lashing across his face as the Norsemen strained, putting all of their effort into every pull on the oars, "You'll never make it, Sigurdsson. You'll fail, just like you did at Stiklestad!"

Hardrada's stomach twisted into a knot of barely controlled rage, but he fought it down, knowing all of his attention needed focusing on the task at hand – to cut off the Arabs as they made for open water, and certain escape. He kept his face forward, striking out his hand, "*Row, boys!*"

Continuing to encourage their efforts, Hardrada rushed back to the tiller, gesturing wildly for the steersman to pull hard and turn their ship about. He saw the dhow skimming across the surface of the sea with the speed of tuna, its great sail billowing in the wind. He spotted the crew, their twisting faces jeering, spitting insults, knowing soon they would be beyond reach. With teeth gritted, sinews straining in his neck, Hardrada added his considerable strength to the tiller, screaming over the surging sea, "Faster, you bastards! We cannot lose them!"

And lose them they did not. The Byzantine dromon, as sleek and as swift as any Norse ship, gained speed as men worked as one, backs straining, muscles bulging, fit to burst. Hardrada, breath coming in rasping gasps, watched the smaller, lighter dhow crossing their bow, hands clamped on the tiller. "We've got them, boys, *we've got them!*"

The distance between the two ships narrowed, the angle of approach working in the Viking's favour. Too late, the dhow responded, attempting to veer away from certain collision. With one final surge, the long ship smashed into the Arab vessel, wooden slats shattering like dried twigs under the tremendous momentum of the dromon. At once, the Norsemen leaped to their feet, gathering weapons, and charged, screaming terrifying war cries.

Sent sprawling by the impact, many Arabs had little time to recover before their enemy assailed their stricken ship. Hardrada, at the head of his men, sprang amongst the Arab corsairs, battle axe swinging through the air to strike without pity. Mad with panic, they smashed blindly into each other, but flight proved impossible. As they backed into one another, assaulted from the front, a blood-soaked bottle neck formed, forcing those fortunate to be separated from the deadly struggle, to throw themselves into the sea. With blood erupting from hacked torsos and necks, the Norse waded through their terror-stricken foes, most of whom were rigid with fear, unable utter a cry as blades, spear points and axes cut into them. A few managed a show of resistance, but soon the sheer ferocity of the Viking onslaught overwhelmed even them.

Hardrada stood amongst the fallen, dragging in his breath, blood dripping from his battle axe as around him, his warriors despatched the wounded and dying. He caught sight of two survivors, cowering under the intensity of his gaze. They lifted their hands in a pathetic show of surrender, saliva drooling from the corners of their trembling mouths. Hardrada stepped over to them and, without a blink, hewed the first one's head with a single blow. The second man howled, blubbering incoherently, a limp rag in Hardrada's fist as the giant Norseman lifted up his quarry.

"You're a hard bastard," came a voice and Hardrada glanced sideways as Bolli Bollason stepped up beside him.

"I do what I must."

Bollason smiled, nodding towards the whimpering Corsair, "I'd keep him alive, if I were you. He could tell us where their camp is."

Hardrada grunted, pulling the captive closer, snarling into his face, "Is that true, my little friend? You have a camp?"

The man nodded frantically and Hardrada shoved him away, sending him clattering to the deck, amongst his dead comrades. He yelped, rolling over onto his feet, blabbering in a flurry of Arabic.

"Get him to tell you where his base is," Hardrada said to one of his men, "then set a course for it." He swung around, looming over Bollason, his voice low, threatening, "You ever say anything about Sticklestad again and I'll kill you."

Bollason cocked his head, feigning dread. "Oh my, your words do set my heart to pound. What's the matter, Harald, the truth too hard to swallow?"

"If you knew anything about the truth of that day, you wouldn't be so quick to judge. You weren't even there."

"No, but I've heard the tales. But you were nothing more than a boy back then..." Nodding his head, he surveyed the dead corsairs strewn across the decks, "I can see you are a boy no longer."

Hardrada turned his mouth down, disgust mixing with anger, and he swung away and barked, "Get these bodies overboard, then work on freeing our ship!"

"Like I say, you're a hard bastard. It'll be your undoing."

Hardrada looked at Bollason again, eyes narrowing, "I'll tell you something, something I want you to take heed of." He took a step forward, noted how Bollason tensed, hand dropping to his sword, and he smiled. "*I'll* be *your* undoing, Boli Bollason."

Bollason's expression this time remained cold, unblinking. "From now on, I'll not call you Sigurdsson, but *Hardrada.* Hard you are, and your rule shall be hard too, I shouldn't wonder. But you'll make enemies along the way and one of them will lay you low." His eyes creased into something akin to humour, "And it might just be me."

"We can end this now, Bollason. Here, or ashore, I care not." His eyes locked onto his shorter adversary, well aware of the man's strength and prowess, having experienced it not so many years before .

"After we've taken their camp, shared out the spoils, you and I can have our reckoning. It is something I have longed for, *Hardrada*." He licked his lips, "Enjoy your life whilst you still can, for today you *die*."

"The General!"

Both of them jumped at the great cry and Hardrada looked past Bollason's shoulder to the Byzantine flagship looming close. He stepped away, "Hurry men, we must get our ship free and make haste to the pirate camp," he chuckled, "before our beloved general puts a stop to our fun!" As his crew scurried around, some lifting up corpses to drop them into the sea, others working at prising their ship from the shattered dhow, Hardrada glanced over to Bollason. "And then the entertainment will truly begin."

Forty-Three

The fleet dropped anchor in the bay and Maniakes sent signals for the captains to assemble on the shoreline. Hardrada, ruffled not only by his altercation with Bollason, but also from having to delay his assault on the corsair's base, waded through the shallows to do Maniakes's bidding.

A group of a dozen or more swarthy, weatherbeaten Byzantine sailors, eyed the approaching Viking with a mix of disdain and curiosity. Hardrada ignored them, pausing for a moment to wash the blood from his hands in the shallows of the crystal clear waters of the bay, before he stepped up to the General to salute him in the time-honoured way of the old Roman Empire. "*Salve,* my lord."

Maniakes lifted his helmet from his head and arched a single eyebrow. "Impressive, Sigurdsson. I watched you overwhelming those bastards, and I'll ensure our divine Emperor hears of your abilities."

"I'm honoured, General."

Maniakes allowed his eyes to settle on Bollason as he surged ashore. "He fared well, Bollason, don't you think?"

"Some," returned the Varangian commander begrudgingly, shaking out his boots. "We still have work to do before victory can be truly guaranteed. They have a camp not so very far. We should assault it without delay, before any word reaches them of what has happened here this day."

"I must make a report to the Emperor," said Maniakes, addressing the other assembled captains. "We have a chance to not only crush this menace once and for all, but to also seize the riches they have stolen. Remember, ten percent of whatever we recover goes into your own coffers." He turned to look at the two Vikings. "That should bring joy to your hearts, eh?"

Bollason chuckled whilst Hardrada remained stoic. "We have the location of their camp, General. We need nothing more."

"Then make sail, whilst we reconnoitre here. We must leave nothing to chance."

"Fear not, General," said Bollason, shooting a glance towards Hardrada, "we shall not fail the Empire."

Maniakes nodded, "Then so be it!"

* * *

They came ashore in the late afternoon. Three ships, the leading two captained by Hardrada and Bollason. Fast, sleek dromons, which the Vikings beached. Behind, in the bay, a much larger Byzantine galleon, anchored, gently bobbing in the calm waters. On its decks, armoured spearmen, waiting for the call, watched the Norsemen hitting the beach at a run.

Running to the left, Hardrada signalled for his men to spread out. The shoreline soon gave way to deep, soft sand, punctuated with clumps of sharp marram grass and, beyond, rolling dunes bordered by a tree line of palms. Hardrada stopped at the foot of the hummocks of sand and, taking in deep breaths, glanced across to see Bollason already plunging into the thick undergrowth.

He turned to the Arab captive shivering next to him. "How many of your men are here?"

The corsair lifted his face to the giant Norseman and, dumbfounded, merely shrugged.

"I don't think he understands," said a warrior standing close by.

"He understood well enough when we took him," spat Hardrada and squinted into the trees. Close packed, they offered little opportunity to pick out any signs more than a few paces within. "I don't like this. We should circle around if we can." He scanned the beach, both left and right. Way over, farther than where Bollason had careered into the trees, a cliff face rose up, giving a commanding view of the bay. "Where in the name of Christ are we?"

It was the other warrior's turn to shrug. "Two days it has taken us to cross from Poros to here. Perhaps this is Serkland."

Hardrada frowned and, without warning, took the cringing Arab by the collar, shaking him as if he were a rag toy. "Is this Serkland? Answer me, you bastard, or I'll cut out your heart!"

A low moan came out of the young corsair's mouth and he sagged in Hardrada's grip, knees buckling as a dribble of urine splattered into the sand at his feet. Disgusted, Hardrada flung him backwards into the sand, where he squirmed, flapping his arms, eyes alive with dread. "*Yes, my lord, yes. It is Serkland! I have been here before and know it well.*"

"Then we had best move with caution," said the warrior, leaning close to Hardrada's ear. "This may be the land of the Caliph of Tunis and if it is, we are sure to be overwhelmed."

"Aye," Hardrada blew out his cheeks, looking out across the bay to the Byzantine galleon. "Get a signal to the captain. We need his men to set camp here whilst we reconnoitre further inland. I'll gather the men and then we move on, with care. Not like Bollason, the fucking oaf. What does he think he is doing, rushing forward the way he did?"

"I think he has been here before."

Hardrada snapped his head towards the warrior. "What did you say?"

"Did you not notice how he took his ship ahead of ours, despite us having the captive?"

"I did, but I assumed he set lookouts to mirror our progress."

The warrior shook his head, "I do not think so. Boli Bollason is renowned for setting out on his own journeys, regardless of orders. He knows there is booty here, all he needed was the opportunity. With the corsairs defeated, he now has a clear run to their base *and* their riches."

Hardrada stared into the depths of the woodland, simmering with rage. The knots tightened in his gut. "Then we cut the bastard off." He glared at the Arab corsair, curled up in a ball, whimpering. "He'll show us the way whilst you get a signal to the Byzantine galleon." He lifted his axe high above his head, "Onward, lads, and keep your wits about you!"

At the given signal, the Norsemen plunged in amongst the trees, Hardrada pushing forward, holding the quaking corsair ahead of him as a form of shield.

Despite their utmost, the sound of their crashing boots amongst the dry, brittle undergrowth amplified through the close, heavy woodland. No birds sang or animals scurried and the heat collected amongst the branches causing progress to slow and sweat to erupt from every pore. Within the space of a hundred paces, every man was drenched.

There seemed no end to it. Every way Hardrada looked, the only sight that greeted him was one of trees. It proved impossible to steer any form of course and soon the company became disgruntled, the men muttering to one another, shoulders slumped, heads hanging low. Hardrada, eyes skyward, managed to navigate some constant direction by keeping the descending sun to his left shoulder. However, as evening drew on, shadows lengthened and the darkness around them grew, his despair gripped him like a foe around his throat and he stopped, holding up his arm. His company gathered around, all of them blowing and snuffling, some gasping.

"Take some time, lads. We'll rest here."

"This is madness," said one of the men, slumping down amongst the sprawling roots of the trees pressing in on every side. "We should go back, Harald."

Hardrada pressed his lips together, knew the sense of the man's words. But to go back … He looked through the trees to the direction they had come. "It's too far, and with the night coming on we'll be hopelessly lost. Best if we rest, then continue."

"But we'll be lost going forward," said another.

"Either way, there is nothing we can do," chimed in a third. "We'd best set camp here."

Hardrada scanned the woodland floor. There was barely room for a man to stretch himself out, but propped up against a tree trunk, it might suffice. At least they would be warm. As if to convince himself, he dragged his arm across his soaking forehead and gazed at the sweat on his skin. "Listen, we'll move on for as long as the light holds, then we'll camp until dawn. For all we know, we might be in reach of a clearing, or even the corsairs' camp."

Voices rumbled. "Bollason knew where he was going. Notice the way he took to the far side without even discussing it."

"Aye, the bastard knows where he is, for sure."

"He's been here before."

"He's been everywhere before. We should have stuck with him, at least his men are safe."

"Aye, and rich by Christ."

"*Enough!*"

Every face turned wide-eyed to Hardrada who stood, feet planted wide apart, his body trembling, hands wrapped around the shaft of his great axe, whites of his knuckles showing through. "Enough, you bastards! Bollason's played me for a fool, hoping we'd lose ourselves in this hellish place, spend days going around and around until we drop and die from thirst. Well, it's not going to happen. We're going to get through and if any of you doubt my words, then speak up now and you're free to go."

The men exchanged glances. A company of almost forty warriors, heavily armed, some with byrnies, four large metal rings connected to a central one, others with lamellar armour, all of them tired, despondent and irritable. As they fell in clumps amongst the roots, many ripped off their armour, casting it aside, pulled off their linen shirts and jerkins and tried their best to relax. Not one took up Hardrada's challenge.

Hardrada pulled the Arab corsair aside, pressing himself up close to the weatherbeaten, cracked leather of the captive's flat face. "How far are we from your camp?"

The man's mouth fell open, revealing worn, blackened teeth, and he whimpered in his strange, sing-song voice, "Not so far, great one. You have come farther than he had left to go."

Hardrada nodded. "Tell me, what do you know of Bollason?" The man frowned and Hardrada, whose patience was brittle at the best of times, gripped and twisted the man's collar, pulling him closer. "The other Viking leader, the one as broad as he is tall. You know him?"

The man clawed feebly at Hardrada's hand, gasping, "*Please*, great one."

Relaxing his grip a fraction, Hardrada retained most of the pressure, unwilling to let the captive think he may yet survive. "Answer me."

"He is known to me, yes. To *all* of us, great one." Another tug from Hardrada and the man became desperate, words tumbling out in a mad scramble, "He came to us, two summers ago, and he spoke with our leader, Abn Haider. They often met, great one, and the Viking we call 'The Bull', would bring gifts."

"*Gifts*? What sort of gifts did he bring?"

"Weapons, for the most part. Maps, charts, sometimes—"

Hardrada unconsciously twisted the corsair's collar tighter, "Charts? By Christ, Bollason told you where to raid? How to get there?"

The man's efforts to disentangle Hardrada's hold grew more desperate, and he kicked at Hardrada's shins, squawking as he tried to wrestle himself free.

With total indifference, Hardrada released his grip and the man fell, clutching at his throat, sobbing uncontrollably. Hardrada stepped over to him and motioned for his men to listen. "Lads, we're not so very far from the camp. It seems Bolli has been here before, which explains his reckless charge through the woodland. If we tarry too long here, he'll take the loot for himself and that I cannot allow. So, gather yourselves, my lads, and keep your weapons close."

"Can we not rest for a few moment- looking warrior slumped against a nearby tree. "Would you allow yourself to sleep whilst the chance of riches goes begging? No, lads, there'll be time enough for sleep after we've filled our knapsacks with treasure." He lifted his axe. "Let's go and meet our dear old friend Bolli!"

Grumbling and sighing, the men climbed to their feet, shaking themselves, breathing hard. Slowly they one by one struck out once more through the trees and Hardrada, watching them pass by, paused and looked down at the snivelling corsair. "If you're lying to me, I'll cut off your balls and hang you from the highest tree."

"I am not lying, great one." He sat up, wiping away his tears with the palm of his hand. "You will see. There is treasure in our camp, enough for all."

"Well, you'd better be right because if Bollason has taken it already, I might just castrate you anyway." He grinned, "Just for the fun of it."

Forty-Four

General Maniakes placed his sword and helmet at the foot of the steps and made his way up to the entrance. From within came the hypnotic chants of the priests and the slight whiff of incense floated through to his nostrils. He gave an involuntary shudder. Churches always caused him discomfort, especially this one. The Hagia Sofia, the finest and greatest church in all the world. After striding through the hallowed halls of the great Imperial Palace, its vaulted ceilings decorated with gold embossed frescoes of the saints, he prepared himself for what awaited him here. He lightly pressed his fingertips against the solid door closest to him and it wheezed open. Taking a breath, he stepped inside.

Lit from the flames of a thousand candles, the enormous space appeared to be filled with liquid gold, every niche, apse, corridor and aisle aglow. And in their seats, the good and the great of Byzantium, their ceremonial robes mirroring the splendour of the surroundings. Bejewelled, magnificent, shimmering, the dignitaries and nobility responded as one to the incantations of the patriarch who stood, arms and face uplifted, at the top of the far off dais. And before him, ready to accept his blessing, knelt the Emperor and Empress themselves.

The priests sang out, voices growing in volume, and it was as if the very building responded.Iits perfect acoustics delivering such awe, such flesh-tingling sensations, Maniakes felt the stirrings of something akin to emotion playing with his eyes.

A movement beside him caused him to jump. He turned, saw who it was, and tried his best not to groan.

John Orphano, chief administrator of the empire, dressed in a plain, short-sleeved white robe, hemmed with royal purple, which barely covered his ample midriff, stood leaning against a nearby pillar. His arms folded, he regarded the general with a slight smirk before he sighed, looked down the nave, and crossed himself three times with a dramatic flurry of his hand. He then motioned Maniakes to follow him outside.

"Your little sortie to the islands proved a great success, so I am led to believe."

Maniakes came down the steps to join the eunuch, struggling to keep the disgust from his voice, "You know a lot."

"Well, I try to keep abreast of the mechanics of our illustrious armed forces." He smiled, his slack lips glistening with something Maniakes preferred not to contemplate. "Where is the booty?"

"We have yet to seize it all. A company of Vikings, with some support from—"

"Varangians?"

"No, a group recently arrived from Kiev. They seem hardy enough, if a little rough around the edges. Bolli Bollason led them, and did well in overpowering one of the Arab dhows that made a break for open water." Maniakes shuffled his feet, growing uncomfortable under Orphano's unceasing stare. "I think he should be rewarded with a command in the Varangian Guard. His loyalty and skill are unquestioned."

"You would have him afforded the title of *manglavites,* just like Bollason himself?" Maniakes nodded. "Well, if he is as capable as you say, I shall mention him to the emperor and we will arrange for the ceremony of the Red Sword for him as soon as he returns."

"That is most gracious of you."

"Yes, it is … isn't it?"

Maniakes stiffened slightly, raising a single eyebrow. "What do you mean by that?"

Orphano shrugged, "Only that I heard it was another who led the attack. A young Norseman by the name of Harald Sigurdsson."

Maniakes sucked in a breath, but stopped himself before he betrayed too much of his surprise. "Indeed, you *do* know a lot."

"I make it my business, General. I am the eyes and ears of the Emperor and his beloved Empress. No doubt His Highness will wish to know why Sigurdsson is not being rewarded ... " His voice trailed away, waiting for Maniakes to offer up an explanation.

"He is brave, but young and headstrong. Bollason took command."

"I see. And then what happened?"

"I ordered them to sail to the mainland and seek out the pirates' camp. They had a captive. No doubt he showed them the way."

"Yes, no doubt." He closed his eyes, turning his face to the sun. "North Africa is not the most welcoming of places. I do hope they return."

"I'm sure they will. And when they return, we will have everything those bastards stole."

Orphano snapped his eyes open and shot Maniakes an angry stare. "General, *please*, you are on the steps of the holiest place in all of Byzantium!"

Maniakes held up his hands, "Apologies. I sometimes forget myself." Inside, he seethed. How dare this overfed upstart chastise him like some prick of a schoolboy! He shuffled his feet and readjusted his belt, anything to give him a moment to quieten his temper before he spoke again. "Sigurdsson is some relation to Olaf, the defeated king of the Norse."

"Yes, so I understand. He was wounded, yes? In the same battle in which his half-brother was killed?"

"Stiklegard, yes. If you're contemplating any form of reward, I would limit it to a commission in the Guard. A squad leader, nothing more. I think the lad will be a thorn in our sides before long."

"Because of his royal associations?"

"Yes. And he seems to have an unsavoury ability to make enemies."

"Yes. Bolli Bollason being one, so I understand."

Is there nothing this man does not know? The General decided to seek out the eunuch's spy and split his tongue, but knew he would have to act carefully. Orphano's reach was long and deep.

"But do not concern yourself too much," continued Orphano, a tiny glint playing around the outer corners of his eyes, "Her Royal Highness has made mention of her interest in this young Norseman. I am to arrange an audience."

"An *audience*?" Maniakes gasped, all patience gone. "But is that wise? The man is a barbarian, a ruffian! He has not the wit or the grace to be in the presence of the empress!"

"Oh, I think you exaggerate, my dear General." He reached over and patted Maniakes by the arm. "All shall be well. Trust me."

And with that, he swung about and returned up the steps to the great doors of the Hagia Sofia. After a few moments, Maniakes followed him, the heat rising to his face and for a long time could not gather his thoughts into one, coherent sentence.

The service drawing to a close now, the congregation rose to their feet, the priests swinging incense as they progressed along the central aisle. Maniakes pressed himself as best he could into a niche between a pillar and the wall. His size gave him away and the Patriarch, on seeing the General, smirked and motioned him to step outside once again.

Without a pause, Alexius took Maniakes by the elbow and took him out of earshot. He glanced back to the doorway where Orphano stood, wringing his hands, bowing and smiling as the procession of aristocrats traipsed by.

"His Highness is not well," said the Patriarch of all Byzantium in concerned, low tones. "I hope you have not brought ill news, General."

"Not at all. Hasn't the eunuch told you?"

"Pah, he keeps whatever he can close to his chest. You know that as well as I. All I know for certain is the corsairs, who have plagued the Aegean for these past months, have been swept away. Is it so?"

"More than swept, Holiness. Destroyed would be a better word."

"That is good news indeed. His Highness will be most pleased." A dark look came over the Patriarch's face. "He had another attack yesterday. I begged him not to attend this mass, but he insisted, saying it might help his condition. You see how he quakes?"

Maniakes turned to the massive doorway. The press of royal dignitaries, ambassadors, courtiers, milled about like bees, with Michael the Fourth, Emperor of the Byzantine Empire in the centre, his face still comely, smiling, accepting the devotions of his ardent supporters. But as he looked, Maniakes saw the quivering mouth, the left eye drooping from one corner, the slow, ponderous way the emperor lifted his hands to make the sign of the cross. Of his wife, the tempestuous Zoe, there was no sign. They rarely accompanied one another nowadays. No doubt she had made her exit through the so-called 'secret' passageway which led to the Imperial Palace.

"He seems confused," said Maniakes. Choosing his words carefully.

"Oh, he is more than that, General. This is a good day. His attacks are becoming more frequent, so much so we have erected a red curtain around his throne, so we may shield him from the gaze of others once his eyes begin to roll." He put his hand on the General's arm once again, "I'm deeply worried, General. I do not have to tell you what might happen to the empire should this great and noble man die."

Maniakes snapped his head around, "Surely to God you don't think—"

"General," Alexius shot a glance upwards, to the great dome of the Hagia Sofia, "*please* do not take the Lord's name in vain. Be aware the emperor grows daily more and more weak, and Orphano tightens his grip on every organ of government. If Michael should die, I fear the eunuch will place his own creature on the throne."

"Zoe wouldn't let him."

"Her Highness has her own mind, for sure, but her interests have little to do with who sits on the royal throne, and more to do with how much money she can spend."

"Or lovers she can bed."

Alexius winced, his voice low with disgust, "Indeed."

"I might be able to help in that regard, Holiness."

"*You?*" Alexius appeared shocked, mouth dropping. "You don't mean that you have desires to—"

"No, Holiness, not *me*." He chuckled. "No, her Highness rebuked my advances long, long ago." He shook his head, allowing the memory to rear up in his mind. Zoe lying on a couch, maids massaging her feet, painting her nails, combing her hair. Maniakes standing before her in a linen robe, the Empress gazing at the bulge so prominent beneath the fine material. How she had gestured for him to move closer. How, as his ardour rose, she licked her lips, then directed one of her handmaidens to lead him into the adjoining bedroom so they all could listen.

"Who then?"

Maniakes blinked, for a moment lost in the images of those satin sheets, of the girl's long, slim thighs. He shook his head, "I have an idea, Holiness. A man, recently arrived in the City. Her Highness has already professed an interest, and Orphano is arranging a meeting. However, I know this man and, given the right encouragement, I feel he could serve us well."

"I don't follow you, General. Serve us well how?"

Maniakes smiled, leaned across and patted the old man's forearm. "In ways your calling does not allow you to dwell too much upon, Holiness. Leave the details to me."

"You play a dangerous game, General. Do not make yourself an enemy of Orphano. As the emperor's brother, his power knows no limits."

"Oh, I'm well aware of that, Holiness. But I am more subtle than I look. The empire has need of me, if my reports are correct. Spies have brought me news of activity in Sicily which does not bode well. I will seek and audience with the Emperor and, whilst I'm at it, perhaps a word with the Empress too. Orphano has designs to use this man for his own gain, but I think I may just be able to outflank him."

"This isn't a battlefield, General."

"Isn't it? I think you'll find it is, Holiness."

He bowed and went to move away, but the Patriarch caught his arm. "Who is this man of whom you speak, General? Do I know him?"

"No, not yet. But I think you soon shall. His name is Harald Sigurds-son, and he is one to watch if we all know what is good for us."

Forty-Five

No one knew how long they spent on the north coast of Africa. They went from one arid, barren place to the next, upturning rocks, exploring caves, ransacking lost villages and as they moved through the land, they accumulated their wealth.

Bollason sat like a king in the centre of the camp, regaling the men with stories of his past adventures, and they listened like children, hanging on every word. In the background, Harald Hardrada steamed, arms crossed, stoic. They all called him Hardrada now. He cared not. Two things alone dominated his thoughts. How much gold was his, and how he could undermine Bollason.

His opportunity came on the evening the Caliph of Tunis finally caught up with them.

At the end of a productive day, the men settled down around several well-stocked fires, some to eat or drink, others to stretch themselves out and ponder what lay ahead. Hardrada stood watching the setting sun, the sky alive with bands of violet and red and something else.

He squinted towards what he at first believed to be a sand storm. Often in that barren wasteland, a sudden eruption of wind would cause great clouds of sand to envelop everything in sight. The speed and intensity of such storms were frightening, but the men adapted themselves well, their Arab captive explaining how to protect themselves. The man had proved his worth more than once and now, as Hardrada stood and peered into the distance, he came up beside him and sucked in his breath.

"Lord, I fear this is no storm."

Hardrada looked down at him. Even in the half-light, his deeply bronzed face seemed as if made from boiled leather, the deep cracks around his eyes and mouth chiselled away from years of exposure to the unrelenting sun. "What else?"

"Riders, Lord." The man shook his head. "They travel fast and their course is clear."

Hardrada immediately drew his sword and went to turn when the Arab held up his hand, "Lord. There is only one such man who has enough riders to produce such a cloud. The Caliph himself." He shook his head. "It would not be wise to provoke him. His reach is long, his power great. *And,* he is a friend of the Byzantine Emperor."

"You know a great deal."

The man shrugged, looking coy, "Lord, I survive. Knowledge is power, is it not?"

Hardrada considered the Arab corsair for a momen. Then, reaching his decision, slid his sword back into its sheath, and took to chewing his bottom lip as a thought came into his head, small at first, but taking root rapidly. He grinned. "A friend of the Emperor, eh?"

"Oh yes. My companions and I often had to run the gauntlet of his ships, but we almost always managed to escape."

"Almost always? What happened when you didn't?"

"He would take his share of the booty, Lord. We had ... an unspoken agreement. Twenty percent."

Hardrada raised his eyes. "Favourable."

"He is a merciful man, Lord. So long as the deal is brokered."

Nodding to himself, Hardrada strode back to the camp. Some of the men smiled or gave a lazy salute, most ignored him. Except one. Bolli Bollason stood outside his tent, drinking from a goatskin gourd. He cocked an eyebrow as the giant Viking approached, smacked his lips and grinned, "You seem pleased with yourself."

"So shall you be."

"Oh?" He put the cork stopper into the gourd and threw it into his tent. "How so?"

"The Caliph's men are on their way. At least a hundred."

Bollason tensed, hand automatically curling around the hilt of his sword. "That many? Are you sure?"

Hardrada motioned to where the cloud of sand spread across the horizon. He also noted the first sounds of pounding hooves, like the distant rumble of thunder. "Look for yourself."

"We'd best break camp, make our way to the hills. The night will cover our withdrawal."

"I've something to tell you."

"Oh? You've always been a man of secrets, Harald. Not all of them good."

"I visited the Caliph some nights ago."

Bollason frowned. "When?"

Hardrada shrugged, "Whilst you slept. I took the corsair."

"Why would you do that?"

"To make a deal. It seems the Caliph expects a share of our treasure."

"A *share*? You mean, you promised him a percentage of our booty, without first consulting me?" The grip on his sword tightened. "I grow tired of you, *boy*. I let you live in order for you to help me in my endeavours. I too have met with the Caliph, *many* times. We made our arrangements then. He is to take ten percent of what we have. Of the remainder, the Emperor wants forty percent."

"That is what he told me, except the arrangements have changed."

"You'd better speak plainly, and quickly." He jutted his chin towards the approaching horsemen. By now, those in the camp aware of their approach, hastily gathered together their weapons, grumbling and scrambling around in the dirt.

"He wants fifty percent and, whatever is left, we share with the Emperor."

"A pox on that."

"I agreed."

Bollason's mouth fell open. "You did *what*?"

"The Emperor knows you've been embezzling him for months. Your unaccounted absences from camp, greasing your palm with stolen, pirate gold." Hardrada shook his head. "Now they've come to take you back, Bolli. The Caliph and the Emperor want your balls on a spit."

The big Icelander took short gasps, pressing the back of his hand against his mouth, eyes wide with doubt, confusion, perhaps even a tinge of fear. "Why have you waited until now to tell me this?"

Hardrada shrugged, "To be honest, I never actually believed the Caliph would come." He swung around. The riders were plain to see now, cloaks billowing in the wind, lances pointing down, all of them blackened silhouettes against the setting sun, tingeing their outlines with a blood red glow. "But clearly, the Emperor is not best pleased with your little schemes, Bolli." He smiled as he turned to face his enemy. "He's willing to pay the Caliph a handsome reward for your safe return."

"You bastard, you wait until now to tell me this? By Christ, I'll split your skull, you bastard."

He drew his sword, but before it had cleared the scabbard, Hardrada was on him, hand gripping the man's sword arm as his knee swung up into his unprotected groin. Bollason yelped and Hardrada took him around the waist, and threw him over his hip to dump him into the hard dirt.

Before Bollason reacted, Hardrada had his knife against the man's throat, "I've grown stronger and quicker, Bolli, whilst you've grown fat and slow."

Bollason squirmed beneath the giant Viking, tears running from eyes screwed up in agony. "Bastard," he hissed.

"No, not so much, Bolli. I'm giving you a chance. Take a horse, and get out of here, now. I'll think of something to tell the Caliph."

Bollason, despite his pain and anguish, gawped at the man straddling him. "I don't believe you."

"Oh, what do you think I'll do? Put an arrow in your back? Why would I do that when I can hand you over to the Caliph right now?"

Bollason, whimpering, blinked and gasped. Slowly, the focus returned to his eyes, and reasoning overcame the agony. "Why would you do this?"

Hardrada shrugged and stepped away, sheathing his knife, "God alone knows, Bolli. I've reason enough to see your head on a pike, but…" He looked across to where the rest of the company were strapping on armour, picking up shields, readying swords and axes, "Stand-to, lads. Those are the Caliph's men. They are not here to kill us." He thrust out his hand towards Bollason, who took it, and hauled himself to his feet. "You'd best go quickly. Take whatever you can in a knapsack, but do it now, Bolli. I can't guarantee your fate if you stay."

Bollason held Hardrada's gaze. "I'll not forget this, Harald." He gripped the young Viking's hand. "I have wronged you in the past and for that I am now ashamed. For you to show such mercy…" He shook his head. "Christian virtue flows through your veins, lad. I am honoured to have known you."

He turned around and slipped away, bent double, crossing to the far side of the camp to where the horses were tethered, mounts captured on one of their many raids during the past weeks. As the sound of him riding away in the opposite direction disappeared into the night, Hardrada, barely able to keep the smirk from his face, went over to the men and stood, hands on hips. "Come on, lads. Get yourself sorted out. Make no sudden moves, and keep your weapons down. We play this right and none of us will be in any danger."

"Where's Bolli?" came a voice from the descending darkness.

Hardrada glanced over to the far side and sighed, "He played a dangerous game with the Caliph. Seems like he tried to swindle the old bastard, and now it's caught up with him."

The men muttered to themselves, some sounding surprised, most accepting Hardrada's words without question.

"Lord," said the Arab corsair, stepping up close to Hardrada. "Is it not you who plays a dangerous game?"

"Maybe," returned Hardrada, "but now the Caliph deals with me, and me alone."

"And if he learns of the truth, Lord?"

"And what truth might that be, eh?"

"He knows Bollason. He will wish to speak with him, as he is the one he trusts."

"I'll come up with something, don't worry."

"As you have come up with the story you have weaved this night, lord?" The man chuckled, "You should be a storyteller, Lord. A *skald*, I think you call such men in your language. Those who write the sagas, create the legends."

Hardrada now laughed, shaking his head. "Is that what I am, do you think? A legend?"

"I believe you will be, lord. Whatever you told Bollason, worked. Now you must continue to play the game with the Caliph. Let us hope your life continues after this night, and your legend too."

Hardrada frowned, fingers creeping towards his knife. This Arab was the only one who knew the falsehood of what he had told Bollason. Perhaps killing him would be the safest course. But before he made his decision, the riders pounded into the camp, horses snorting, weapons and armour jangling, the ground rumbling as they surrounded the anxious Norsemen, with Hardrada at their head. His eyes burned into the Arab. "Tell me your name," he said.

"Taymur," and he gave a small bow.

"Well, Taymur, you say one word, and you're the first to die."

Another slight incline of the head and then he stood, as silent as the rest, and waited.

Forty-Six

The royal physician came out of the Emperor's bedroom, face lined with worry. He could not force himself to look at John Orphano, who stood a little way off, head tilted, severe. "Well?"

The physician shook his head, "He is not good, my Lord."

"I could tell that much myself, you ass!"

The man quailed, seeming to shrink inside himself. "Lord, the attacks grow more frequent. I fear the stresses and strains of government are too much. He needs to be quiet, to rest as much as possible."

Orphano grunted and stepped forward, "*Rest*? He's the Emperor of New Rome, you ass. How is he meant to rest?" He blew out his cheeks and looked past the physician to the two bodyguards who flanked the entrance to the room beyond the double doors. "You cannot give him a potion? Something to still the heat in his blood?"

"I have bled him, my Lord, and he appears better for it. Perhaps a purge…" He cupped his chin in his fingers. "Tomorrow. If his condition is not improved, I shall evacuate his bowels. But in the meantime, as I said, he must rest." He bowed, "My Lord."

Orphano watched the little man scurry away into the vastness of the imperial palace, his soft sandals making no sound on the marble floor. He glanced across to the guards. "No one is to enter, you understand?" The two men straightened their backs, slamming shields against their chests in a form of salute. "And if the Emperor wakes, or makes any move to leave this room, you come and fetch me. At once!"

He turned about and strode through the broad corridors towards his apartments, passing courtiers and government officials on his way, dismissing their attempts to question him with a flurry of his hand. He had no time for their fake mutterings of concern, not now. Not with the news he received that very morning still playing around in his head.

Bursting through the door he made straight for the wine jug set upon a marble topped table and poured himself a generous goblet. As he drank he gazed across to the open balcony, the vista before him of the great city often stilled his heart, cleared his mind. But not this morning. He let the wine swill around his mouth, enjoying its sweetness. Good Italian wine, infused with herbs and spices, meant, like the view, to bring him a sense of well-being. He closed his eyes, swallowed, concentrated on the banging of his heart. There were some who said it was possible to lessen the heartbeat if one focused. Focused. He could do nothing but focus.

Damn those bloody Saracens.

A low moan came from his bedroom and he remembered, with a jolt, the lithe youth he'd left beneath the sheets when the guards came running with news of Michael's latest attack. Smiling, Orphano put down his wine and went into the other room.

The youth reclined in the bed, bedclothes thrown back, barely covering his lower abdomen. A thrill ran through Orphano as he recalled the treasure which lay there. He stepped forward and looked down to the fur rug on the far side of the great bed, and the girl lying there in a foetal position, naked, her soft breasts rising and falling, exhausted. The young man had made love to her throughout the night, her cries of pleasure ringing out around the room as he took her in more ways than Orphano thought possible.

"You discovered all of this for yourself?" asked Orphano when the youth took a moment to lie back, sample wine, rest his hand on the well-rounded buttocks of the girl, index finger swirling over the taut flesh.

"I lived in India," he said, "as my mother came from there. They have a tradition of using physical pleasures as a means to reach paradise."

"Indeed?" Orphano sat down on the corner of the bed and stared at the girl's smooth curves. A longing to be able to reach out, flip her over, and plunge into her soft, willing flesh, overcame him and he almost cried out with frustration. They'd taken his balls, those bastards, and he'd writhed in a makeshift bed for days, the pain overwhelming him. Two old men administered to him, cleaning the wounds, applying fresh bandages every few hours. They forced foul tasting solutions down his throat, ensuring him they would ease the pain. It may well have done, but nothing could relieve the sense of shame, the awful knowledge that love, and love-making, were things he would never experience again. How many years ago was that now? A hundred? It felt like it. "Physical pleasure for me is an impossibility. But I take comfort in knowing I can watch such a lover as you give so much pleasure, so selflessly."

As if taking the hint, the youth put away his wine, rolled the girl onto her back, and dipped his lips towards her sweet sex.

And now, here he was, sitting, smiling with such self-confidence, Orphano took almost as much pleasure in that as he had at observing his lustful thrusts. "I would give anything to be you," he said quietly.

"But, my lord," said the youth, leaning forward, "you have the whole world at your feet, riches beyond imagining, power beyond dreams! I, in comparison, have nothing."

"No," Orphano shook his head, a single tear rolling down his face. He gripped the cover and threw it back, and stared down at the youth's long, thick manhood, lying like a club against his thigh. "You have *everything*." He spent a long time gazing down at the youth's manhood before suddenly jumping up, anger replacing admiration. "Get dressed and get out. And take this whore with you."

"Lord, if I have offended you, then—"

"You haven't offended me." Orphano turned away, biting his lip, fighting back the tears. He did not wish the youth to see how affected, even jealous he was. So, keeping his back to him, Orphano went over to the far side, unlocked an intricately carved cabinet of seasoned teak, and brought out a large box. Another key, which he kept on his belt, allowed him to delve inside and he turned and threw the youth a leather purse bulging with coins.

The youth caught it, weighted in his hand, and beamed. "You are generous, lord."

"You will come again, in three days." He nodded to the girl who was slowly rousing herself, stretching out her slim form like a cat. "And bring her. What is her name?"

"Leoni, lord. But she is nothing but a scullery maid. If you prefer, I could find—"

"No. I want her. I've never seen such a body and if I am to be so punished watching you make love to someone else, I would rather it was someone as delicious as she. Now go, and not a word of this to anyone or I'll have you both drowned in the Horn."

They both scurried out, the youth pulling the girl out of the apartment by the wrist, gathering up bits of clothing as they went. Orphano flopped down on the bed, brought the sheet to his nose and breathed in the scent of sex. When the door banged shut to leave him alone, he allowed the tears to come unchecked. He folded himself up into a ball, twisting the material of the bedclothes tightly around him, and wept until his eyes grew puffy and raw.

* * *

The tentative knock on his door caused Maniakes to look up from the piece of parchment laid out on his desk. He grumbled, "Enter," and finished the sentence he was on before sitting back in his chair.

"Jonas," he said.

The youth shuffled in, bowing his head. "General."

"You have news?"

"Only that the Lord Orphano was called away early this morning, by Imperial bodyguards."

"Don't call him 'lord', Jonas. The man's a worm. Call him 'Orphano' if you must, but not 'lord'. It sticks in my craw."

"Yes, General." The youth bowed his head again.

Maniakes caught a movement beyond the heavy scarlet drapes separating the inner area of his tent from the annexe. Maniakes, although private apartments waited for him in the Imperial Palace, chose to make his campaign tent his place of work whenever he was in the City. It helped remind him of who he was; a rough, low-born soldier who had risen by his abilities, not by privilege. "Who is outside?"

The youth half turned, "A girl, General. It was … *Orphano's* wish that I took her to his bed and ravished her whilst he watched."

"Dear Christ, the man is a degenerate." Maniakes smirked. "Bring her in. I'd like to take a look at her."

Without hesitation, Jonas dipped through the gap in the curtains and returned with the girl.

Maniakes gaped. She stood in a long, virtually transparent white shift, which concealed nothing of her superb body, the full breasts, slim waist, rounded hips. And her legs … as long and as slim as any he had seen. He stood up, his eyes bulging, throat drying, loins pulsing. "My God," he managed.

Jonas drew her forward and she stood, face turned down, hands playing with the thin cord of blue around her waist, coy, subservient.

Maniakes came around his desk. He towered over her and as he stood, he sensed her body stiffening with uncertainty, perhaps even fear. He gently put his hand under her chin and lifted her face towards his. "Do not be afraid, child. I am General Maniakes, supreme commander of the Imperial forces. What is your name?"

"Leoni," she said, her voice low, soft.

Her eyes, round and huge, drew him in and as he stared, his knees trembled slightly, his heart fluttering. He tried to dismiss such sensations, but the girl possessed some secret power, some unknown device to take hold of his emotions and trap them in the infinite loveliness of her face.

Her face…

Did any other land in any other part of the world possess anything as lovely as she?

His hand dropped from her chin and she looked away. Jonas reached out to lightly brush the General's arm. "General, sir..."

Maniakes heard the voice, but it sounded a hundred leagues away. He took a few uncertain steps backwards until he banged against the edge of his desk, which seemed to bring him back to the present. He blinked several times and grinned, more through embarrassment than anything else, "Forgive me, I..."

Leoni's eyes came up once more and now it was her turn to smile. "There is nothing to forgive, my General." She bowed and left, without waiting for his permission.

His eyes followed the swell of her buttocks. He would not have minded if she had run all over his enclave, knocking over his belongings, rifling through his communications, drinking his wine, anything she wished to do. He wouldn't care.

"General," said Jonas, stepping closer, frowning, "if you wish, I could bring her to you again, in private?"

Maniakes nodded, his gaze fixed on the gap in the curtains as if he hoped for one more glimpse. "She is a servant to some official?"

"No, sir. She works in the kitchens."

Maniakes almost laughed aloud, "The *kitchens*?"

"Aye, General. I'd seen her once or twice, noted her beauty, and as I knew Lord—" He stopped himself, coughed, tried again, "as I knew *Orphano* wished someone young, lithe, supple, I chose her. She was reluctant at first, but the opportunity to earn some money eased her decision. She is not a whore, General. I do not believe she would agree to such things for just anyone. I courted her for weeks, made her believe I had feelings for her which went beyond the physical." He shrugged, "I am the whore, sir. I sold both of us for a handful of gold."

"You did what you had to do. I do not judge you, or her." He sucked in his bottom lip, thinking. "Leoni. She is more lovely than any woman I have ever seen."

"I agree with you, sir. An angel."

Maniakes nodded, forcing himself to think of other matters. "Tell me, this news Orphano received. What was it about?"

"The guards said something about the Emperor being taken ill, sir. Then Orphano ran out, in something of a panic."

"Another attack. Dear God, I wonder how many more he can suffer without..." He shot a glance towards the youth, as if realising, for the first time, he was there. "Jonas, you have served me well these past months. Earlier today, word arrived that the various factions in Sicily were breaking out in open revolt, *against* each other. I tasked you with allowing this to slip out in conversation with Orphano."

"Which I did, General."

"And his reaction?"

Jonas shrugged, "Neutral. Almost as if it were of no surprise."

"But he heard it?"

"Oh yes."

Maniakes smiled. "Orphano keeps much of his reactions and feelings well hidden. But as long as the seed is sown, the wheels will turn." He waggled his finger in front of the young man's face. "But you, my dear Jonas, you know a great deal about my plans. Can I trust you?"

"Of course General! I am not an idiot. I know full well what my fate would be if I dared to cross you."

Maniakes clapped Jonas on the arm. "Aye, that you do. If I get a single whiff of any lapse in your loyalty..."

"You will throw me into the Horn?"

Maniakes's eyes twinkled, "Nothing so mild, my dear Jonas." He titled his head. "Orphano might resort to such threats, but for myself, well..." He leaned forward, mouth close to the young man's ear, "I think to lop off that cock of yours and set you upon a pike in the Harbour of Theodosius might be more *fitting.*"

Jonas turned green and teetered to the side, about to topple over, when Maniakes caught him around the waist, holding him close. "Never underestimate me, Jonas. I have spies other than you. You remember, and keep your loyalty to me, and *for me only.*"

Maniakes released him and Jonas swayed away, groping for the curtain and left without another word.

Forty-Seven

The man sat cross-legged before the camp fire, swathed in a voluminous black robe, another next to him picking at the remains of a cooked bird, skewered on a wooden stick. This man forked small pieces of flesh into the first's mouth, juices running down his chin, but he seemed to care not, all of his attention on his food. Until Hardrada stepped in front of him, then he stopped munching. He shot the other a glance, the carcass dropping into the flames where it sizzled and cracked. The second man then slipped away into the night. Without looking up, the man in the black robe gestured for the Viking to sit.

There were at least a hundred armed Arabs in the camp, most of them armed with spears and bows, now trained towards the gathering of Vikings who stood, twitching, fingering their swords and axes nervously. It was a fight they could not win, if they chose to do so. Hardrada knew the odds were stacked against them, so when he approached the man by the fire, he left his weapons behind. He felt sure the gesture would not go unnoticed.

Hardrada sat, settling himself amongst the scree and sand and peered at the man across the crackling fire. When he noticed the man had no hands, he almost gasped out loud. He stared, unable to stop himself, but the man appeared not be in any way offended. "Both my hands were cut off many years ago, Viking."

Hardrada held the man's black eyes, saw the intelligence there, the supreme confidence.

"My servant does everything for me and my saddle and horse bridle are specially adapted. You are shocked?"

"Surprised. My apologies for staring."

The man shrugged, "Those who I have not met before always stare. I am Ali bin Ahmad Jarjarai, or Al-Jarjarai for short, and I am Vizir of this region. Tell me Viking, where is Bolli Bollason?"

The suddenness of the question almost wrong-footed Hardrada, who gagged, stumbled over his words, and did his utmost to appear unruffled. He knew he failed. "Bollason? I-he-we talked and when..." He shrugged, spreading his arms outwards, "I don't fully understand..."

"It's quite simple," smiled Al-Jarjarai, not in the least affected by Hardrada's discomfort, "We had a deal, one we hammered out over many meetings. I would give him free range to roam across these lands, ferreting out the ill-gotten gains of pirates, and he would give me a share of the spoils. A share, which I hasten to add, will go straight into the coffers of the Caliph. So, I ask you again, where is he?"

"He's gone."

Al-Jarjarai titled his head to one side, "I grow tired of you, Viking. Tell me *where* he has gone."

All at once it became clear to Hardrada they were no longer alone. As if through some power of thought, several armed men pressed in close, vicious looking curved swords in their hands. Hardrada eyed the blades then looked through the flames to Al-Jarjarai. "I am protected by the Emperor of Byzantium. Kill me and both you and your Caliph will find yourselves on a spit."

Al-Jarjarai was not impressed. He sneered, his eyes unblinking, his voice low, full of venom. "Do you seriously believe anybody cares about you, Harald Sigurdsson? I could crush you like the insect you are and no one would ever know."

"They care about the gold. Out in the bay is a Byzantine war-galley, one of many. You may not fear me, but I know you will fear the commander of the fleet. General Maniakes."

He felt it then. The tiniest change in the Vizir's mood, a chink in his otherwise impassive nature. His eyes looked away, albeit briefly, but enough for Hardrada, emboldened, to press on. "Bollason had no desire to share the captured riches with you, or the Emperor. So, when your approach was seen, he gathered whatever he could and left."

"Where?"

"South, or so I believe. He didn't stop to tell me. When I went to his tent to tell him of your arrival, I found it empty."

"If he has gone south, he is a fool. There is nothing for him there but sand. He took much of the treasure?"

"Not so very much, no. He had no time to take all that he wished."

"I see." Al-Jarjarai studied Hardrada carefully for a moment before lifting his eyes to the soldiers and dismissing them with a flash of his eyes. When they drifted away, he looked again at the Viking. "You have not made a plan, have you? With Bollason? That as soon as we leave, he sneaks back to camp and together you resume your treasure-hunting?"

"I would never make any deal with that bastard."

Al-Jarjarai nodded, mulling over Hardrada's words. "He is not your friend? Or family, perhaps. I understood your Norsemen were all related."

"Then you heard wrong. The Norse is a vast area, the home of many people. He is from Iceland, I am from Norway. A distance as great as the one from here to Constantinople."

"I see. So, his leaving was a surprise."

"Very much so. And if I had known, I would have prevented him."

"Really? And how would you have done that, I wonder."

"By killing him."

A silence fell between them and for a long time, Al-Jarjarai stared into the camp fire, lost in thought.

"I will strike a new deal with you, Viking. You will give me forty percent of the treasure you have amassed. I think this is fair."

Hardrada's eyes rose up from the embers of the fire. "I do not believe this was the deal you made with Bollason."

"That was yesterday. Now, with Bollason gone, a new agreement is to be made. I believe it is a good one. Forty percent."

"The Emperor would never agree with such a thing."

"The Emperor is not here. Besides, I could kill you all and take the whole lot. Who would know what had happened to your little band, out here, in the endless wastes?"

"They will know once Bollason returns. And when he does, the Emperor's wrath will know no bounds. The corsairs took what was his. If you take it, you will be no better than them and he will crush you."

"Yes, but you would be dead."

"And so will you, very soon afterwards."

Al-Jarjarai remained impassive, arms folded, the cruel legacy of his punishment hidden beneath the folds of his robe. Hardrada wondered how a man of such authority survived without any hands. For his part, he knew he would rather be dead.

"A deal has to be made, Viking. The one I had with Bollason proved profitable enough. For two years or more he wandered these lands, weeding his way into the trust of the corsairs. Where does he hide his cache?"

"I have no idea. If I did, it would already be mine."

"Forty percent."

"Twenty-five, and I know that is more than you agreed with Bollason."

The Arab sneered. "You know *nothing*, Viking. You insult me. This is my Caliph's land and it is only through his good grace that you are allowed to move across it." He chewed away at his bottom lip, leaning towards the fire, burning low by this time. "I have a certain problem, which you might be able to help me with. In return, I will reduce my percentage to one-third. The emperor has sent the Caliph a request, to give safe passage to two of his bride's sisters to the holy city of Jerusalem."

"The Empress? I wasn't aware she had sisters."

"You have never met Her Highness?"

"No, never."

"Then you are a lesser man for it. Her beauty is beyond compare. Her sisters, however..." He shrugged, a flicker of amusement playing around his mouth. "I would not put them in quite the same category. They are pious, and dowdy for it. It is something I do not understand about you Christians – why you regard sexual pleasures as something to be avoided."

Hardrada shifted uncomfortably upon the hard ground.

"Ah, I see I have stirred up something. You have guilt about past sexual unions, perhaps?"

Hardrada looked around for something to grab hold of. A stick perhaps, anything to keep his mind otherwise occupied.

"How old are you Viking? Twenty summers?"

"Eighteen."

Al-Jarjarai raised his eyebrows. "Really? You appear older. Eighteen…" He sniggered. "I remember those years, when my loins burned with such fire I would couple with anything that moved on two legs!" He laughed, shaking his head. "Before I lost my hands, of course. One must have hands if one is to pleasure a woman properly. Would you not agree?"

Hardrada shrugged, keeping his face downturned to avoid the Arab's penetrating stare.

"Ah, I think I understand…" He lifted his head and barked out an order in Arabic. A soldier immediately appeared from out of the darkness and bowed down next to the Vizir, who whispered something in his ear. The man leaned backwards, hesitating for a moment, and Al-Jarjarai snapped something in their own language and the man retreated, cowering a little, giving Hardrada a sideways glance before he disappeared once more.

"So. If you are in agreement, you will escort these two women to the holy city, and in return I shall take a third of the booty."

Hardrada shook his head and looked up at last to study the man opposite him. "For such an undertaking, I would only ever agree to twenty percent."

Al-Jarjarai eyes darkened. "And I could never agree to such a figure … so … we will rest this night, Viking. In the morning, we will talk again and reach our decisions."

He climbed to his feet, yawning loudly. "My men have pitched their tents on the perimeter of your camp. Any attempt to escape, we will hunt you down."

"There will be no attempt to escape."

"Which will be your tent, Viking?"

Hardrada shrugged, getting his feet, rubbing his arms. The fire was by now almost dead and the bitter cold of the desert night bit deep into his exposed flesh. "I think I will sleep in Bollason's. But let me tell you, Al-Jarjarai, we Norse sleep lightly. I will post sentries. We will meet any attempt to slit our throats in the night with full and bloody resistance from us all. We will make you pay dearly, have no doubts about that."

Al-Jarjarai shook his head. "You exhibit such little trust, Viking."

"It is what keeps me alive, Arab."

The man gathered his robe about him and shuffled off into the night, laughing loudly whilst Hardrada stood and studied the few remaining embers of the fire, wondering what the Vizir said to his guard.

Forty-Eight

As a newly appointed officer in the Imperial Guard, Nikolias marched somewhat self-consciously towards the sprawl of the Valens Aqueduct, adjusting and readjusting his belt as he went. Accompanying him were two burly soldiers, neither of whom seemed particularly happy to be out at this time of night. The streets and houses pressing in around them were dimly lit, but full of noise as citizens gathered around the dinner tables to feast. Tension crackled in the air. Soldiers were mistrusted at the best of times, but mainly at night. This was not a safe quarter to be in.

The massive edifice of the Aqueduct loomed out of the darkness, two storeys of arches, the evidence of recent repair work, begun under the previous emperor, Romanos III, all around. Indeed, it was thanks to such maintenance that prompted the delivery of the report to the regional office of the Emperor. Three workmen found the body swinging from one of the arches earlier that morning. It had taken until now for Nikolias to respond to the report, for no one believed the poor unfortunate warranted such investigation. Until, that is, they discovered the letter in his satchel, a satchel which the vultures descended upon before the body was yet cold. At the sight of the seal of General Maniakes, most of them scurried off to their hovels. One of them, a wizened bald old coot, believing some reward may be pending, alerted the guards. He stood there now, trembling as Nikolias stepped up to him.

Over to the left, the workers had lit an iron brazier and a bunch of them huddled around it, far from happy. Nikolias nodded towards it and said to his men, "Go and warm yourselves, lads. I'll talk to this old fool."

The men grunted but did not argue. Nikolias squinted through the shadows towards the body gently swinging from its rope. "You were the one who discovered him?"

"Aye, lord. Is there a reward?"

Nikolias sighed, "That depends." He put out his hand. "A letter, you said?"

The man reached inside his threadbare blouse and brought out the screwed-up paper and handed it over.

Nikolias turned to the brazier, to use some of its feeble light to identify the seal. It was indeed the General's. As an Imperial Guardsman, although his superior officer was the General, his particular duties were the protection of the Emperor. With this letter, the General may in some way be implicated in the death of the poor unfortunate swinging from the broad arch of the aqueduct.

He folded the letter and slipped it beneath his lamellar hauberk. He stepped closer to the body.

Even in the half-light he could pick out its details. A young man, lean and muscular, almost like an athlete. Naked, his flesh as cold and as white as marble, Nikolias rested his eyes on the man's finest attribute and pursed his lips, impressed.

"He's quite a man, isn't he?" said the old man sliding up next to Nikolias.

"*Was*," said Nikolias, his voice betraying some of the bitterness he felt rising in his craw. This was not the sort of investigation he would have chosen for his first official duty. To have Maniakes's name associated with this death might cause any number of complications. "Where are his clothes, do you know?"

"No, lord. This is how we found him."

"And the letter?"

"In a satchel, lord, which hung around his neck. The letter was inside, but nothing else."

"Curious. Why would he strip himself before throwing himself off the ledge ... and why keep the satchel?"

"For the letter, lord. A note perhaps? I have heard it said suicides often leave notes, to explain their sinful act."

Nikolias looked down on the bald pate of the old man. "You're not some humble, babbling peasant, are you."

"I was a scribe in the Imperial Courts, lord. Many years ago." He shrugged. "My wife ran off with my pension and since then, I've scraped out an existence amongst the whores and scoundrels of this great city."

"That's a sad story, old man. What is your name?"

"Theonidas, lord."

"Then, given your background, Theonidas, it is clear that you can read?"

"Yes, lord. Naturally."

"Did you read the letter?"

The old coot turned his mouth down, looking away, "A little. Curiosity. You know how it is."

"My men will escort you to the Imperial barracks. I want to question you further, but not in this Godforsaken place."

The old man hesitated, shifting his weight from one foot to the next. "I-er-wonder if you might..." he smiled, rubbing his hands, "It *is* cold, and anything I might receive to warm my bones would be gratefully received."

"You'll get your reward, Theonidas, on that you can be certain. But *after* I have questioned you further. Now, go with my men." He looked up towards the body again. "How in the name of God did he manage to string himself up from there?"

* * *

Nikolias poured out a goblet of spiced wine and pushed it across the table towards the old man who took it gratefully and drank it down.

Nikolias stretched out his legs and turned his face to the fire blazing in the grate. He'd pulled off his lamellar armour and bronze helmet as soon as he came through the door, dismissing his servant with a curt nod. Now, sitting here in the warmth, he gave a silent prayer of thanks to God for having delivered him to his present position. He knew full well his father's position was the reason for his promotion, but he also knew his future was dependent on how well he carried out his duties. Father was dead. There would be no protection from him, at least not in this world.

Whispering 'Amen', Nikolias poured himself a small measure of the wine and considered it for a moment before swallowing it in one. "So, Theonidas," he said, "was there anyone else lingering in that soulless place when you came across the body?"

"No one, lord, save for the workers. They were working some way off, on another archway. When I saw the young man, I called out to them and it was one of them who alerted the guard."

"And the body was exactly as you found it?"

"Exactly, lord."

"And you are certain no one else was there?" The old man shook his head, staring down into the bottom of his goblet. Nikolias reached over with the jug and filled up the man's cup. He watched as Theonidas took a gulp. "Who paid you to alert the city guard?"

The old man shrugged, "I don't know his name, but—" He snapped his head up in horror, the colour draining from his face.

Within a blink, Nikolias was across the table, seizing the old man by the throat. He twisted him around and slammed him on the tabletop, a knife appearing from nowhere, pressed against his scrawny throat. Nikolias hissed through gritted teeth, "I would have stuck you like a pig back at the arches, but I knew every viper in that nest would appear to overwhelm us. But I'll do it here and now, so help me. So, I'll ask you again, *who paid you?*"

The man squirmed underneath Nikolias's grip, the colour return-ing to his face, brought about by the pressure the young officer applied. From sallow yellow, to rich ruby red. He gagged, "For the love of Christ!"

Nikolias shook him, "I'll slit your throat and drop you in the Horn, you old, feckless bastard. Now tell me!"

The man spluttered and wheezed, bobbed his head numerous times and squawked, "I will, I will."

Nikolias released the pressure, stepped back, and listened to what the old man had to say.

* * *

The guards outside the tent entrance snapped to attention as Nikolias stepped up close. "Inform the General I am here on urgent Imperial business."

One of the men swung his arm across his chest in the time-honoured salute and dipped through the heavy curtain. Muffled voices came from within and, after a slight pause, the guard reappeared looking somewhat flustered. "The General will see you."

Nikolias nodded and stepped inside.

Maniakes sat on his truckle bed, dressed in a simple linen robe, his hair in disarray, his eyes still thick with sleep as he turned to face the young Imperial officer. "This had better be good."

Nikolias took a step closer and, without a word, produced the letter.

Maniakes frowned and took it. Slowly he unfolded the paper and, as he read, silently mouthing the words, he grew more tense. When he finished he sat, staring into the distance, the paper held in both hands. "Where did you find this?"

"Upon the body of a young man, sir. We found not a few hours ago, swinging under the Valens Aqueduct."

Maniakes looked up. "Murdered?"

Nikolias shrugged, "I believe so, although the perpetrators tried hard to make it look like suicide."

"And this note. Who else has read it, apart from yourself?"

"The man who found the victim. But you have no need to worry about him, sir. His body is already floating in the Horn."

The General pushed himself to his feet and Nikolias took an involuntary step backwards as the man's sheer size seemed to take up almost the entire room. "I spoke with him, only yesterday."

"The victim, sir?" Nikolias looked aghast at the General. "So, you did know him?"

"Not in *that* way, you idiot!" Maniakes screwed up the note in his hand and threw it on the bed. "He was an agent of mine. I secreted him into Orphano's service. Clearly that bastard got wind of it and ended Jonas's life, in the hope someone would find the note and incriminate me." He chuckled, "What a devious little shit, he is."

"Orphano?" Maniakes nodded. "I think dangerous would be a more fitting description, sir. If the contents of that note were made public…"

Maniakes allowed his shoulders to drop and he went over to his side table and poured himself some wine. He stood with his back to the young officer and quietly drank. "To dirty my reputation by branding me a sodomite," he said, his voice trembling, "I'll have his eyes for this."

"Sir, if I may…" Nikolias stepped forward, his pulse throbbing in his throat. "Orphano is the most powerful man in the Empire, after his Royal Highness. Even the Patriarch, Alexius is subordinate to him. You cannot move against him, sir."

"No." The General's voice sounded flat, unconvinced.

"Sir, it might be best to wait."

"Wait?" Another sharp chuckle. He finished his wine and turned. "Wait for what, eh? A mistake? A fall from grace?"

"He clearly sees you as an obstacle, perhaps even a threat. Once he realizes this particular plan has failed, he might try something else. As long as we are prepared—"

"*We*, Nikolias? I take it then that you are with me?"

Nikolias blinked, "How could you think otherwise, sir? You are my supreme commander."

"But you have been enrolled into the Imperial Bodyguard."

"My loyalties lie primarily with the Emperor, yes, but you are my commander-in-chief, not that damned effete clerk!"

Maniakes grinned, "By Christ, that's a fitting moniker. I'll have to remember that ... *effete clerk.*" He shook his head, laughing. "No, you're right. To wait is the best strategy. He will make a mistake, overstep his mark, perhaps..." He frowned, "To be honest with you, we all know the Emperor's health is fading. There are rumours that even now Orphano is grooming another ... he may well pick the wrong side."

"His Highness is not dying, sir. He has a falling-down sickness, nothing more."

"Yes. As Caesar did. I know my history, lad. We all know what happened to him."

Nikolias cleared his throat, becoming tense, "Sir, I don't think you should—"

"Don't worry, lad," Maniakes clapped him on the arm, "I'm not in any way suggesting Emperor Michael is about to be assassinated. He is much loved and has done enormously well after the death of Romanus, but ... the Royal throne is a strange thing..." He smiled. "Nikolias, keep your ears open and report back to me about anything you find out. Orphano had some plan to introduce a young Viking adventurer to the Empress, but nothing has come of it. I left him in Africa, together with Bollason, to mop up the last remnants of the corsair threat. Already they have been gone far too long. They may even be dead. But," he leaned forward and gripped the young officer's bicep, "if and when this wild man from the north enters her bedchamber, I want to know, you understand."

Nikolias swallowed and tried to keep the disgust out of his voice. "If I must, sir."

"For the good of the Empire, eh lad?"

Nikolias brought his heels together and gave a slight bow before turning to go. He stopped, his eyes settling on the screwed up note on the General's bed. "Shall I take that, sir?"

"No, I think not. Leave it with me."

"And what should I put in my report?"

"Suicide, found swinging under the Valens Aqueduct. Not witnesses, *no note.*"

Nikolias flashed his eyes across to the General, who returned his look without a single flicker of emotion. "As you wish, sir."

He went outside, waved the guard away as he came to attention, and wandered a few steps towards the entrance to the barrack square. He stop, considered what Maniakes had said, about Orphano's over-stepping the mark, of choosing the wrong side. *What if it really did come to that? The sudden, unexpected death of the Emperor, who would follow? With no obvious heir, might Orphano champion someone of his choosing, somehow persuade the Empress to give her support ... and by subtle means, gain control of the entire Byzantine Empire?*

He looked back towards the General's tent, his mouth open, barely able to breathe. What if he had already made the wrong choice? By taking the note to the General had he, in fact, sealed his doom, by choosing the wrong side himself?

Forty-Nine

Hardrada snapped open his eyes, every sense alert, body tense, coiled like a spring. His fingers crept towards the hilt of his seax, the broad-bladed knife which he always slept with. He waited, holding his breath.

The slight swish of material of the tent flaps pulling apart was what brought him instantly awake. Now, rigid, straining to hear, he picked out the low, tremulous breathing of the intruder. Whoever it was moved slowly, creeping forward.

Creeping.

On hands and feet. Like a snake, sliding ever nearer, to strike.

The intruder moved, a hand slipping under the cover, and Hardrada swung around, grabbing the wrist, throwing all of his weight on top of whoever it was, rolling them over, the seax already finding the throat.

A soft, slender throat.

"Don't kill me, lord."

He froze, unable to comprehend who it was, and her other hand deftly lifted his own, moving the knife away. It clattered to the ground from fingers numb with surprise.

"The Vizir sent me, lord. As a gift."

Her features were difficult to make out in the dark, but her voice flowed like warm honey, and when her lips pressed against his own, they tasted of sun-kissed oranges. Her perfume filled his nostrils, set his head spinning, and he groaned as her fingers ran through his hair, raking his scalp.

She pushed him over, all of his strength gone and she straddled him, slipping off her thin robe. He gazed at her, the outline of her body nothing more than a smooth, rounded form of black. When her fingers ripped away his thin jerkin, he did not resist.

"I will give you such a night, my lord. One you will never forget."

He stretched back his head, arched his back, and groaned, his manhood pulsing beneath her, harder than he could ever remember. This must be a dream, one he'd always longed for. To couple, to blend, to become as one.

And such a one.

Her young, soft body slid over him, fingers deftly bringing him out into the night, to curl and roll over his blood-engorged flesh. And then her mouth, Sweet, warm, engulfing him, her lips, tongue … he cried out and she muffled his moans with kisses, and she took him, pressed him against her, and he slid into her.

From that point on, time blurred, the night vanishing, the single most important thing the sensations overpowering his loins.

* * *

The morning light filtered through the thick canvas of the tent and he flickered his eyelids, shrugging off the dregs of sleep, and he sat up, rubbing his face. He looked down at the imprint of her body, placed the flat of his hand over it and thought he felt the slight memory of her warmth. Reassured, he smiled to himself. No dream. The most perfect reality.

He stood up, naked, and ran his hand over his flaccid manhood. The slight tingling, the tiny friction burns. She had loved him any number of times, bringing him to hardness again and again, until her cries outdid his own. She curled up beside him, kissing his chest, her hand on the flat of his belly, and she purred, "And you have never done this before?"

"Never."

"Then I am indeed the fortunate one."

He laughed and she snuggled up closer to him. He draped his arm around her, held her close, and they slept.

And now, she was gone.

He went over to the washing bowl, splashed water over his face and paused, hands over his eyes, the sweet memory returning again. Who was she? Would he recognise her if he ever met her again? Her voice might betray her, the litheness of her limbs, the sweet taste of her lips … but he never saw her eyes. How could he know her?

He put on a jerkin, tied the leather thongs loosely, and pulled on his breeches. The day was pressing; already voices from beyond were lifted in greetings. Arab, Greek and Norse. The mingling of tongues. The spread of Empire. Bootless, he stepped out into the sun.

A few faces turned his way, some smiling. A large black-robed Arab warrior loomed close. "My master would speak with you."

Hardrada grunted, shuffled across the arid dirt towards where Al-Jarjarai sat, in his usual way, his manservant dipping figs into yoghurt before popping them into the Vizir's mouth. When he saw Hardrada he smiled, spoke to the servant, who mopped his mouth with a soft cloth, then scurried off, leaving the figs behind.

"Please, have some breakfast."

Hardrada frowned at the figs and flopped down with a grunt. "I think I'll pass."

"They are good for the bowels, Viking. One should always keep the bowels working. My father used to tell me—"

"Please," said Hardrada, putting up his hand, "spare me the details."

"Your voice is hoarse, Viking. Have you not slept well?"

"I slept perfectly well, what little I had of it."

"Ah!" Al-Jarjarai sounded amused and his eyes twinkled with boyish glee, "You were busy, then, eh?"

"I was."

"And, I hope, you found the experience enjoyable."

"Very much so." Hardrada couldn't help but smile. "You're a remarkable man, Al-Jarjarai, and a most generous one."

The Vizir squeezed his lips together, smug, contented. "I wanted your first time to be memorable, my friend, not some dirty grope in a filthy dockside brothel. She is a luxury, that one. A beauty like few others. Thighs of silk, and a sex of pure, liquid gold. Do you not agree?"

"I did not think such pleasures were possible." He smiled again. "When you see her…" He looked away and decided, despite his misgivings, to try a fig. He chomped away, trying to keep himself occupied.

"Yes, my friend, have no fear. When I see her, I shall tell her you were more than *satisfied*."

"You, er, don't think…" He picked up another fig, studying it with great intensity, "You don't think she might…"

"No, my friend. She was yours for one night, and one night alone. From this point, you must make your own way and travel the road of pleasure wherever it may take you."

"I see." Hardrada dropped the fig and sighed. He stared for a long time into the distance and the Vizir waited, without comment, until the young Viking was able to lift his head and speak. "I suppose we should turn our minds to the deal we made."

"Yes, my friend, we should. And here it is. You will stay here for three more nights, collecting the booty under the watchful eyes of my men, half of whom will remain here with you. You will then divide the cache, setting aside a quarter of it for my caliph. By the third morning, the holy sisters Theodora and Eudocia should have arrived, under escort. From here, you and your men will accompany her east to the Holy City."

"For how long?"

"You should stay in the city? Who knows. Until the sisters have finished whatever devotions they wish to carry out. A month perhaps."

Hardrada put his face into his hand and shook his head. "A month? It will take longer than that to travel there, then the return. Three months all together?" He dropped his hand and stared at the Vizir. "I'm beginning to wonder if this deal was such a good idea."

"You could always refuse. I will stake you out in the sand, after having your eyelids sliced off, and take every item of your collected treasure for my caliph. A simple choice." He smiled.

Hardrada blew out his cheeks. "When this is over, and I am safely back in Constantinople, I hope these holy sisters make it known to the Emperor the service I have done."

"Oh, I'm certain of it, my young friend. I believe they will herald your name throughout every street and forum of the great city. Who knows," he raised a playful eyebrow, "perhaps even the Empress herself will show you her gratitude. She is a fabled beauty, my friend."

"And you , my *friend*," said Hardrada, waggling his finger in front of the Vizir's face, "play this mating game too well. In fact, if I didn't know differently, I'd say someone unseen was pulling your strings."

"Indeed? And who do you think that person might be?"

"Someone who would like to have me under their control too. I can name a number of candidates."

"You're brighter than you look." Al-Jarjarai smiled and leaned back, shooting a quick glance towards the figs. "Would you feed me a fig, my friend? I will forever be in your debt."

Hardrada reached over, picked out a fig and slipped it between the Vizir's teeth. "And I am forever in yours."

"I hope you will not forget my kindness," Al-Jarjarai said, slowly chewing down the fruit.

"Oh no," said Hardrada, sitting back, "I *never* forget anything."

Fifty

Constantinople, some months later

The warm summer sun beat down on Hardrada's face as he stood in the prow, the position he always took now. The ship skimmed across the surface, a slim, black dart on the silver of the sea.

Jerusalem, the Holy City, was weeks behind him. The sisters, as silent as ghosts, faces unreadable, as plain and as dowdy as sand, pressed a leather purse in his hand when he left them. He rooted himself on the place the wily Arab guide told him was Golgotha and he peered across the sprawl of that legendary place.

They said the walls were gold, the streets embedded with jewels.

None of it was true.

No stirring rolled through his guts, no tears sprang from his eyes, though he tried his best to gather up some response to what he saw. A hundred thousand souls, mingling together in the cramped, narrow passageways, voices of a hundred different tongues clattering together. None of it made sense to him. He hated cities, longed for home and the wilderness of the North.

He was glad to leave the Holy City far behind.

Taymur, who accompanied him through the bustling streets, sat silent and sullen next to the keelson. Hardrada studied the corsair, wondering not for the first time why the Arab had not taken the chance to escape. Opportunities to do so had arisen on many occasions during their journey, but not once did the man ever attempt to slip away. Now, crossing the Sea of Marmara with the great city of Constantinople rearing across the horizon, Hardrada considered what awaited them both. A hero's welcome for the Viking, an audience with the Emperor himself... and a stretched neck for Taymur. Unless a way might be found to enrol the Arab in the Varangian Guard, or have him as a servant. No one would agree to either suggestion.

Hardrada moved over to the Arab and sat down next to him. Taymur did not flinch.

"You are worried?"

He shook his head, eyes dropping to the deck. Around them, the grunts and gasps of the oarsmen, straining to make speed, the promise of warm beds, a woman's caress, copious amounts of imported English ale bringing renewed energy to their weary bodies.

"My fate is sealed, Lord. You could have killed me many moons ago, but you did not, and for that I am eternally grateful."

"You could escape." Hardrada nodded to the distant harbours of the great city. "You could easily slip away, unnoticed. No one would ever find you."

"But if any did, I would end up in a gutter, my throat slit. You know it as well as I." He tugged at his plum coloured trousers. "I am who I am, Lord. I would not last a week."

"Then I will give you safe passage," said Hardrada with steely determination in his voice. "Why did you not remain in Egypt? You could have survived."

"But not as I was. For years I sailed these seas, pillaging, doing all manner of things I would rather forget..." His voice trailed away, lost amongst the sea spray and the straining sounds of the men.

"I will keep you safe, Taymur. It is the least I can do."

"Lord, perhaps this is where my life has brought me. The choices I made, the wrongs I have done. Allah, in His infinite wisdom, turns the wheel of the great machine, and my end is in sight. My only prayer now, is that I will not suffer too much, for I have heard the Greeks are experts at inflicting pain. Something they inherited from their Roman cousins, yes?"

"They're still Romans, in their souls. If they have any."

"Do you? Forgive me, Lord, but I often watched you in Jerusalem, the way your eyes clouded, as if in great thought. Did you find your God there?"

Hardrada measured the Arab with a flat stare, considering not for the first time how it was he could ask such things, without fear. No one else ever engaged the Viking in such conversation and Hardrada realised, with something of a jolt, that friends and confidants were as alien to him as salt water in his lungs.

"My brother, Olaf, tried to continue the work of his father, and fought long and hard to bring the teachings of the White Christ to my land. Some say a vision came to him one night, of the Christian God, guiding him in what he should do. But he failed. The far north is still the land of the old gods. Odin, Thor." Hardrada shook his head, "I do not think they will ever be totally forgotten, for they live in our hearts, our minds. The manner of our death. Olaf died believing in the righteousness of his efforts, but I have often asked *if* what he attempted was the Lord's work, then why was he abandoned at Stiklestad. I asked God the same question at Jerusalem, as I stood alone in those holy places, places where the White Christ walked and died. I received no answer."

"Allah does not always speak with words, Lord. Perhaps you will receive your answer at a later time. He is wise and merciful; we cannot hope to understand Him, merely trust in His divine magnificence."

"But you see, Taymur," Hardrada gave a wry smile, "as I came away, disillusioned and confused, I looked up to the sky and amongst the clouds I saw the shape of a drakkar, sailing across the firmament. I knew at once this was Odin speaking to me, telling me I am and always will be a Viking."

"A drakkar is a ship such as this," Taymur swept his hand before him, "your Viking longship."

"A serpent ship, used in war. Much bigger than this one. I saw it plain, there is no question in my mind what it meant."

"You must be careful, Lord. Such thoughts could bring about your fall. I have heard it said if any question the authority of your god, they can be burned."

"Or have their eyes cut out."

Looking out to sea, Hardrada now grew silent himself. The Arab's words brought him little comfort. The Holy City had done nothing but cast him into a world of confusion. The sisters, silent and pious, were serene in their faith, unquestioning and content. He wished he possessed a fraction of their certitude. Perhaps then he would gain some sense of peace, at least in his heart. However, the Viking way dominated, as it always would. The searing desire for revenge, against all those who had wronged him. Talk of Olaf rekindled it all and he gritted his teeth, knowing the Christian creed of forgiveness would never be one he could embrace.

* * *

At the dockside, they raised oars and eager hands hauled in ropes to secure the ship to the harbour wall. The gangplank came down and the crew disembarked, Hardrada having dismissed them, giving the men freedom to visit whatever taverns and whorehouses they so wished. With their voices lifted in eager anticipation, they called out their farewells and Hardrada stepped onto the dockside, catching the eye of the Byzantine guard commander standing a little way off, half a dozen armed soldiers in a neat group half a pace behind.

Hardrada clapped his hand on Taymur's shoulder. He'd forced the Arab to change his clothes, rough sewn breeches replacing satin pants, a stout leather jerkin and belt in place of white, billowing blouse and rich blue sash. The man could almost pass for a European, especially with the iron helm pushed down over his oily-black hair. The nasal bar and looped eye-protectors proving an effective disguise.

"Make as if you're with the other lads," said Hardrada and shoved a purse of coin inside the man's jerkin, "then do whatever you need to do to survive."

Taymur's eyes behind the helmet grew moist. "Why do you do this for me, Lord?"

Hardrada shrugged. "Perhaps … someone showed me kindness once, saved me from the hell of Stiklestad. This is my way of repaying that debt. Who knows? When I saw that ship, I realised I could only ever be a Viking. I may appear Christian, but in my heart, I am not. Vikings do not show pity, Taymur, nor do we forgive. This is my one act of kindness, my token Christian gesture." He squeezed the Arab's arm. "You served me well and now I free you."

"I will serve you again, I think. And I will do it willingly." He took Hardrada's hand, pressed his forehead against it, then turned and disappeared amongst the throng of dockworkers and other assorted humanity milling about the pulsating harbour of Theodosius.

"Sigurdsson," came a gruff voice.

Hardrada turned to face the owner of the voice, the officer, and said, "They call me Hardrada now." He chuckled. "Not that it matters much. Maniakes sent you?"

The office bristled, "If you mean *General* Maniakes, then yes, he did. You have the booty?"

Hardrada nodded towards the gently bobbing longship. "It's all there. My share is in the smaller of the two bundles. Make sure you do not mix them up."

"The General would speak with you. Two of my men will escort you to his command tent."

Hardrada nodded and glanced out to sea, fighting the urge to dive into the water and leave everything behind. But the Viking way, imbued with the power of the fate goddess, Urd, reclaimed Hardrada and he closed his eyes, sighed, and fell in behind the soldiers as they marched to meet Maniakes.

Fifty-One

Close to the Forum of Constantine, with the crowds bustling and jostling amongst the many market stalls, the soldiers stopped abruptly, exchanged looks, then turned to speak with Hardrada. Pausing to pick a piece of fruit from one of the traders, the Viking frowned at the men. "What is it?"

Without a word, the soldiers stepped aside and Hardrada found himself staring into the florid face of a large, plump official, bobbing his bald head, a greasy smile splitting his face. His hands were lost within the folds of his voluminous saffron robe and when he produced one, Hardrada noted the splendid, glittering rings covering each stubby finger. The man bowed slightly.

"At last," he said, his voice light, soft, "I have the good fortune to meet you, Harald."

Hardrada tilted his head, "You have me at a disadvantage."

"Yes. No doubt." The man's smile broadened and he waved the soldiers away, linked his arm through the Viking's and steered him away from the Forum towards one of the subsidiary entrances to the palace complex. "I am John Orphano, chief administrator of the Empire, and brother to the Emperor."

Hardrada stopped and the little round man shot him a look of alarm. "Do not fear me, Harald. I assure you, I am concerned only for your welfare. The Empress herself has heard of you and has expressed a desire to meet with you."

Hardrada swallowed hard, gaping at the man. "The *Empress*?"

Orphano chuckled, slipped his arm through Hardrada's once again, and tugged him forward, sniffing loudly. "Come along, Harald. What the empress so desires, she usually gets, but we can delay your meeting for a little moment, in order for you to have a bath." He laughed aloud and Hardrada allowed himself to be led forward, conscious of how people bowed and stepped aside. Here was power and Hardrada liked how it felt.

* * *

Inside the great marbled halls, the mad press of citizens seemed as if they were from another, distant land. Here, all was serene and calm. Courtiers moved through the broad corridors with measured steps, as if floating. Guards stood silent and aloof, and the sweet tang of citrus invaded the nostrils, sweetening the air and contributing to the overall atmosphere of luxury and timeless opulence.

Having bathed and dressed in a simple unbleached linen robe, Hardrada walked with Orphano along the corridors towards the private apartments of the ruling elite. The Viking craned his neck, taking in an endless ceiling covered in frescoes of heavenly scenes. Saints and emperors, of warriors astride winged horses, of angels spreading out their arms, and everywhere the shimmer of gold.

"Come Harald," said the soft, liquid velvet voice of Orphano, gripping Hardrada's arm. They were before two enormous doors, studded and banded with bronze. Guards stood either side, impassive, bristling with lamellar armour, massive oval shields decorated with portraits of Jesus Christ.

"This is beyond anything I ever imagined."

Orphano breathed a contented sigh. "Ah, Harald, your innocence is most alluring. How old are you now?"

"Nineteen summers."

"Nineteen…" Orphano smiled, tracing a forefinger along the Viking's bare bicep, "You are so strong for one still so young. I believe you will please her Divine Majesty, more than even she thought possible. You have seen her before?"

"No, never."

"Ah, then you are in for something of a treat, my young friend. She has often spoken of you, the tales of your exploits exciting her. She wished to meet you before you left for the Islands and has grown somewhat *impatient*." His eyes danced with a kind of impish playfulness. "When you have … *completed* your audience, I would very like you to visit me. We have much to discuss."

Intrigued, Hardrada was about to speak when the doors creaked open and Orphano put the flat of his hand in the young man's back and thrust him forward into the inner sanctum of Empress Zoe's chamber.

He stood unblinking, rooted to the spot, drinking in the scene before him. Every part of the room stretched out before him gleamed with richness, ebony pillars soaring to the vast ceiling, ruby red curtains hanging heavy, a broad dais, reached by black, marble steps, topped by an onyx throne, padded with a purple cushion. Vacant, waiting.

On all sides, sumptuous couches and chairs, richly decorated and thickly padded, with foot stools, animal skin rugs. Braziers on slender stems, flames lapping gently, sending out plumes of swirling grey, brown, blue and red smoke, perfumed, making the air thick with the scents of eastern spices.

There was no living thing in the room, nor any evidence of anyone inhabiting it for some considerable time. Everything appeared new, fresh. The intensity of the silence pressed in on him and he wondered if Orphano had made a mistake, and brought him to the wrong place.

He edged forward, running his finger over the smooth, solid surface of one of the pillars. He wondered how such constructions were possible. Such opulence. To have the means, the desire, the vision. Shaking his head, he took it all in, turning himself around, picking out every detail, every painting adorning the walls, every piece of furniture, the ceiling, pillars and floor. The finest materials, the most exquisite craftsmanship. And all for her. The Empress. To warrant such excess, she must be the most wondrous of all rulers.

And the most beautiful.

There came the slightest sound, of material swishing across the marble floor, and he swung around and saw her.

Zoe, Empress of Byzantium.

She stood as if from a dream, a vision in white silk, a simple gold cord, loosely tied around her slim waist, the only nod to her royal personage. Her arms of burnished bronze were bare, long, tapered fingers clasped before her, raven hair stacked up in ancient Greek style, loose ringlets cascading heavily down either side of her finely chiselled face. Eyes, as soft and alluring as a fawn's, captured and drew him to her and he moved closer, the strength leaching from his limbs, all liquid, nothing of any substance or form. She neither spoke nor moved, but seemed nevertheless to call him. He obeyed, without question and when her perfume enveloped him, clean and fresh, of cucumber and lime, he closed his eyes and breathed deeply. His mind whirled, his stomach turned over, and his loins burst into flame. When he opened his eyes again, it was to see her rich lips slightly parted, her fingers reaching to his face, her head tilting.

"I heard the stories of your size," she said, her voice that of an angel, sending his senses soaring, "but I never guessed."

She pressed herself against him, her full breasts against his chest. He glanced down. Rich, sun-kissed flesh, flawless, brimming with health. He wanted to answer, but no words came, the power of coherent speech having deserted him. His throat, dry and constricted, refused to work. All he could offer was a grunt and she smiled, seeming aware of the effect she had on him.

Zoe took one of his hands in hers and lifted it, studying it with a strange intensity. "I hear you Vikings are men of violence, quick to anger, full of hate and vengeance. Is that so?"

She looked up into his face and all he could think of was her eyes, how they drank him in, how, if the whole world came crashing down around him, this would be the one thing, the one memory he would take with him.

"I have read your history, of how your forefathers raided distant shores, overcame others with your power and strength. How you butchered the menfolk, carried away the children, raped the women. But also, how those acts soon became needless, for no one could resist you, so they surrendered and submitted…" Her fingertips trickled across his face, cooling his skin, but sending the blood surging through his loins. "Submit," she whispered, pushing herself upwards to stand on tip-toe, her breath floating across his lips. "Wouldn't that be the most wondrous feeling, Harald?"

He swallowed hard and managed a single nod.

She smiled, dropping back down on her heels. She still held his hand. "You are young, Harald and yet your body is hard, like seasoned oak. Like your ships, yes? Sleek, yet strong. I have need of a sleek, hard man, Harald. And seeing you, despite my having thought many times about you, I never guessed how beautiful you are."

Without warning, her hands sprang to his head, gripping him by the hair, nails raking against his scalp, and she forced him down to her waiting lips and she kissed him. He moaned as her tongue slipped into his mouth and found his own, and his hands folded around her taut, full buttocks, his whole body aflame with desire.

They fell to the marble floor, ignoring the hardness, the cold, and he pulled apart her thin robe, exposing her flesh. Desperate, impatient, he brought himself out and slid into her, a wild frenzy overcoming him. His only thought to burst deep within her golden, giving body, to dampen the urgent need, the raging flames of desire.

Her slim thighs wrapped themselves around him and she arched her back, throwing her head from side to side, letting out a stream of gasps and tiny cries as he drove into her. He bellowed like some great, wounded beast, and collapsed on top of her, gulping in his breath and she held him, like a child to her breast, and waited for the storm to pass.

They made love a second time more slowly, mouths exploring flesh, fingers seeking out areas of intense sensitivity. Their groans filled the throne room before he took her to the inner chamber of her bedroom where they lay amongst the silk sheets until the morning.

Fifty-Two

On the morning of the third day someone tentatively knocked on the double doors. One or two servants had wandered in like ghosts every now and then, bringing refreshment, but nobody dared disturb the Empress in her bedchamber. This time, however, urgency overcame fear. She ripped open the door to confront the person standing before her, the words of outrage catching in her throat when she recognised the serious expression, the proud eyes, the arrogance she always found so infuriating.

"I need him."

She whirled around and Maniakes came in behind her, casting his eyes across the dishevelled, the floor littered with items of clothing, bedding, upturned furniture. He looked up to watch his empress slip off her thin robe and stand, naked, in front of the spread-eagled Hardrada, deep in sleep.

"Poor lamb," she said, looking over her shoulder to the impassive Maniakes, "he's worn out." She grinned and lay down next to the Norseman, her hand resting on his manhood. She stretched her body like a cat, moaning softly and Maniakes, breathing in short gasps through his open mouth, fought hard to keep his pulse from engulfing his throat. He forced himself to turn away.

"We have received reports, Highness. The many Saracen factions on Sicily have broken out in armed conflict with each other. The Emperor has ordered a force to sail there, seize this opportunity, and retake control of the island. I need Sigurdsson and his Varangians."

"I'm sorry to hear that, General. How long will you be gone?"

"I cannot say. As long as it takes."

He heard her kissing Hardrada. The Norseman groaned, moved, tongue sounding thick in his mouth when he mumbled, "I want you."

Maniakes closed his eyes and sighed. "Within the hour," he snapped and strode out without a backward glance.

Outside, he leaned back against the double doors, gulping in air, struggling to rid his thoughts of her lithe body, the way her hips rolled as she walked, those long, slender legs, smooth as silk. "Dear Christ," he muttered and strode off down the imposing main corridor of the mighty Imperial Palace.

He needed a drink.

Orphano caught up with him in the formal gardens, the scent of jasmine thick in the warm morning breeze. Amongst the serried ranks of fragrant trees, dissected by manicured pathways, Orphano glided forward, paused, pressing a bay leaf against his face and closed his eyes in rapture. Maniakes stifled a groan as the grand administrator turned and sidled up to him, an oily smile dominating his round face. "My dearest General," he said, "I trust you are well. How goes it with Harald?"

Maniakes arched a single eyebrow. "I thought your hand would be in it somewhere."

"I thought we agreed the Norseman should serve Her Highness in whatever capacity she deemed fit."

"Aye, but not to such excess. He's been with her for three days."

"I know," his eyes twinkled, "my servants have been taking them food and drink." He laughed, "His appetites match hers admirably."

"I can't begin to understand how you think this might profit us, Orphano, but I need him to command a contingent of Varangians on our campaign."

"I would have thought Bollason would have been better suited."

"Bollason is nowhere to be found. I thought your spy network would have told you that."

"They have, my dear General. I am merely stating a wish, that is all. I know full well Bollason took off when in Africa. Strange, don't you think? A man who has served us so well for so long should suddenly take it upon himself to simply ... *disappear.* I have some suspicion our friend Harald had something to do with it."

"To what purpose?"

Orphano shrugged, "To feather his nest, of course."

"And you've certainly made it a damn sight more comfortable for him, haven't you. You play a dangerous game, Orphano. Sigurdsson is of royal lineage and he grows stronger, more dangerous by the day."

"They call him Hardrada now, so I understand. *Hard Ruler,* although what he rules is somewhat difficult to understand. I understand his share of the booty he seized is impressive. The man is rich. If he should use these riches to recruit men..." He left the implications of his words to hang in the air whilst he studied the General with an expectant gaze.

"He has no designs on the Empire. All he wants to do is to go home and exact his revenge."

"If he lives."

Maniakes frowned. "Why are you so anxious to have him in the Empress's bed?"

Orphano looked away for a moment. He took a deep breath. "This is a most tranquil and evocative place, don't you think?"

"Answer the question."

Orphano sighed. "The Emperor's sickness continues to rage through him, weakening both mind and body. It is becoming increasingly difficult to keep his condition from the Senate. Already rumours of his imminent death circulate unchecked and there are many who would use the situation to their advantage." His face, when he turned to Maniakes again, was tense. "Can I trust you, General? You have the ear of the Patriarch. I know his wish is for Theodora to rule when Michael dies." He gritted his teeth. "Such an outcome would be disastrous for the Empire. I need you to talk with His Holiness, to bring some common sense to his thoughts."

"Alexius is guided by God, Orphano. I have little sway over him."

"But you could *try*. Plant a little seed, General, that is all I ask. We have to be ready to install a new Emperor without delay. These are perilous times, as well you know. I fear this expedition to Sicily is the precursor to something far more dangerous."

"The Normans, you mean."

"Their reach is long, and their ambition limitless. His Holiness is incapable of appreciating the importance of strength. His faith is commendable, but often it blinds him to what is required."

"The army gives the Empire its strength and—"

"And by that you mean your good self, General."

Maniakes narrowed his eyes. "I have no ambitions other than to serve to the best of my abilities. I have no designs to rule, Orphano."

The eunuch put up his hand, "No, no, of course not. I merely point out that the Empire requires someone who can lead, General. An emperor of strength, foresight, and good health! It has been too long since we have had consistent good leadership, General. We must not allow Byzantium be to be set adrift, without direction. That would never do."

"I assume from all of this you have someone in mind, if the tragic day should arrive when one of His Highness's seizures prove fatal?"

"From what his doctors have told me, that may well be sooner than we think. But yes, I have someone in mind. I shall not go into any specific details just yet, but needless to say any decisions will rest with Her Royal Highness. As the ruling family, she has the ultimate say."

Maniakes smiled, bobbing his head, "Ah, now I get it. You hope that by clouding her senses with desire she will agree with whatever advice you pass her way? You're a devious one, Orphano."

"And you are wise, my good friend. Together we could ensure Byzantium grows stronger, not weaker, with the Emperor's passing."

"Well, you could be right," Maniakes rubbed his chin, allowing himself to ponder for a moment on what might happen if Michael were to suddenly keel over. Orphano had his plans already set in place. Who might be his creature, this 'new' emperor whom he would manipulate and control? Perhaps there could be a way to put his plan of action into place, to undermine Orphano's ambitions. He would have to think hard, find a way. "Of course," he said, chuckling, "this is all very well. But what if the Emperor doesn't die. What then, eh, Orphano? All your schemes will come to nothing. He could live for years."

"You think so? Have you seen him lately? He was once heralded as the most beautiful man alive, now he is nothing more than a bloated, purple-veined abomination."

"Have a care, Orphano," said Maniakes, surveying the surroundings, "you never know who might be listening."

"I say no more than is openly discussed in the Senate. The Emperor has not long for this world, and well you know it."

"Yes, but *if* he lives, we have a duty to maintain the security of the Empire at all costs. It is my duty to shore up the borders, prevent incursions, and build up our strength in the face of threats from a host of enemies. Michael is coherent and well aware. We cannot act as if our feet are stuck in mud."

"Which is precisely why I have put my plans into place. The transition to a new emperor will be swift. All I need is Her Highness's agreement, and that will be forthcoming, do not doubt it."

"Maybe you'll get Sigurdsson to guide her hand as she signs the mandate?"

"Hardrada, General. I have him where I want him, safely ensconced between the Empress's thighs. As I said," he rubbed his hands together, "everything is in place. Good luck in Sicily. Don't do anything stupid like getting yourself, or dear, sweet Harald killed. That really would be a tragedy."

He bowed and left, laughing to himself and Maniakes watched him go and wondered how he might outflank this most treacherous and resourceful of adversaries. He needed a weapon. His only problem was where to get it.

Fifty-Three

The Kontoskalion Harbour thronged with a mass of soldiers and sailors, boarding ships and moving stores. Everywhere, the air was thick with confused shouts and the scream of horses as men struggled to force the terrified animals across gangplanks onto the waiting galleons. Hobnailed boots crunched, armour and weapons clattered, the sun not yet even brushing the horizon. And over on the far side, arms folded in nonchalant ease, General Maniakes stood next to the Iron Gate and studied it all.

A great roar came up from over to his left. He turned to see the Varangians pushing and shoving their way onto their waiting ships, and by their coarse actions and derisive curses aimed towards nearby Byzantine troops, Maniakes knew most of the Norsemen were drunk, their laughter the loudest of all. He sighed, shifted position, and spotted Hardrada, standing at the head of a more disciplined and patient bunch, well-armed, their great two-headed battle-axes heads down on the dockside wall. These were the giant Viking's hand-picked guard, men who had followed him from Kiev down into Africa. Somewhat aloof, there could be no doubting their martial prowess. They looked the part, almost akin to the well-ordered ranks of the Byzantine troops, whose officers barked and threatened. The Varangians continued to roll onto their ships and Maniakes thanked God they were on his side, for he knew how ferocious they were in battle.

He edged his way through the press of men and approached Hardrada who, with his eyes set straight ahead, appeared indifferent to the chaos around him.

"Well, Harald," said the General as he moved within earshot, "the great adventure is almost upon us."

Hardrada pulled off his bronze helmet and held it in the crook of his arms as he studied the great general. He wore an unbleached lamb's wool jerkin, with brown breeches and a simple leather belt fastened around his waist from which hung a sheathed sword. He wore no badge of rank, nor any armour, in stark comparison to Hardrada in his well-polished lamellar armour, fringed linen jerkin, and stout leather boots. Across his back he slung his axe and, with two swords at his belt, he seemed more than ready for a fight. He arched a single eyebrow, as he studied Maniakes from head to toe. "You're travelling incognito, General?"

"My plan is simple. As the main forces under *Protospatharios* Kekaumenos hit the shore, I and a hand-picked force will skirt the west, taking a circular route to catch the Saracens in the rear. You, Harald, will hold the beachhead at all costs. Kekaumenos will appear to withdraw, sucking the Saracens into the trap. Whatever happens, *you* must hold."

"I'll hold, General, have no fears."

"But I do, lad. I'm entrusting you with the security of the empire. We must seize the island, secure trade routes and bolster our borders against the Norman threat. The Saracens are a minor inconvenience, but if the island falls to those French bastards, the Mediterranean will become once more an area of major concern. The Emperor is determined to win it back, so your duty is clear."

"I'll not fail you, or the emperor. I've seen battle before, led men and—"

"This is not some rampage across the desert in search of booty, Harald, this is major military action. I need to know you are up to it. With Bollason's disappearance I have little choice in the matter."

"I fought in the Polish steppe, General, don't forget. I engaged Pechenegs and—"

"That was an ambush in the night, and," he held up his hand quickly, "before you tell me about Stiklestad, you were nothing but a boy then, however brave you may have been. No, this is a major engagement, Harald. If you fail me, then..."

"I won't. If I do, you can have my head on a pike."

Maniakes smiled, but there was no humour in it, just sneering cruelty coupled with, perhaps, a hope. "Oh, believe you me, lad, I'll put more than your head on a pike. Talking of which, how is the Empress?"

Hardrada stiffened, the colour draining from his face. "Have a care. I may forget my position."

Maniakes held the Viking's glaring gaze for a moment before looking away. He sighed, "Grow up, Harald. As soon as she's tired of you, she'll spit you out like a grape pip." He turned again, "With as little conscience."

"You speak from experience, General, or is that envy I hear in your voice."

The General's look grew dark. "Now it is time for you to have a care, lad. The Empress is chosen by God to be the leader of His people. Who has chosen you? Odin?" His eyes narrowed. "I see the remnants of your pagan beliefs burning in your eyes, Harald. It will be your undoing." He tilted his head. "What did you do with Bollason?"

Hardrada frowned, taken aback by the unexpected question. "*Do* with him? I did nothing, he took off."

"Of his own volition? I heard you made a deal, over the share of the stolen treasure."

Aghast, Hardrada could not prevent himself from allowing his jaw to slacken, his eyes bulge. "Who told you that?"

Maniakes shrugged, "I have my ways and means, lad. Just as I know how many times you've fucked the Empress." He winked, "There are no empty rooms in the Royal Palace, you'd best remember that."

"If you weren't—"

"Harald, never threaten me. You have friends in high places for the moment, but as soon as you fall from grace, I'll crush you like a beetle. So, be wary, lad, watch your back, and make sure you win that beachhead."

Hardrada, trembling with barely contained fury, went to speak but stopped as a well-turned out officer of the Imperial Guard strode up and snapped to attention. He thrust out a rolled up piece of parchment. "Begging your pardon sir," he glanced towards the General, "but I have an urgent communication from Her Divine Majesty."

Maniakes grunted and went to take the roll, but the officer moved it away slightly, "Apologies, sir, but it is for the Norseman."

"Is it, by Christ?"

Hardrada couldn't help but smile. He took the roll with a grunt and read the words. His smile grew broader and when he had finished, he folded it up and thrust it inside his jerkin. "Tell Her Highness I shall be there directly."

The soldier saluted, turned on his heels and strode off. Maniakes blew out his cheeks, "We haven't got time to have you indulging your passions."

"Orders are orders, General," he smiled, leaning towards the General, "no matter how unsavoury they may be. Eh?" He winked and quickly fell in behind the Imperial officer, well aware of Maniakes rumbling on the quayside.

* * *

Within the darkened chamber, a shape moved and he stood still, every fibre, every sense rigid, locked on that shadowy corner. For he knew what was waiting there and the thought thrilled him to the very core of his being.

His heart pounded in his throat, the searing heat raging within his loins. She stepped out of the shadows and he saw the form of her body beneath the thin, silken robe, and he almost cried out. In two strides he was on her, folding his great arms around her slim waist, pulling her close, his mouth pressing against hers. The sweet smell of her perfume filled his nostrils, invading his mind, sending him into a kind of warm, misty bliss, filled with thoughts of her.

She pushed him away, gasping, and her round eyes, full of lust and longing, held his own. "I had to see you one last time, before the sea takes you away from me."

"My Lady," he croaked, barely able to speak, his tongue thick in his mouth, the flames of desire overcoming him, "I am lost in my need for you." He slipped his hands beneath the delicate material separating her body from him, and he cupped her smooth, full breasts and groaned, "Dear Christ, but you are beautiful."

She arched her back, head lolling to the side, eyes closed, and he swept her up in his arms and carried her to the bed. He ripped away her robe, gazed for a moment on her slender waist, her heaving breasts, strong, bronzed thighs, and tore away his breeches, to free his pulsing manhood. She gazed, wide-eyed, and licked her lips. "Make it quick, and make it hard, Harald."

And he did, without hesitation. She squealed as he thrust into her, holding onto his back and buttocks as he drove with such fury, such passion, she felt sure the bed would break beneath them.

He roared out her name and she gripped him hard, sinking fingernails into his flesh, as his loins tensed and went into spasm. Whimpering, he collapsed on top of her and she massaged his scalp, kissed the top of his head, and held him close.

When he rolled off her, breathing hard, she propped herself up on one elbow and smiled across at him. "I want you to be careful, Harald. Let nothing happen to you, you understand."

"I won't get myself killed. Don't worry about that."

"But I do," she said, running the back of her index finger along the line of his nose. "I worry about it more than you know. Do what needs to be done and get yourself back to me as soon as you are able. I want you as whole and as strong as you are now."

"I shall take care, have no fears."

"And watch that Maniakes. The man is a snake, Harald. He thinks I am ignorant of his machinations, but I am not. They all underestimate me, Orphano, the General, even my husband. It will be their undoing, you see if it is not."

"As long as you don't count me in with that lot, my Lady."

"As long as you never betray me, my sweet." She smiled and stood up, pulling her torn robe around her body. She laughed. "Look what you've done to me. You're an animal, Harald." She leaned over him, arms either side of his lower abdomen, "I'll count the moments until we're together again." And she lowered her head and kissed his flaccid penis. "I can't wait!"

He stepped out into the sunlight and stood at the top of the broad steps, which led to the entrance to the royal Palace. It was a glorious morning and, far off in the distance, the Sea of Marmara shimmered as if made of gold. Soon he would cross that sea and voyage across the horizon towards the island of Sicily. The greatest adventure of his life, and perhaps the most dangerous. But perhaps not as full of danger as her words, which rang in his ears and brought a coldness to his heart. *As long as you never betray me, my sweet.*

He closed his eyes and moved down the steps towards his destiny.

Fifty-Four

Northern Byzantium, 1042

The sun had barely broken across the eastern sky when Andreas came out of the stable, yawned, stretched and shuffled over to the watering trough. A stagnant dribble settled on the bottom of the roughly hewn trough. He couldn't remember when the rain had last fallen and the brown scum on the surface made him hesitate. Sighing, he skimmed the dirt away with his hand and threw what water he could over his face, keeping his eyes and mouth firmly closed.

He took up the hem of his tunic and dried his face before turning and tramping through the extensive stable yard to the villa, its glaring walls reflecting the rapidly ascending sun. Already the heat played at the back of his neck as he walked and he knew the journey would be a long and arduous one in such ferocious heat.

The manservant looked up from preparing the table as Andreas stepped through the open doorway. The man stiffened, bowing from the waist. "You require some breakfast, sir? I have figs, olives, some sweet wine."

Andreas grunted and sank into a chair. "Where is Nikolias?"

"The new master sleeps, sir."

Andreas sniggered, "*Master*? Is that what you call him now?"

The man servant averted his eyes. "A messenger arrived in the early hours, sir." He turned his gazed towards Andreas, his face hardening. "The news is grave, sir."

"Grave? How so 'grave'?"

The man busied himself loading up a platter of food. "I have not been privy to everything, sir. I am sure my master will give you the details." He placed the figs and olives in front of the Byzantine Officer. "I can wake him if you insist."

Andreas picked up an olive. "But you said 'grave'?"

"Yes, sir. Master Nikolias appeared unsettled when the messenger relayed the news."

"But you do not know what this *news* was?" He popped the olive into his mouth, slowly chewing it before spitting the pip onto the floor.

The manservant studied the pip, not a flicker of emotion on his face. "I'm afraid not, sir." He took a cloth from the side table, dipped down and scooped up the discarded pip. Andreas grunted before choosing a fig this time. "Would you like me to wake the master?"

Andreas nodded. The servant poured him a goblet of wine, bowed, and scurried off.

Andreas leaned back in the chair and peered at the ceiling. *Sclerus lived well*, he mused. *The man's estates were vast, bringing in a healthy income. Now he was dead, and Nikolias had slipped in without a blink. You really had to admire his front. From an officer of the Imperial Body-guard to a landowner of wealth and influence, his rise was breathtaking. But once Maniakes found out …* He chuckled to himself and took a long drink of wine.

* * *

Nikolias sat up, a hand curling around the hilt of his sword. The manservant gasped.

"Sorry," said Nikolias, "old habits." He swung his legs out of the bed and ran his hand over his face. "What is it?"

"I would not have disturbed you if it weren't important, sir, but the army officer is breaking his fast, and he is anxious to know the news."

"Is he? Did he say why he is so anxious?" The manservant shook his head and wrung his hand, looking awkward. Nikolias stood and crossed to the veranda, a thin veil across the opening. He squinted towards the sun. "It's damned early. What is his mood?"

"Sir?"

Nikolias turned. "Is he angry, suspicious...?"

"I'm not at all sure, sir."

"Well, he's going to be when I tell him what has happened." He nodded to the bed. "Make sure nobody disturbs Mistress Leoni."

The manservant nodded, and quickly crossed to where Nikolias's linen coat hung. He helped his new master put it on, then stepped aside for him to leave.

Nikolias, not used to being waited upon, could not conceal his smile. He wondered, not for the first time, what the man would do now that Sclerus, his true master, was dead. When he and Leoni first arrived, there were at least half a dozen retainers mingling around. All, save this one man, left within days. Perhaps they feared the General's wrath? If they did, they had nothing to fear anymore.

He found Andreas at the table, picking at olives. "You're up early."

"I plan to leave."

"Oh?" Nikolias poured himself some wine. He took a sip and pulled a face. He sat down. "And where are you going?"

"It is as I said. North."

"You are still determined to pursue Hardrada?"

"To the ends of the Earth if need be."

Nikolias put his face in his hands. He was tired of this. Tired of the intrigue, the suspicions, the hate. He had tried to convince Andreas of Hardrada's innocence in the killing of the girl, but Andreas would have none of it. Consumed by hatred, blinded by it, he probably had nothing else in his lonely, desolate life. He dropped his hands. "Very well. Do what you must. I have no interest in any of it."

"Not now you have this place."

"That is by no means guaranteed. I was hoping you might return to Constantinople, relay a message for me to the Empress."

"I go north. Hardrada is already well ahead of me, and I have little knowledge of where his destination lies."

"He will sell himself, as he always has. I hear the Normans employ mercenaries in large numbers. Perhaps he will go with them, travel back to Sicily. Now wouldn't that be ironic?"

"I care nothing for where he has been, or where he is going. I seek his death, nothing more."

"And if he dies before you reach him?"

"That will not happen."

"How can you be so sure?"

"Because I have prayed long on it, and God will not abandon me."

Nikolias arched a single, sceptical eyebrow. "I am not convinced God would approve of murder, Andreas."

"Murder?" Andreas bristled, fists either side of the wooden platter before him, squeezing hard. "Is that what you think it is? I seek *retribution!*"

"And I've told you what Leoni said!"

"She would say anything."

"Careful, Andreas. You may be so hate-filled that your reason is blurred, but do not think you can say whatever you wish."

"That assassin would tell her anything, to sew discord. That is what I meant, and you know it. I have no dispute with you, or her. Only the Viking. He saw I had feelings for... " He turned away, biting his lip, closing his eyes. A fist came up and he pressed it into his mouth. Nikolias studied him, confused by the man's behaviour, disturbed by his hate. *Why would he not accept the truth? Was there some other reason other than the killing of the girl?*

Andreas took a breath and stared towards Nikolias. "I leave as soon as I can," he continued. "You'll have to go back to the City yourself."

"Things are different there now."

"Oh?" Andreas leaned forward. "The servant told me a messenger arrived in the night?"

"Aye. He brought news for Maniakes's wife, but because of the lateness of the hour, he came here first, as we were still awake. He sleeps in the barn. You wish to talk with him?"

"No. I want you to tell me what he said."

Nikolias nodded, considered taking another mouthful of wine but decided against it. Instead, he reached over and took the last remaining fig from Andreas's platter. "Maniakes is dead."

Andreas's face went white and for a long time he seemed to have lost the ability to move, his eyes alone growing wider and wider as the enormity of the news sank in.

"He raised an army in the hope of overthrowing the new Emperor, Constantine Monomachus," explained Nikolias. "Whether it was because of superior numbers, or sheer bad luck, I know not. All I know is, Maniakes is dead and they stuck him on a donkey and paraded him through the streets of the capital."

"Dear God," muttered Andreas.

"It gets worse." Nikolias sat back, arms folded. "Monomachus is married to Zoe. But he lies with his mistress." Andreas gaped. "And his mistress is none other than the sister of our late friend, Sclerus."

"The owner of this estate?"

"The very same."

"But…" Andreas shook his head, bewildered. He reached for the wine jug and poured himself a generous measure, his hand shaking, forcing him to concentrate hard so as not to spill any. He drank deeply, sat and fell into deep thought.

"So, you can see, I am not so sure if my presence in the City would go down particularly well right now."

"You have the protection of the Patriarch, you could—"

"Alexius took his life, Andreas. The old order has gone. Wiped out. Zoe is the one remaining vestige, and I am not confident of her support."

"But you served her well!"

"Aye, I did. But Maniakes used Leoni for his own ends. Zoe will be distrustful of me because of my love for her. I shall have to tread carefully."

"It's a vipers' nest, Nikolias. You're better off out of it."

"But I cannot remain here. Scleriana, the Emperor's mistress, will want to acquire this estate for herself. I have not long, perhaps a couple of days."

"You and I are both disposed now, Nikolias. How far we have fallen."

"I have family in Hadrianopolis. We shall go there."

"I envy you, Nikolias. A beautiful woman, a family..." He shook his head, a rueful smile playing around his lips. "You have the chance to disappear, to start again."

"You could do the same."

Andreas stared. "No. Not until I have fulfilled my destiny." He stood up. "I must gather what things I have and leave."

"I will instruct my servant to prepare some supplies. You will need food, plenty of water, bedding. And two horses."

Andreas lowered his head. "You are too kind, Nikolias. I could not ask you for—"

"We once served the Empire, Andreas, we had a common cause. Fate has torn us asunder, but we can still retain our dignity, our loyalty to what once was."

"But I seek another man's death. I know you cannot accept that."

"We have both done regrettable things, Andreas. I have to live with what I have done. I hope you can do the same."

"My conscience is clear."

Nikolias made a sad smile. "I wish I could say the same."

He watched Andreas go out and absently turned the goblet around by its base, considering how hatred and the need for revenge clouded the mind, forcing rationality to hide in the deepest, most inaccessible corners of the mind. But then, had he not also been controlled by blind hate when he found his mother's corpse and Leoni gone? He did not wait for a moment to consider who might have carried out such a heinous crime, nor why. All he desired was Maniakes's death and a young, innocent man had lost his life as a consequence.

"What are you thinking, my love?"

Nikolias sprang upright in surprise, knocking over the goblet, then laughed at his clumsiness as Leoni glided over to him, her silk night-dress gossamer thin, revealing every curve of her delicious body. He curled his arm around her waist and she sat on his knee, tussling his hair. "You startled me," he said, unnecessarily.

"Andreas frightens me," she said.

"But he saved your life."

"I know, but nevertheless ... he is a driven man."

"Driven by hate."

"Which makes him unpredictable and dangerous."

"Well, as long as he doesn't hate us." He leaned over with some effort and upturned the wine goblet. "I must go and speak with the General's wife. We may have to leave here, sooner than we expected."

"I overheard some of what you and Andreas were discussing." She kissed the top of his head. "We will go to Hadrianapolis, as you originally intended. We shall both be safe there."

"Is it what you want?"

"To be safe?" She raised her eyebrows then laughed, cupping his face in her hands and kissing him. "Oh Niko, stop being so worried about what I want! I want *you* and I don't care where we go, as long as we are together."

He pressed his face into her warm, soft breasts. "Where have you been all my life?"

"Right here, my love. Always."

Fifty-Five

The distance between the two estates was short. Olive and orange groves ran side by side, in some places separated by rough wicker fences, in others, open. The vineyards, which covered the surrounding hillsides, had boundaries clearly marked. A rough pathway ran from the Sclerus's villa to both his neighbours' homes. Along the one leading to the General's, Nikolias strode, dressed in a simple green tunic and sandals. A short sword dangled from his belt, and he carried it more out of habit than for personal defence, although he was wary of other 'visitors' assailing him, sent by the Empress. The message the man brought in the night unsettled him. With Maniakes dead, his association with the great man may put him in great danger. How ironic, that it was from fear of the General's retribution that he had taken Leoni and fled to this place. No matter which side he chose, events would always contrive to make his choice the wrong one.

Already the morning heat, trapped in the closeness of the pathway, bordered by orange and lemon trees, caused the sweat to trickle down the back of his neck. He wiped his forehead as he stepped out from the trees and stopped to admire the view of the General's impressive, single-storey villa.

A body lay just inside the main entrance, sprawled across the path face down.

Nikolias held his breath, steadied himself, hand taking hold of the sword hilt, drawing it slowly from the scabbard.

The only sound the occasional song of a nearby bird, or the faint rustle of a mouse scurrying between the trees. Nothing else. Senses alert, he moved forward, measuring each step, ready for any assault.

He reached the main entrance, flattening himself against one of the adjacent ornamental pillars and waited. His eyes swept over the trees and the pathway from which he had emerged. If the attacker had left the villa, then the orange grove was the only way back to Sclerus's estate. Unless he had made his escape across country, going farther north.

His other thought was an unsettling one.

The attacker might still be inside.

He sprinted, doubled-up, making his way along the approach path to the broad steps which led to the main building. It was a large villa, with adjacent outhouses on either side. Nikolias did not stop, giving the body a fleeting glance before he pounded up the stairs and continued into the entrance hall to the bright, airy interior. He veered left, never having visited the place before and not knowing which doorway led where. He pressed himself against the far wall, breathing hard, and scanned the area.

The wide, rectangular hallway opened up into the dining room, with a shaded veranda with views of an ornamental garden. There were doors on either side of this entrance, a door next to him and one opposite. All were closed. There was no sound, no evidence of anyone living there. No sign of a disturbance, all neat, clean, tidy.

And yet somebody had been here, and murdered the man outside.

With his heart pounding in his head, he gripped his sword, curled his fingers around the door handle, and eased it open.

The heavy woodwork of the door swung wide, creaked on its hinges, the sound echoing horribly throughout the house, warning anyone, if they did not already know, that Nikolias was here.

He paused as the weight of the door banged against the adjacent wall. Taking a breath, he chanced a peek inside, before darting back, fearful of an arrow.

A bedroom, the bed carved from Far-Eastern black wood, the raffia mattress thick. The body lying upon it, wide-eyed, dead.

He counted the seconds, took another peek, then went inside in a half crouch, sword at the ready.

She was naked, white as alabaster, throat slit, the blood not yet congealed. Nikolias groaned. She had to be the General's wife. So, the imperial court had let loose its dogs, Monomachus intent to remove all shreds of Maniakes from the Earth.

And then it all fell into place.

The messenger. An assassin, sent by the Emperor, and he had discovered, by sheer chance, Nikolias in hiding here, Nikolias, servant to the Empire and one of General Maniakes's principle officers. And Leoni's lover.

With all thought of personal safety banished from his thoughts, Nikolias charged out of the villa, and ran with all his strength back along the pathway leading to Sclerus's villa, to Leoni, alone in the house with the assassin so close and so deadly.

* * *

Andreas saddled his horse. It was well fed and watered, the manservant having done well to brush the mare down, ready her for the journey. The second horse was perhaps not as well bred, but seemed sturdy enough. He placed supply bags and a bedroll on it, securing them tightly with leather straps. He wore lamellar armour, but his bronze helmet he decided to leave behind, choosing a wide-brimmed sun hat instead. A sword and dagger were at his belt, and a short bow, constructed from bone, hung from his saddle, together with a quiver of arrows. A shadow fell across the stable entrance and he tensed, whirled around, hand falling to the hilt of his sword.

"Stay your hand, sir," said the stranger, his hands held out to show he was unarmed. He stepped closer. "I am the messenger, from Constantinople. I understand you have some questions for me?"

"Not now," said Andreas, relaxing, returning to securing the second horse. "Nikolias has told me it all."

"I must go to see the General's wife before I return to the City. My orders originate from the newly instated Commander of the Imperial forces, General Kekaumenos."

"I know little of him," said Andreas, throwing a second bedroll over the horse's back. "My orders always came from other quarters." He chuckled at that, remembering how both Maniakes and the empress used him as a pawn, and in his last command, to send Bolli Bollason off to Sicily to almost certain death.

"He sends his greetings."

Andreas froze in that instant, knowing he was already a dead man.

* * *

He saw him as he rounded the last bend, crossing the yard to the stable building. In his hand was a knife, its blade long and curved. Nikolias stopped, regaining his breath, gulping in the air, creeping forward, not wishing to startle the man, giving him a chance for escape. He needed to question him first, get some information, find out how much the new emperor, what his intentions were.

Muffled voices. The man stood in the wide entrance to the stable, talking to someone inside. Nikolias crept closer, noting the blade, how clean it was. He almost cried out in relief. This had to mean Leoni was safe. Unless he had strangled her, squeezing the life from her, cruel fingers wrapped around her soft throat. He put his fist in his mouth, confused. Should he check the house first, and where was the manservant? Dead already. Nikolias shot a glance at the house. Nothing stirred. So like Maniakes's household. Dear Christ, surely the same nightmare vision did not await him in there?

"My orders originate from the newly instated Commander of the Imperial forces, General Kekaumenos," Nikolias heard the man say.

Kekaumenos? The rising star of the Imperial army, groomed by Maniakes, destined for greatness.

Father of assassins.

The man lifted his knife. "He sends his greetings."

Nikolias drove forward, all thoughts of interrogations forgotten, the blade of his short sword plunging into the man's flesh, driven deep, slicing upwards through lungs and heart. He gripped the man by the throat, holding him close, unrelenting, twisting the blade, hearing the blood gurgling up into the mouth, the body going into spasm, legs and arms twitching. The knife clattered to the ground, the knees went slack, and Nikolias let him drop, lifeless.

"Dear Christ."

Nikolias dragged his eyes from the corpse to see Andreas, ashen, lips trembling, eyes unblinking, wide with terror.

"I never…"

But Nikolias was no longer listening. He ran, pumping his arms, blasting into the villa, whirling around, frantic, screaming, "*Leoni!*"

And she was there, coming out of the bedroom, alarmed, arms open, falling into him, gasping, "What is it, my love?"

He held her close, sobbing into her shoulder, unable to explain, no words forming, only relief flooding every sense, every thought. Consumed by her, the press of her body, the warm, smoothness of her skin, her perfume. He kissed her, never wanting it to end, the tears pouring down his face to settle around their joined lips.

"Oh dear God," he managed at last, taking in rapid breaths, allowing himself to relax, to accept she was unharmed, that he had saved her. Saved them all. Except for the General's wife. God rest her.

He took Leoni outside and they sat, he with his elbows on his knees, staring at the ground, her hand stroking his head.

Andreas came and he appeared grim. Nikolias looked up and they stared into one another's eyes for a long time before Andreas cleared his throat, averted his eyes and muttered, "I owe you my life."

"You owe me nothing, Andreas. There is no debt between us."

Andreas nodded, glanced back towards the stable, to the body of the assassin, a dark patch of blood around him. "Others will come. They will not stop."

"I know it." Nikolias took hold of Leoni's hand and squeezed it. "We will leave, make our way to Hadrianapolis."

"Once the Emperor receives reports of what has happened here…"

Andreas shrugged.

The manservant came out of the house, drying his hands on a cloth. He looked from one Byzantine soldier to the other, pursed his lips. "I shall bury him, clean the stables. No one will know."

"They will suspect," said Nikolias.

"Suspect what, sir? Nobody knew you were here. And I shall not tell them." He caught Nikolias's frown and added, quickly, "If you will allow me, sir, I would accompany you and the mistress to your destination. In your service."

Nikolias breathed hard through his nose, and Leoni picked up his hand, kissed it. "My love, it is an admirable plan. It would help us in beginning again. An anonymous couple, looking to lay down new roots. No one would ever suspect."

"And I know where the money is, sir."

"Money? What money?"

"That Master Sclerus kept, as a reserve, in case of emergency. It is not a fortune, but it is enough to purchase some land, build a farm."

"I could never—"

"Yes, you can, Nikolias," interjected Andreas. "This is God's work, my friend. They will ransack this place, and the General's, and they will loot whatever they can find. Monomachus will fill his pockets and he won't give a fig for whose money it was. Think of it as your revenge."

"And what of yours?"

Andreas smiled, swung on his heels and looked out across the rolling hills. "I have no need of money, Nikolias, or love. I have no ambition, no dreams of peace. All hope of that was taken from me." He sighed. "His only course would be up the Dneiper, to the Northern Lands. To Novgorod, and the land of the Rus."

"And if you do not find him?"

Andreas turned and his smile glistened with the promise of death. "Oh, I'll find him. And when I do, he will die."

"However long it takes?"

Andreas nodded. "Yes, my friend, however long it takes…"

About the Author

Stuart G Yates is the author of a eclectic mix of books, ranging from historical fiction through to contemporary thrillers. Hailing from Merseyside, he now lives in southern Spain, where he teaches history, but dreams of living on a narrowboat in Shropshire.

Books by the Author

- Varangian

- King of the Norse (Varangian Book 2)

- Origins (Varangian Book 3)

- Unflinching

- In the Blood (Unflinching 2)

- To Die in Glory (Unflinching 3)

- A Reckoning (Unflinching 4)

- Blood Rise (Unflinching 5)

- Bloody Reasons (To Kill A Man 1)

- Pursuers Unto Death (To Kill A Man 2)

- A Man Dead (To Kill A Man 3)
- Lament for Darley Dene
- Minus Life
- Ogre's Lament
- The Pawnbroker
- Sallowed Blood
- The Sandman Cometh
- Splintered Ice
- Tears In The Fabric of Time
- The Tide of Terror

Printed in Poland
by Amazon Fulfillment
Poland Sp. z o.o., Wrocław

57469145R00202